ALL ALONE WITH YOU

Also by
Amelia Diane Coombs

Keep My Heart in San Francisco

Between You, Me, and the Honeybees

Exactly Where You Need to Be

ALL ALONE WITH YOU

Amelia Diane Coombs

SIMON & SCHUSTER BFYR
New York London Toronto Sydney New Delhi

An imprint of Simon & Schuster Children's Publishing Division
1230 Avenue of the Americas, New York, New York 10020
This book is a work of fiction. Any references to historical events, real people, or real places are used fictitiously. Other names, characters, places, and events are products of the author's imagination, and any resemblance to actual events or places or persons, living or dead, is entirely coincidental.

For information about special discounts for bulk purchases, please contact Simon & Schuster Special Sales at 1-866-506-1949 or business@simonandschuster.com.
The Simon & Schuster Speakers Bureau can bring authors to your live event. For more information or to book an event, contact the Simon & Schuster Speakers Bureau at 1-866-248-3049 or visit our website at www.simonspeakers.com.
Interior design by Krista Vossen
The text for this book was set in Calisto.
Manufactured in the United States of America
First Edition
2 4 6 8 10 9 7 5 3 1
CIP data for this book is available from the Library of Congress.
ISBN 9781534493575
ISBN 9781534493599 (ebook)

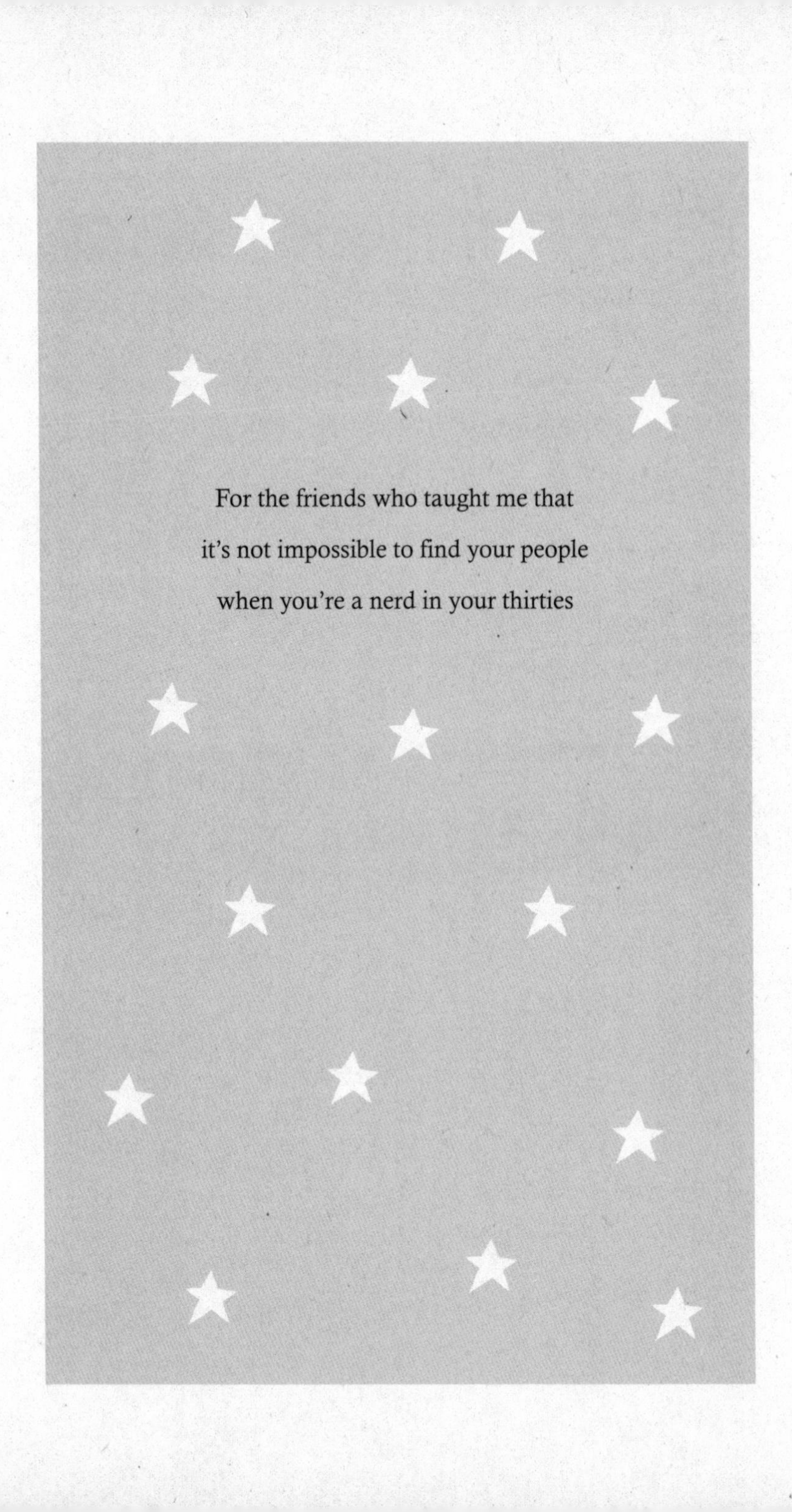

For the friends who taught me that
it's not impossible to find your people
when you're a nerd in your thirties

But listen carefully
To the sound of your loneliness
Like a heartbeat drives you mad
In the stillness of remembering what you had
And what you lost

—Stevie Nicks, "Dreams"

ONE

This loneliness will cease in a heartbeat
All my mistakes turned us bittersweet

—The Laundromats, "Aftertaste" (1981)

Senior year was always destined to be a dumpster fire, but today takes it to a whole new level.

I frown at the pamphlet and handout my guidance counselor, Ms. Holiday, slides across the desk. The pamphlet is for some retirement home; the glossy trifold shows an elderly woman sitting alone in a rocking chair, staring forlornly out a window. I shift the pamphlet aside and pick up the handout.

"You really think *community service*"—I don't bother hiding the derision in my voice—"will help my application stand out?" I stare at the handout so intently, I'm amazed it doesn't burst into flames.

"For the scholarships? Yes, I do." Since it's the first week of school, Ms. Holiday looks frazzled as hell. Her ponytail is sliding down the side of her head, and no fewer than five mini cans of Dr Pepper clutter her desk. And this is the woman in charge of my academic future. "Your grades and test scores are fantastic. You have a great shot. But *everyone* applying to USC—both for freshman year and for scholarships—has equally good numbers. The rep I spoke with over the summer emphasized community involvement, especially for scholarship applicants."

My dentist keeps warning me about bruxism, but I grind my molars anyway. For the last three years, I've had one goal: getting into the University of Southern California. Until last month, I was intent on laser-focusing on my fall grades, playing video games in my spare time, and senioritis-ing my way to graduation once that acceptance pinged my inbox. Then Dad lost his job.

Now it's either loan city or scoring a scholarship if I have any chance at affording a private, out-of-state college like USC.

"And there aren't any scholarships based on academic achievement?" I scan the handout Ms. Holiday put together for a second time. As if there's some secret code, a solution to my problems, to unlock.

But the handout is just a summary of what I've done so far for my college apps, and what needs to be done before now and the end of November. SAT and ACT scores: 1520 and 33, respectively. My current GPA: 4.1. Class rank: second—but watch out, Mindy Channing, I'm coming for valedictorian. Extracurriculars: Computer Science Club Secretary. But the black hole on this sheet of paper is the space beside Community Service.

"Academic achievement doesn't cut it anymore, Eloise. You know that. If you want the full-ride scholarship, you're gonna have to round out your application—with something *non*academic."

I lift my eyes from the handout, my stomach already twisting and turning into little anxiety knots. "How many hours?"

Like most guidance counselors, Ms. Holiday is preppy and cheerful, and most of her office is either pink or covered in glitter. Sometimes both. There's even one of those kitten-hanging-from-a-branch posters on the wall to my left, which I thought only existed in corny nineties movies. But she doesn't bother hiding her sigh of annoyance as studies me from the other side of her desk.

I wouldn't be surprised if Ms. Holiday talks about me and my attitude problem in therapy.

"There's no magic number. Most schools ask for anywhere from fifty to two hundred hours, but USC is looking at more than just metrics. They're looking for investment and involvement. A true passion for helping your community."

I frown. Because I might be the least involved student at Evanston High. Or in the Seattle area altogether. I've never volunteered a day in my life, I don't talk to anyone—my fellow peers, bus drivers, baristas, our mail person—if I can help it, and I don't give a shit about the neighborhood. "So. Like seventy-five hours or . . . ?"

"If numbers are *that* important to you, Eloise, sure, shoot for seventy-five hours to start. I'm not telling you all this to be a pain in the you-know-what. I'm saying this because you're smart and any college would be lucky to have you." She gives me an imploring look, like the bigger her eyes, the easier it'll be to get through to me. "But sometimes you have to jump through some hoops, especially if you're looking to land a full ride. They don't give those out to everyone with a 4.0."

"4.1," I correct, and Ms. Holiday's left eye twitches.

The literal definition of high school is jumping through arbitrary hoops. Grades and tests and placement exams. Numbers that will mean absolutely nothing in a year. But the University of Southern California has been my dream since freshman year, when I built my first computer. Since I fell in love with computers and coding and video games like my favorite MMORPG, *Realm of the Ravager*. USC has one of the—if not *the*—best computer science programs in the world for video games. They even offer a BS in Computer Science Games. Why would I go anywhere else?

My parents have stressed, ad nauseam, that they don't want me taking out loans for college. Especially with a solid school like University of Washington fifteen minutes from our house, in-state tuition included. And I get it—my parents *still* have outstanding student loans—but USC is my dream. I'll gladly go into debt until my forties for my dream, but a scholarship would probably be less devastating to my future credit score.

"I really think you'll love LifeCare," Ms. Holiday says once she realizes I'm not going to reply, and nudges the pamphlet closer. "It's a great program—"

"No need for the hard sell, Ms. H." I shove the paperwork into my overstuffed backpack. "I don't really have a choice, do I?"

"Ever the pragmatist, Eloise." She sighs again and types, her glittery fingernails punching at the keyboard. "But yes, LifeCare is your best bet. They're the only program paired with Evanston that can provide the number of hours you'll need. The coordinator is named Donna, and she'll email you about coming in this weekend. Sound okay?"

"Yeah." I tug the zipper of my backpack shut and lift the bag from the floor. "Can I go?"

"One sec." Ms. Holiday rests her elbows on the table and props her chin with her hands. "Are you . . . How're you doing? Is senior year treating you better than last?"

"Considering it's been five days, it's kind of too soon to tell."

I try to keep the snark out of my voice—I know better than to openly antagonize my teachers and administrative staff—and force a smile onto my face to show her that I Am Totally Okay.

The worry on Ms. Holiday's face eases. "Excellent," she says with a tentative smile. "Well, don't let me keep you! I'm here if you have any—"

But I'm already out the door. No offense to Ms. Holiday or anything—she's nice enough—but I'm low-key panicking. If I want to shoot for seventy-five hours, that's about six hours a week on top of my AP classes, homework, babysitting my trashball of a little sister, and living my life. And by living my life, I mean playing *Realm of the Ravager* with my guild during every moment of my free time.

The guidance counselors' offices are in Evanston High's creepy sublevel basement, and I begin my ascent up the linoleum-tiled staircase. Panic sweat gathers beneath my armpits and against my lower back, causing the fabric of my skull-patterned button-down to cling to me. Gross.

Since Ms. Holiday sent me a note to meet her right after my sixth and final period, the hallways are nearly empty. Evanston High is three stories—four, counting the probably haunted administration basement—with brick and ivy and stained-glass windows. The kind of high school you see in movies and teen dramas. I used to love Evanston. But lately, its halls just fill me with an unshakable sense of dread.

Most things do, honestly.

I cross the hallway and push open one of the heavy double doors leading outside. We're less than a month away from fall, and the maple trees lining the cobblestone pathway to the street hint at their turn, green leaves dulling in brightness, rusting around the edges. Even though I'm dying to move south, I'll miss the weather. *Especially* fall. The turning of the leaves and maple lattes and how the city comes alive once summer comes to an end.

The breeze feels good against my bare arms as I hop down the stairs, and I try to calm myself with each step. Seventy-five hours isn't unrealistic. Totally doable. And working in a retirement home probably will consist of handing out Jell-O cups and calling bingo. I ignore Ms. Holiday's note about *passion* and *investment*. If I have the hours, the scholarship committees won't know the difference.

The street that runs in front of Evanston has bumper-to-bumper traffic since the elementary school is down the road, and I hit the crosswalk button with my elbow. Seattle drivers are notoriously passive-aggressive. Meaning they'll go out of their way to break traffic laws in the name of being nice, which inevitably causes traffic jams, which then causes people to lay on their horns or run red lights. It's chaos.

As I wait, I dig out my headphones from the side pocket on my backpack. They pair to my phone, and I pop them on, but not before noticing the car to my left, stuck in the long line of traffic. It's just a navy Camry, but I'd recognize that dented bumper anywhere.

I can only see the back of their heads. But the sight of Lydie's sleek black bob and Jordan's sporty blond ponytail is enough to make my stomach sour. When the crossing light turns, I dash to the other side of the street, taking short, quick steps—even though I want to break out into an asthma-attack-inducing run—until I'm out of view. I shouldn't care if they see me, walking home all by myself on the first Friday of senior year. And I *don't* care. But that doesn't mean I want to make accidental eye contact or anything.

I hit play on one of my newest playlists, full of loud, angry perfection, as I head home. We live between Greenwood and Ballard, in an old neighborhood with equally old houses. Although half have been remodeled into weirdly vertical, modern town houses. Nothing is uglier than a house built in 1920 beside an all-angles town house with solar panels, but here we are.

The more distance I get from Evanston High, the calmer I become. The vague nausea in my stomach fades, although it's not completely gone. My psychiatrist said this is because of my anxiety disorder—you have a ton of neurons in your gut, releasing all sorts of neurotransmitters. While my depression has become my most debilitating disorder, the anxiety is the most constant. A low-level hum in the background of my everyday life.

When I reach my house, I'm relieved to find the driveway empty. Since our house was built in the early 1900s, our garage is better suited for tiny cars and horse-drawn carriages—not my mom's massive minivan. And my dad bikes everywhere. *Everywhere.* He wears those gross spandex shorts and everything. After he lost his job, Dad made biking his life. Mom jokes that it's a midlife crisis, but there's a nugget of truth at the core.

No car in the driveway or bike locked to the porch railing means no one's home to ask if I sat with anyone at lunch today or what my weekend plans are.

I dig my keys out of my backpack and let myself inside.

"Hello?" I call out, just to be sure, and no one answers.

I kick off my Doc Martens before I drift into the kitchen, fill up a mug with cold leftover coffee from this morning, and grab a protein bar. Then I head to the basement.

My room used to be upstairs, next to my parents', but when my mom had my sister, they turned my bedroom into a nursery and banished me belowground. Just kidding. Sort of.

Mom and Dad handled the situation well—considering Ana was an accident, a fact I can't wait to rub in her face when she's older—and made sure I found my banishment fun and exciting. We remodeled the old office space into my bedroom, decorated it and everything. Now, at seventeen, I'm glad I don't share a bedroom wall with my parents.

I set my snacks beside my computer and dump my backpack onto the floor.

The room isn't large by any means—it's narrow and the ceiling is six inches shorter than it is in the rest of the house, for no reason whatsoever. My double-sized bed is tucked into one corner beneath the egress window, and the dark-blue walls are covered in one-of-a-kind prints for my favorite video games and movies that I found on Etsy. And the love of my life sits before me: my computer.

I boot up the tower, turn on my display, and then sink into the cushion of my gaming chair. Log in to Monsoon—the gaming client for *Realm of the Ravager*—and wait as it updates. *RotR* is my go-to whenever life becomes too much—and let's face it, senior year is off to a shitty start. Plus it's Friday, and I've earned endless hours of gaming.

When I'm focused on leveling my rogue, I don't have to think about going to LifeCare this weekend. I don't have to think about Lydie and Jordan, best friends forever. I don't have to think about anything. Because that's the beauty of video games. You can slip into a different world. You can become someone else. You can be a hero—or a villain.

I even have some friends on *RotR*. No one I know in real life, but people in Unarmed Rage, my guild, who I play with several times a week. Online, I'm less awkward. Online, I have control over who I interact with, and I always have an escape route. Unlike in real life.

Needless to say, I prefer my virtual life over my current reality.

That'll change next year, though.

Come next August, I'll pack my bags for Los Angeles and never look back.

TWO

You can stay golden
And I'll turn tarnished

—The Laundromats, "Midnight" (1977)

Here's the funny thing about depression: I'm tired *constantly*, but most of the time, I can't sleep. For whatever reason, I almost never fall asleep once it's lights out. Usually, I toss and turn myself into a big blanket-tangled ball of misery. But whenever I *can* sleep, I have a go-big-or-go-home mentality. Basically, I don't believe in alarm clocks, and I'll sleep in for as long as humanly possible or socially acceptable.

On Saturday, I wake up a little after ten thirty, roll out of bed, and slide onto the bench seat at the kitchen table. In a sleepy haze, I alternate spoonfuls of Lucky Charms with long gulps of coffee. My phone, resting between the bagel basket and container of orange juice, buzzes halfway through my breakfast.

I swipe to check the notification. Then groan. "Fuck."

"Jar," my little sister, Ana, snaps, arranging her pots of paint in a neat row. Ana's eleven and Mom put her in this after-school art camp for the year. Now we all have to act like Ana's blob-like paintings are super awesome and precocious. They're really not.

"Seriously?" I glare at her. "Mom didn't even hear me." Our mom is bathing a dog in the laundry room off our kitchen; she runs a pet grooming business offering both mobile services and "salon" services out of our laundry room.

Talking Heads thumps into the kitchen from behind the shut laundry room door. I love my mom, but she's one of those self-made businesswomen who unironically uses the phrase "girl boss" and will pet a stranger's dog without permission.

Ana glances up. Her white-blond hair is so unlike my dark-brown locks, and she has the face of an angel, even if she might be a demon. "It's the *rule.*"

I get up, grab a dollar from my wallet, and make a performance out of shoving it into the bedazzled Swear Jar on the hallway table. Then I slump back into my seat at the kitchen table and reread the message.

The email is from Donna, the super effusive and excited volunteer coordinator! She ends every sentence with an exclamation point! She's so excited that I'm volunteering at LifeCare! And can I come by today for my orientation?! Whenever's clever!

Yeah. This was a *huge* mistake.

After playing *Realm of the Ravager* until two in the morning and passing out, I kind of forgot about volunteering, Donna's impending email, and LifeCare. I've only been awake for fifteen minutes, and I have to reread the email a few times until my brain catches up with my eyeballs.

What're my odds of USC and a scholarship if I bail?

According to Ms. Holiday, not good. Probably . . . really, really bad.

Sighing, I lock my phone and finish my cereal. Ana hums

to herself as she begins painting a gray blob that I think is supposed to be a dolphin. But I don't want to ask for clarification and crush her fragile artistic ego. Not because I'd feel bad, but because Ana would tattle on me in under five seconds. Once all I'm left with is pink milk, I slide off the bench and dump my bowl into the sink.

"Gonna get dressed," I yell over my shoulder at Ana as I head downstairs. "Don't set anything on fire." I'm not even joking. Over the summer, she started a small fire when she lit one of Mom's candles unsupervised. My little sister mumbles something in response but I'm already halfway to the basement, regretting the sugary cereal. My stomach hurts.

In the solace of my bedroom, I flop onto my bed and open the email again.

Donna wants me to come in today, but the procrastinator in me is whispering to postpone. To tell Donna I can come in tomorrow. Anything to delay the impending awkwardness. Because I can already feel it. The anxiety slowly rising. My psychiatrist, Dr. Bailey, who I see once a month, says I have social anxiety, but honestly, I have everything anxiety. I have anxiety over just *existing*.

Dr. Bailey thinks I need a therapist, but after a few failed sessions in sophomore year after my diagnoses, I tapped out. Sure, I like to talk about myself, but I don't need therapy. I'm *fine*.

I hit reply and stare at the blank email, considering my options. But then my gaze wanders around my room. The University of Southern California banner over my desk. A stuffed Traveler, the USC mascot horse, on my bed. The mirror that used to be framed with photos, which is now plain except for my old Emerald City Comic Con wristbands from the past six years. I rub my fist over my eyes, then drag my fingers through my sleep-tangled hair.

I type out a response to Donna, agreeing to come in today. Then I shower in my tiny basement bathroom, blow-dry my hair, and spend thirty minutes braiding the strands into a crown. The braiding is methodical, almost mathematical, and has become a hallmark of my personal style. Eyeliner? I'll poke my eyeball out. But braids? Braids I can do. And I do them well.

Once my hair is done, I choose my Schrödinger's cat button-down (the pattern is a bunch of cats and boxes and question marks) and roll up the sleeves to my elbows, and I pair it with jeans. And after I take my morning antidepressant and anti-anxiety medications, I run out of reasons to procrastinate. Time to sign away my free time for the foreseeable future.

Mom's playlist has made a depressing shift to Joy Division, and I go upstairs and knock on the closed laundry room door. "Safe to come in?" I ask. Sometimes, if a dog client is skittish, they bolt for the hallway when the door is opened. Once, I had to chase a Jack Russell terrier named Terrance around our house, following a sudsy trail he left along the hardwood.

"Safe!" Mom yells, and I step inside.

The laundry room is cramped, with a massive industrial sink currently housing a Cavalier King Charles spaniel, who I know from past appointments is named Doug. "Hi, buddy," I say in my doggo voice, scrubbing his wet ears. Then to my mom: "I'm headed out."

Mom swipes her hair back with her wrist, her face flushed. She's wearing a T-shirt dress and a gingham apron on top. Her blond hair, similar to Ana's, is tied back with a bandanna that doesn't hold back her flyaway bangs. "Where to?"

"My lack of volunteer hours has come back to haunt me," I say as if it physically pains me. And given my stomachache, it kind of does. "Ms. Holiday told me I needed to volunteer if I wanted a fair shot at that USC scholarship."

Mom brightens, and she returns to shampooing Doug, massaging soap behind his ears. "Really? Where at?"

I lean against the counter. "Some place called LifeCare? It's over in Fremont. It's a retirement home or something. I honestly don't care."

My mom ignores my ambivalence. "Why don't you take my car?"

"You sure? I don't mind taking the bus."

"Nah." She begins spraying down Doug, and I jump back to avoid the splash zone. "Your dad's biking with his buddies and won't be back until dinner, and I'm booked up all day. I don't need it."

"Thanks." I lean in and kiss her cheek. "Best of luck with Doug."

Doug whines upon hearing his name, and Mom chuckles. "Have fun, baby."

Doubtful, I think, but I smile and nod. Mom wants me to be happy—and it's not like I'm unhappy. But I don't want to give her any ammunition to worry about me again. For the last nine months, my depression has stayed steady and manageable; I don't want her to think otherwise.

"Bye, Mom." I shut the laundry room door behind me and grab Mom's keys from the side table in the hall. After shoving on my Doc Martens, I yell, "I'm leaving, Ana!"

"I don't care," Ana yells back.

I lock the door behind me and trudge over to Mom's minivan.

The sky above is thick with white-gray clouds, and the thought of rain makes me smile. People have this misconception that Seattle is one torrential storm. But in reality, it doesn't rain here more often than in many other cities. Our rain is spread out—drizzly days broken up with pockets of sunshine—and after our sticky, hot summer, I'm ready for fall.

Mom's minivan is a mess, and I shove loose wrappers and empty coffee cups into the small car trash bag I put in her Christmas stocking last year, not like she ever uses it. According to Google Maps, LifeCare is an easy ten-minute drive. Twenty minutes by bus, which isn't bad. During the week, I rarely have car privileges. Mom has clients at the house during the weekend, since she can't leave Ana, but usually does her whole mobile schtick during the week, while we're at school.

I connect my phone and crank up one of my playlists, then work my way out of our neighborhood. Saturday afternoon traffic isn't terrible, and I drive over to LifeCare's neighborhood. Fremont is unironically hip, with boutiques and bars and, inexplicably, a sixteen-foot bronze statue of Lenin. But there are loads of businesses down by the water, and I follow the directions until I pull alongside a row of brick buildings off Thirty-Sixth Street and parallel park.

I double-check the address, then peer out my window.

When Ms. Holiday mentioned LifeCare, I assumed it'd be some dumpy retirement home. I mean, that pamphlet screamed "My grandchildren don't visit me anymore" in bold font. But I seriously doubt a retirement home would be above a coffee shop and a weed dispensary called Best Buds.

I smooth my palm over my braided crown for flyaways, grab my bag, and hop out of the car. In Donna's email, she gave me the building's door code, which I punch into the keypad mounted beside the street-level entrance. The door beeps as it unlocks, and I use my shoulder to nudge it open. The vestibule is small—just a wall of mailboxes and a narrow staircase—and thanks to Best Buds, it smells skunky. A wall placard reads LIFECARE with an arrow pointing up the stairs, and I grudgingly begin my climb.

The staircase ends at the second-floor landing, right in front of LifeCare's frosted-glass door; on either side of the door are fake potted plants layered in dust. After stalling for as long as possible, I take a deep, anxious breath and push the door open.

Unlike its dusty exterior, the inside of LifeCare is large and airy, with exposed brick walls and large windows overlooking Fremont and a slice of Lake Union. The office is open concept, with a half-dozen empty workstations, and a hallway curves around the corner and out of sight. A front desk faces the entrance.

This place is *nice*. But it also kind of looks like a call center.

I deeply regret not doing Google recon last night.

Since there's no one around, I sit in one of the armchairs flanking the entrance. *Ten minutes,* I tell myself. I'll give them ten minutes, and if Donna doesn't show, I can leave, go home, and play *RotR*. I can leave knowing I *tried*. That's reasonable, right?

While I wait, I reread Donna's email, confirming that she'd be around all day and that I could show up whenever was most convenient.

"Are you Eloise?"

A boy my age exits the hallway and strolls in my direction.

Both hands are tucked into the front pockets of his skinny jeans, and an oversized sweater engulfs his lanky frame, sliding off his left shoulder.

I lock my phone, slip it into my bag, and then frown. "You're not Donna," I say bluntly, because Donna probably isn't a Korean American teenaged boy. I mean, it's possible. Just unlikely.

The boy grins. "Nope. But consider me Donna's stand-in. I'm Austin. I help Donna train new volunteers."

My anxiety is *not* enjoying this change in plans, and I manage a flat, "Hi."

Austin grabs a clipboard from behind the front desk and walks over. He plops into the armchair beside me, crosses one ankle over his knee, and then hands me the clipboard. "Donna stepped out for lunch, but she asked me to show you around until she got back."

"How fun for you." Clipboard and pen in hand, I begin filling out the form. It's long and detailed, asking for availability, a copy of my driver's license, my criminal history, etc.

I scowl at the sheer number of questions.

"Cheer up." Austin hops to his feet and spreads his arms wide. "LifeCare is a happy place."

I lift my gaze from the clipboard and wrinkle my nose. "Is this a cult or something?"

"Not to my knowledge," he says with an easygoing laugh. "Why would you think that?"

"You're . . ." I hesitate, choosing my words carefully. "Very upbeat."

Austin leans against the front desk with his hands tucked back into his pockets. "Wait. Are people in cults happy?"

"Historically speaking." I return my attention to the form. "At least, you know, before the Kool-Aid."

"Huh. Interesting," he says contemplatively. As if I didn't inadvertently insult him.

Even when I'm not looking at him, I can sense his energy. It's hard to ignore. Austin *exudes* positivity, and he hasn't stopped smiling since he walked into the room. It's unnatural for anyone to be this happy, and despite what he said, I'm not buying that this place *isn't* a cult.

When I'm done filling out the form, I pull my wallet from my bag and slide my driver's license out, setting it on the clipboard. I get up and hold the materials out to Austin, who's been standing by the front desk like a tall, smiley scarecrow.

"Wonderful! Thank you, Eloise." He rounds the desk and opens the lid of the scanner on the counter. After turning the machine on, he places my ID against the glass. "Hey, is it cool if I call you Lou?"

"Nope."

"You look like a Lou, though."

I narrow my eyes. "What does that even mean?"

"Also," Austin says, continuing as if I hadn't spoken and hitting the button on the scanner, "we have several clients named Eloise—it's a pretty old-fashioned name. Could get confusing."

"I'll take my chances."

The scanner is done, and he hands me back my ID, which is warm to the touch. "Whatever you say." Austin grins, as if I'm enjoying this conversation. As if his golden retriever energy is cute. "Lou."

I return my ID to my wallet. LifeCare might be a cult. Or Austin might be the most unfailingly positive person I've ever had the misfortune of coming across. Has this boy ever had a bad day in his life? He's like a walking, talking sunshine emoji.

Since Austin seems impervious to my snark, I change tactics and plaster on my biggest, fakest smile. The one I've used daily at school for the last year. "Okay, what will I be doing here exactly?"

Austin shuffles my paperwork and the photocopy of my ID into a folder before tucking it into a filing cabinet beneath the desk. "Donna didn't explain?"

"Obviously not."

"Volunteers usually call our clients and talk to them. Some of us do house calls."

So *not* Jell-O or bingo, then. "Is that it?"

Austin tilts his head to one side. "Is that it?" he repeats with an incredulous laugh. "Our clients have lost their loved ones, their families. We talk to them! Keep them company! We foster the power of human communication." He smacks the counter for emphasis. "They're *lonely*, Lou! And it's our job, as LifeCare volunteers, to cheer them up."

Yup. I've definitely made a huge mistake.

THREE

The seams of your discomfort
Unravel before my eyes

—The Laundromats, "I Am Not Afraid" (1973)

Austin insisted on giving me a tour of the building—a tour I did not ask for and barely paid attention to. I considered asking where the bathroom was and making a break for it, but the dude's barely let me get a word in edgewise. I'm not sure if he's taken a breath in the last ten minutes. His commitment would be impressive if it weren't so annoying.

Even though I don't really have a say in the matter, my mind is spiraling with ideas of how to get out of this. Because I'm beginning to think LifeCare was my guidance counselor's pathetic attempt to socialize me. Good game, Ms. Holiday, but I'm not that easily fooled.

But as the tour winds down, I've decided three things:

1. LifeCare doesn't sound inherently awful—you can literally *phone* in (har har) your community service. The only problem? I hate talking on the phone. Maybe more than I hate talking to people face-to-face.
2. I have never, ever met someone with as much energy

as Austin. Sure, some might find his attitude uplifting and pleasant, but I am not his intended audience. I mean, he volunteers for *fun*. Who does that? Serial killers? I mean, Ted Bundy volunteered at a suicide hotline, so anything's possible.

3. Ploy by Ms. Holiday or not, if I want my hours, I need to begin ASAP . . . and LifeCare might be my best, if only, shot.

"Your desk is right over there," Austin says once the tour is finally and mercifully over, and points to a desk near the big windows overlooking Lake Union. He plops down at a desk catty-corner to mine, gives his chair a spin. "This is me, but I usually go on house calls. Most of us do on the weekends, actually, which is why it's so quiet. Once Donna's back, she'll go over everything else with you."

"Can't wait." I slump into my desk chair and cross my arms. *USC,* I repeat to myself over and over again.

Austin, who's still spinning side to side in his wheely chair, slows to a stop. "Hey, uh, are you okay?"

I lift my gaze from my Doc Martens. "Peachy."

That should have been the end of it. But Austin apparently thinks we're having a two-sided conversation, and he nods to my shirt. "I feel bad for Schrödinger's cat. But at the same time, I don't."

"Funny." Mental note: wear only non-conversation-starter shirts in the future.

Before we can continue this scintillating back-and-forth, a small woman in her forties bustles into the center, carrying several large packages. Austin jumps up from his seat and hurries over to relieve her of two boxes from the top of the stack.

"Thanks, Austin," the woman says, and he gives her a two-fingered salute. She unloads the other boxes onto the counter and when she finally notices me—my arms crossed, face pained—she does a double take. "You must be Eloise!"

Ah. Donna of the exclamation points. "Yeah, hi," I say, and push up from my chair.

Donna beams. "How wonderful! Isn't this space gorgeous? We moved in last year! Now, Eloise, did Austin do a good job showing you around?"

"Oh. Yes. It was . . . *wonderful*. He's an excellent tour guide."

From the corner of my vision, I catch Austin grinning on his way into the break room. As if he knows I'm full of shit.

"I'm glad!" Donna can't be more than five feet tall and has curly red hair. Her voice is husky and warm, and similar to Austin, she's bubbly and high-energy. She bustles behind the desk and begins rooting through the drawers. "One sec. I have your welcome packet in here somewhere. . . ."

I eye the exit forlornly, then wander back to my desk.

While I wait for Donna, I rack my brain, trying to remember what car Ms. Holiday drives, because I'm definitely egging it. The more time I spend here, the more I worry that I'm going to be absolute shit at this. I'm the opposite of these people. Would the elderly even want to talk to someone as sarcastic and . . . well, *negative* as I am? How am I supposed to keep people from being lonely when I have exactly zero social life? If anything, I might make them even lonelier.

Austin strolls out of the break room and says, "You're going to love it here, Lou."

I give him a withering glare.

Donna walks over to me, welcome packet in hand. "Sorry, hon—do you prefer to go by Eloise or Lou?"

"Eloise," I say quickly, and take the proffered packet. "No one calls me Lou."

Donna's brow puckers in confusion, but she doesn't comment. "Okeydoke! Your client list and numbers are all on the computer, and everything else you'll need is inside the packet. But really, it's simple. Our clients are lonely. They just want someone to talk to."

I swallow hard. "Right. And . . . I'm going to talk to them."

Donna makes her way back to the front desk. "Most importantly, have fun! Our clients love talking to our younger volunteers. You have a thirty-minute break, and our shifts run in two- or four-hour blocks. Austin can help you out if you have any questions, okay?"

"Okay." I flop the welcome packet onto my desk with a satisfying smack. The cover has a picture of the same lonely lady that's on their pamphlet, and I flip it open.

I scan the first handout, which has instructions and technical FAQs. I have a Bluetooth headset and a directory on the computer, which is hooked up to the center's landline, to make my calls. The handout behind the first has tips on questions to ask. Topics to avoid. Things of that nature. And the longer I stare at the list, the more I panic.

Well. Might as well get this disaster rolling.

I pop my Bluetooth into my ear and remove the tip sheet with prompts and conversation starters, resting it against a cactus in a clay pot that has PLEASE DON'T DIE engraved on it, for easy reading. Then I click the first name in my log and hit call.

The next forty minutes pass in a blur.

Sometimes, my anxiety slows things down to a crawl, but today, it hits fast-forward. That or I've officially entered a fugue state, which I learned about in AP Psychology last year.

My first phone call was with an elderly woman named Edith. I followed the prompt sheet. I tried asking her about her kids (estranged—if they spoke to her, why would she be talking to me?), her friends (dead for years), and her favorite activities (making me squirm, apparently). My second was with an eighty-year-old vet who regaled me with stories of his time during the Vietnam War in graphic and racist detail. The third went worse than the first two. All I'm going to say is I accidentally made a ninety-year-old woman cry.

After the third call, I take a break and rest my face in my sweaty palms.

Then I hear it—the squeak of desk chair wheels against hardwood—and drop my hands from my face. Seriously?

"How'd it go?" Austin rests his elbows on my desk, somehow *still* smiling.

"Aren't you supposed to be on a call or something?" I mutter, and turn back to my screen.

He's quiet for a moment. A miracle. But then he says, "I have an idea."

My attention flicks to him. "Does it involve me not having to pick this phone back up?"

"Actually, it does. Wanna make a house call with me?"

"I think I'd rather make another old woman cry."

Austin's perma-smile droops. "You made someone *cry*?"

"What? I didn't do it on purpose."

"Hey, don't stress. It . . . happens." The way he says this, though, makes me think it's never happened before in LifeCare's history. "And I think you should reconsider. Ms. Landis is a fucking *trip*."

I shake my head. "Pass."

Austin wheels closer to me. "Lou."

"Yes, Memphis?"

I never claimed to be mature. If Austin won't call me by my first name, I won't call him by his. And since Austin has no real nicknames (Aus? Aussie? Yeah, no.) I can think of on the spot, I'll cycle through all the name-worthy cities in America.

Austin blinks in confusion before his mouth stretches out in an unbearable grin. "Ah. *Clever*." But wisely, he doesn't wheel himself any closer. "Come meet Ms. Landis with me. It'll take until the end of your shift."

"I should tell Donna I quit." I gesture meaninglessly at the computer.

He drags his fingers through his messy black hair and says, "We both know you're not quitting. Donna told me this morning your guidance counselor sent you here, right? For your college application to USC?"

Oh yeah, I'm definitely buying a value pack of eggs at Fred Meyer on the way home.

"Isn't that a privacy violation?" I lean my elbow on the desk and slump over. This is terrible. Way worse than I could've ever imagined. And here I thought volunteering with old fogies was all bingo and Jell-O. I *yearn* for bingo and Jell-O.

Austin blinks at me. "What? No." Then he nudges my bag on the floor with his shoe. "Besides, you have a University of Southern California iron-on patch on your bag. Not exactly subtle. *Anyways*." He makes an exasperated noise, which, for some reason, makes me want to smile. Maybe terrorizing

Austin, a ray of sunshine in human form, will make my stint at LifeCare somewhat bearable. "Not everyone is cut out for the phones. Ms. Landis is my client, but I think she'll like you."

"Why? No one likes me."

"That can't possibly be true." Austin pushes both feet to the floor and wheels himself back to his desk. "But you both have a lot of . . . moxie, which she'll dig," he calls over. "I'm heading out in a minute. Come with me if you want."

I rest my chin in my palm and stare at the computer screen. The long list of names I'm tasked to call and cheer up. But if my history is any indication, I'm no better in person than on the phone. Because when it comes to social situations, I'm a Human Disaster. But I *definitely* don't want to do another cold call. The thought alone makes me want to anxiety puke.

When Austin strolls up to my desk with a messenger bag slung over his shoulder a moment later, I power down my computer and gather my belongings. "Lead the way."

Donna's on board with our excursion and shows me how to download the LifeCare app her wife developed. Volunteers can check in through the app to log their hours ("It's location-based, so no cheating!"), and the system helps keep tabs on the house-call volunteers. For minors, it's required if we ever leave headquarters.

After we're all squared away, Austin leads me downstairs, through the vestibule, and out onto the street. He parked a block north of where I left Mom's car, but I stop in my tracks as he unlocks the driver's-side door.

"Yeah, not happening." I nod my chin to the grungy, windowless van. "That right there, Memphis, is a murder van."

Austin glances over his shoulder. "How is this a murder van?"

"No windows. Peeling paint. A faint aroma of terror."

"I'm not going to murder you, Lou." Austin hops inside. I assess the van and the boy behind the wheel. The vehicle truly looks like a creeper van. And someone as cheerful as Austin *probably* has some hidden dark secret like being a serial killer. I walk to the driver's-side door, and he rolls down his window. "Yes?" he asks, and I get the tiniest thrill that he sounds annoyed.

"What's up with the murder van?"

"The van is for moving musical equipment." Austin starts the engine, and it turns over a few times. "No one, to my knowledge, has been murdered in this van. But I did buy it at a police auction, so I can't make any promises."

I consider this. Better than being inside making old women cry, I guess. I walk around the van and open the passenger-side door. The inside of the van smells faintly of weed and french fries. I plop into the passenger seat and, before closing the door, check to make sure it opens from the inside. Once that's confirmed, I click my seat belt.

"Here." Austin waves something at me. It's his driver's license. "If you're *that* worried about me murdering you, take a picture of my ID and send it to one of your friends. Then if you go missing—"

I pluck the ID from his fingers. "They'll know to look for one Austin Yang who lives on Fletcher Drive?" As I scan the ID, I note that he lives in my neighborhood, a few streets from my house. Not like I have the school district zonings memorized, but there's a good chance he goes to Evanston High. Ugh.

"Fair?"

I snap a photo of his ID and then hand it back. "Fair," I

agree, but I *don't* tell him the person I'm texting is my mom. After attaching the photo, I thumb out a quick text and send the message.

ME:
Had to go off campus at LifeCare. Here's the person driving me in case I end up murdered.

I might be fine with my loner status, but too often people find my lack of a social life pitiful. Or a situation in need of a remedy. You can be alone and not be lonely.

A few months into junior year, my depression began to flare, and by winter break—after weeks of me dodging plans and not responding to texts—Lydie and Jordan were over it. Over *me*.

During break, Mom carted me to my psychiatrist, who tweaked my doses. Once we were back in school, I tried to rally, to be a good friend. Like yay, three cheers for store-bought serotonin! Yeah, that didn't work.

I *know* that it didn't work because, not long after, Lydie texted our group chat. I'm fairly sure that it was an accident, that she meant to text Jordan instead, but who knows. Lydie said that I was faking the depression and that I liked attention. Jordan sent a laughing emoji and a "Seriously, right?" in response.

I wanted to reply. To ask what kind of person would fake depression. To point out that I hated attention so much, I got hives and threw up in a trash can during my tenth-grade Honors Core History presentation. But I never replied. Jordan had the audacity to try to talk to me in the cafeteria during lunch the following week; I didn't even acknowledge her. I just reached around her for a pudding cup and left.

In their eyes, I was shitty and selfish for withdrawing. And they were right. But the truth still stung. Jordan had been my best friend since the sixth grade. We'd met during my *very* brief stint in Girl Scouts; I got too competitive during cookie sales season and was kicked out. Then Jordan met Lydie freshman year, and everything changed. Jordan changed.

Despite this, Lydie and Jordan were the only friends I had—until I didn't have them anymore. Lydie, who elevated our social circle to popular-adjacent since she was this charismatic mishmash of jock and president of our school's fashion club. Jordan, whose shared history of sleepovers, movie nights, and awkward puberty firsts like buying tampons together kept me relevant.

Turns out, one major depressive episode was all it took to make me irrelevant. To make me not worth the effort anymore. And I don't blame them. During those dark weeks, I didn't want anything to do with me either. Nearly a year later, it's fine. . . . I mean, I'll have all of college to make friends, right?

Good thing I'm kind of awesome at being a loner.

FOUR

They say no man is an island
But this woman's moving upstream

—The Laundromats, "Upstream Woman" (1977)

As we drive toward the mysterious Ms. Landis's house, I survey the interior of Austin's van. Cliché fuzzy dice hang from the rearview mirror. There aren't any seats in the back, and true to his word, it's packed with a random assortment of musical equipment. When we hit a speed bump, the amp thumps into the side of the van and a set of hi-hats rattle.

"I'm in a band," Austin says, glancing over at me. He drives like a grandpa, both hands on the wheel, shoulders hunched.

"Good for you." I shift back in my seat and stare ahead at the road. Austin being in a band doesn't quite align with my image of him. Maybe it's one of those creepy Christian bands that sing about love and god's forgiveness? Yeah, that could track. "So. What can you tell me about Ms. Landis?"

He huffs a laugh. "She's hard to describe. I think it's best if you just meet her."

We dip into a pothole, and the fuzzy dice bounce into each other. "Why so vague?"

"Why so persistent?"

I roll my eyes and begin picking at my chipped blue nail polish. Then Austin turns on the radio and the car is filled with some pop-indie band I don't recognize, and we don't bother talking. The silence is . . . awkward. But compared to cold-calling, this is better. At least right now I don't have to talk to anyone.

Austin doesn't look up directions once as he navigates the murder van. We merge onto Aurora and head north, driving past Woodland Park Zoo, and exit near Green Lake. Since the sun's out, the path around the lake is busy and the street's full of cars, but eventually Austin finds a spot next to a house shrouded by tall hedges.

"Wait. *This* is where Ms. Landis lives?" I peer out the window. "More like Ms. Moneybags, huh?" Because the houses along Green Lake are *nice*. Like multimillions-of-dollars nice. When I was a kid, we used to drive over here for trick-or-treating, since everyone hands out full-size candy bars. One house even passed out pizza slices.

Austin chuckles. "Come on," he says, and steps out of the van. "Trust me, there's more to Marianne than meets the eye."

Marianne. Marianne Landis. Something about her name pricks at my brain, but I can't figure out why. I tilt my head back. The house is above street level, and—because of the stone retaining wall and the hedges—only the roof is visible from the sidewalk. But consider my interest piqued.

Austin hops up the stone steps leading to a wooden gate nestled in the hedges and flips open the plastic case on a keypad, punching in a code.

I follow Austin through the gate, which clicks shut behind me. Ms. Landis's house is a well-kept Victorian. It's two stories and painted teal blue; the front door is a pop of yellow, and the lawn is wild, overgrown. Austin's already at the front door and I hurry to catch up. The porch is small and cluttered, with a welcome mat and an odd array of items. Jars of sea glass. A trio of ceramic frogs. A small Buddha statue, his belly cracked due to weather and age.

Austin nudges one of the ceramic frogs to the side and unearths a house key.

"You know her gate code *and* where her Hide-a-Key is?"

He unlocks the door. "Yeah. We have a set schedule, and she doesn't mind me letting myself in. Take off your shoes, though."

I sigh and hobble on one foot as I shuck off my boots. The front door opens into a hallway. The house smells like dust and clove and tobacco, with a hint of cat litter.

"Marianne?" Austin sets the Hide-a-Key on the side table.

"In the sunroom!" a voice hollers.

Immediately to my right is a spiral wrought-iron staircase, the wall it runs against covered in so many mismatched picture frames that we might as well be in a thrift store. But Austin leads me past the stairs and deeper into the house before I can snoop further.

Austin catches me surveying the mess. "She keeps firing her house cleaners," he says by way of explanation.

I follow him into another hallway full of closed doors, and we turn right into a bright kitchen. The walls are a creamy white, and the backsplash behind the sink is mint-green tile. An old-fashioned wood-burning stove sits in one corner and a rectangular glass kitchen table is tucked into the other. The shelves along the walls are heavy with bowls and plants and what appears to be—

"Is that a *bong*?" I point to the shelf in disbelief. It's one of those massive bongs too, its glass a swirl of blues and pinks. Someone means business. Serious stoner business.

Austin glances over his shoulder. "What? She grew up in the sixties." Then he points to the kitchen door. "Through here," he says, and pushes it open.

We step out into a sunroom, where the walls are floor-to-ceiling glass windows with sliders to let in fresh air. Plants are everywhere. On the floor in big bohemian pots, on wall mounts beside the kitchen door. Hanging from the ceiling. And between the plants is expensive-looking patio furniture.

"Hey, Marianne," Austin says cheerfully, and walks over to a woman lounging on a chaise and reading a book. A black cat is curled up beside her bare feet.

I don't know exactly who I was expecting Marianne Landis to be, but this *definitely* wasn't it. The woman draped on the chaise is in her seventies, dressed in patched jeans and a turtleneck with a lace shell on top. A mustard-yellow shawl is looped around her shoulders, and her bone-white hair is wild down her back.

"Austin!" Marianne tosses her book on the mosaic-tile coffee table. Her voice is deep, husky. Like she spent her youth chain-smoking. Her bright-blue eyes flick over to me, still standing in the doorway with my arms crossed. "And who's this?"

"Marianne, this is Lo—*Eloise*." He fumbles over my name and sits in a rattan armchair across from her. "She's new to LifeCare."

Marianne groans to her feet. She's tall—even taller than me, and I'm an abhorrent five-nine—but she moves gracefully as she approaches. "Eloise," she repeats, as if committing the name to memory, and nods. "Why don't you remove the stick from your ass and take a seat? I'm making tea."

I blink at the old woman as words fail me, which is a rare occurrence. Finally, I manage to say, "What?"

Marianne pats my arm, then steps around me on her way into the kitchen. "As my mother used to say, you look more uncomfortable than a nun in a cucumber patch." As the door shuts behind her, she yells, "I hope you like Earl Grey!"

"Told you," Austin says once we're alone. "She's indescribable."

"No. She's an asshole." I lower myself into the armchair beside him, beneath an overgrown spider plant.

"You two should get along wonderfully, then." Austin crosses his ankle over his knee and smiles serenely.

I lift a brow, impressed with the comeback.

Before I can reply, Marianne drifts back into the sunroom. "Here we are," she says, and slides a tray with three mugs and a tea diffuser onto the coffee table.

Austin and Marianne pour themselves tea, but I hesitate.

"Eloise, it's tea, not poison," Marianne says. "Drink up."

As if to prove a point, Austin takes a big sip of his tea and winces; I hope he burned his tongue. But I reluctantly pour myself a cup and sniff—black tea that smells vaguely vanilla-y—and lean back in my chair, trying to appear relaxed.

Marianne is chaotic, which would usually stress me out—and it does—but I also want to see what she does next. Despite the snark, there's something almost likable about her. Or, if not likable, *interesting*. And I'd prefer interesting over likable any day.

"Hope you don't mind Eloise tagging along," Austin says. "Today's her first day, and I thought I'd show off the best of the best. LifeCare's VIP."

Marianne snorts. "I already told you that I'm not writing you into my will." But she winks, then adds, "Please, keep the compliments coming. Maybe I'll have a change of heart."

How long has Austin volunteered with Marianne? Because their dynamic is seamless, more like two friends, not a volunteer and his client for the afternoon. Their ease makes me even *more* uneasy, so I sip my tea and glance around the sunroom, through the windows and into the lush backyard.

When I turn back to Marianne, I find her staring at me as she absentmindedly pets the black cat curled beside her. Unlike the LifeCare clients I stumbled through conversations with earlier, Marianne is vibrant. Physically and mentally. Why does she need LifeCare and voluntarily keep the company of someone like *Austin*?

"Let me guess. You're wondering why I'm a LifeCare client, aren't you?" she asks, and I'm one hundred percent creeped out that she's right. Maybe she's a witch.

"I mean . . . yeah? Not like I have a ton of experience, but you're not like the other clients I spoke with."

Marianne grabs an ashtray from the coffee table, then slides an unlit cigarette from behind her ear. "I live in this big, fancy house all alone—no offense to Nox." She motions to the cat with a flick of her bony wrist. Sparking the cigarette with an old-fashioned lighter, she blows a plume of smoke in my direction. "But the thing is, no one starts off alone, Eloise. Everyone I've ever loved is dead. And I'm lonely as hell."

★

An hour later, I climb the narrow staircase to LifeCare's headquarters with Austin. Inside, Donna's packing up for the day, sliding her laptop into a sleek messenger bag.

"Hey, you two," she says, pausing to twist back her red curls. "How was Marianne's?"

"We had a blast!" Austin ducks into the break room for the leftovers he forgot in the fridge.

Donna turns to me. "Wonderful! She's quite a hoot, isn't she, Eloise?"

I linger by the front desk. A hoot? What is this, 1954? I lean my elbows on the desk. "Sure, yeah. So, I was wondering about logistics. I need seventy-five hours by the end of November. Is that doable? Ms. Holiday said it was."

Donna purses her lips for a second, then says, "Very doable, but I heard that, well, that you made someone cry on the phone today?"

How is it my fault that some old lady can't control her emotions? Not like I take pride in making an old woman cry, but *come on.* "Yeah . . . I mean, it was an accident?" I try to smile, but it probably looks like a grimace.

Donna rounds the counter and stands beside me. I'm a foot taller than she is, and it's awkward as she places a comforting hand on my forearm; her nails have little rainbows painted on them. "We'd love to have you as a volunteer, truly, but incidents like this are worrisome."

I chew on the inside of my cheek. "Right. Yeah. I get it." My heart rate quickens, and my palms moisten with panic. Unfortunate doesn't even begin to explain this situation. Of course my lack of social skills will be my downfall. I feel USC slipping from my sweaty fingers.

Austin returns with his leftovers, a grease-stained paper bag from a nearby burger joint. "You know, Marianne and Eloise really hit it off today."

Donna doesn't hide her surprise. "Really? That's . . . well, that's wonderful to hear!" She turns toward Austin. "Do you think Marianne would be open to Eloise joining you two?"

"Um, hold on—" I begin to say, but they talk over me. As if I'm not literally standing in between them.

"Yeah, totally. She said Eloise was welcome back anytime."

"Wonderful," Donna says again, like it's the only positive adjective in her vocabulary. Then she turns to me and adds, "Maybe the phones aren't for you, Eloise. Some people connect better in person."

Oh, now *that's* funny. Someone grab my inhaler because I'm going to have an asthma attack. But instead of breaking down into a fit of self-deprecating laughter, I ask, "If I volunteer with Marianne, can I get my hours by the end of November?"

"Can't see why not!" Donna circles back behind the desk and continues packing up. "If you ever need more hours, let me know, but I think this is a wonderful solution!"

Austin elbows me, and I flinch. "What d'you say, Lou? Tuesdays and Thursdays after school for two hours, plus Saturdays. You in?"

I readjust the strap of my bag and sigh. "Sure. It's going to be *wonderful*."

"Now that's the spirit!" Donna gives me a thumbs-up. She's so earnest, I almost feel bad for making fun of her. Almost.

My computer monitor is in split-screen mode—one half has *Realm of the Ravager* pulled up and the other has my college application essay draft, with its grand total of sixteen words. I'm stuck. And ever since coming home from LifeCare, I've felt restless, too.

Marianne's words from earlier rebound inside my head, almost like they're haunting me. She didn't explain, didn't elaborate, after telling me everyone she'd ever loved was dead. Instead, she turned to Austin and changed the topic of conversation. Like that one line was sufficient explanation for why she signed up for LifeCare, when all it does is unleash an endless stream of questions.

I guess I don't want to think of life that way. That the elderly become lonely because they're the only ones left. That every other person in their life is just *gone.* People talk about growing old and their golden years, but no one wants to be the last one standing.

With a groan, I drop my head into my hands for a moment, then stare at the whiteboard calendar above my desk. I scheduled a few hours to work on my college application essay tonight, but my brain feels like some old cartoon character running into a brick wall.

It's like spending one afternoon at LifeCare broke me.

I sit up and open a new window, toggling over to Google.

Then I type in *Marianne Landis.*

Eight million results pop up.

Eight. Million.

I click on Wikipedia and read.

Marianne Rae Landis (born June 7, 1950) is an American singer, songwriter, and producer best known for her work with the band the Laundromats. . . .

Holy shit. No wonder her name sounded familiar. The

Laundromats were a huge band in the seventies and eighties—my mom has some of their greatest hits on rotation when she's working. That explains the expensive-as-fuck house and her aura of effortless cool. People who are in bands are usually, by default, kind of cool. Excluding Austin, that is.

I scan the rest of the Wikipedia article, which is annoyingly vague. It recaps sales numbers and tours and that, upon the band breaking up in 1986 during their European tour, Marianne retired to her hometown of Seattle, Washington, where the Laundromats were first discovered, and where she lives a private life.

There's a photo beside the Wikipedia entry. A version of Marianne forty years younger than the woman I met today. Her hair is golden brown instead of white but just as long, and her face is softer, rounder. Dressed in a crocheted crop top and flared jeans, she stands in front of the band with her head tipped back and eyes shut, lips parted in song.

The caption beneath reads:

Marianne Landis, lead singer of the Laundromats, during the final stop of their 1975 tour at Seattle venue the Showbox.

After talking with Donna and reluctantly partnering up with Austin, I did the math. If Austin visits three times a week for roughly two hours, that's six hours a week. If I want to hit that seventy-five-hour minimum by the end of November (yes, I'm ignoring Ms. Holiday's comment about the metrics of it all and plan on grinding out these hours), those thrice-weekly visits alone will take care of it.

And if I need to fudge about the community and how much it means to me . . . What sounds better on a college application than helping out an old, lonely woman? Especially if said old, lonely woman is a famous recluse?

LifeCare was probably some elaborate way of Ms. Holiday forcing me to socialize, but the thing is, I'm fucked without these hours. And Marianne is the easiest, quickest way to lock in a scholarship. Nothing on my college app says I need to befriend people or play nice or even enjoy myself. I just need hours.

"Eloise, baby," Mom hollers down the basement staircase, "it's time for dinner!"

I shut off my monitor and push back from my desk, grabbing a black hoodie off the floor and yanking it on as I head upstairs. Once a week, my mom forces us to have family dinner. And by family dinner, I mean that Mom orders delivery and puts it on real plates for us to eat at the dining room table. No one in my family cooks. I'm convinced we'd die within days if there ever were an apocalypse; we're city people.

The tradition started before I can even remember. Until Dad was let go, his life revolved around work. Most nights, he never made it home before eight. See: weekly dinner. One night a week, Dad would have to leave his office in Redmond early enough to make it home by six. The tradition stuck, even though Dad's been unemployed for over six weeks now.

I'm the last one to the table, sliding onto the bench seat beside Ana. Our dining room is a tiny offshoot of our kitchen, and the table is this massive, refurbished picnic-table-style made of shiny, polished wood. For a moment, it's quiet as we serve ourselves, just the clanking of utensils, the slurp of spaghetti plopping from take-out container onto plate. My parents, no doubt, scraping the sides of their brains trying to come up with something to say to me.

I have a good relationship with my parents, but more often than not, I don't feel like their daughter. I just don't . . . fit. Our interests don't overlap. Our passions have never aligned. They love me, but sometimes, I wonder if they even know me. If I'm even worth knowing—one foot already out the door, even if graduation is still nine months away.

Ana, on the other hand, is as open as the book in her hand. She reads as she eats, blindly spiraling spaghetti around her fork and flecking sauce everywhere. A splotch lands on my hoodie. Ana is essentially a mini version of our mom. Absentminded and extroverted, they even look the same—fair and blond and freckled. While I physically take after my dad, that's about it. The parallels between my home life and my lack of a social life aren't lost on me. If anything, the fact that I don't fit in with my own family is more fuel on the Eloise Deane Is Destined to Die Alone fire.

Once I have my plate of spaghetti, I dig in like the carbs might fill the void of unease in my chest.

"So, El," Dad says from across the table, and smiles warmly over a basket of breadsticks. He's in one of his performance-wool sweaters, his hair damp and combed back, glasses crooked on his nose. On Saturdays, Dad straps his Cannondale onto his buddy's bike rack, and they drive outside the city to sweat their balls off. Just another difference between us; I can't even walk three blocks without succumbing to an asthma attack. "Your mom said you started volunteering today?"

I grab a breadstick and take a bite. "Um, yeah," I say around the dough. "It's with LifeCare? I thought it was a retirement home, but it's actually a nonprofit that pairs volunteers with the elderly to keep them company."

"Oh!" Mom lifts a brow, her face frozen in apprehension. "You'll be working one-on-one with someone?"

Some kids might be offended by this. But my lack of social skills isn't exactly a secret around here. I nod slowly. "I'm actually, um . . . I'm working with Marianne Landis. From the Laundromats?"

Dad laughs. "No sh—way," he says, casting a glance at Ana, even though she appears to be immersed in her book. If there's one thing I've learned about little sisters, it's that they're always paying attention.

Mom stills her glass of wine mid-sip, and her hazel eyes widen. "Really?" She sets her glass down and leans forward. "What was she like?"

I think of Marianne's house—gorgeous and cluttered and messy, but empty of anything with substance—and that one terribly depressing statement I can't seem to get out of my mind.

"Lonely," I say, and dig into my spaghetti.

FIVE

I'm jealous of all that empty space
Surrounding you when I'm far from here

—The Laundromats, "Hitchhike" (1979)

On Tuesdays, my sixth period is free—technically, I have study hall, but as a senior in good standing, I'm allowed to study off campus or even go home early if I want. And as much as I want to go straight home, I take the bus to LifeCare. I would've preferred going straight to Marianne's, but I have to drop off a parental consent form, and Donna told me that Austin would meet me here at three thirty. Guess he's my LifeCare babysitter.

Not eager to make awkward small talk with Donna while I wait, I shove the form into the mail slot affixed to the front door, then duck into the coffee-shop-slash-bookstore, Lost the Plot. The decor is farmhouse meets influencer—all folksy, with creamy walls that serve as perfect Instagram backdrops, kitschy light fixtures, local art in handmade frames, and a section for pretentious books in the back. I order a latte before claiming a seat beside the bookshelves.

It's only the second week of senior year, but I'm finding my groove. Kind of easy when you have absolutely no social life or friends to manage. It's just me, my classes, and my college applications. Between the handouts Ms. Holiday has given me to keep me on track, the whiteboard above my desk, and the customized planner I ordered online over the summer, everything has been broken down into digestible chunks.

I lug out the planner—it's like three inches thick—pop my headphones on, and begin reviewing my schedule for September. But I've barely made it through next week before I hear, through my music, someone calling my name.

Well, not my full name.

There, on the opposite side of Lost the Plot, is Austin, his hand lifted mid-wave. Ugh. He's early. Thanks to those long, gangly legs, he crosses the café with his coffee and is at my table in five seconds flat. Part of me wants to ignore him until three thirty. But after having spent several hours with Austin over the weekend, I'm confident that ignoring him will only make him stronger.

I pull off my headphones and toss them on top of my planner. "What?"

Austin's wearing a wool vest over a T-shirt, his black jeans ripped at the knees. And, because it's Austin, he's smiling that toothpaste-ad-worthy smile. He should seriously get an endorsement or something.

"Fancy running into you here," he says, and sits in the seat opposite me before I can, I don't know, hook my ankles around the legs of the chair and prevent him from pulling it out. "Do you get out of school early on Tuesdays too?"

"What do you want, Boston?" I ignore his question. The less this dude knows about my personal life, the better.

Austin tilts his head at me. Like a dog. *Uncanny*. "We're still on for Marianne's, right?"

I fuss with my headphones. "I am here, aren't I?"

He sips his coffee, then says, "We can leave early, if you're ready to go?"

I shove my pens, planner, and headphones into the side pockets of my backpack and lug it into my lap. "Let's get this over with."

Austin hops to his feet and makes an *after you, madam* gesture. One that I grudgingly follow. In the last half hour, it's begun to rain. I don't know what it is about rain, but it's calming. The slow, lazy drizzle instantly puts some of my discomfort at ease.

"You okay with me driving? Or do you want to drive?" Austin fishes his keys out of his messenger bag, light raindrops plinking on our shoulders and dampening our hair.

"I took the bus." The coffee's helping, but his overall eagerness and energy is taxing. Almost like clockwork, I have an energy crash after school; seems like the exact opposite happens for Austin. How fun for me.

"The van it is." Austin clicks his key fob, and the van's lights flash from up the street.

I climb into the passenger seat, dump my bag by my feet, and take a long sip of coffee. The rain picks up as Austin slides behind the wheel and starts the engine. We sit for a moment as he turns on the wipers; they squeak with every swipe across the windshield.

"How was the rest of your weekend?" Austin asks once we're on the road and headed toward Marianne's.

I shrug one shoulder. "Fine. I guess."

"Mine was great," he says brightly, as if I asked. "Went to Golden Gardens with my bandmates for a little beach bonfire. Then we had rehearsal."

"Mmm." I nurse my coffee and stare straight ahead. "Fun."

"It really was!" Austin turns onto East Green Lake Drive. "What'd you do?"

I consider my options. Lie and pretend like I have a social life. Tell the truth and show my vulnerable underbelly. "Not much," I say, going with the underappreciated "evasion" tactic.

"Keeping the mystery alive, I see," he says thoughtfully. "Fair enough."

Normally, I'm against car crashes. But I wouldn't complain about one right now. Nothing catastrophic or hospital-worthy—a low-key fender bender or a scrape against the side of a parked car. Anything to distract Austin from me and my life. But his line of questioning ends without a car crash intervention, and we park alongside Marianne's curb.

I have major déjà vu as we head through the wooden gate. He locates the key, and we enter the house. Only this time, Austin tells me that Marianne's probably in the basement.

"Marianne's a pack rat," Austin explains, untying his sneakers by the front door. "I've been begging her to let me organize the spare room in her basement—it has all these mementos from the Laundromats, like lyric notebooks, old photos, and letters. Stuff like that. She finally agreed after that storm two weeks ago; the basement window leaked and damaged a bunch of boxes. But it's slow going. We could really use your help."

I frown. "Wait. I thought working with Marianne was all about hanging out and talking? *That* was the sales pitch. You never said physical labor was involved."

"Do you really consider organizing old boxes physical labor?" Austin rubs his hand through his damp hair. Not sure what the intended effect was, because now his hair is sticking out in about fifteen different directions.

"Yes, Boston," I say solemnly. "Yes, I do."

Austin sighs.

I smirk into my coffee cup.

I pay closer attention to my surroundings as we walk deeper into the house. Some of the frames on the walls feature Marianne at the height of her fame. Others are newspaper or magazine clippings. All the clutter is dusty, but beneath the mess, everything is nice and clearly expensive. And I count no fewer than three pianos—two in the study and another in the dining room—during our trek through the hallway and down a flight of stairs.

Marianne's basement is finished, like ours at home, but way bigger. A fancy washer and dryer are tucked beneath the staircase, and the hardwood is covered in thick, expensive-looking rugs that overlap and lump. Bookshelves stretch from floor to ceiling. Heavy wooden trunks line one wall. A worn corduroy couch is in the center.

And sitting on it is Marianne.

Today she's wearing a pale-blue sweater that looks like cashmere—but is pockmarked with moth holes—and a maxi skirt. Her hair is tied back in a messy bun, strands escaping as she leans forward over a stack of photographs in her hands, her lips a slash of dark burgundy.

"Hey there, Austin." When she looks up and notices me, she lifts a pencil-thin brow. "And Eloise. I was hoping to see you again."

"Congrats on being the first person to ever feel that way," I say flatly, uncomfortable with the spotlight focused on me.

"Funny," Marianne says with a small smile. Her blue eyes narrow, and the spotlight intensifies.

"She's sarcastic and self-deprecating." Austin brushes past me to join Marianne in the center of the basement. He sits on one of the chests and leans forward to adjust his sock. "Not funny."

"Excuse me," I say, pretending to be affronted. Which I kind of am—not because I actually think I'm all that funny, but because Austin has me pegged, and I *don't* like it. "I'm hilarious."

"Don't listen to Austin. Those are both valid self-defense mechanisms." Marianne says this casually, and my cheeks warm in response.

I just got owned. Twice.

This is my nightmare.

USC, I remind myself, and force a big, tortured smile onto my face. "I'm so happy with my life decisions right now."

Marianne laughs, a rough and throaty noise, but she's focused now on the stack of photographs in her hands. I wander over to the center of the basement, set my backpack on the floor, and lower myself onto the opposite end of the couch.

In the moment of silence, all my muscles tense; the anxiety and unease are creeping back in. Not like they ever really left. Even though I chose to be here, I can actively *feel* myself becoming overwhelmed. Social anxiety is always worrying you'll say the wrong thing, so you spend hours planning conversations in your head. Society anxiety is assuming everyone hates you and you're embarrassing or boring or stupid—

"Okay!" Austin claps his hands together, wrenching me away from my thoughts, and I flinch. "Eloise and I are early, but we can stay until six. What were you thinking for today? We can help you work on Project Nostalgia."

"Project Nostalgia?" I repeat with a grimace.

"The organizational project I was telling you about. The spare room is back there," he says, and nods his chin behind me.

I look over my shoulder at the open door on the other side of the basement. From this angle, all I can see is a wall of cardboard. Literally floor-to-ceiling. All stacked boxes of various shapes and sizes. All covered in dust and water stains. All haphazard and precariously balanced. I want to sneeze just looking in its general direction.

"Yikes," I mutter, and turn back around.

"Isn't he adorable? Came up with that name all by himself." Marianne gestures to Austin with the stack of photos, and I pretend I don't exist on this ethereal plane. When I don't reply, she places the stack of photographs on the coffee table and stretches her arms overhead; bangles slide down her bony wrists. "Thank you for the offer, but I've been down here since lunch. I'm bored of looking at the past."

"Any preferences, Lou?" Austin asks, his chin propped up in his hand. "And don't say leaving. We're here until six."

I scowl at him. "Nope. Just do . . . whatever you guys normally do. Pretend I'm not here."

"Game day it is," he says cheerfully, and hops to his feet. "What're you thinking? Uno? A little Jenga? A fifteen-hundred-piece puzzle?"

And then it hits me.

Maybe I don't hate Austin Yang at all. Maybe I'm incredibly jealous of him. Jealous of how at ease he is here—or anywhere, really. The way his shoulders aren't tight, up to his ears, like mine. How his jaw isn't clenched; I doubt *he* has to wear a night guard. Nothing forced. Nothing uncomfortable.

The realization makes me twitchy. Like it exposed a raw nerve.

"You really don't have a preference?" Marianne readjusts herself beside me on the old couch. She smells like tobacco and vetiver.

Overly aware of how I'm grinding my teeth, I release my jaw. "Oh. Um." I shrug helplessly. Most, if not all, of my gaming takes place behind a computer screen. And I hate making decisions, especially if they affect other people. "Whatever works. I don't care."

"Jenga it is," Marianne declares. "Austin, why don't you go get the game? It's in the great room somewhere. You'll find it."

"On it!" He gives Marianne a two-fingered salute and jogs upstairs.

Leaving me alone with Marianne Landis.

I grip my coffee cup tight as a slither of unease makes itself at home around my chest. What am I supposed to say to her? I try to remember the tip sheet Donna gave me, which is currently shoved beneath a stack of comics in my bedroom.

"Um—"

"Eloise"—Marianne shifts to face me and rests one arm along the back of the couch—"tell me about yourself."

My throat tightens. "Aren't I supposed to be, um, asking you questions or something?"

"Not necessarily. I'm boring."

"You're . . . *famous*."

Marianne leans in a little closer. "Exactly. You're new. We'll start off easy. How old are you? Everyone below the age of thirty looks the same to me."

"Seventeen." I'm wearing my shoulders like earrings and try to relax.

"Seventeen. That's a good age."

I snort. "Yeah, not so much."

Marianne quirks a brow. "Why not? Look at you. You're *young*! I'd kill for half your collagen."

Self-conscious, I touch my cheeks. They're plump, round. *Chipmunk cheeks,* Lydie laughed when she did my makeup once. Then she spent a half hour trying to contour my baby fat away. "Thank you?"

Marianne grabs a mug from the coffee table; I wrinkle my nose at the burning scent of vodka that wafts my way. Tilting her head, she takes a sip, then says, "Why're you volunteering if you hate it?"

"That obvious, huh?" I push back some loose strands from my braid and shrug. "College apps. I need some . . . nonacademic accomplishments, according to my guidance counselor."

"Don't you worry, we're very nonacademic here." Marianne winks, and something inside me softens.

A thump comes from upstairs, and we lift our gazes to the ceiling.

"Do I need to check on him or something?" I ask. "That was loud."

"And here I thought you weren't too fond of our Austin."

I look down from the ceiling. "Oh, I can't stand him. But he's my ride. So."

Marianne laughs, tipping her head back for a moment. "I like you." Her smile is dazzling as she meets my gaze again. "And I don't like many people."

The corner of my mouth tugs with a smile of my own. "Same here."

"Cheers to that." Marianne taps her mug of way-too-early vodka to my to-go coffee cup.

Austin comes bounding back down the basement stairs a moment later, his dark hair flopping like the ears of an over-eager golden retriever. In one hand is a beat-up Jenga box, and in the other is a plate of cookies. He sets the cookies on the coffee table and dumps the Jenga box upside down beside it.

I take a cookie, then hand one to Marianne.

"Holy shit." My mouth's so full of cookie that crumbs land on my jeans. I'm a disgusting monster. "These are *amazing.* Did you bake them?"

Austin looks up from the pile of wooden blocks. "Don't sound so shocked. I'm more than just a pretty face, Lou."

No one should have this much self-esteem. But I'm too impressed by the cookies to knock him down a peg, and I take another bite. "I hate to admit it, but these might be the best pumpkin cookies I've ever had."

"Spooky season is upon us. Felt appropriate."

"It's still September."

"What's your point?" He starts building the tower. "I said what I said."

I roll my eyes, but I can't complain. The cookies are legitimately delicious. When Austin's not looking, I grab four more off the plate and stuff them in my backpack.

Once the tower is ready, Austin picks up the torn, old directions and reviews them out loud. Honestly, I don't think I've ever played Jenga before, but the competitiveness inside me is flaring. Between having a task—something to win—and my conversation with Marianne, I don't know, I'm almost comfortable in this cluttered basement. Not actually comfortable. But headed in that general direction. Comfortable-adjacent. In a nearby zip code.

"Whoever topples the tower loses," Austin says, and sits on the floor across from Marianne and me, resting his elbows on the coffee table.

"Let's do this." I roll up the sleeves of my button-down, then crack my knuckles.

He watches me from the other side of the tower. "Someone means business."

Eyeing the wooden blocks and planning my strategy, I say, "I'm extremely competitive."

He holds both hands up in surrender. "Somehow, I have no trouble imagining that."

"What does *that* mean?"

"Lou, you're stubborn. You kind of scare me. And it makes sense that you'd also be cutthroat in a game of Jenga. You know this is a children's game, right?"

I open my mouth, then close it. "Hold up. I *scare* you?"

"Have you ever been on the receiving end of your scowl? Yeah, didn't think so."

My mouth twitches. But I don't want to give him the satisfaction of me smiling.

Marianne glances between us before saying, "You two done? Because I'm the reigning Jenga champion, don't you forget."

I tamp down the strange, light feeling in my chest and say, "Bring it on."

SIX

Every room I'm in, every street I stroll
Is the same without you beside me

—The Laundromats, "Not Knowing" (1981)

Our school has an actual bell. This loud, clanging thing that the front-desk secretary rings over the PA system to signal the end of the day. My response is straight-up Pavlovian now that it's senior year. Today, though, the bell doesn't fill me with its usual level of joy. Because Thursday means more LifeCare. And, *okay*, I didn't totally hate hanging out with Marianne on Tuesday. Even if she did beat me in Jenga.

Today sucked, and all I want to do is curl up in my gaming chair in my favorite hoodie and play *Realm of the Ravager* until my eyeballs dry out and my fingers cramp into dinosaur claws. Socializing sounds like the worst kind of torture right now. Because today Jordan and I were assigned as lab partners in AP Bio.

When I walked into class last week and saw her in the third row with that sporty blond ponytail, I froze up. Honestly, it shouldn't have been surprising to see her in one of my Advanced Placement classes. After all, Lydie, Jordan, and I were in honors classes freshman and sophomore years together.

Now Jordan and I pack up our Fast Plants materials in stilted silence. We barely spoke throughout the Artificial Selection lab, except when necessary. But I won't let Jordan knock me off my game. I need an A in AP Bio if I want to nudge out Mindy Channing for valedictorian, former failed friendships be damned. Good thing Ms. Ivers is open to lab partner swaps; I plan on emailing her tonight.

"Here." Jordan holds out the pen I let her borrow.

I pluck the Bic from her fingers and shove it into my backpack. "Thanks."

Jordan steps away from our lab table, then pauses, her blond ponytail swinging against the base of her neck. Then she turns back to me and says, "You know you don't have to act like I don't exist, right? We were best friends for, like, five years." She digs her thumb into the sleeve of her cardigan, her hazel eyes focused on me. "It's kind of messed up, Eloise."

A dozen different replies flit through my brain as I stare at Jordan. Angry, sarcastic, cruel—take your pick. But all I say is, "Can you move? I have to catch the bus."

Jordan's nostrils flare as she turns on her heel and steps into the aisle. I brush past her and nearly trip on my loose shoelace in my attempt to escape the classroom. Nausea burns my esophagus as I enter the crowded hallway, and I dig my hand into the front pocket on my backpack for a ginger chew, then shove one into my mouth.

Jordan can think what she wants, but what's *actually* messed up is what she and Lydie did last year. Like, I get it, I suck. I make a great lab partner but a shitty friend. So who cares that Jordan and I were best friends for five years? Our friendship ended when she agreed with Lydie that I was a faker, crying *depression* for attention.

The ginger settles my stomach, and I shoulder my way through the crowd and out the exit. I walk down the maple-lined path, pulling a hoodie out of my backpack and shrugging it on, then search through my backpack for my headphones. The bus stop is only a block away; I can see it up ahead, the sidewalk already crowded with students.

The sky is gray and thick, but there's no rain, and I shiver at the breeze tickling the back of my neck. I take a few deep breaths—easier now that the walls of Evanston High aren't closing in around me like a scene from a horror movie—and swallow the rest of the sticky ginger chew.

Before I can unearth my headphones from the piles of text-books and loose scraps of paper in my bottomless backpack and properly shut myself out from the world, someone honks their horn. And to my left is a white, windowless van that crawls at a snail's pace alongside the curb.

I stop.

The van stops.

Austin rolls down the passenger-side window and says, "Hey! Want some candy?"

"Are you trying to lure me into your van?" I bite the inside of my cheek to keep from laughing as a group of elementary school kids ahead of me on the sidewalk cast horrified glances at the windowless van and run to the safety of the bus stop.

Either Austin doesn't notice the elementary school kids or has no issue with the van's license plate being reported to the police, because he leans over to pop open the passenger-side door. "Sorry, bad joke. I have an extra coffee, but that really doesn't have the same ring to it. Anyways. Want a ride? And some coffee?"

The coffee? Yes. The ride . . . I'm not so sure about.

Something itchy claws at my insides as I stare at the open car door. And no, it's not my latent stranger-danger instincts kicking in. Because, like it or not, Austin Yang is no longer a stranger. I study him—as if visually, I can key in on why he annoys me so much—sitting there expectantly, half leaning across the van with one hand braced on the passenger seat. And I think back to my revelation in Marianne's basement. The one I don't want to look at too closely.

Austin's nice. I'm the asshole. The jealous, miserable asshole. But Austin's so nonthreatening. He looks . . . *kind*. And I guess, if we're getting technical, he is. The imploring brown eyes. The messy dark hair. The doofy, lopsided smile. All that golden retriever energy. But I don't know why he's being kind to me.

Maybe that's what annoys me the most. Not that he's a ray of sunshine. That he's a ray of sunshine *toward* me, while I'm actively being an asshole to him. During junior year, I learned that if you snarl at people enough times, they'll eventually leave you alone.

However, this logic doesn't appear to work with Austin Yang.

"I'm not asking you to enter a murder-suicide pact." Austin leans back into his seat. "Want a ride or not? I can't imagine I'm any worse than public transportation."

With a performative sigh, I say, "Okay, fine," and climb into the van.

As promised, a disposable coffee cup is sitting in the center console, *Lou* written across the side in a barista's Sharpie scrawl. But the stamped EHS logo on the side is what snags my attention. Austin bought this from the coffee cart in the quad.

Which means he *definitely* goes to Evanston. We have over eight hundred kids in our senior class alone, so it's not exactly shocking that Austin and I have never crossed paths. Until now. Maybe I'm cursed.

Yeah. That would make sense.

Because I can't escape the dude.

I dump my bag at my feet and the weight makes the fuzzy dice hanging from the rearview shudder.

"Holy shit, Lou," Austin says, turning on his blinker. "Do you have the Ark of the Covenant in there?"

"What?"

He glances sideways at me. "*Indiana Jones*? No? You know what, never mind."

I get the reference—my dad is obsessed with *Indiana Jones*—but I like to see Austin suffer. Another point in the Eloise Deane Is the Worst column I keep inside my head. Austin's kindness, while overbearing and weird, is a living reminder of how not cut out I am for something like LifeCare.

Get in and get out, I remind myself. I don't have to belong. I'm not here to make friends. Just to log my hours.

"You're at Evanston?" Austin says after a minute of awkward van silence.

I rest my arm on the side of the door and stare out the windshield. "Yep."

"Me too." He taps out a beat against the steering wheel. "Small world, huh?"

I grunt in response, trying to end this conversation before it gains any traction. Because the last thing I want is Austin poking into my private life. Asking me questions about classes and friend groups and what I want to do with my life. If he keeps this up, there's nothing stopping me from pushing open the door of this van at the next stoplight and running until my lungs give out.

My lack of verbiage finally breaks Austin, who turns on the radio after our silence becomes too loud.

We don't talk for the rest of the drive to Marianne's.

Marianne Landis might live a private life, but she has no qualms about handing me a box of personal photographs from the basement's spare room to organize. While Austin helps Marianne water her plants in the sunroom, I sit at the kitchen table and pore over the photos. No one gave me any instructions on how to organize them, but I try to group the photos by decade. Someone has to bring order to this chaos. And that person is going to be me.

I shuffle through, careful not to smudge them with my fingertips.

My favorites are candid shots of Marianne.

Marianne in her thirties, smoking a cigarette on the Studio 8H stage when the band performed on *Saturday Night Live*.

Marianne as a teenager, sitting on a beached kayak on Bonnie Lake with her older brother.

Marianne on a camping trip, a fire roaring in the background, as she leans against a curvy white woman with thick dark curls, their hands woven together. I pause on this one. Because I've seen the woman before, in several framed photos around the house. I flip the photo over, but there's only a processing date on the back: 1975. The mystery woman is unnamed.

Marianne's Wikipedia page mentioned that she never married or had any long-term partners. There were rumors.

Marianne dating her bandmates or fellow musicians. An actor or two. A tabloid photographer even caught her on vacation in South Africa with some British prince between the release of the Laundromats' third and fourth albums.

I glance at the photo again—the two women's obvious intimacy and love frozen in time. Well. I guess not even Wikipedia knows everything. Setting the photo down in my 1970s pile, I stand up and grab my to-go coffee from the kitchen counter. I take a sip, glancing out the window above the sink. Nox lounges in a rare sunbeam on the floorboards. Fresh air blows through the cracked kitchen door, the breeze damp with last night's rain, and I check my watch, then groan. Not even an hour down.

Out in the sunroom, Austin waters the various plants while Marianne and a trail of her cigarette smoke follow. From what I've been able to glean, Austin's volunteered with Marianne for over two years, and it shows. How close they are, how they lean into each other like confidants. Like a grandmother and her grandson, if said grandmother had absolutely zero maternal instincts and chain-smoked constantly.

I'm about to return to the table when I hear Austin say my name. Just barely. They're too far away for me to hear anything else, but my insides seize up. The thought of them talking about *me* when I'm not around makes me want to throw up. They aren't Lydie and Jordan—they couldn't be more different, and the rational part of my brain knows that—but I feel the same. The one on the outside, the third wheel. And it makes my skin itch.

Even if Marianne said she likes me, I don't fit in here.

Marianne and Austin make their way toward the kitchen,

and I slump back to the table, to the mess of photos I've barely made a dent in. I flip through a new stack and pretend to look busy as they step inside. Marianne laughs at something Austin said. She's not laughing at me. She's not.

But what if she is?

"How's Project Nostalgia going?" Austin grabs his coffee from the counter and slides into the seat across from me. Apparently, me agreeing to help organize photos means I'm a part of Project Nostalgia. Love this for me.

I don't look up from the photos in my hand. "Fine."

"I've warned Austin, but I haven't gone through those in years," Marianne says casually, "and I can't guarantee that a few personal photographs haven't snuck their way in."

I glance up at Marianne, who's leaning against the kitchen counter, my self-pity panic forgotten. "Personal photos? Like . . . *nudes*?"

Marianne cackles and takes another drag of her cigarette before dropping the butt into the sink.

"I can't tell if she's kidding," I say to Austin.

He lifts both brows and sips his coffee. "Welcome to my world."

"If you find any, set them aside for me," Marianne says as she drifts out of the kitchen and into the hallway, her flowing skirt tangling around her legs.

I shudder and drop my stack onto the table. "Ew."

"If it makes you feel any better, I've been through hundreds of these photos, Lou. Everyone is usually clothed."

"Usually?"

"Well, it *was* the seventies."

We're alone in the kitchen, the only sound coming from

the starburst-shaped wall clock above the fridge. "Were you and Marianne talking about me? Outside?" The question pops out of my mouth before I can fully realize what I'm asking, how vulnerable and insecure the question sounds in this quiet kitchen.

Austin tilts his head for a beat. Then he says, "Not really? Marianne asked how my day was going. Said I ran into you outside Evanston and that we go to the same school."

"Oh. Okay." I hate that I'm relieved right now. Hate that I care, the tiniest bit, about what was said behind my back. I blame Jordan and the whole AP Bio Awkward Fest. Before he can mistake my moment of insecurity as an invitation to make personal small talk, I point to the camping trip photo. "Hey, who is that?"

Austin peers at the photo in question, both hands wrapped around his cup. "That's Georgie."

"Who's Georgie?"

He glances toward the hallway and lowers his voice. "Georgie was Marianne's lover."

I choke on my coffee. "Oh god. Don't. Lover is the *grossest* term of all time."

Austin gives me a bemused look. "How about partner? Is that acceptable?"

"Acceptable," I say with a nod.

"Georgie was Marianne's *partner*," he says slowly, his lips curving into a smile. "She passed away forever ago. In 1985, I think? I'm not sure on the details."

My chest squeezes tight. "Shit. That's sad."

"Yeah. Marianne will talk about Georgie, but only in stories. The highlights. Never about losing her, though. She's . . ." He trails off, pausing for a sip of coffee. "I don't know. Marianne is kind of weird about grief."

My palms are sweaty against my cup. "Aren't most people weird about grief?"

Austin stares at the overlapping photographs on the table. "Yeah, probably. No one likes to talk about losing people they love. It's depressing as fuck. But it's healthy, you know?"

And the award for the most well-adjusted seventeen-year-old goes to Austin Yang.

"Right." I stare down at the photographs, suddenly longing for the ease of joking about Marianne's nudes.

None of this information about Marianne is surprising. She already told me everyone she'd ever loved was dead—that's the only reason why Austin and I are even here. But seeing a photograph of Marianne, caught both in time and in love, gives me goose bumps. An uneasy, panicky feeling in my chest. Death is such an abstract concept to me. One of my grandparents passed away before I was born; the rest are still alive. No one I've known personally has died.

I don't know how people do it. Losing people sounds worse than spending an eternity alone.

"Grief can fuck you up if you don't deal with it," Austin continues, and pushes aside some of the photographs to set his cup down. "When my dad died, my mom made us all go to therapy. At the time, it sucked, but now I'm glad. It helped me cope, you know?"

I blink at the boy across from me.

Austin's . . . dad died? The sunshine emoji in human form lost his *dad*? This new information doesn't fit my mental image of Austin, who acts like he's never had a bad day in his life.

Like, this is actively distressing but for all the wrong reasons. "I'm—um, sorry about your dad. Was it . . . recent?"

"Me too," he replies simply. "But no, years ago, when I was ten. I mean, it still sucks, and I still cry about it sometimes, but I can't change what happened."

"I'm sorry," I say again, because what else am I supposed to say? I don't know how to talk about death or grief. Even thinking about it fills me with intense existential dread. "Seriously. I had no idea."

"It's okay, Lou," Austin says quietly, and strangely, he smiles. "Really."

Marianne returns to the kitchen, and we luckily drop the subject of dead dads before I can say "I'm sorry" ten more times, focusing on Marianne as she works through the photos, regaling us with stories. Like how she and Georgie met.

"June of 1975. We'd just wrapped up our first tour at the Showbox. I was supposed to be in the greenroom for an interview, but I snuck out back for a smoke. And there she was. Georgie," Marianne says, smoking her fourth cigarette since we arrived. "She wore this yellow shirtdress with white sandals and was losing a battle with a Bic lighter. I offered her a light and walked away with her number."

Stories upon stories upon stories. I feel like Marianne has hundreds, maybe thousands, of these stories. And strangely enough, I want to hear them all.

As we go, I set aside the photos Marianne wants help digitizing—I volunteer the idea and offer to help, since computers are really the only thing I'm good at—and spend the rest of our visit in the kitchen.

Thankfully, no nudes are found.

"Austin," Marianne says when we wrap up, "can you do me a favor and bring in the packages by the garage? Should be a few cases of Nox's food. They're too heavy for me."

"Sure thing," he says with a salute, and disappears down the hallway for his shoes.

The door closes a moment later, and it's just me and Marianne in the darkening kitchen, the only light coming from the garden lamps out in the sunroom.

"From an untrained eye, it almost looks like you and Austin are getting along," Marianne says as I collect our empty to-go cups. "A week can really change things, can't it?"

I snort, rinsing the cups out in the sink. "Are you high? Nothing's changed."

"Sadly, I'm sober at the moment," Marianne says with a wink as she stands up, stretching both arms overhead. "But Austin could use a friend like you."

"We barely know each other." I toss the empty coffee cups into the recycling bin beneath the sink. "Just because we both volunteer here and go to the same school doesn't mean he wants to be my friend. He probably can't stand me."

Marianne's big, orb-like blue eyes narrow their focus on me, the spotlight bright and unrelenting. "You know, the whole poor self-confidence, woe-is-me schtick isn't as cute as you think it is."

I cross my arms over my chest, heat flushing my face. "Fuck you, I don't have a *schtick*."

The room falls silent, and I brace myself. I really doubt Donna's tip sheet recommends telling your clients to fuck off. But then Marianne laughs. A shock wave of noise. A contagious noise that makes me smile.

"Fuck you too, doll. But we're getting off track," she says with a lazy wave of her hand. "I know you probably see an optimistic, happy-go-lucky kid, but Austin's an onion."

"A what?"

Marianne gives me a pointed look, reaching into the pocket of her skirt for her cigarettes. "I heard you two talking about his dad. Austin's got layers. Don't write him off. That boy doesn't have a mean bone in his body. Schtick or not," she adds with a quirked brow, "you could use a friend. And so could he."

Austin chooses this very moment to return to the kitchen through the sunroom, carrying a stack of cardboard boxes. Some part of me is annoyed. I don't want to think of Austin as someone with layers. I don't want to know deeply personal details about him, because it's way easier to write him off this way. To write off this whole weird volunteer situation, honestly.

But as Austin and I say our goodbyes, donning our jackets and shoes, I realize something. When I was talking to Marianne, I never told her that *I* didn't want to be Austin's friend. I just said he wouldn't want to be mine. Both statements are true, though. I have zero interest in befriending Austin. What would even be the point of that?

"Penny for your thoughts?" Austin asks me as we walk down Marianne's cobblestone path toward the gate. He accidentally bumps into my shoulder as he tugs on a knit beanie.

"Nothing," I say, but I'm pretty sure Austin knows I'm lying.

We listen to music on the drive back to our neighborhood, and when he offers to drive me home, I say yes. Whatever will get me home the fastest. When we pull up in front of my house, he idles on the curb.

"Um. Thanks for the ride," I say, gathering my stuff from the floor of the van. I eye the glowing living room window, hoping that my mom's watching TV and not looking outside. She's really wanted me to make more friends since Lydie and Jordan dropped me. I don't want her getting the wrong idea.

As I hop out of the van, Austin rolls down the passenger-side window. "Hey, want me to pick you up on Saturday? We can carpool and save the earth together."

I rock back on my heels, feeling about ten different types of conflicted. Austin isn't turning out like the stereotype inside my head, and I hate it. Austin might be an onion, but I'm a cactus. "I don't want you going out of your way."

"I live literally two blocks that way, Lou." Austin hitches his thumb over his shoulder. When I don't reply, he grabs a receipt and pen from the cup holder and writes something down. "Here," he says, and leans across the van.

I step closer and grab the receipt, holding it gingerly like the piece of trash it is. "What is this?"

"My number. Text me if you want a ride Saturday, okay? Beats the bus."

Rain plinks onto the receipt, smearing the ink. I shove it into my pocket. "Thanks," I say, and start up my driveway. "Have a good rest of your night. Or whatever."

"Have a good rest of your night or whatever too," Austin says with a laugh, then drives off.

I linger on my driveway. Anxiety is multiplying inside me like a germ. For no good reason other than the fact that I'm freaked out. Freaked out that I like talking to Marianne. Freaked out that Jordan's comment got to me. Freaked out that Marianne can read me like a fucking book. Freaked out that Austin is nice to me, even though I've given him every reason not to be.

Luckily, Mom didn't see Austin's creepy van drop me off, and I'm spared from an inquisition into my social life. Dinner is low-key and serve-yourself, so after doing homework, I bring my bowl of butternut squash chili down to the basement. My room is ice-cold, and I click on my space heater before booting up my computer.

I spoon chili into my mouth as I check my notifications on Monsoon, shooting off a few replies to the members of Unarmed Rage, promising I'll be online in an hour. As I eat, I tidy my desk and end up tugging the welcome packet Donna gave me out from beneath a pile of comics. Flipping it open, I thumb through the handouts.

The first has a list of suggested reading, the top title being *Together: The Healing Power of Human Connection in a Sometimes Lonely World* by Vivek Murthy. Beneath that sheet is a list of facts and figures. I tuck my feet beneath me on my desk chair and read the fact sheet while I finish eating.

Chronic Loneliness Can Lead to Adverse Health Consequences, Such As:

- **Depression**
- **Poor Sleep Quality**
- **Poor Cardiovascular Health**
- **Substance Abuse**
- **A 30 Percent Increased Chance of Stroke**

Recent studies of over 580,000 people showed that chronic loneliness increases the risk of premature death upward of 50 percent from every

cause, regardless of race. Loneliness is as lethal as smoking fifteen cigarettes a day.

Why Does Loneliness Increase Health Problems?

It seems as if loneliness can lead to long-term "fight-or-flight" responses, which negatively affect the immune system. Lonely people have less immunity and more inflammation than those with stronger social structures. Being lonely isn't the same as being alone. Humans need alone time and solitude, but in order to be healthy, being alone needs to be a choice. In particular, the elderly are at an increased risk for health concerns stemming from loneliness. They're more likely than other age groups to experience the physical and emotional effects of loneliness.

The Bottom Line? Loneliness Kills.

Yikes, Donna, laying it on a little thick?

I set the handout on my keyboard and scrape my spoon against the sides of my bowl for leftovers. Scare tactics aside, I had no idea that loneliness was that, well, unhealthy. Good thing I'm a loner—*not* lonely. All my alone time is by choice. But the line about the elderly really gets me thinking about Marianne. About how I'm not dreading Saturday nearly as much as I thought I would.

I shift until I can wiggle my hand into my pocket and yank out the crumpled receipt Austin gave me earlier. Mom already told me that she needs the car this weekend, and even if it's annoying to admit, the murder van *is* better than the bus. I definitely don't believe in fate, but the fact that we live so close to each other is kind of convenient.

Flattening the receipt against my leg, I frown at the numbers. Is that rain-smeared digit a seven or a nine? A nine. I think.

Well. Here goes nothing.

ME:
Pick me up Saturday?

Then I toss my phone onto the comforter like it's a grenade and pad into my bathroom to take a shower. As I wash my hair, I wait for the regret to ping at my chest. The backtracking. The anxiety. But it doesn't arrive. Because, whether I like it or not, Austin is now a part of my life. An annoying part of my life, to be sure, but I might as well get free rides out of the situation, right?

When I'm out of the shower, I pull on my pajamas and grab my phone from my bed.

AUSTIN:
Lou?

I groan, not that he's around to hear me, and plop onto my mattress.

ME:
Do you usually give strangers your number and offer them rides?

Wait. Don't answer that. You do, don't you? You're *that* good of a samaritan?

AUSTIN:
I'm not a rideshare, if that's what you're asking. just making sure it wasn't a wrong number 🙃

ME:
Amazingly not a wrong number. You were right

AUSTIN:
excuse me? 😮

ME:
Riding with you is better than the bus, okay? Don't take it personally. The bar is really low

Last week some tech dude in the back row jerked off to porn on his phone. Without headphones on. I'm scarred for life.

AUSTIN:
1) what the fuck 🥴 and 2) want some bleach for your brain?

ME:
Think I'm going to try repressing it

AUSTIN:
that sounds healthy. 10am Sat? 🌞

ME:
You use too many emojis

AUSTIN:
😱

ME:
10am works though

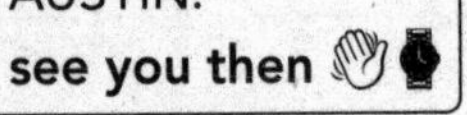

AUSTIN:
see you then

SEVEN

Blooming along the edges
Of becoming someone new
Because of you

—The Laundromats, "Sunflower" (1981)

I sip my fizzy water and click through a series of articles for my US Government and Politics class project in Evanston's computer lab Friday afternoon. Located on the third floor, the student station section of the lab is pretty nice for a public school—the computers aren't new, but they're not ancient, either. The big desk up front, usually occupied by Ms. Deaver, is empty. I've known Ms. Deaver since I was a freshman, and to my knowledge, I'm the only student with eating-in-the-lab privileges. Most kids knock over sticky sodas or get Cheetos crumbs in the keyboards. But Ms. Deaver trusts me. Good thing, too, because for the last year, I've eaten lunch here.

By myself.

Just the way I like it.

The lab's out of the way and usually empty. Sometimes Ms. Deaver munches on her salad and chats with me over the rows of computers. Other times, she reminds me to power down my computer when I'm done and gives me a warm pat on the shoulder on her way out. During lunch, I can catch up on homework or obsess over the USC subreddit.

Today, the lab is silent except for the hum of CPU fans—my favorite kind of white noise.

I jot down some notes in my Google doc for when I get home tonight.

On the other side of the lab, the door clicks open, and I glance up from the screen.

Austin is standing in the doorway, his brows so high they've nearly disappeared beneath the rim of his beanie. If he didn't look shocked to see me, I might think he was stalking me.

Not, like, *seriously* stalking me.

I'm way too boring to be stalked.

"Hey," he says, and sounds genuinely surprised.

"Hi." My hackles lower slightly. I haven't spoken or even thought about Austin since our text exchange last night. I mean, why would I? The texts were purely transactional, and today's been too much of a clusterfuck of assignments and boring classes to think of anything LifeCare-related.

"What're you doing in here?"

I hold up my drink. "Lunch."

Austin wanders between the rows of computers to join me. "Does Ms. Deaver know you're eating in here?" he chides, nodding to the NO FOOD OR DRINKS signs she's plastered around the room.

"Yep." For good measure, I shove a chip into my mouth.

Austin leans one hip against the desk beside mine. "Is she around?" He holds up a folder. "Dropping off sign-ups for the food drive next week."

I wrinkle my nose. "Huh?"

"The annual food drive?" he says, his tone as if I've been living under a rock for the last three years. "We do it every year for the Ballard Food Bank. Ms. Deaver helps coordinate . . . ? None of this is ringing a bell, is it?"

"Erm. No." Until this moment, I had no idea we had a food drive. Wow. I really am a shitty person compared to Austin, huh? Even when I had a modicum of a social life, I did my best to steer clear of all school-sanctioned events. Lydie and Jordan were the well-rounded ones, not me.

Austin pulls out the desk chair beside me and sits down. "We could always use an extra hand—"

"Nope. Nice try. LifeCare is an anomaly. I'm not a . . . *helper*," I explain, and hold out the bag of chips toward him. Ew. Did I just quote Mister Rogers?

"Thanks." He grabs one, then pauses and glances suspiciously between me and the proffered chips. "Lou, you're not going to start being nice to me because of what I told you about my dad, right?"

"Wouldn't dream of it."

Austin pops the chip into his mouth. "Okay, cool. Because I'd really prefer you to be an asshole to me forever. I find the consistency very comforting."

I set the chips on the desk and pull my sandwich from my backpack. "Luckily for you, I can arrange that."

He laughs, grinning wide. Neither of us says anything for a moment, the sound of the CPU fans humming loud, and awkwardness prickles at me. I shift my attention back to the monitor. Waiting for him to leave.

But then he says, "I'm gonna hit up the taco truck. Wanna come with?"

"Um." I hold up the sandwich. "That's okay."

"Lou, you're eating all alone in the computer lab. Save the sandwich for later. Besides, tacos beat sandwiches."

Lunch only started ten minutes ago. Technically, I have time. And Austin's right. Tacos are way better than the soggy peanut butter and jelly in my hand. But this is weird. Austin and I don't hang out. We're forced together because of LifeCare. We don't *choose* to be around each other.

"Don't you have friends to eat with?" I ask, my tone coming off grumpier than I intended. Is this pity? Did he see me here, eating all alone in the computer lab, and feel compelled to invite me? Doesn't seem wildly out of character for someone like Austin.

"Nah. I usually eat in the music room or go off campus." He drums his hands on his thighs. "Most of my friends—the band—go to Brickline."

Brickline is the fancy arts school in Shoreline; it has major theater-kid energy. "Oh." Like most pieces of Austin Information, this doesn't fit. The Austin inside my head is popular and gregarious. But the boy in front of me is . . . looking at me hopefully. Like I'd be doing *him* a favor.

"Tacos, Lou. You could be eating tacos right now," Austin says, nudging my Doc Marten with his sneaker. "Please? I hate eating alone. It's depressing."

Dead dad or not, I kind of doubt Austin knows what actual depression feels like.

But I toss the sandwich into my backpack. "Okay. Let's go."

Austin's perma-smile widens. "C'mon, you miserable lump of a human being," he says, hopping up from his chair. "Let's go get tacos."

Maybe it's Austin calling me a miserable lump of a human being, but I'm almost enjoying this conversation. Or that could be the promise of tacos speaking. I shrug on my backpack, and after Austin leaves the folder for Ms. Deaver on her desk, I follow him out into the hall.

The third floor is quiet during lunch, and the tile squeaks beneath the soles of our shoes. We walk side by side, but far enough away so we don't accidentally bump into each other. "Do you usually eat up here?" Austin asks.

I hold on to the straps of my backpack, anxiety sweat dampening my bra. Every cell in my body is urging me to turn around and go eat my soggy-ass sandwich in the computer lab.

"Um," I say, and my brain starts buffering. Do I tell him the truth? Lie? If we're going to be spending time together with Marianne, he'll probably figure out my loner status sooner or later. Not like I'm ashamed or anything. People get the wrong idea and seemingly can't understand the concept of being alone by choice. *Shit.* I'm taking too long to answer. "Pretty much. The extra time to work on homework is nice."

"What? Your friends don't miss your sparkling personality during lunch when you're cooped up here?" Austin asks, and we begin walking down the stairwell. We pass a handful of teachers on their way to the teachers' lounge, which is beside the computer lab. Half of them say hi to me, because yes, I'm *that* student.

My shoulders tense. But Austin is bound to learn some personal details about me if we're going to work together for the next few months. Might as well have control over the narrative. "I don't—" My mouth goes dry, and I try again. "I don't really have many friends at school either." Or at all. But baby steps.

"Seriously?" Austin's brows arch, like this is surprising and new information.

"Seriously." I busy myself with tugging my hoodie out of my backpack; it's pinned beneath my Calc textbook. We reach the main floor and duck through the side exit closest to the student-teacher parking lot, where the taco truck sets up on Fridays.

We cross the parking lot, and I count my steps, waiting for Austin to badger more details out of me like I'm a human piñata. Or make fun of me. But neither happens. And I guess this one piece of Austin Information *does* fit. He's kind. Like Marianne said, I doubt he even knows how to be mean.

Really makes me wonder why he's hanging out with me, but okay.

We reach the taco truck, and any conversation about friends—or lack thereof—ends.

"Okay," Austin says, rubbing his palms together as he studies the menu. "What're you thinking?"

"Um." I squint at the chalkboard menu. "The chicken tinga tacos are pretty good."

Austin bumps his arm against mine, and when I look at him, he smiles. "Way better than that PB&J, huh?"

I pull on my hoodie and don't reply.

The line is long, but it moves fast. The taco truck guys come prepared to feed all of us unruly teenagers, and they have their system down pat. Austin and I order, pay for our respective meals, and wait off to the side while they're made.

Once we have our cardboard-box trays with our tacos, Austin gestures for me to follow him closer to the street. He plops down on a mow strip, stretches his legs out into a parking space, and balances the tray on his lap. I lower myself beside him and dump my backpack at my feet, but I glance around before digging into my tacos. Because eating outside is way, way more exposed than eating in the computer lab. It's almost *social.*

Doesn't help that I haven't eaten out here since before winter break of junior year. Nearly a year ago. Depending on the weather, Lydie, Jordan, and I bounced between the indoor cafeteria and a picnic table on the other side of the taco truck, beneath a gigantic maple tree. From Austin's spot on the mow strip, I can just barely see the old picnic bench. Just barely see Lydie and Jordan.

I turn back around and stare at the tacos in my lap.

"Something wrong?" Austin asks, pausing mid-bite. A chunk of al pastor falls onto his jeans.

"Nope." And it's the truth. Because nothing's changed. Nothing's new. Lydie and Jordan are exactly the same, down to their chosen seats at the exact same picnic table they've been eating at since freshman year.

I pick up a taco and try to turn my brain off.

After one bite, I have to admit that Austin was right. They're worth braving the outside world.

"What're you up to this weekend?" Austin shoves an entire folded taco into his mouth. "Other than volunteering, that is."

Truthfully, other than my pile of homework awaiting me, nothing. Blissful, amazing nothingness. Marianne's will take a chunk of Saturday, but after I wrap up my homework, I'm planning on playing *RotR* all weekend and never leaving the basement.

I swallow some chicken tinga and sip my fizzy water. Then I say, "Mostly homework. Senior year is off to a brutal start. But um, other than that? Probably video games."

"What games do you play?" He uses a compostable fork to shovel some leftover al pastor onto his last remaining street taco.

My insides tighten. Why? Because most people mock MMORPGs. They think they're the epitome of nerdiness. Like everyone who plays lives in their mom's basement or something. I mean, I *technically* live in my mom's basement, but I'm also seventeen. Not the same thing.

"*Realm of the Ravager*," I finally say, because I don't care what Austin thinks of me.

"Seriously?" Austin laughs, and my insides tighten even more. Maybe I was wrong about Austin not knowing how to be mean. But then he adds, "I used to play with my older brother all the time."

"Really?" I glance sideways at him, then fixate on my tacos. He doesn't look like someone who'd play *RotR*. But I guess that proves my point.

Austin wipes his hands off with a napkin and sets the tray beside him. "Really. But Ethan—that's my brother—is in college and started dating this girl last year who thinks it's too dorky, so he refuses to play with me. I haven't logged in in a while." He shrugs. "It's not as much fun solo."

I began playing *RotR* in the eighth grade. Jordan was never interested, despite my many attempts to get her hooked on the game. She never judged, though; it just wasn't her thing. But Lydie? Lydie definitely thought it was dorky and never let me forget the reputation *RotR*—and MMORPGs—have. Since they ditched me, I've upped my playtime to unhealthy levels. I've definitely seen my mom reading "So Your Kid Is Addicted to Video Games" articles when she thinks I'm not looking.

But I've never, ever played *RotR* with real-life friends before.

I use the game's built-in group finder or ask my guild; we usually voice chat over Discord. "Well, to your brother's girlfriend's credit, the game *is* pretty dorky."

Austin laughs, leaning back on his hands. "Fair. But that's what makes it fun, right?"

I grin. "Exactly. That's part of the charm."

"What's that on your face?"

"Probably guacamole," I say, reaching for a napkin.

"Yeah, that's not guac. If I'm not mistaken, that's a smile." Austin is, predictably, way too happy about this. "I didn't think this was possible. Or you knew *how* to smile. Hold on, let me get my phone so I can document—"

"Stop!" I shriek in horror, and cover my face as he aims his phone at me. "It's not a big deal!"

"This," Austin says seriously, "*is* a big deal. The biggest deal! I've known you for a week and this is the first time you've smiled. Wow. I made you smile. Who would've thought."

"*Realm of the Ravager* makes me smile. Not you." My cheeks heat with embarrassment, and I busy myself with collecting my trash. Beneath my breath, I mutter, "This is why I don't leave the computer lab."

Austin gets up to dump our trash into the compost bin on the other side of the mow strip. "You know what, Lou?" he says, and sits back down beside me. "I think you're full of shit. Admit it: you're having fun."

The words are smug and confident, and I resist the urge to shove him into the parking lot on the off chance a car might come and run him over.

I roll my eyes so hard it makes me dizzy. "Fine. You're okay to hang out with. I guess."

"'Okay'?" he repeats. "I was expecting something along the lines of 'awful' or 'super annoying.' You know what? I'll take it."

As super annoying as Austin is, he's right. I *am* having fun. The ache behind my sternum that's almost always present from eight to three on weekdays has faded into a phantom pain. The whole situation is too weird for words.

Austin and me, having stuff in common? Hanging out of our own volition?

"If I'm okay to hang out with, does that mean you might want to play *Realm of the Ravager* together sometime?" Austin zips up his messenger bag. The warning bell clangs, reminding us to get to class or else. "I've missed it."

I stand, groaning as I lift my backpack onto my shoulders. "Um. Maybe," I say, and I'd shrug if it weren't for the fifty pounds of textbooks weighing me down.

Austin and I fall into step, heading back to the towering brick building. "Cool," he says cheerfully. "And I'm still picking you up tomorrow?"

I bob my head in agreement. "Sure. Whatever works." The second warning bell clangs and I wave, heading off to Calculus. The classroom is upstairs, and I keep my head down to avoid any accidental eye contact as I make my way toward the staircase.

Austin is a lot of things. But he's also surprising. When people are nice to me, I assume it's out of pity or obligation. For whatever reason, Austin seems genuine. Almost painfully so. Like he wants to be *my* friend. That, or there's a sign on my back that says HEY, I'M LONELY, LET'S HANG OUT. I can do this—be nice to Austin. Forge a friendship with him.

Sure, Austin will eventually realize that I'm a shit friend.

But until then, maybe I don't have to eat alone in the computer lab anymore.

EIGHT

The greatest mistake I'll never make
Is what happened between you and me

—The Laundromats, "One for the Road" (1984)

With a solid week of community service behind me, the second one passes uneventfully. Austin, Marianne, and I walked along Green Lake with hot chocolates last Saturday, and we spent Tuesday and Thursday working through boxes of old photographs with her. Austin's given me rides every single LifeCare day, either picking me up from the curb in front of my house on the weekends or meeting me in the upperclassmen's lot behind the school.

Today, Marianne had no interest in working on the basement, and it's too stormy to go on a walk. Instead—when she heard that I'd never seen a live performance of the Laundromats—she asked Austin if he could pull up some old videos online. Hard to believe I'm getting volunteer credits for half paying attention to old rock performances, but hey, I'm not complaining.

We're all in the "great room," as Marianne calls it. Not sure what's so great about it; the room is no less cluttered, spider-web-filled, or eclectic than the rest of the house. The hardwood floor is creaky and cold. There's an old teaching skeleton in the corner wearing a field jacket that Marianne *claims* belonged to Patti Smith; a snuffbox with what looks like forty-year-old cocaine caked inside, perched on the mantel beside Marianne's Grammy; giant framed posters from the Laundromats shows lining the walls; and a grand piano with a crystal gazing ball sitting off to the side of the fireplace.

It's like a drugged-out antique store.

But Austin stoked a fire to life in the mother-of-pearl-inlaid fireplace, and it's cozy. Rain lashes against the stained-glass windows that face the backyard, and the chandelier above our heads casts the room in a warm, buttery light.

"This was our first show," Marianne says from her spot on a gold-threaded love seat. Nox purrs, molded against the curve of her legs, partially covered by the velvet blanket draped over her lap.

The TV is old, boxy. Like something from before I was even born. It's perched on a cedar chest, the screen covered in a fingerprint-smudged layer of dust. Austin's clearly done this before, because he pulled an adapter out of his messenger bag and hooked up his laptop to the ancient machine. Makes me wonder how often Marianne does this, watches old videos of herself.

I can't tell if it's a power move or just sad.

"Well," Marianne amends with a tilt of her head, "the first one recorded. I think. We played constantly, all over the city. Usually for drunks. Or friends. Or drunk friends."

"How old were you?" I ask, because the Marianne on the boxy TV is young, only a few years older than me and Austin. No longer a teenager but definitely not an adult. Shifting in my armchair, I glance between the girl on the screen and the woman sitting beside me.

Marianne hums beneath her breath for a second. "Nineteen or twenty," she says, almost to herself. Then: "That sounds right. Twenty. We signed our first record deal a few weeks after my twenty-first birthday. The record exec was in the crowd that night."

Twenty-year-old Marianne is similar to the girl from the photographs I saw in the kitchen, and the Marianne who shows up online. Tall and imposing—hard to miss or turn away from—but at the same time, there's something delicate about her. Onstage, she's wearing a denim jumpsuit with platform sandals, flowers braided in her hair. She smiles as she sings, and you'd never, ever expect a voice so rich and so deep to come out of a girl like that.

"Everyone was playing at Lindon's," Marianne continues, and there's this spark to her voice. Like she's happy to have an audience. Even though I'm sure Austin's heard her stories a thousand times before, I haven't. And I'm a snoop, so naturally, I want to know everything. "Dumb luck we ended up on that stage. Our drummer's cousin—or was it his brother?—was a janitor there. The opener's bus broke down outside Portland hours before the show, and he hounded the booker into giving us a call. And I thought, in that moment, it'd be the highlight of my career."

Marianne doesn't strike me as the modest type, but it's clear—even with my lack of musical knowledge—that the Laundromats were something special. That the Lindon's show was just the beginning. Other than the talent, which they clearly possessed, they had that unknown factor, that *charisma*. They were a big band—two guitarists, one drummer, one bassist, one backup singer and tambourine player, and one Marianne Landis. Sure, they were talented as a group, but Marianne was the front woman for a reason. She was the thread knitting them all together.

"You guys were incredible," Austin says from the floor, leaning forward with his elbows on his knees. He clasps his hands together and rests his chin on them. Completely enraptured, even though he's seen this video before; I saw the entire YouTube playlist of the Laundromats performances on his account earlier. "Ol's bass work is . . ." He lets out a happy sigh.

"Did you know who Marianne was before you started volunteering?" I tuck one of my legs beneath me.

"Nope. As Bob Ross would say, it was a happy accident." He glances sideways at me, his chin still on his hands. "She was on my call list as Marianne L., and I didn't recognize her name at first. But I eventually put the pieces together. When Donna told me Marianne requested house calls, I jumped on the opportunity to hang out with her."

Marianne chuckles, smiling fondly at Austin. "Austin took me by surprise. I wasn't expecting someone so *young* to know our music. After we broke up, it's not like we were forgotten. But musical trends change, new talent emerges . . . People cover our songs, and my manager convinced me to license the lyrics to 'Upstream Woman' for a Nissan commercial. But this"—she juts her chin toward the screen—"was a lifetime ago. That's the weird thing about fame. It's like love: intense and loud and over before you know it."

Marianne doesn't sound sad or wistful about this. If anything, she sounds relieved.

Even though the concert hasn't ended yet, the TV snaps off and Marianne sets the controller down on the couch beside Nox. "Well, Eloise, what do you think?"

"You were amazing," I say, and it's the truth. No snark, no bite. Just the truth.

The corner of Marianne's mouth twitches. "Past tense?"

I roll my eyes.

Austin laughs and pushes up from the floor. "You're still amazing, Marianne." He unplugs his laptop. Tucking it beneath his arm, he says, "I'll grab lunch."

Even though I, oddly enough, want to follow Austin, I stay curled up in my armchair. I know how to talk to him, even if he's a chirpy little ball of sunshine. I'm still figuring Marianne out. Unlike Austin, she's . . . unpredictable.

Fascinating, but also terrifying.

Marianne sits up and wanders across the great room to a small wet bar in the corner. Glasses clink as she pours herself a drink; then she turns and leans against the bar and says, "Sometimes, watching those videos is like a portal, a step backward into my memories. But other times, it unleashes everything I've tried to forget." She tips back her drink, smacks her lips.

"What? Being famous wasn't everything you wanted?" I joke, because fame is my actual nightmare.

Marianne raises her brows. "No one knows what they want when they're twenty years old."

"That's fair." I shift in my seat, watching as the older woman pours herself another drink. "Why'd the band break up? There's almost nothing online about what happened."

"The short story? Our lead guitarist, Mark, had an affair with our drummer Billy's wife. And secrets like those?" She snorts, shakes her head. "There aren't any secrets in a band, not for long. Billy was devastated when he found out. We were on tour in London, backstage at the Rainbow Theater. Billy punched

Mark. Allison—that was Billy's wife—flew back to the States with their kids. Tour was canceled. Billy and Mark refused to be in the same room together. It was a mess, so we called it. But we were all done years before that. That kind of lifestyle burns you out. Burns out the people around you, your loved ones . . ."

Marianne trails off, something shifting in her expression, and she takes another sip. Smacks her lips together again. I bite my tongue to keep from asking about Georgie, how she fits into this messy puzzle of music and relationships. But I don't want to hurt Marianne either. I don't trust myself to be gentle and tactful like Austin.

Instead, I ask, "Have you spoken to any of them since?"

Marianne shakes her head. "No. But that's for the best. We all fucking hated one another at the end. You always do."

"I was going to ask you for a pep talk before the battle of the bands," Austin says as he returns with three soup bowls balanced on a serving tray, "but now I'm not so sure."

Marianne barks a laugh. "Austin, you're impossible to hate. And why is this the first I'm hearing about the battle of the bands?"

Austin sets the tray onto the coffee table. "Because we only confirmed our spot last night," he says with an uncharacteristically nervous smile.

"That's amazing. Don't listen to me. I'm washed up and jaded." Marianne returns to the love seat, then jabs her finger in his direction. "You'd better record every second of that show."

"Or you could come watch," he says, pumping his eyebrows as if enticing her, and grabs a random dining chair from the corner, pulling it into our semicircle around the coffee table.

"In addition to washed up and jaded, I'm old. Too old for

a battle of the bands," she says with a dismissive wave of her hand. "Thank you, but I'll pass."

"Just think about it," Austin says, digging into his soup. "It's not until the end of October."

Marianne makes a noncommittal noise and eats her lunch.

I take a bowl and lean back into my armchair. "So. Um, Phoenix, what instrument do you play?" This is me making an effort. The question feels weird and forced coming out of my mouth. But I've known Austin for two weeks and I feel kind of shitty for never asking before this, since the band is, like, his life.

Austin's taken to his nicknames far easier than I have—my blood pressure rises every time he calls me Lou—and doesn't hesitate over being called the state capital of Arizona. "The bass and occasional keyboard. Some vocals."

"You sing?" This surprises me, and I smother the urge to smile just in case he tries whipping out his phone again.

"Hey, I have a great singing voice," he says in mock defense.

I chuckle. "Uh-huh. Sure."

Marianne points at me with her spoon. "Believe it or not, he's telling the truth. Austin, show her one of your performances. The one you showed me, on your Insta-whatever."

Austin lifts his brows at me. "Lou, would you like to watch a video of my band performing?"

"I'd rather eat glass," I say cheerfully. "But thank you for asking."

"Oh, anytime. My pleasure."

Marianne glances between us with a smile.

"What?" I'm suddenly self-conscious, holding my bowl of soup close to my chest.

"Nothing," she says. "I'm glad you're here, Eloise. Austin was getting a little dull on his own."

Austin looks up from his soup. "I'm sitting *right here*."

Marianne leans over and pats him on the forearm. "Don't worry. You're still my favorite."

"For now," I add in a singsong voice. "I'm competitive, remember?"

"You two are the worst," he mutters, but he's grinning.

And I'm grinning too.

Because this is the best Saturday I've had in a while.

Later that night, I look over my planner after dinner. I've logged almost fifteen hours with LifeCare. Not too shabby. My application essay is still plagued by the blinking cursor of doom, though. I open the word processor, click over to my essay document, and reread the prompt at the top of the page:

> *USC believes that one learns best when interacting with people of different backgrounds, experiences, and perspectives. Tell us about a time you were exposed to a new idea or when your beliefs were challenged by another point of view. Please discuss the significance of the experience and its effect on you.*

I sigh, raspberrying my lips, then massage the space between my brows. My brain is drawing a spectacular blank. There are only three prompts to choose from and this one seemed the easiest. And yet . . . I have no fucking idea what to write about. Most of the time, I'm able to *not* think of what'll happen if I don't get into USC. But the panic settles in my chest as I sit in my basement bedroom, the only light coming from my monitor.

Mom wants me to apply to University of Washington, and I get it—UW is a great school. And Seattle has loads of opportunities for gaming internships. But how am I supposed to start over and move past all the bullshit and friendship failures if I never *leave*? I groan and rest my head on my desk.

Ding.

I unstick my forehead from the desk and check my Monsoon notifications. The gaming client for *Realm of the Ravager* is pretty much always running in the background of my computer, but now it has a little red dot on the dashboard icon. I click on the icon.

User **baselessinseattle** sent you a message. Accept/Reject.

I usually don't read messages from randos. But I have a feeling I know the rando in question, and I hit accept.

baselessinseattle 7:51 p.m.
Lou! I reupped my subscription. want to start new RotR characters with me?

esioledoesntcare 7:51 p.m.
How'd you find my username?

baselessinseattle 7:52 p.m.
the "Add Friend" function can search by phone number

esioledoesntcare 7:52 p.m.
You could've just texted me and asked

baselessinseattle 7:52 p.m.
that . . . would've been easier. wasn't sure if I could text you about non-LifeCare stuff

esioledoesntcare 7:53 p.m.
You can

baselessinseattle 7:54 p.m.
good to know ☺

esioledoesntcare 7:54 p.m.
Oh no you found the emojis

baselessinseattle 7:54 p.m.
🧙🐉🗡️

esioledoesntcare 7:55 p.m.
I'm blocking you if you keep that up

baselessinseattle 7:55 p.m.
okay, I'll stop. so, you down?

I lean back in my chair and stare at the screen. While we've hung out during our rides and at Marianne's, he hasn't brought up *RotR* since Taco Friday. Which was over a week ago. I assumed that he wasn't serious about playing. That, in the moment while we scarfed down tacos, he was trying to be nice. Because that's what Austin is—*nice*. But I was wrong. He's here, harassing me with his emoji usage, and actually wants to play.

I guess . . . it could be fun playing with someone I know. Might as well try. The block button is just a click away if this is terrible, right?

esioledoesntcare 7:58 p.m.
Do you have Discord?

baselessinseattle 7:58 p.m.
send me a friend invite

Then Austin sends me his username.

I open Discord and pause, my mouse hovering over the green add friend button. I'm not even friends with the members of Unarmed Rage; we have a server we use to communicate and coordinate. But I paste in Austin's username and send the friend request, which he accepts in less than five seconds.

Then I pop on my headphones and turn on my microphone.

"Hey." Austin's voice is both familiar and foreign coming through my headphones, disembodied and deep. Out of place in my dark bedroom. "Can you hear me?"

"Yep." I readjust my volume. "You're good."

There's a shuffling noise as he adjusts his microphone, and he says, "This is weird."

My stomach clenches like a fist. Maybe this *is* too weird, us playing a video game together. "Um—"

"I haven't used Discord in so long. I forget how to change my push to talk. Help."

The fist releases. *Way to go jumping to conclusions,* I think, and force myself to relax. Austin was the one who asked me to play. He started all this, so if it's a hot mess, it's his fault—even if I'm the socially incompetent one.

"Go to user settings, then voice and video." I switch screens to *RotR*. I log out of my main and return to the login screen to make a new character.

Austin types for a moment—a rhythmic clacking—before he says, "Got it. Thanks, Lou. Okay! What race are we going with?"

"Moon Elf?" I suggest because they're my go-to.

"Awesome. Moon Elves are awesome." He sounds giddy, like he's excited to play.

"Any class preference?" I work on my character's looks. *RotR* has pretty basic customization, and I scroll through the face options. All the different faces remind me of that meme from *The Office* where both pictures look the same.

"Ethan and I always played rogues. Fair warning, I'm going to be pretty rusty. But maybe less so on a rogue?"

I click on the rogue symbol (two crossed daggers dripping with blood, very original) to lock in my class. "Rogue it is," I tell him, then finalize my character creation.

I listen to Austin's endless stream of commentary as he creates his character, and I find myself smiling. As much as I like my guild, we're strictly business. Questing and raids and PvP. This is . . . relaxed. Fun, even.

"Okay," Austin says a few minutes later. "I'm in the starting zone. My character is Zadreal."

I navigate Fasia, my character, through Mareglen, the magical, woodsy town where all Moon Elves begin their starter quests. Since we're in the same realm, I find Austin's character and add him to a group so we can quest together and share progress. His character jumps up and down on the screen, then does a bowing emote.

"Nerd," I mutter, but I'm smiling even wider now. This is weird but not altogether terrible.

In the game, I make my character curtsy, and Austin laughs, the sound booming against my eardrums.

"Oh god, I'm going to die constantly, aren't I?"

I snort. Maybe this'll be even more fun than I thought. "I'll help you out. If you have questions, let me know. I spend, like, ninety-five percent of my nonschool life on this game. I've been playing since the Blood Lord expansion."

On-screen Austin jumps up and down as he walks toward the quest giver, trying to get his character to do a backflip, which occurs on random chance. "Thanks for playing with me."

"Um. Yeah." In the game, I run up to the quest giver and accept our quest. Austin does the same, and we head off into the twilight-dappled forest to kill some diseased wolves. "Thanks for playing with me too."

I hate to admit it, but Austin's right: playing with friends is way more fun.

NINE

What if we're only temporary?
Here for an hour, gone in another?

—The Laundromats, "Like Yesterday" (1984)

The following Tuesday, Austin and I help Marianne work on Project Nostalgia for two hours after school. And for those two hours, I use the portable scanner I brought from home and digitize photo after photo. Honestly, Project Nostalgia is busywork. But—busywork or not—organizing the chaotic pocket dimension that is Marianne's spare room still counts as volunteer hours. Hours that will be proof, to the USC application committee, that I care about my community.

Eloise Deane: helper.

While we work, we listen to music on the ancient record player, laugh at bad hairstyles, and listen to Marianne's stories, and it's not terrible. As I organize and scan photos by year, I pay special attention to those featuring Georgie.

"What's the story behind this one?" I ask, angling the photo in my hand toward Marianne. In it, Marianne's perched on the back of a gigantic yellow speedboat that looks straight out of *Baywatch*, in a gingham-checkered bikini, legs kicking into the water. Behind her is Georgie, in a pinup-style bathing suit—dark curls spilling from a bun—as she's caught mid-pop of a champagne bottle, the spray arcing over Marianne's head.

She plucks the Polaroid from my fingers. Then laughs. "Georgie's birthday. Her twenty-second or twenty-third, I can't remember. But we rented a boat, stocked it with all the champagne I'd brought back from France during our latest tour, and spent the entire day on Lake Washington. Drunk and warm and . . . happy. She looks so happy here, doesn't she?"

I study the photograph and smile. "You both do."

Maybe it's morbid, but Marianne's history—and losses—fascinate me. Austin lost his dad and he's still standing, growing up without one of his parents. Marianne lost her partner, and she has to exist in a world without her. I don't get how you move on from a loss that heavy.

I put the photo facedown on the scanner and upload the copy to my laptop, then move on to the next. Photo after photo. Memory after memory. I easily lose myself—and track of time—as I work through the photos. And before I know it, our visit is over.

"It's almost six," Austin says from the other side of the lumpy rug we've commandeered as our work space for the evening. "Wrap up, then head out?"

I motion to my stacks of photos. "Yeah. I have everything organized—roughly—between 1973 and 1975 so far. . . ." In addition to the scanner, I brought a packet of catalogue envelopes from home to store the originals. I slide the 1973 stack of photos into an envelope and use a Sharpie to scrawl the year on the outside. Then I pass it to Austin so he can put the corresponding fan mail, mementos, and miscellany with the photos. I repeat the process for the 1974 and 1975 photos.

Marianne pushes up from the couch, displacing Nox from

her lap. About an hour ago, she began coughing. Probably due to the dust and the fact that she chain-smokes like someone pays her by the cigarette. But after she disappeared upstairs for a mug of honeyed tea, she returned and stretched out on the couch, telling us to carry on without her.

Ten bucks it's all a ploy to get out of organizing.

"Austin," Marianne says, wandering over to take a look at our progress, "do you still want that recipe? I think I have it in the kitchen somewhere."

Austin brightens and hops to his feet. "Hell yeah. Perfect timing. My mom's birthday is next week."

"Recipe for what?" I ask.

"The best apple pie, Lou! Marianne has a killer recipe."

"My *mother* had a killer recipe," Marianne says, smoothing back the wild strands of bone-white hair from her cheeks. "I don't cook. Or bake."

"Or clean, by the looks of it," I mutter.

Marianne narrows her eyes into a glare. "Eloise, if the mess bothers you so much, by all means, have at it."

"Considering I haven't had my tetanus booster, I don't think that's a good idea."

"God, you're a little shit," she says with a ragged laugh, and pats me on the cheek as she heads for the staircase, Nox following her like a dark shadow.

I collect the envelopes before climbing to my feet and stack them on the coffee table. It's raining again today—guess fall decided to get a head start, and I'm not complaining—but thanks to the gas fireplace, the basement is sleepy-warm.

"Ready to go?" I lift my backpack off the ground and heft it over my right shoulder.

"Yep." Austin grabs his messenger bag, which was on the couch, and loops it over his head. "Hey, *RotR* was fun the other night."

I head for the stairs. "Yeah. You only died seventeen times while questing."

"You *counted*?"

"What? It was funny."

Austin follows me up the creaky basement staircase. "Glad my fictional deaths bring you so much joy."

I sigh wistfully. "Me too."

We reach the top landing. "Well, if I wrap up my homework early tonight, I'd be down to play. Run that raid you were talking about?"

"You're nowhere near ready for raiding."

"You're missing the point, Lou," he says as we head toward the kitchen. "Just imagine how many times I'll die."

Even though I've tried implementing a strict No Smiling Around Austin rule, I can't help but grin. Because watching Austin die in *RotR* is extremely entertaining. There's commentary over Discord and dramatic emotes. "I should be done with my homework by nine."

"Awesome. I'll be there." Austin nudges my shoulder with his and steps into the kitchen, but I hang back.

Playing *Realm of the Ravager* with that goof was the highlight of my weekend, and while I'll never tell him that, it's . . . nice that it wasn't one-sided. When Lydie befriended Jordan—and me, I guess—it became so clear, so fast, that the things I loved weren't *cool*. And I became ashamed.

Not only of *Realm of the Ravager*, but of my unironic love for 1980s campy slasher films, and of the fact that my wardrobe consists of roughly twenty button-downs. Ashamed of the medications I'd hide in my bag during sleepovers. Ashamed of how I couldn't fit in, no matter how hard I tried.

Hanging out with Austin is effortless.

And I *really* don't know how I feel about that.

"Eloise," Marianne calls, and I walk into the kitchen.

"What's up?" I cross my arms defensively over my chest. As if Austin might be able to tell I'm having real-life feelings about playing a *video game* with him. Yeah, I'd never live that down.

Marianne's seated at the kitchen table, flipping through one of those old-fashioned recipe boxes that look like they're from the fifties. "I was just reminding Austin I'll be gone Thursday."

"Oh." Marianne . . . goes places? Honestly, until this very moment, I was convinced she didn't leave the two-mile radius around her house and the lake. Not like I'm a psychologist, but I hadn't ruled out agoraphobia. "Where are you going?"

Marianne plucks a recipe from the box and hands it to Austin, who stows it in his front pocket. "I have a yearly retreat in Colorado I like to attend." She grabs her cigarettes from the table and lights one. "Very *woo-woo*. Some of the workshops are ridiculous, but the food's good and the body workers are phenomenal."

"Sorry, I should've told you sooner." Austin kneels to scrub Nox behind the ears as she winds against our legs. "Marianne goes every September, but I totally blanked. But we're on for Saturday?"

Marianne exhales, the smoke coiling from her nostrils. "We'd better be," she says, then points at me with her cigarette. "I'll need someone to talk shit about the New Age yogis with. Eloise, that seem your speed?"

"Shit-talking usually is," I say with a bob of my head. But on the inside, I'm far less chill. No Marianne means I'll have to be on the phones if I want to keep up with my weekly hours. So far, I'm on track, and I'd like to stay that way.

Despite my unease, I tell Marianne to have a good time, and then Austin and I lock up behind us and return to the van.

"I have to swing by Pequeño's to pick up dinner for my mom," Austin says, checking his phone before dumping it into the cup holder. "You okay with tagging along? It's on our way home."

"Yeah." I click my seat belt. "I might order something for pickup too. My family really doesn't do dinner." Pequeño's is this local Mexican restaurant that advertises their burritos as "baby sized." Not small. The actual size of a newborn baby. They're gigantic and amazing.

Austin glances across the van. "You don't do . . . dinner?"

I laugh at his expression. "Calm down. I get fed. We just have an informal approach to dinner. We eat together once a week, otherwise my mom puts a frozen casserole in the oven or warms up soup for us."

"I can't tell if that's practical or depressing."

"Both?"

"Do your parents work full-time?"

"Um." I fiddle with my phone, pulling up Pequeño's online ordering. "My mom owns her own dog- and cat-grooming business. My dad used to work at Microsoft, but he was let go over the summer."

"Bummer. About your dad, not the grooming business, which is kind of awesome." He pulls onto the road, tracing the familiar path toward our neighborhood. "I didn't know you could groom cats."

"Oh, you can definitely groom cats. But that's why I'm doing community service." I focus on my phone and order a burrito the size of a small child. "I need a scholarship. Bad."

"Hold on. You're not hanging out with us out of the kindness of your cold, black heart?"

I flip Austin off, and he chuckles.

"Shitty circumstances aside," Austin continues, pausing at a four-way stop, "I'm glad you're volunteering with me. I like hanging out with you, even if you're the worst sometimes."

Through the online app, I submit my burrito order, and then I'm left with nothing else to pay attention to except the boy sitting beside me. After locking my phone, I drop it into the cup holder beside Austin's. I expect a jolt of anxiety or discomfort, but . . . that doesn't happen. *Why* doesn't that happen? Like with *RotR*, this is easy. "If you keep talking like that, someone might think we're friends."

"You are my friend," Austin says simply.

I glance across the van, headlights illuminating his profile. The anxiety I should've felt a minute earlier tenses my body, knocks me off-balance. Because this wasn't supposed to happen. Austin is the kind, layered one—an onion, if you ask Marianne. I'm prickly and shut off and I spend most of my waking hours hating myself. This doesn't make sense. But at the same time, this makes so much more sense than the last three years of Lydie and Jordan.

"Sorry, I didn't mean to freak you out," he says after a minute of *extremely awkward* silence. "You're under no obligation to be my friend or anything. We can have a one-sided friendship. That's cool."

A weird, strangled laugh escapes my lips. "No, it's not that. Um. I don't really do friendship."

"Okay, let me get this straight," Austin says, bemused. "You don't do dinner, and you don't do friendship."

"I used to do friendship," I admit, unsure of what I'm doing. Or why I'm still talking. "My two best friends ditched me last year and it sucked pretty hard."

"What happened?" He sounds genuinely interested. And that's the thing about Austin. He's so soft and open and easy to talk to. It also helps that I'm not looking at him. Just staring straight out the rain-streaked windshield.

I'm not the kind of person who is comfortable advertising their mental health struggles. I get why some people do it. To destigmatize it or help people feel less alone. But I'm not that person. Maybe things are under control right now, but I'm nowhere near having any kind of ownership over my disorders. But if Austin wants to be my friend, then he should know what he's getting into. That way, he can tap out now and save us both the trouble.

"I have pretty bad anxiety and depression. Sometimes, during the winter, it gets worse, and last year, it was bad. Really bad. Um." I hesitate, not going into the details. Don't want to utter the words *suicidal ideation*, that moment when I wasn't sure if I wanted to be here anymore. "My mom had to call me in sick a bunch before winter break because I wouldn't get out of bed. I also stopped replying to my friends' texts. They said I ghosted them."

I rattle off the entire story as matter-of-factly as possible, tucking away the emotion. I've never told anyone this before. I mean, I told my old therapist and my psychiatrist. But I've never told anyone that . . . matters. Loath as I am to admit it, Austin *matters*. I care about what he says next, and all that caring makes me feel raw, flayed open.

Austin's quiet. Just the swish of the windshield wipers and the sound of the cranky heater fill the van. Then he says, "What the fuck, Lou? That's messed up."

Shame fills me. "Yeah, I know. I don't know why I didn't text them—"

"No," Austin interrupts me, his voice hard and sharp. "What they did was messed up. Would they have done that if you had pneumonia? Or you couldn't go out because you broke your ankle?"

"I—" My mouth opens and closes. I don't know what to say. When my mom found out what happened, she urged me to go back to therapy, but . . . I don't know. There's no big mystery to be solved. I'm not stupid. Lydie and Jordan were closer with each other than with me. But they were still my friends. My *only* friends. "I was a bad friend, end of story." The van lurches to a halt and I brace myself against the glove compartment. "Why're we stopping?"

Austin nods to the side. The glowing neon of a dancing burrito sign washes over the van's dim interior. "We're here. But hold on." He looks imploringly at me, and I force myself to make eye contact. "Lou, tell me you know it's not your fault. Even if you could've handled things better, you weren't a bad friend."

Of all the things I thought Austin was going to do, defending me wasn't one of them. Not even in the top five, really. "You don't know that."

"Maybe." He shrugs. "Maybe not. But you're a good friend to Marianne. You show up three times a week and—before you say it's just for community service, that doesn't matter—you make her *laugh*. You played *RotR* with me even though I spent eighty percent of the time asking stupid questions and getting ganked."

"You should probably turn off PvP mode."

Austin's intense expression softens into a smile. "Probably. But hey, those friends? They weren't your friends if they ditched you like that. Okay?"

I drop my gaze from his, feeling all mixed up inside. "Okay." Right now, in this moment, I don't believe Austin. What happened with Lydie and Jordan was one of those cuts that don't heal. They infect and scab and they're always, always tender. But the thing is, I *want* what Austin said to be true. I want to believe him, to take his word as fact.

"Thanks." My voice is quiet and broken.

"Anytime." Austin turns off the van and flips up the hood of his rain shell. "Now c'mon. There's a burrito the size of a two-year-old in there with your name on it."

TEN

All I want to do
Is come undone around you

—The Laundromats, "For Today" (1981)

Whether I like it or not, something changed between me and Austin while we sat parked in front of that neon dancing burrito sign. If you'd told me weeks ago that I'd be willingly buddying up with Austin Yang—an actual ray of sunshine and sentient smiley emoji—I would've laughed myself into an asthma attack. But here I am. Openly (and by openly, I mean to myself, not out loud) admitting to enjoying Austin's company.

But even Austin's weirdly comforting presence doesn't erase my dread about today.

No Marianne.

Austin parks the van a few blocks from LifeCare for our Thursday shift, and I begin to panic. Maybe I should've bailed and taken up extra hours some other day. Besides, Ms. Holiday said the numbers don't matter as much as the effort. But when I tried bailing last night while playing *RotR*, Austin talked me into it. He said it'd be *fun*.

"I'm really not looking forward to this, Denver." I hoist my backpack up from the floor of the van. "Last time I tried to be on the phones—"

"You made someone cry," he cuts in. "Trust me, I haven't forgotten. But I can give you some tips. It's really not all that different from hanging with Marianne."

Today, the sky is an uncharacteristic blue. I'm wearing one of my button-downs—patterned with little lightning bolts—and jeans, my hair pulled back into reverse-braided buns. I climb out of the van and wait for Austin on the sidewalk. "Maybe I can pretend to be on the phone all day."

"The calls are logged in the computer." Austin locks the van and grabs me by the shirtsleeve, tugging me toward the entrance. "C'mon."

I shake him off. "Great," I say bitterly, and wait while Austin punches in the key code to the building. "RIP whatever self-confidence I've gained at Marianne's. Will Donna even let me near a phone again?"

Austin chuckles and opens the door for me. "You'll do fine. And don't worry about Donna—you redeemed yourself with Marianne."

Upstairs, the center is busier than I've seen it. A handful of other volunteers sit at desks, chatting away on their headsets.

"Afternoon, kiddos!" Donna calls from her spot behind the front desk.

"Happy Thursday," Austin volleys back, a literal spring in his step. "Two volunteers, reporting for duty."

"Ugh," I mutter as I pass Austin and drag my feet to my neglected desk space in the back. I dump my bag on the floor and lower myself into my chair.

Austin settles at his desk, catty-corner to mine, and waves.

I lift my fingers weakly.

He wheels himself over and leans his elbows on the edge of my desk. "Hey, I have an idea."

"Is it drugs? Are you on drugs? Because that'd explain so much."

Austin pulls the sleeves of his striped cardigan down around his hands and laughs. "What?"

"How do you have so much energy? We just got done with eight *mind-numbing* hours of school and you're, like, bouncing off the walls." I frown at my computer screen. "I want to take a nap."

"I'm not on drugs, thanks for asking." He fiddles with the cactus on my desk, which looks dehydrated. Am I supposed to be keeping that thing alive? "Pretty sure I was born this way."

I snort at the mental image of a hyperactive baby Austin. "Okay, fine. What's your idea?"

"I bet that you can't get a higher satisfaction score from your clients than me."

"They give us feedback?" Horror ripples through my soul. I figured my first day fuckup was an anomaly—that clients don't frequently check in with Donna about how the volunteers are performing. "No one told me that!"

"It's in the welcome packet. Which I'm guessing you barely touched?"

"I think you know the answer to that question."

Austin continues as if I hadn't replied. "Feedback is a strong word. When we end our call, they're prompted to give us a score between one and ten. It's . . . quality control. Anything below a three gets a check-in call with Donna." He grins at me, then pumps his brows. "What do you say?"

"Are you really trying to entice me through competition?"

"You're competitive," he says. "Other than coffee and free food, winning is your only motivator, from what I can tell."

"I am," I say warily. "What are we betting?"

"We're betting . . ." He trails off in thought. "Bragging rights?"

"Nope, that's boring."

"Okay, okay. Obviously, this wasn't well thought out. Do you have any ideas?"

I stare at Austin and consider my options. "Well. I'm leaning toward the loser having to do something embarrassing." I *really* want to see if it's possible to humiliate Austin Yang. Is it possible to embarrass someone with this much self-confidence? He has no shame.

"Like?" He rests his chin in his hand and lifts one brow.

"Like . . ." My brain can't function right now. "It'll be a secret."

"You can't think of anything, huh?"

"I'm brain-dead after three. It's not my fault."

"Fine. We're betting an undisclosed, embarrassing punishment for the loser." Austin sits up straight and holds his hand out. "If you get a higher cumulative score than me when the day is over, I'll take your punishment. If you get less, you'll have to take mine."

"Fine." I shake Austin's hand. Some good-natured competition does light a fire beneath me. I hate losing, as Austin has learned at Marianne's. "May the best volunteer win."

Austin grins. "Oh, this is going to be fun."

Austin is a liar. Talking on the phone with new clients is nothing like chatting with Marianne over tea as she chain-smokes and watches videos of herself from the seventies. Oh no. It's just as bad as I remembered from my first day. But I'm hopeful I can pull through. After my first semi-disastrous call, I learn the power of "active listening" and asking leading questions.

Sure, the elderly want someone to talk to them, but they also want someone to *listen*.

But I'm not entirely sure how well I'm doing.

I haven't made anyone cry, but that's an incredibly low bar.

The first call was semi-disastrous because I failed at finding common ground with the client. I asked about movies and music and pastimes. Turns out client number one only liked to watch *Dateline* and binge Fig Newtons. So . . . not a lot to work with. It was awkward. Not a full-blown disaster. Just unpleasant for everyone involved.

The second, I asked some impressive (if I do say so myself) leading questions and listened to a woman named, comically, Eloise—Austin did warn me they had clients with my name—talk about her college years as one of the few women in her graduating class and working as a librarian, as well as our shared name. Overall, a success. I'm pretty sure I have at least one positive rating. The third and fourth go well, but I don't have much to say and end up making a ton of listening noises.

Then it's my fifth and final call, and I'm eager to wrap up this nightmare. The elderly man is nice enough but has a thick Midwestern accent, and between that and his slow drawl, it's a struggle to follow him. We chat about his favorite pastime—hunting, which is a big nope in my book. But for twenty minutes I pretend to enjoy killing rabbits for fun.

Because I can't let Austin win. I'm far too competitive for that.

Which is annoying because he knew that.

Austin is blatantly playing me. But whatever. I'm going to win.

When the final call is over, I remove my Bluetooth and exhale heavily, leaning back in my chair. Socializing is *exhausting*—and I was already tired. I don't know how extroverts do it. Luckily, Marianne will be back this weekend, and I'll get to ditch the phone calls in favor of tea and boxes of memories and stories.

Austin's still wrapping up his final call, so I push up from my desk.

Donna's up front eating a salad for dinner, and I catch her attention as I walk up.

"Austin said we can check our scores?" I stop in front of her desk. "How'd I do?"

Donna holds up her finger and finishes chewing. "Let's see. . . ." She sets her salad aside and pulls up a program on her computer. "You did great!"

I toss Austin a smirk. "Really? What's my score? Cumulative, from all the calls?"

Donna clicks through the LifeCare logs, checking my numbers. As she does, Austin hangs up and walks over to us, his hands tucked into his pockets. He looks far too confident for my liking.

"Three of your callers gave you ten out of ten," Donna says, and beams at me like I'm a newborn doe who's learned how to walk without eating shit. "One gave you a six out of ten, the other a five out of ten. That's wonderful, Eloise! Quite the improvement."

So . . . forty-one out of fifty. Normally, a B would give me hives. But I'll take it.

"What'd I get?" Austin joins me in front of the counter.

Donna glances between us. "What're you two up to?"

"Nothing—" I begin to say, but Austin cuts me off.

"We made a bet."

Donna tuts. "Technically, I can't stop you. But you do realize we're talking about lonely seniors who just want some company, right?"

"Yeah, yeah, get on with it." I crane my neck to get a look at her computer screen. "How'd Austin do?"

Donna sighs, but her lips twitch in a smile. "Austin got . . ." She pauses and clicks her mouse. "Tens across the board."

"That's a perfect fifty, Lou," Austin says, as if I've lost the ability to do basic arithmetic.

"I hate you." I push past him.

He lopes behind me. "No, you don't," he says in a singsong voice.

I stop at my desk and swivel to look at him. "You wanna bet?" I sling my backpack over my shoulder. At least the day is over.

"Sure. I'll probably win again."

"You're insufferable."

"And you're a sore loser." He walks over to his desk and gathers his stuff. "You want a ride home?"

My dignity is telling me to take the bus. But I just missed it, and I don't want to wait around for the next one. I shove my dignity aside and nod. "Okay, *fine*."

As we walk out of LifeCare, waving goodbye to Donna, I glance over at him. "Why're you smiling?"

"Because I'm thinking about what your punishment should be."

I groan. "How bad is it going to be?"

"You'll find out Saturday." Austin unlocks the van with his key fob and we both climb inside. "Marianne will be back in town."

"Well, that's one thing I have to look forward to," I mutter, clipping my seat belt.

Austin starts the van, then pulls away from the curb. We drive in silence for a moment, until he says, "You have to admit it: you did better today."

I lift one shoulder in a lazy shrug, watching the traffic from a right-hand-only turn lane beside us. "I guess."

"You're not nearly as incompetent as you pretend to be, Lou."

"I don't pretend," I say. "I'm sure, with certain people, I do fine in social situations. But if I learned one thing from my best friends dumping me, it's that I'm not for everybody—or most people." The second the words leave my lips I want to wilt and die.

Austin's silent beside me, and I cross my fingers, hoping he'll breeze over my embarrassing word vomit. But he says, "There's nothing wrong with being an acquired taste."

I wrinkle my nose. "Acquired taste? I'm a human being, not cilantro."

"Not everybody's going to like you, Lou. Not everyone likes me," he says. "And, clearly, your two friends weren't your people."

I don't look over at him, instead focusing on looking out the window. As annoying as Austin can be, he's wise sometimes. Like his extroversion and positivity are superpowers. "Yeah . . . maybe."

After Tuesday night, I thought about what Austin said. I even tried to internalize it. That what happened between me and my former best friends wasn't all my fault. That maybe they were always going to drop me, and all I did was hand them a good excuse.

Today, the words sink in a little easier. Maybe it's because I want to believe them so bad. That there isn't something inherently wrong with me, something so unlikable that no one could ever dream of becoming my friend. Or *staying* my friend. That maybe, just maybe, I haven't found my people yet. It's a nicer thought, a hopeful one.

As we sit in traffic along Fifteenth Avenue, Austin drums his hands on the steering wheel. Then he says, "Question. Do you like music?"

While thankful for the change in topic, I lift my brows in confusion. "Who *doesn't* like music?"

"Monsters."

"Yes, I like music. Why?"

"Well, if you're not a music-hating monster, then you should come to one of our shows."

"And why would I want to do that?"

"Lou"—he glances at me from across the center console—"we're friends now. Right?"

I sigh and look up at the roof of the van. "I mean . . . Why do you even want to be my friend? You said it the other night. I'm the worst sometimes." The light's green and we roll forward a few inches, the road a sea of brake lights as the light quickly turns to yellow, then red again. Leaving me stuck in traffic hell and a conversation that's turning my stomach inside out.

Austin falls quiet on the other side of the van. Then: "Sure, you're the worst sometimes. But not *all* the time. You make me laugh. You also don't care what anyone thinks, which is kind of badass."

Thankfully, the van is dark and the nearest streetlight is on the fritz, because heat flushes from my chest up to my face. I almost want to laugh. Or cry a little. Because that's a lie. I care too much about what other people think. But all I say is, "I'm mean to you." I've never been able to take a compliment.

"Actually, you're not? You're just . . . prickly."

"Like a cactus?"

"What?"

I tug at a loose thread on my seat belt and stare out the windshield. "Nothing."

We finally make the light, only a few blocks away from our neighborhood now. Neither of us says anything for a moment, and I let the conversation settle around me. Austin's my friend. For some masochistic reason, he likes hanging out with me. I really shouldn't be questioning this, questioning him. I don't exactly have friends to spare these days.

Austin clears his throat, then says, "Well. The offer stands. Live shows are stressful. It's nice to have a friendly face in the crowd."

I gesture to my face as he parks outside my house. "This is *friendly* to you?"

He grins. "If I squint hard enough."

Despite it all, I laugh. "Touché."

"No pressure, though. Just thought I'd put it out there."

I settle for an awkward and stilted, "Um, thanks. I'll think about it."

"We're still on for *RotR* later?"

I scoop up my bag and open the door, pausing to look back at Austin. His forearm rests against the steering wheel, his body canted slightly toward me. The sleeves of his cardigan are too long, covering his knuckles, and his hair is as messy as ever. But the thing I can't look away from are his eyes.

"Yep. I can't wait to see if you break your record of seventeen deaths in one session."

Austin laughs, waving as I slide out of the car and shut the door behind me.

After he drives off, I stand there on the sidewalk in front of my house.

What I didn't tell Austin is that his live show invite was the first time someone, outside of my family, has invited me to do something social in a year—well, ten months, but close enough. I honestly couldn't remember how I'm supposed to react. I've been half-assing my way through our new friendship, but my social skills are beyond rusty.

Even if I've gotten somewhat comfortable with Austin and Marianne, this is different. Austin inviting me to get tacos or sending that friend request through *RotR* is one thing. But him inviting me to do something outside school or a video game—inviting me to do something in *his* world—feels like a big friendship step.

Maybe that doesn't sound so scary, but . . . what happens when Austin gets to know me—because he doesn't know me yet, not really—and he doesn't like what he finds? What if he realizes what everyone else already has? That I'm not worth the effort. And what if what happened with Lydie and Jordan happens again? One depressive blip and I'm *out*? I press my eyes shut, rocking back on my heels as I try to quell the panic inside my chest.

I like being a loner.

Then why am I panicky at the idea of no longer having Austin to good-naturedly torture three times a week?

ELEVEN

Take a chance and make it last
Do it for the story

—The Laundromats, "Memory" (1979)

I'm nervous as I pick at my breakfast Saturday morning.

Last night over Discord, I drilled Austin for clues about whatever punishment I'll be enduring today. But he refused—and on top of that, he sounded positively gleeful during our voice chat. Even more gleeful than usual. It's going to be bad. At least we'll get to see Marianne. If possible, I want to avoid the phones between now and when I wrap up with LifeCare.

"More coffee, baby?" Mom holds up the carafe. Tilting her head to one side, she adds, "Am I a bad mom for forcing caffeine on you? Is this bad parenting?"

I tear at a chunk of bagel in my hand. "I'm five-nine, so it's not like the caffeine stunted my growth. Besides, I read online that coffee actually has more beneficial properties than negative ones."

Mom brightens at this and tops off my mug. Sliding into the seat across from me, she asks, "You okay? You're shredding that bagel."

"Oh, yeah." I shove the bagel crumbs into my mouth, then

give her a thumbs-up. After swallowing, I add, "I lost a bet to Austin and today I find out my punishment."

Mom lifts her brows. She knows about Austin, but if I have my way, I never want them to meet. Because, *okay*, there's still something in the back of my head that's worrying everything might fall apart. Then what? Mom peppering me with questions about what happened, like she did with Lydie and Jordan?

"What'd you bet over?"

"Who could do better on the phones since Marianne was out of town. In hindsight, I shouldn't have taken the bet. He's way more well-versed in likability than I am."

Mom smiles.

"What?" I shove more bagel into my mouth and wash it down with coffee.

She shakes her head. "Nothing. You've seemed . . . happier the last few weeks."

The doughy bagel and coffee combo turns to cement in my stomach. The past year has been hard. Even if I did get my depression under control, I lost my friends. If you could even call them that. I haven't been depressed or unhappy, but I haven't been happy, either. I've just been . . . existing.

But am I *happy*? Like, right in this moment? The question throws me off-balance. I've been running in neutral for so long, I think I forgot what happy feels like. How it feels in my body.

"LifeCare hasn't been terrible," I say, skirting around the *h* word.

Mom lifts her mug to her lips. "Good. And I'm still waiting for my Marianne autograph."

"I'll get right on that."

My phone buzzes on the kitchen table. Austin's on his way, and considering it takes him less than a minute to drive to my house, I say goodbye to my mom, grab my bag, and wait on the curb. Not even thirty seconds pass before the murder van rolls up, nearly knocking into our trash cans.

I hop to my feet and open the passenger-side door. "Long time, no chat." I slide into my seat. Austin and I played *RotR* until one in the morning last night, and we voice chatted the entire time. If you discount him stonewalling me about my punishment, it was . . . fun.

"Good morning!" Austin says, and as I buckle my seat belt, he leans into the back of the van and grabs something.

"What's that?"

"This"—he hands me a bundle of yellow fabric—"is your punishment."

I take the fabric and unbundle it. It's a T-shirt. A plain yellow T-shirt. "I think I'm missing something."

"Turn it over."

And I do. "Oh, *hell no.*" Because on the yellow shirt is RAY OF F☺☺KING SUNSHINE arched over a rainbow. It's also three sizes too large.

Austin is smiling so wide that I can see, like, all his teeth. Either he had braces or has great genetics. "You lost the bet, which means you have to wear that shirt all day."

"Please no." I drop the shirt into my lap and turn to Austin. Widen my eyes. "I'll do anything else."

"It's just a shirt, Lou." He bites his lip, as if trying not to laugh.

"No, it's the ugliest shirt known to humankind!" I hold it back up and shudder. "Where did you even find this?"

"I had it made," Austin admits, and finally breaks, his words dissolving into laughter.

"You had it *made*?" The level of commitment to the bit is almost admirable. Almost.

"I went to that print shop on Market after school yesterday. The rush order cost double, but this is so going to be worth it." He's still cackling like the asshole he is.

"This is cruel. And deeply fucked up." I'm wearing one of my cuter button-downs—it has printed cat paws on it, which I thought Marianne would appreciate—and I begin to unbutton it.

Austin stops laughing and his face reddens. "Oh. Uh. You don't have to change—"

"I'm wearing a tank top underneath," I say with an eye roll, and undo the remaining buttons. As I slide off the button-down, Austin's gaze shifts from my bare shoulder to out the driver's-side window and he drums his hands on the steering wheel. I pull the shirt on over my head. "If you had this made, why is it so big? I can fit four of me in here."

Austin finally looks back over, the flush in his cheeks fading. "The only yellow shirts they had in stock were that size. And the shirt *needed* to be yellow. It's such a cheerful color, don't you think?"

I shake my head, folding my button-down and tucking it into my bag. I spread my arms wide and show off the front of the shirt, which will probably hang to my knees when I'm standing and is so ugly that my eyes hurt. "Happy?"

"The happiest, Lou. You have no idea."

I sigh heavily and stare down at my chest. "I hate it."

"I know." Austin starts the van, and we're off. "That was kind of the point."

"You're cruel and unusual, Houston." I roll down my window since it's sunny this morning, cool air whipping into the van.

"Hey, you've hit Texan names," he says. "You're not far off from Austin."

"I'm not moving geographically." I smooth my hand down the shirt. Ew. Are there rhinestones bedazzled on the rainbow? "First one that popped into my head." This is a lie. I bookmarked a website with a long list of all city names for babies, and I've been working my way through it.

We pass a coffee shop along Green Lake on our way to Marianne's, and Austin slows down, then pulls to a stop on a nearby neighborhood street. "I told Marianne I'd bring her a matcha latte."

I look at my shirt, then back at Austin. "Yeah, I think I'll wait here. Can you get me a large latte?"

Austin shakes his head. "If you want a coffee, you'll have to get out of the van."

"Are you kidding? I am not going out in public like this."

"Do you want coffee or not? I'll pay." The fact that Austin has me pegged so well is deeply disturbing. He gestures toward the coffee shop. "After you."

Glaring, I hop out of the van and resist the urge to fold my arms over my chest. The shirt hangs down to my mid-thigh, the sleeves hitting past my elbows. Austin rounds the van and pauses, looking me up and down. He grins.

"Shut up," I mutter, heading toward the coffee shop.

"I didn't say anything."

"You didn't need to." I motion to his face. "Your facial expression said it all."

"My face always looks like this," he says with—somehow—an even bigger smile. My humiliation brings him way too much joy.

I flip Austin off, then pause outside the entrance to the coffee shop and look at my tormentor. "Don't make me do this."

He steps closer and whispers in my ear, "C'mon, Lou. Listen to the shirt."

I snort and push him back. "What?"

"The shirt is the first step of my plan to turn you into a positive person. Embrace it."

Even though I'm still laughing, I scowl. "I'm not going to embrace the shirt, you freak."

"You're no fun," he says with a sigh, as if he's disappointed in me. Holding up the van's fob, he locks it twice and it beeps. "I'm going to get some coffee, then. Feel free to stand outside and wait." Then he turns around and pushes open the door.

Letting out a frustrated groan, I follow him inside.

Because what's weirder? Me lurking on the sidewalk in front of a very busy street wearing The Shirt, or me being in a coffee shop in The Shirt? At least if I have Austin, I can use him as a human shield to keep people from seeing me. The second option also includes free coffee.

The door clatters shut behind me. To my right are a few tables with people on laptops. A handful look up and give me weird looks—one person even laughs, reaching for their phone. I march past them, fighting the rising heat in my cheeks, to stand beside Austin in line. "I'm only here because I want coffee. I'm *not* embracing the shirt."

"What is it," he asks, reaching for his wallet as we move up in line, "that makes you insistent on being a misanthrope?"

"Wow. I'm a misanthrope now?"

"If the existential shoe fits."

I cross my arms. "What makes *you* so insistent on being positive?"

Austin shrugs and looks around the café, with its low ceiling and crowded tables. There are at least twenty people in here. Twenty witnesses to my humiliation. "Why waste energy being pessimistic when you can look on the bright side?"

"Maybe," I say, and approach the counter, "some people find that it takes more energy being positive? Have you ever thought of that?"

The barista—a girl with locs and a lip ring—stares at my shirt, her mouth agape.

"I lost a bet. A sixteen-ounce latte, please." If Austin's paying, then I'm not skimping out. "Oh, and a chocolate scone."

The barista laughs. "Sure thing." She turns to Austin. "And for you?"

"A twelve-ounce mocha and a sixteen-ounce matcha latte," he says, and slides his card across the counter. Then he looks over at me with a little shit-eating grin. "Positivity is linked to longer life expectancy."

I press my eyes shut in annoyance because *does he ever let up?* Just when I'm finding him tolerable, he dives off the deep end.

"Did you get that from one of Donna's pamphlets?" I ask, opening my eyes.

"Maybe." Austin hands me a small wax-paper bag with my scone and adds, "It increases your life span eleven to fifteen percent."

We step aside to the pickup area, near the little counter of creamers and cinnamon shakers. "By that logic, you're going to live forever."

"One can hope," he says. "I'm pretty awesome."

I thunk my head back against the wall and cross my arms over my chest like Ana when she's throwing a tantrum. "Can I go hide in the van now?"

Austin leans against the wall beside me. "Once our coffees are ready."

I turn my head toward him and glare. "I should've never taken the bet."

He smiles. "Nope."

The barista calls Austin's name, and he grabs the coffees from the counter. I stay behind because my embarrassment has made it too difficult to move. When he returns, he stands in front of me, the toes of his Converse touching the toes of my Doc Martens. "Your hard-earned coffee, madam," he says, and presses the latte into my hands, folding my fingers around the cup.

I lift my gaze from the cup to Austin's annoyingly cheerful face, and for a beat, all I can feel is the pressure of his fingers on mine. "I hope you're enjoying this." I pull back and step around him, booking it for the exit and ignoring all the curious stares that follow me.

Austin trails me and puts his and Marianne's coffees on the roof as he unlocks the van. "Did I tell you that shirt looks great on you?"

My entire body is hot from embarrassment. "Shut up, Houston."

"I was being serious, but okay." He mimes zipping his lips, grabs the coffees, and climbs into the van.

For once, I really can't wait to get to Marianne's.

TWELVE

We are all alone together
Don't forget you're my tether

—The Laundromats, "Storied" (1979)

Austin and I eat lunch together during the school week now. Not on purpose. It sort of started happening after we played *RotR* for the first time. Like our gaming was a friendship gateway drug. Since Evanston High is massive and confusingly laid out, he usually texts me so we can coordinate. Sometimes we eat outside. Other times we brave the cafeteria together or share our packed lunches.

Unlike my mom, Austin's packs him meals with more than three soggy ingredients. I'm almost a hundred percent positive he only offers to split with me because he feels bad, and not because he's been "craving a peanut butter and jelly sandwich lately." But his mom's a killer cook, so I have no qualms about eating pity chicken bulgogi.

As resistant as I first was, it totally beats eating in the computer lab while Ms. Deaver picks kale out of her teeth and talks about her divorce proceedings.

But on the Thursday after The Shirt, Austin doesn't text.

I should be the one not texting him after that humiliating stunt, but I grab my phone and check in.

ME:
Hey where are you? Last time I ate in the computer lab Deaver got weepy about her divorce and I'd rather not listen to a grown woman cry about sharing custody of her dog for thirty minutes

I perch on the edge of my desk and wait for a reply. AP English just let out and my teacher, Mr. Carson, is cleaning the whiteboard while a few students chat at their desks. My stomach growls. Pretty sure Mom packed me another peanut butter and jelly, one of two sandwiches she knows how to make. Maybe I'll brave the cafeteria if Austin's down.

My phone buzzes twice.

AUSTIN:
shit I'm the worst, I forgot to text you this morning

Too many late nights playing RotR caught up with me

ME:
Nerd burnout? Carpal tunnel?

AUSTIN:
nope. I'm at home sick 🤒

The disappointment I feel is heavy and strange.

ME:
That sucks

Real eloquent, Eloise!

AUSTIN:
yep, I'm miserable. which probably makes you happy, huh? think you can hack Marianne's on your own?

ME:
I can definitely try. Feel better.

Then I lock my phone and shove it into my bag. The heavy, weird disappointment multiplies as I hurry out of the classroom and head for the back stairwell. That knee-jerk instinct to assume I'm at fault is strong. But Austin doesn't lie. If he didn't want to eat with me, he'd tell me. He's sick and it has *nothing* to do with me.

Ms. Deaver's at her desk when I knock on the doorframe.

"Hey, Eloise!" She smiles and waves me in. "I haven't seen you in a while. How're you doing, girl? How's that USC application going?"

I slide into a nearby station and unpack my lunch. "Good. Things are . . . good."

Until recently, lunch up here was one of my favorite times of the day. But as I pick at my sad peanut butter and jelly, I can't escape the fact that I'm . . . lonely right now. No offense to Ms. Deaver. But I miss Austin. It's not like we even really do anything during lunch. Mostly we talk about *Realm of the Ravager* or Marianne or the crackpot theory that our principal is being *Weekend at Bernie's*-d. Obviously it's nonsense. But hilarious nonsense.

Ms. Deaver starts up about the dog custody situation again, and I utilize my active listening skills from LifeCare—making contemplative noises but not really paying attention.

Because all I can focus on is this weird new emotion that's stupid as hell and doesn't make sense: I miss Austin.

As much as I like Marianne, we've never been alone for more than fifteen minutes, and I'm kind of freaking out. I haven't felt this much anxiety about going to her house since my first LifeCare day. Which, according to the massive planner I have in my lap while I ride the bus, will be a month ago this weekend. A *month*. I've been tracking and logging my hours, sure, but a month hits different. An entire month of senior year, gone. An entire month closer to graduation. To USC. I thought LifeCare would turn every Tuesday, Thursday, and Saturday into a crawl, but time is speeding by.

The bus drops me off two blocks from Marianne's, and when I reach the wooden gate, I stop. Because I don't know the code. Only Austin does. Shit. I squint at the keypad—like I'm in some spy movie and I'll be able to figure out which keys are more worn down than the others—and quickly give up, hitting the buzzer.

A moment later, a cantankerous *"What do you want?"* crackles through the speakers.

I shift awkwardly, clutching my backpack straps. "Um. Hey, Marianne. It's Eloise? Eloise Deane?"

There's a lengthy pause. Then the gate clicks open. Marianne doesn't say anything else, and I step through the gate, shutting it behind me. The yard is as overgrown as ever, and I pick my way up the cobblestone pathway, the stones slick with this afternoon's rain. But before I can remember which frog statue is concealing Marianne's house key, the door opens wide.

"Eloise." Marianne leans against the doorframe and

motions me inside with a roll of her wrist. "Come on in."

I step onto the porch and slip past her, pausing in the hallway to unlace my Doc Martens. "Sorry about the intercom. Austin's out sick today and I don't know the code."

"Oh, you're fine," she says, and wanders down the hallway to the kitchen. "I get tons of solicitors. Girl Scouts. Mormons. Gotta keep them at bay somehow. A little growl usually does the trick."

I can't help but grin—old people get to be assholes as much as they want, and no one calls them the worst—as I set my backpack down beside my shoes and head into the kitchen.

"Is Austin okay?" Marianne pauses by her fancy Italian coffee maker and holds the carafe up to me; I nod. She knows I prefer coffee to tea, which I appreciate, since not all caffeine is created equal.

"No idea." I lean my hip against the counter. "He just said he's sick. So . . . okay enough to text?"

"Well." Marianne pours our coffees, adds the creamer. "We'll have to have fun without him."

I grab my mug, that familiar flame of unease burning my chest. Because what am I supposed to talk to Marianne about for two hours? This is my social anxiety nightmare. No escape. Societal expectations I can't meet. A sense of obligation I can't shake.

Marianne stares at me and sips her coffee. Then her eyes brighten. "I have an idea. Follow me."

Thankful she's taking the lead—literally—I follow Marianne back into the hallway and to the spiral staircase. In the month I've volunteered here, I've never gone upstairs. Just to the basement and the main floor. The snoop in me is eager to poke around. The allergy-prone clean freak in me is prepping for disaster.

The stairway opens up to a small landing, a giant picture window to our right, overlooking Marianne's yard, and a long hallway to our left. Marianne motions to the hallway. "Down here."

Like the rest of the house, the second floor is cluttered, from the paintings on the walls to the piles of tchotchkes in the other two rooms I manage to peek into. At the very end of the hall is a set of double doors, thrown open to expose the master bedroom.

Marianne's bedroom is cozy in the way attics are cozy. But I wouldn't expect anything less. A four-poster bed, complete with a canopy that would've made eleven-year-old Eloise drool with jealousy, is in the center of the room. Nox sleeps curled up against a folded blanket at the foot of the bed. Gauzy white curtains hang from the windows, and a patterned rug stretches across the hardwood, worn and pilled. A vanity with a giant beveled mirror sits off in one corner, and a mint-green velvet fainting couch is tucked into another. The smell of vetiver and tobacco is even stronger up here, clinging to the curtains and rug and blankets.

"When I was packing for Colorado," Marianne says as she crosses her bedroom, "I couldn't find a thing. My closet is a mess, and most of the items I haven't worn in decades." She slides open a door beside the vanity and reveals a deep walk-in closet.

I peer over her shoulder. "What the fuck? This is bigger than my bedroom."

"Well, that's depressing," Marianne says dryly.

The closet is octagonal, with a tufted cushion in the center in the same shade of mint green as the fainting couch in the bedroom. A vintage chandelier hangs above it, softly illuminating the walls of clothes, the shoe cubbies, the chest of drawers, the jewelry dripping off stands. And it's a *mess*.

"I thought you could help me organize everything." Marianne drifts into the walk-in. She glances over her shoulder at my button-down, my neatly braided hair. "You strike me as the . . . organized type."

"One of my few positive qualities," I say, and she wheezes a laugh.

With Marianne's permission, I begin hauling the clothes from the closet and spreading them out on her bed, displacing a disgruntled Nox, who darts off down the hallway when I accidentally cover her with a pair of bell-bottom jeans. Marianne supervises as I comb through decades' worth of clothing, organizing them into piles for keep, giveaway, or her storage unit downtown.

I don't consider myself overly feminine. Sometimes, I wish I were. Wish I felt comfortable in dresses and makeup, showing off soft skin and flowy hair. But it's not *me* and it never has been. Another wedge between me, Lydie, and Jordan, actually. For a while, I tried, if only to fit in. But dressing like Lydie made me feel like I was wearing the wrong skin.

"Are you even listening to me?" Marianne asks loudly from her spot on the fainting couch.

I look up from the array of vintage sundresses. "Um. Yes?"

She snorts, then sips the drink she poured herself from the tiny wet bar in the closet. "You're a bad liar. Where'd you go?"

Heat reddens my cheeks, and I shrug. "Nowhere . . . I was just thinking of my old friends. They would've loved these," I say, gesturing to the dresses.

"And you don't?" Her eyes narrow. "What's wrong with my clothes?"

I laugh, setting the dress into the keep pile. "Nothing. I'm not a dress person."

"I'm not either."

I glance toward the closet. "You so sure about that? You own, like, two hundred."

Marianne tips back her drink, then sets it aside. "For shows. Events. The label and my manager were always lecturing me about being more feminine, more *appealing* to our male audience. And they'd never listen when I said sex appeal or femininity has jack shit to do with whether or not you're in a dress." She stretches out on the tiny couch, then adds, "In my opinion, a dress's only upside is that you don't have to wear underwear."

"Too much information, Marianne," I say, and shake my head. But something in my body releases, softens. Lydie and Jordan never got it, never understood, but Marianne does.

"Your friends," she says, smoothing her palms over the velvet. "What happened to them? I doubt you meant old like *moi*."

I play with the lace edging on a fancy-looking gown. "They're . . . not my friends anymore."

"What happened?" Her tone is softer now, and it's embarrassing.

Like she can sense the hurt, right there, beneath the surface of my words.

"Last year, I was really struggling. And I sort of went MIA for a while. Until my meds got sorted out and I could get out of bed again. Guess four Eloise-free weeks showed them they were better off."

"Well," Marianne says after a moment, "that's their loss. Because you, Eloise Deane, are pretty great."

I force myself to look up from the dress. "Thanks," I tell Marianne, even though my insides are kicking and screaming at me to tell her she's wrong. To snark. To lower her expectations of me. But I don't.

Marianne nods in acknowledgment. Then she says, "Austin's a good kid. He'd never—"

"Yeah, I know." I cut her off even though it's rude. But everything about this conversation is making me uncomfortable. "I told him about the mental health stuff, my ex–best friends, all of it. And he still wants to be my friend. It's weird."

"Weird how?"

"What are you? My therapist?"

"You couldn't pay me enough to deal with a teenager's problems," she says with a pointed look. "But this, dear Eloise, is called a conversation."

I flip her off, and she chuckles. "I don't know. I just don't have a good track record with friends, okay?" Then I duck back into the closet for another armload of clothes and dump them on the bed. "Historically, people don't like me when they get to know me. So I guess I'm trying not to get attached." The last part of the sentence slips out of me, and my face heats up again. But I realize it's the truth.

"Hate to break it to you, but you're already attached." Marianne uncurls herself from the fainting couch to join me by the bed. Her fingers flit over the pile of sweaters and jackets. "And getting attached isn't a bad thing. It's the only thing that matters—how we connect, who we connect with . . ."

I watch her hands graze the fabric. The only part of her that really shows her age. Thin, papery skin covering ridged veins. The heavy, thick rings crowding delicate fingers. Deep down, I know she's right. I'm attached to Austin. I'm attached to Marianne. But I'm also stubbornly attached to the version of myself inside my head.

"Thanks." I say this quietly, unsure of how else to respond.

Marianne squeezes my shoulder. "You're too hard on yourself, doll."

I grunt. She laughs.

Then Marianne tugs an item of clothing out from beneath the pile. "Aha! I knew I kept this." She holds out the item—a buttery leather jacket with giant star appliqués. "Here."

I lift both brows. "What?"

Marianne hooks her arm through mine and drags me over to the vanity. "Put it on. You're about my size. Or my size fifty years ago."

When I hesitate, she nudges me. So I shrug the jacket on. And she's right—it's my size. The jacket is fitted, tucked in around the waist, the leather soft beneath my fingertips. "It's beautiful," I say.

Marianne adjusts the sleeves a little, then smiles at me in the mirror. "I want you to have it."

My eyes widen. "No. I mean, I appreciate it? But I can't take it."

"It's not real leather, if that's what you're worried about. I don't fuck with PETA."

I rub my thumb over the appliqués. "Are you sure?"

"Yes, Eloise, I'm sure. I'm seventy-three. Not senile." She turns from the mirror and adds, "Just say thank you."

"Thank you," I mutter, but I'm grinning. This jacket is kind of badass.

I slip off the jacket and carefully hang it on the banister in the hallway so I don't forget it later, and then I resume my task, picking through the mess of outerwear. "Keep, toss, or storage?" I ask Marianne, and hold up an olive-green belted wool cardigan. The sleeves are moth-eaten, it's missing more buttons than not, and it reeks of cigarettes. Toss. Definitely toss. I lean down to dump it into the trash bag by my feet, but Marianne tugs the cardigan from my hands.

"What do you think you're doing? This was Georgie's."

I want to point out that there's literally *no way* for me to know that, but I apologize, then ask, "Do you have a lot of her things?"

Marianne runs her thumb across the wool. "No, just a handful. She loved this cardigan, wore it everywhere. She was always cold. When she came with the band to New York City in December, she practically refused to leave the hotel room because of the weather!" She snorts fondly.

I lean against the nearest bedpost. "Did Georgie tour with the band?"

"No," Marianne says quickly, and shakes her head. "The boys . . . they didn't mind. They loved Georgie. But the label was very concerned about *optics*. Most people saw two women together and just thought we were friends. But there were rumors."

"That you were a lesbian?"

Marianne carefully folds the cardigan. "Mm-hmm. And things were very different then. Our record label didn't think that my sexual orientation was 'on brand.' Remember that I was supposed to be appealing for our male audience. Attainable. So, for the most part, Georgie stayed here. She stayed out of sight."

"Let me guess," I say, "the label was a bunch of old white guys?"

Marianne cackles. "Oh, you don't know the half of it. I was the only woman in the room, doll." She smiles and brandishes the cardigan. "Thank you for this," she says, even though I thought the sweater was trash and almost threw it away.

The grandfather clock downstairs tolls six times, and Marianne says, "Suppose it's time for you to wrap up?"

Strangely, I'm a little disappointed that our time is up. But I put away the clothes we haven't yet organized and tidy the giveaway bags in the hallway before folding up the jacket and heading downstairs.

"We can finish on Saturday?" I slip on my Doc Martens, retying them.

Marianne's bright eyes sparkle. "That sounds like an excellent idea. Thank you for your help, Eloise." She hesitates, then touches my arm and adds, "If you don't have to go straight home, maybe you should check on Austin? Bring him some soup?"

This is why I'm a shitty friend. It never occurred to me to bring Austin soup or to check on him. I grumpily texted him to feel better and left it at that. "Won't that be weird?"

"Bringing your sick friend soup? No. It'd be nice."

"Nice is weird for me," I point out, swinging my backpack over my shoulder.

Shaking her head, Marianne opens her front door and shoos me out. "You're impossible. Get out of my house."

I laugh and hop down the front porch steps. "See you Saturday."

Marianne leans against the doorframe, backlit from the hallway light, and crosses her arms. "Bye, Eloise."

Standing in her front yard, I sigh and use my phone to search for nearby restaurants.

I climb off the bus at my usual stop, a bag with a to-go container of chicken noodle soup in my left hand.

Ever since I handed over my debit card at the café with an impressive soup bar near Marianne's house, I've doubted myself. But she's right. This is what friends do. And if I'm going to start making an effort, this is a good place to start. I debated texting Austin and giving him a heads-up, but I like having the option of doorbell ditching the soup on his front porch if I wimp out.

Instead of turning down my street, I walk up two blocks and turn left onto Fletcher. I'm about to pull up the photo of his ID that I forgot to delete to find his address when I spot the murder van parked in the driveway of an old Tudor. Bingo.

Pocketing my phone, I hurry up the sidewalk and stop in front of Austin's house. It's painted a deep, rusty red and has an A-line roof. The yard is tidy but fairly barren—just grass and a few bushes. The van's parked in front of the garage, which is up a steep driveway, separate from the house.

The bag of soup hangs heavy in my hand, and I roll back my shoulders. Walk up to the porch and push the doorbell. Before I can panic and ditch the soup, the front door opens, and standing in the doorway is a tall, gorgeous woman. Her black hair hangs to her mid-back and she's wearing a nice pair of sweats and a matching sweater.

"Hi, I'm—"

"Oh wow, you must be Eloise!" the woman says with a glowing smile. She motions me inside. "Hi, I'm Binna, Austin's mom."

Unnerved by this welcome, I step into the house. "Hi. Sorry to, um, show up like this. But I brought soup for Austin. I heard he's sick, so . . ." Helplessly, I lift up the bag with the soup container.

"How sweet of you! He's upstairs. Second door on the right."

The front door opens into a small entry hall with a staircase; another hallway leads to a living room. The air smells like pumpkin candles. And everything is so tidy, much tidier than our house. The framed photos on the walls are perfectly straightened and dusted. There's no junk table with mail or piles of shoes anywhere. But it's warm and cozy and exactly the kind of house I imagined Austin living in.

"Thanks," I say, bobbing my head awkwardly.

Binna chuckles and waves her hand. "Thank *you*. You saved me from having to make him dinner."

Smiling, I head up the creaky staircase, slowing slightly to look at the framed photos of Austin through the years. There's a lot of braces and *Star Wars* shirts. Dork. A few feature his brother, Ethan, who is bigger than Austin—taller and wider—and equally dorky. There are only a few of the whole family together with his dad. In them, Austin is young, so unaware that he'll lose his dad before he enters middle school. My heart hurts for younger Austin.

I force myself past all the photos and follow Binna's directions, walking down a carpeted hallway and pausing outside the second door on the right. Well. Here goes nothing. I knock, and a moment later a stuffy voice says, "Yeah?"

I push open the door slowly and step inside. Austin's room is more or less what I expected. A bass and a portable keyboard are on one side of the room. A gaming computer on a desk is in one corner, a bed in the other. Austin is propped up in his bed among a sea of tissues.

"Hey." I hold up the bag as I walk into the room. "I come bearing soup."

Austin has a serious case of bedhead and is wearing a sweater and checkered pajama pants. He squints at me. Like I'm a mirage. "Lou?"

"You're not having a fever dream, if that's what you're thinking." I glance around the room, unsure of what to do or say. Didn't really think this far into my plan. Shit.

Austin begins clearing all the used tissues, stuffing them into the trash can. "Sorry about the mess." His nose is red, but his cheeks are darkening too.

I laugh awkwardly. Very, very awkwardly. "I'm the one who showed up unannounced." I probably should've texted. This is weird. I knew it'd be weird. Fuck Marianne.

After using a squirt of hand sanitizer from his bedside table, he swings his leg over the side of the bed and smooths out the comforter. "Uh. You can sit if you want."

I hesitate for a moment, which is ridiculous—a bed is literally just a couch you sleep on—then drop my backpack and perch on the edge of the mattress. "The aforementioned soup," I say, holding the bag out.

Austin grins, despite his red nose and tired eyes. "You brought me soup."

"It's not a big deal," I mutter, studying the posters on his wall.

"You brought me soup," he says again, and takes the bag. "Thanks."

I look back at Austin and his smile is gone, and he's looking at me with an unreadable expression. Like he's trying to figure me out or decipher if he's actually having a fever dream. "If this is weird," I say, "blame Marianne. It was her idea, okay?"

"Way to throw Marianne under the bus." Austin's gaze slips from mine as he opens up the container and grabs the compostable spoon inside the bag. "How was she?"

I pick at my fingernails. "Good."

He spoons soup into his mouth and shifts on the bed so he's facing me with his legs crossed. "What'd you do?"

"I organized her closet, which was a chaotic mess, for two hours. But we mostly talked. It was kind of weird without you."

Austin pauses, his next spoonful halfway to his mouth. "Do my ears deceive me or did you miss me, Lou?" He seems absolutely delighted at this.

I groan, rolling my eyes. "So what if I did?"

"Wow. You admit it." He puts the spoon back in the bag and sips the soup like tea. "And here we are. The ice caps haven't melted. The bees haven't died off. The world continues to turn even though Eloise Deane has *feelings*."

"Yes, I have feelings. I'm not a robot."

Austin raises a brow over the container of soup. "That's exactly what a robot would say." When I flip him off, he nudges my knee with his. "I'm just kidding. I missed you too."

I can tell he means it. My dead, cold heart warms. "What's wrong with you?"

Austin laughs. "Sinus infection. I'll probably feel better by Saturday, before Marianne's. Honestly, it's not that bad. Probably looks worse than it is."

"Mr. Positivity," I say with an annoyed sigh. "What's the upside of a sinus infection?"

"I mean. You brought me soup."

"Marianne's idea. Not mine."

"You're a nice person, Eloise Deane. Admit it."

This time, I flip him off with both hands.

While Austin eats—drinks?—his soup, I gaze around his bedroom. It's way too clean in here. Leave it to Austin to be the one clean seventeen-year-old boy on the planet. The only semi-mess to be found is on his desk. But what catches my eye is an information packet for University of Washington propped up against his CPU.

I turn back toward Austin. "Are you applying to UW?"

"Yeah," he says, and wipes off his mouth with a napkin. "That's the plan, anyways."

"Am I a selfish asshole? Because I don't think I've *ever* asked you what you're doing after graduation." This lapse in social norms shouldn't upset me, but I genuinely feel bad for never asking—which is very unlike me.

"Selfish? No." He sets the empty soup container on his bedside table. "Asshole? Yes."

"Fair enough." I chew on the inside of my cheek. "What do you want to study?"

"I'm not sure yet. That's what college is for, right?" The thought of beginning freshman year of college *without* a four-year plan makes me seriously anxious. But Austin seems perfectly fine with his lack of a plan and yawns, his eyes watering. "Thanks again for the soup, Lou."

"Yeah, well, don't get used to it. This is a onetime thing."

"Whatever you say." Austin reaches for a tissue and blows his nose. "Gross. I'm sorry."

I slide off the bed. "I should go home anyways. You should . . . rest. So you can get better."

This makes him smile. The whole image is deeply pathetic, his nose all red and hair mussed. "You worried about me?"

"Who will I eat lunch with if you die?" I joke, suddenly nauseous. "I'm not going back to the computer lab five days a week. Shit's getting weird with Ms. Deaver and the dog custody situation. *Really* weird."

Austin laughs, then coughs. "Thanks again for the soup. It hit the spot."

I awkwardly drum my hands on my thighs. "Um. Yeah. I'll see you at school."

"I'll try to log on to *RotR* tonight if I don't pass out in a NyQuil coma." He shoves the used tissue into the trash bin and pulls the blanket at the bottom of the bed around his shoulders like a cape. "It's fifty-fifty at this point."

I scoop up my backpack and hoist it onto my shoulders. "Feel better, okay?" Then I wave and hurry back downstairs, luckily not running into Binna, because I can't small talk right now.

Not when all I can think about is what happens if I lose Austin as a friend. I wasn't kidding when I said I don't want to go back to the computer lab. That I missed him.

Befriending Austin is, without a doubt, the best and worst thing to happen to me this year.

THIRTEEN

There are love letters I never sent
In the backseat, and I'm broken for you

—The Laundromats, "The Backseat" (1984)

Austin recovers from his sinus infection by the weekend, and we fall back into the ease of our routine. Because we have a routine now, and even I can admit it's kind of nice. Austin's absence last week made me realize how much I depend on him and our strange, mouse-befriending-a-tiger-viral-video friendship.

On Tuesday, I finish organizing Marianne's walk-in. It's only taken me roughly five hours and six bags, but I pull off the impossible. I've arranged the different racks into four categories: dresses and skirts, tops, pants, and evening wear. All her shoes have found their pairs, buddied up in cubbies. I've detangled necklaces, dusted shelves, and even vacuumed the carpet. If this whole USC thing doesn't pan out, maybe I should look into a career as a home organizer.

Austin and Marianne have spent the past two hours downstairs, working on Project Nostalgia. Yes, I've given in to the name. I wrap up my task with fifteen minutes to spare. After turning off the light in the walk-in, the chandelier dimming, I head downstairs.

Marianne's in the kitchen feeding Nox, and I continue into the basement. Austin's seated on a lumpy rug, resting against the back of the couch, surrounded by envelopes, smushed cardboard boxes, letters, and photos.

"Hey." I lower myself onto the carpet across from him. "It's almost six."

Austin looks up from the pile of letters in his lap, his dark eyes bright. "Where's Marianne?"

"Kitchen. Why?"

"Guess what I found?"

"Please don't say nudes."

"No, you perv. An entire stack of letters to and from Georgie."

I perk up. "Seriously?"

"Yeah. Check it out." He grabs a pile of envelopes—different shapes and colors, some stained by water or wrinkled, torn along the edges. Some of the letters are written on fancy stationery, others on scraps of paper, dozens on different letterheads from hotels around the world. "How cool are these? Look at all the foreign stamps."

I pick up one of the letters. It's on stationery from Claridge's in London, from March 19, 1981.

Dear Georgie,

Sorry for the delay! Billy picked up our mail when we were in Germany and left it in his guitar case, like the absolute dumbass he is. Anyways. Enough excuses. To answer your question, Europe is fabulous! The food alone, Georgie! Why can't you be here with me? I'm kidding. Mostly. Every time I see something you'd love, I turn to the person beside me, as if I'm expecting it to be you. Shit, I miss you. It's not the same here without you. And I get it. Your mom isn't getting any better. But . . . please don't make me answer you—

Austin rips the letter out of my hand. "What're you doing?"

"Reading?" At his incredulous expression, I throw my hands up. "What? Aren't you curious?"

"Yeah, no shit I'm curious. But we can't violate Marianne's privacy." He shuffles the letters together and stuffs them into an empty envelope folder.

"Oh my god, you're so boring," I groan. But he's right. Violating Marianne's privacy is a moral gray zone at best, even if all I want to do is snoop.

"Hey, I'm as curious as you are. But we shouldn't read them."

"Uh-huh. Like I said: *boring.*"

Austin slides the folder onto the coffee table, where we've stacked the other semiorganized envelopes and mementos from Marianne's past. "Let's go."

Upstairs, Marianne's still in the kitchen; Nox happily munches away on her wet food from a bowl on the table.

"We're headed out," Austin says. "Anything you need before we go?"

Marianne looks up from the sink, where she's washing off the can opener. "No, I'm fine. Thank you both for all your hard work today. Eloise, I'm sure the closet looks gorgeous."

"Yeah, no problem. Austin also found—" I yelp as he steps on my foot.

Granted, neither of us are wearing shoes, but still. "I found more amazing pictures. Right, Lou?" Austin gives me a warning glance.

I narrow my eyes at him. "Yep. So many . . . pictures."

Marianne sets the can opener on the drying rack, completely oblivious.

We both say goodbye, confirming we'll stop by on Thursday, then slide on our shoes and head out.

"Why did you step on me?" I ask once we're on the front porch, the door shut behind us.

Austin bugs his eyes out at me. "Marianne's not the most organized person in the world, but those letters were probably stuffed into boxes for a reason."

"Are you still trying to convince me not to read them? Because you should know this is having the opposite effect."

"We're not here to pry into Marianne's personal life, Lou. Marianne might act all tough and untouchable, but I'm sure there are parts of her past that she'd prefer to *stay* in the past, you know?"

The fact that Austin is right—and so caring toward Marianne—irks me. Also, I'm a low-key hypocrite. Marianne might be prickly like me, but that also means she's just as soft beneath the thorns.

"You're right."

Austin pauses with his hand on the garden gate. "Excuse me?"

I push past him. "You heard me. I'm not repeating it. Now, c'mon."

"All right." He laughs, a bright and clear sound now that he's no longer sick. His nose is still a little red and cracked, though. Probably doesn't help that the weather is changing, turning cold and stormy and dark.

Austin starts the van and I sign out of my shift through the LifeCare app, doing the same for him when he passes me his phone. The drive home is quick—we somehow manage to hit every green light—and then he's pulling to a stop in front of my house.

I undo my seat belt and unzip my backpack. I sweep my hand around the bottom of my bag, the little side compartments. "Shit. My keys."

"You forgot your house key?" Austin shifts the van into park.

I raspberry my lips and groan. "Seems that way. But someone should be home. . . . I'll see you later, okay?" I hop out of the van and wave, but Austin stays on the curb.

"I'll wait here." He sits back in his seat. "Just in case."

Even if it is a nice gesture, I roll my eyes. I walk up the path and try the front door. Locked. I knock, then wait a moment, but nothing. As I duck through the side gate, I call my mom. But the call goes to voicemail. So I shoot off a text as I try the back door. Also locked.

ME:
Where is everyone?!

I resist the urge to kick the nearby planter in annoyance. I've been gone all day. School for eight hours. Marianne for two. I'm hangry and I just want to do my homework so I can play *RotR* with Austin. But I'm locked out.

MOM:
Ana's parent-teacher meeting! I left a note on the fridge.

ME:
Well I can't read it because I'm LOCKED OUTSIDE

I retrace my steps to the front of the house. Austin's still parked on the curb.

MOM:
Oh baby, I'm so sorry. Want your dad to leave early to let you in? He could be there in thirty or so. Otherwise it'll be another hour or two.

Austin rolls down the window. "I take it you're locked out?"

I approach the van and rest my forearms on the frame, leaning inside. "Yep. My parents are at my little sister's parent-teacher meeting. My dad can leave early, but that'll still be a half hour."

"Do you want to wait at my house? I'm having band practice, and I have it on good authority there'll be pizza," he offers, and it hits me: he's been waiting here, on the curb, to offer this. *Just in case.* Stupid, nice boy. "Me. I'm the pizza authority, if that wasn't clear."

My stomach growls and he laughs. "Shut up," I mutter—not sure if I'm talking to him or my stomach. "Hold on." Before climbing back into the van, I text my mom.

ME:
That's okay. Going to Austin's. Text me when you're home and I'll walk back

MOM:
Oooh! That sounds fun, baby!!!

I make a face at my phone and shove it into my pocket, then haul myself back into the van. Great. Mom's going to be up my ass about this later, but right now, I'm too hungry to care.

A thirty-second van ride later, we're parked in Austin's steep driveway.

"Fair warning." Austin pockets his keys and tosses his messenger bag over one shoulder. "The band . . . they'll be excited to meet you. And I know that you hate any level of enthusiasm, especially from strangers."

I stop in my tracks. "Why, pray tell, do they want to meet me?"

"I've told them all about my supercool friend from LifeCare. Our drummer, Mac? They totally think I made you up."

"You *told* them about me?" I reach out to smack Austin on the arm, but he dances out of my range. "Why would you do something like that?"

"Believe it or not," he says, "I don't have any friends outside the band. Unless you count Marianne. They were happy I found someone to hang with at school."

I drop my arm by my side, swallowing hard. "Oh."

What's more surprising? The fact that Austin told his bandmates about me, or that Austin isn't the social butterfly I thought he was? I mean, he flies solo at school, I knew that. But I guess I didn't realize, until this very moment, that my friendship might mean as much to Austin as his does to me.

"That okay?" He tugs at a fraying zipper on his bag.

"Yeah." The answer catches us both off guard, but Austin covers up his surprise with a smile.

We walk up the rest of the steep driveway to the garage, which has an opened old-fashioned tilt-up door. Inside, the garage is decent sized, with a couch along one wall and a mini fridge and a folding table on the other. The center of the room is cluttered with a bunch of musical equipment that I vaguely recognize from rattling in the backseat of the murder van.

On the couch are three kids.

The *band*.

"Sorry I'm late," Austin says, loping up to the open door. "But I brought company. This is Eloise."

I reach the garage a few seconds after Austin, pausing at the entrance beside him. Three pairs of eyes land on me, and unease tightens my sternum. Every single part of me wants to turn around and run home. To disappear. To be anywhere but here.

Fuck social anxiety. Seriously. This is the worst.

I think I'm dying.

Every part of my body is telling me I'm dying, but I know I'm not dying.

But I might be dying.

"Hey." My voice sounds too loud, too high-pitched. I lift my hand in an awkward wave before crossing my arms. "Um. I got locked out of my house, so Austin said I could hang. If that's okay . . ." I trail off, waiting for one of the three bandmates to tell me to fuck off.

But Austin grabs me by the backpack strap and leads me into the garage. "They don't mind. Right?"

A pretty Indian girl with wavy dark hair and curves for

days hops onto her feet. "Hey, I'm Shyla. You can call me Shy, though. Hugs okay?" Apparently, I nod—or she doesn't respect personal boundaries—because she gives me a one-armed squeeze. "It's nice to finally meet you!"

I resist the urge to go into panic mode and force a smile. "Yeah, you too."

"I'm Winston," a tall, lanky white boy with red hair says, waving.

"Mac." They're much less lanky but also have a shock of red hair, tied back into a short ponytail. "We're related. If you can't tell. Twins."

"The hair was a tip-off," I say with a nervous laugh. Winston and Mac smile identical smiles, even though they're fraternal. "Nice to meet you both."

"Now you've met"—Austin hands me a paper plate buckling beneath the weight of three slices of cheese pizza—"everyone in the Coinstar Rejects."

I loiter beside a stack of Christmas decorations in clear plastic tubs. "Sorry, what's a Coinstar reject? Please don't tell me that's your band name."

Shy snorts and offers me a soda, but I shake my head. "Told you it was a bad name," she says to Austin.

Austin's cheeks redden. "You know, those coin machines in grocery stores—"

"I know what a Coinstar is," I interrupt. "That's not the issue. What's a Coinstar *reject*? Like when the machine doesn't accept foreign currency and buttons and shit?"

Winston and Mac start cracking up, and Shy plops back onto the couch with her pizza. "Basically, yeah. Worst band name ever." The twins chorus their agreement.

Austin points at his bandmates. "But look, we're having a conversation about it! The worst band names are forgettable."

"I wish I could forget it," I say before I can stop myself, but . . . everyone laughs. Heat rises in my cheeks before I realize they're not laughing at me. Or upset at me for shitting on their band name. Some of the tension in my shoulders releases.

Austin motions for me to follow him, and I sit on the far edge of the couch. They all launch into a conversation about the battle of the bands at the end of the month, and I eat my pizza in silence.

Honestly, it's not terrible. And I don't mean the pizza, which is very delicious. But *this*, hanging out with Austin and his bandmates. I thought I'd feel way, way more out of my element. No one's made me feel like an outsider, though. They just accepted my existence and moved on.

Almost like I belong here just as much as they do.

Mom texts me thirty minutes later as the Coinstar Rejects set up and test all their equipment. I have the couch to myself; I even shucked off my Doc Martens and got comfortable. Look at me, assimilating.

MOM:
Just got done and heading home! Should be there in 30min. How's Austin's? Did you have dinner?

I flip my phone around in my hands, thinking.

ME:
Good and yep, there was pizza

MOM:
That's great! Stay as long as you want but I'll text you when we're home and unlock the back door, okay?

ME:
Ok

My mom's level of excitement about me hanging at Austin's makes me want to die inside. It's *so* cringey. A year ago, she would've never given me a pass on hanging out on a school night for as long as I wanted. Guess she's that desperate for me to have friends, huh? I'm not sure if I should be embarrassed or grateful.

I set my phone on the empty cushion beside me and sit upright, crisscrossing my legs. Austin's tuning his bass, perched on the edge of a gigantic orange amp, his messy hair flopping into his eyes. He keeps having to pause to push it back.

"So." Shy uncoils a length of microphone cord, then kneels down and plugs it into one of the other amps. "You met Austin through LifeCare?"

I smile a tiny bit. "Yep. I'm volunteering for a few months for my college applications."

"Austin's obsessed with that place." Shy hops back to her feet and taps her finger to the mic; feedback echoes and we all wince.

I pull the sleeves of my sweater over my hands. "Yeah, it's surprisingly not terrible." I'm doing my best to be social, but I feel off. Like my socialization is a muscle that's weak from disuse. "Marianne's kind of amazing."

Shy groans dramatically. "I'm jealous. Lead singer of the

Laundromats?" She pretends to swoon, pressing the back of her free hand to her forehead.

"For real." Mac slides onto a padded stool behind the drum kit. "Austin won't let us meet her."

"Really?" I turn to Austin, who's done tuning his bass. Withholding joy seems very un-Austin-like. "Why?"

"Technically, it's a breach of LifeCare confidentiality." Austin walks over to us. "If you ever read Donna's paperwork, you'd know that. I shouldn't have told them about Marianne to begin with, but . . ." He trails off with an unapologetic shrug.

"Ooh, I'm going to tell on you." I'm not-so-secretly thrilled that Austin broke one of Donna's rules.

Austin loops the strap of his bass over his chest, then kneels down to grab an electrical cord and plugs it into the bass. "You know what, Lou?" He looks up at me through his lashes. "I'd like to see you try. Donna loves me. Besides, you'd hate it there without me."

"Please," I scoff, and pretend that he's not right. "This is all part of my master plan to get Marianne all to myself."

Shy laughs, sweeping her hair back into a bun. "Are we practicing or what? We have twenty-five days until A Scare Is Born, people!"

"What's A Scare Is Born?"

"Battle of the bands," Austin reminds me, and struggles to tug his cardigan off without removing his bass. "It's on the twenty-eighth, the Saturday before Halloween? It's themed. Get it? Like a star is born . . . ?"

With everything going on lately, I've been losing track of time. Halloween—also known as my favorite holiday of all time—is creeping up.

"Break a leg?" That's what you say to people, right?

Austin tosses the cardigan onto the couch; he's wearing a T-shirt underneath with some obscure cartoon on the front. And . . . Austin has biceps. *Okay*, no shit he has biceps, but the sleeves of his tee are tighter than I would've ever imagined. Not like I've given any thought to Austin's arms before. It's just . . . weird, that's all.

"You could come." Austin turns to me. "Cheer us on. Friendly face, remember?"

"What?" I hate that my cheeks are hot right now. "You want to have at least one fan in the crowd?"

Austin staggers backward like I've punched him. "You wound me, Lou."

"We have fans," Shy says with a tinkling laugh. "Not many. But they exist."

Mac drums their sticks against their legs. "We have less than ten but more than five."

I can't help but laugh. "I'll think about it, okay?"

"That's all I ask," Austin tells me with a grin, then turns to his bandmates.

The conversation shifts into musical jargon that I don't follow as they warm up. They're kind of messy, stopping and starting, asking questions between notes. Small tweaks and corrections, some good-natured arguing. Then they launch into their first song. And okay. Austin wasn't wrong—they're not bad. Not bad at all.

Shy is the lead singer, her voice high and sweet. For the first two songs, Austin plays his bass. And I don't know anything about music, but over a month into visiting Marianne, I've seen a lot of the Laundromats' performances. He's *good*. Honestly, they all are. In sophomore year, Lydie, Jordan, and I went to an open mic night because Jordan's brother was performing, and those bands were objectively terrible. The Coinstar Rejects are objectively good.

Even if their band name is awful.

For the third song, Austin sets his bass aside and sits down at the keyboard. It's a slower song, a ballad. Shy sings, but then Austin joins her in a duet. The dude wasn't lying—he *can* sing. My knee-jerk reaction is to make fun of him, but I'm too impressed for that. I can't even sing in tune when I'm in the shower.

Austin catches my eye and shrugs, his fingers gliding across the keyboard.

I smile and shake my head, mouthing *Loser* at him.

Thirty minutes of practice and several songs later, Shy checks her phone. "I need to wrap up and get the car back to my dad. Sound okay to everyone?"

"Yeah." Austin turns around on the bench so he's facing Shy. "And we're feeling good about those first three for A Scare Is Born?"

Shy starts coiling up the microphone cable, looping the length around her wrist. "I think so. We only have ten minutes up there, but it's a tight set. We can play around with the order, but I'm down with these three."

"Sounds groovy." Mac begins packing up their bag.

Winston kneels on the ground beside his guitar case and unlatches it. "The band democracy is in agreement, then."

I stretch my arms overhead, then grab my phone. Holy shit, it's eight thirty. I've been here for two hours. Probably overstayed my welcome. "You sounded great," I say, even though the words are awkward and clunky coming out of my mouth. "Not like I know much about music."

Austin's cheeks flush. "Thanks, Lou," he says, then busies himself with breaking down the instruments. He explained earlier that they practice twice a week—Tuesdays in the garage and Sundays at Shy's, since Austin's house is off-limits on the weekend. Binna hosts book club on Sundays, and apparently, forty-something women don't enjoy listening to amateur musicians while discussing the latest Reese's Book Club pick and getting drunk on rosé. Go figure.

I throw away all the pizza-grease-stained plates and stack empty soda cans in a neat pile for recycling.

Shy walks over to me as I'm tidying up the folding table. "Thanks for cleaning up."

"Oh, sure." I wipe down the table with a napkin and pretend like making myself useful isn't how I'm currently dealing with my anxiety. "No problem."

"I had a genius idea. My birthday's this Thursday and I'm having a party Friday night. Do you want to come?" She leans her hip against the table. "Sorry if that's weird. It's just—it's awesome that you and Austin are hanging out, and you seem really cool."

"I'm not cool," I say flatly, confused by this girl inviting me to her birthday party.

Shy just laughs and smacks my arm. "And you're funny! C'mon. Please?"

I glance across the garage, but Austin's talking to Mac. My stomach hurts, but it's not from all the pizza. I want to ask Shy *why*. We talked a little tonight, sure, but she doesn't know me. Now that I think of it, that's probably why she's inviting me—she doesn't know any better. "Um. I don't know."

"Austin," Shy shouts across the garage, "tell Eloise she needs to come to my birthday party."

Austin swivels his attention toward us, his face stretching in a grin. "Oh man, Lou, you gotta come. It's at Retro Rink."

I blink. "Huh?"

"The new roller rink," Shy explains. "Eighties themed. It's going to be so much fun. And you should come. If you're Austin's friend, then you're my friend too."

"Can I—can I think about it?" I ask, my throat oddly tight.

"Yeah! Gimme your phone."

I hand her my phone, and she enters her number with a few taps. "Text me for details, or you can ask Austin. But it's this Friday at six. There's a snack bar at the rink or you can eat beforehand. There'll be cake, though."

"Yeah, um. I'll try to make it," I say, hoping it sounds like I have a social life. But that seems to be enough for Shy, who smiles and hugs me goodbye before bounding down the driveway to her car.

I lift my backpack off the ground. "Hey, I'm gonna head home."

Austin clicks his bass case shut. "Want me to walk you?"

"It's two blocks. I think I'll be okay." Besides, Winston and Mac are still here, and I feel extremely awkward asking Austin to leave his actual friends to walk his volunteer buddy home.

"You sure?" He hops to his feet and pulls on his cardigan.

"Yeah." I turn to the twins, who're dismantling the drum set. "Nice to meet you both."

Winston nods his chin in response. "You too."

"Yeah, likewise," Mac says, and lifts their hand for a high five.

I awkwardly high-five them—for what reason, I do not know.

"See you at school," I tell Austin, then duck out of the garage. But I don't even make it to the sidewalk before I hear his footsteps slapping the concrete.

"Hey!" he calls. I turn toward Austin, who's all backlit by the light from the garage. "Was that, uh, was that okay? I know my friends can be a lot and they all just kind of came at you—"

"All good." I tuck my hands into my hoodie pockets and rock back on my heels. "They were . . . nice."

Austin squints at me. "Yeah?"

"Surprisingly, I'm okay. It wasn't as bad as I thought it'd be."

"You thought it was going to be a disaster, didn't you?"

"I have very low expectations in life."

"Does that mean you'll come on Friday?" He gives me a hopeful grin, then bops his shoulder against mine. "Shy *already* texted me that she thinks you're awesome. And I think you're awesome. There's no reason why you shouldn't come."

My face heats up, but thankfully, it's dark out on the sidewalk. Last thing I need is Austin trying to photograph me blushing to add to his Embarrassing Eloise Album, which I know for a fact exists on his phone. I'm legitimately afraid he might start an Instagram account. "Do I have to dress up?"

"Is that a yes?" That hopeful grin stretches wider, and for whatever reason, it makes me smile too.

"Yes, fine. But I'm *not* dressing up."

"Do you even own anything other than jeans and button-downs?"

"Oh, yes. I happen to own the world's ugliest shirt."

Austin laughs.

"Yo, Austin," Mac yells from up the driveway. "Where's that screwdriver?"

"Shit," he says, and holds up the screwdriver in his hand. "I gotta get back up there. I'll see you tomorrow, okay? And no bailing on Friday. I'm holding you to this."

I wave him off. "Yeah, yeah. I'll see you tomorrow," I say, grumbling, and then I take off down the sidewalk toward my house. But I'd be lying if I said I wasn't smiling the entire walk home.

FOURTEEN

I'll never know, never escape
The way you made me your fate

—The Laundromats, "Daydream" (1979)

I sit on my bathroom floor trying—and failing—to breathe. Trying to fight the roar of discomfort inside me, the nausea of anxiety, the pounding headache behind my eyes. Because why the fuck did I agree to Shy's birthday party? Was the pizza laced? Was there a carbon monoxide leak in the garage?

Groaning, I rest the back of my head against the cabinet.

When Austin dropped me off after school today, I promised him that I'd be there. Because at three in the afternoon, the six o'clock party felt like eons away. And I've replied to his not one, not two, but *three* follow-up texts making sure I won't bail. But now it's 5:31 p.m. and all I can think about is how this is a huge mistake.

I reach out for my phone and grab it off the bath mat beside me. Hold it up to my face and open my messages. Stare at the string of text history between me and Austin. The last text he sent was over an hour ago, double-checking that I had a ride. He left an hour early to pick up Shy's birthday cake from this gluten-free bakery in West Seattle. Either I had to leave early with him or I had to find a ride; it didn't make sense for him to double back to our neighborhood. Even if he was willing.

Mom volunteered to drive me, positively gleeful that her daughter had been invited to a birthday party, like I'm in the fourth fucking grade. Right now, I'm glad I turned down riding with Austin. Almost like I subconsciously knew this bathroom breakdown was coming. Like I knew I'd bail at the very last minute.

Hi, I'm Eloise Deane, and I'm the fucking worst!

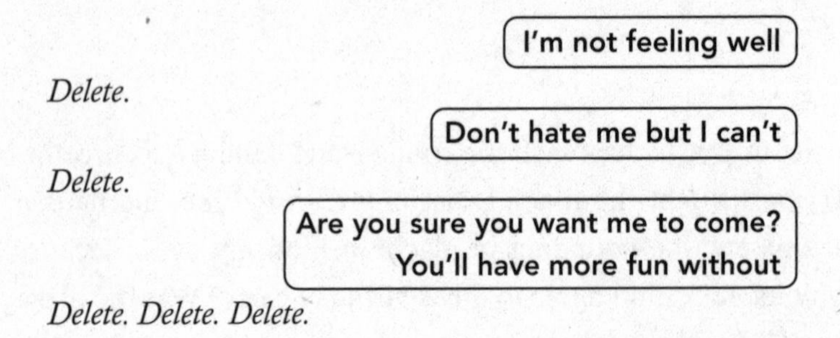

Delete. Delete. Delete.

I toss my phone onto the fuzzy bath mat and dig the heels of my hands into my eyes.

Why is this so hard? Why can't I let myself be excited for tonight? Why do I always, always feel like an outsider, even when people go out of their way to include me? I fucking hate this about myself. I'm constantly analyzing and picking apart and preparing for the worst. Waiting for the moment when someone I care about will realize that I don't belong.

This soft, eager part of me wants to go tonight. To have fun. To try to be something, *someone*, different. But that would require getting off the bathroom floor.

"Eloise?" Mom knocks on the door. "Are you okay? We should leave soon if you want to get there on time. . . ."

"Fine," I manage to say, even though my throat's all tight.

Mom's quiet on the other side of the door. Then: "Can I come in, baby?"

I lean over and unlock the door for her. She was working today—she's dressed in her apron and smells like the lavender dog shampoo she always uses—and her face crumples. "What's going on? Are you sick?"

I shake my head. "*Really* anxious. Bad anxious."

She sinks down beside me on the bathroom floor. "About the party?"

"Mm-hmm." I pull my legs to my chest and rest my chin on my knees.

Mom smooths back my hair from my sweaty cheeks. "What's going on?"

"It's just . . . I haven't done something like this in a year. What if it's terrible? And I fu—mess up whatever friendship I have with Austin? All I want to do right now is text him and say I'm not going."

Mom taps my phone, still on the bath mat where I tossed it. "But you haven't. Why not?"

"Because . . ." I trail off and stare at my hands, my anxiety-chipped nail polish.

"Because you *want* to go?" Mom guesses gently.

"Yeah. I guess. . . . But what if it's a disaster?"

"What if it's *not* a disaster?" Mom lifts my chin so she can look me in the eye. Those light-blue eyes are soft and loving. "You need to stop assuming you're the problem. You can't control what other people think of you or if they like you. The right people will show up. But you have to show up for them, too. Don't let what happened with Lydie and Jordan ruin a good thing. Those girls already took enough from you."

My phone lights up on the pale-green bath mat and Mom kisses my cheek before handing it over.

AUSTIN:
just got the cake! Text me when you're on your way, okay? 🛼🕺🎂

The corner of my mouth tugs with a reluctant and stubborn smile.

Retro Rink opened downtown over the summer, and generally speaking, I'd rather walk over hot coals than go roller-skating. But Mom drops me off near the massive windowless building fifteen minutes after six. The wooden exterior is painted navy, the roof is domed, and RETRO RINK flashes in pink neon above a matching set of pink doors.

Before I can turn and run back to the minivan, Mom drives off. Stranding me with my bag, a pocket full of ginger chews in case my stomach acts up again—seriously, having an anxiety disorder is like one intestinal wreckage after another—and enough nervous energy to power a small city.

October air brushes over me and I shiver.

Austin's joke about me not owning things other than button-downs wasn't far off. But I was able to put together a slapdash outfit in under ten minutes. Black leggings beneath jean shorts (that I wear for approximately three days every summer) paired with a purple T-shirt that I forgot existed; I bunched up the material and knotted it in the front. I side-braided my hair, and the finishing touch is Marianne's starry leather jacket. No idea if it's from the eighties, but it's old. That should count for something.

Sure, I look ridiculous. But you can't say that I didn't try.

I walk toward the entrance.

Then stop.

Austin's perched on one of the benches outside, his elbows on his knees as he stares at the ground. He's wearing acid-washed jeans and a white T-shirt tucked into the waistband, Ray-Bans looped through the collar. The toe of his Converse taps energetically against the concrete, and my heart quickens with the beat.

When I'm ten feet away and he hasn't noticed me, I call out, "Hey, Chandler! Party's inside."

Austin looks up and his grin is full-on sunshine. He hops to his feet, his gaze traveling from my face all the way down to my combat boots. "Whoa, Lou. You—"

I hold out a hand. "Shut up. I look ridiculous. Like the final girl in an eighties movie."

"That's not what I was going to say." Before I can ask him what he was going to say, Austin steps closer and tugs on the sleeve of my jacket. "Hey, is this Marianne's?"

"Yeah. Payment for delving through the nuclear fallout zone that was her walk-in closet." I glance over his shoulder at the roller rink, then back at him. "What're you doing out here? It's fucking freezing."

"What do you think?" Austin shoves his hands in the front pockets of his jeans, tilts his head slightly. When I don't reply, he sighs. "I was waiting for you."

Heat pricks my cheeks and that soft, eager part of me thinks, *So this is what it's like to have people*. But I say, "What? Worried I'd take one look at this place and flee?"

"You could just say thank you, you know." The more

exasperated he sounds, the wider I smile. "C'mon. Let's get our skate on."

Reluctantly, I follow Austin through the pink double doors and into Retro Rink.

The interior is everything I dreaded it would be—it's loud and neon and still has that toxic fresh-paint smell since it's only been open a few months. The doors thunk shut behind us, and I survey my own personal hell.

To our left is a row of lockers, a bunch of those coin-operated rides you see in malls or outside grocery stores, and three pinball machines. To the right is the snack bar, some schoolyard-style tables, and several kitschy vending machines. Straight ahead is a check-in counter with a wall of cubbies stuffed with skates; beyond the counter is the rink itself. The lights are low, lasers flashing patterns across the crowded floor.

Austin's hand brushes mine, and I glance beside me. "You okay?" he asks.

I raspberry my lips. Then I shrug. "Sure?"

"Very convincing," he says with a laugh.

We grab our skates and plop onto a bench by the lockers. I've only laced up my first skate before Shy glides over.

"Hey, you made it!" She sits beside me but leans over to Austin to say, "I told you she'd come."

Austin shifts forward to lace his skates, his head ducked low so I can't see his face, and mutters, "Thanks for that."

Shy rolls her eyes, then says to me, "Anyways. Hi. You look fucking amazing."

"Um, thanks," I say with an awkward laugh, and finish lacing my roller skates. My side-braid falls over one shoulder, the strands tickling my bare neck. "Happy birthday."

Shy flips her crunchy, crimped hair over one shoulder. She's in a full-on Madonna getup, black tutu and all. "Thank you! I'm finally, officially eighteen. Lotto tickets, army drafts, and cigarettes, I have arrived."

I tuck my shoes into a locker along with my bag and stand up, testing my balance.

Austin does the same, both of us wobbly-kneed and clutching onto the nearby animatronic horses for balance. Fifty bucks that tonight ends with one of us breaking a limb. Money's on me, since Austin's steadier than I am—but that's not saying much.

Shy twirls in a circle around us, then skids to a stop and gives us an expectant look with her hands on her hips. "Okay, come on! This isn't a stand-around-and-talk party. It's a roller-skating party. Winston and Mac are out there, but so are, like, a ton of our other friends. Don't worry, Eloise, they'll all love you."

I shoot Austin a panicked look, clutching the animatronic horse's snout for dear life. *More* friends? "Don't worry," he repeats, and takes shaky steps toward the rink.

"But I'm so good at it," I whine, and Austin just reaches back, his fingers looping around my wrist before he wheels me behind him like a rolling suitcase.

Once we're on the rink, Shy does a little spin—*someone's* roller-skated a lot in their life—and takes off.

"I'm going to eat shit," I yell at Austin over the music, which is true to the theme, all eighties synth pop; "Take on Me" by a-ha blasts from the speakers. He's still holding on to my wrist with one hand—his fingers are hot against my skin—but the other clutches the safety railing that circles the rink. We're near the on-off ramp, and people zoom and zip past us, laughing and dancing and talking.

"I mean, same." He laughs and shrugs.

"What?"

"You showed up."

"I said I would, didn't I?" I say, as if I wasn't bemoaning my decision on the bathroom floor less than an hour earlier.

"I'm just happy you're here."

I pretend to vomit.

Austin's fingers lace with mine as he takes tentative steps forward along the side wall of the rink. "Come on, you miserable asshole. If you're gonna eat shit, then I'm eating shit with you."

I stare at our hands—fingers woven, palms cupped—and wonder why I'm not pulling away. Austin holding my hand so I don't trip and fall is a kindness that *should* make me pretend puke again. Or real puke. But I just take a deep breath and push away from the wall.

At first, I struggle with my balance as I keep pace with Austin, but once we're skating side by side, I let go of his hand. The first lap is rough, but after we've circled the rink once, we gain confidence and pick up speed. We're still a hot mess, though, laughing as the other almost falls. Which happens. A lot.

On our sixth lap, we ran into (not literally, luckily) Shy, Mac, and Winston, and the twins cheered when they saw my terrible outfit. Like Shy had warned, they had a whole other group of friends with them, but between the music and general roller-rink chaos, introductions were pretty useless.

"Are you having fun?" Austin glides beside me. He's stuck close lap after lap, his arms bumping into mine. Probably so he can drag me down with him when he falls.

"Yeah!" And the thing is, I *am* having fun. Like a stupid amount of fun. Even if I'm a little wheezy from asthma and my calves burn and my big toes hurt because my skates are a half size too small. Doesn't matter, because the music is poppy and loud enough that I don't have to think too much. And Austin is good company, but I already knew that.

"Me too!" Austin shouts back, but even if the music drowned out his words, I'd still be able to tell from the goofy look on his face that he's having just as much fun as I am. Something catches his attention and he adds, "Shy's waving us over. You hungry?"

I nod, comically out of breath. Shit, I should work out more.

Austin reaches for my hand again, and after hesitating for a half second, I thread my fingers between his. If we get separated out here, I'll become roller-rink roadkill. The second we hit carpet, I let go, and we wheel ourselves over to a big table in the back corner by the snack bar. The group has grown. More unfamiliar faces crowd the tables, eating french fries and drinking sodas, laughing and chatting.

"You want anything to eat?" Austin pushes back his hair from his forehead.

"Um." I squint at the menu for the snack bar. "Maybe fries? I don't know. What do you want?"

"We can split. I'll get a large, okay?"

"Sure. My wallet's in my locker with my shoes, though."

Austin waves me off. "I got you," he says, and then rolls over to the small line.

I hobble over to the table and slide onto the bench beside Shy.

"Hey," I say, still out of breath.

Shy shoves a garlic fry into her mouth. "Hey! Are you having fun?"

I'm really not used to this many people caring if I'm having fun or not. This is weird. "I had my reservations, don't get me wrong, but this is awesome."

"Austin was so happy you agreed to come," she says, and slurps her soda. "He was seriously worried you'd bail."

I make a face. "No offense, but it's just a birthday party. Me being here isn't a huge deal."

"None taken." Shy pops another garlic fry into her mouth, then shrugs. "But try telling Austin it's not a big deal. He sent me a dozen emojis when you agreed to come."

"Yeah. The dude has a problem."

Shy chews on her straw and gives me a funny look. I glance over at the snack bar, watching as Austin opens up his wallet and pulls out some cash, his hair flopping forward again into his eyes. Annoyed, he shoves it back. He needs a haircut.

Setting her soda down, Shy says, "So. You and—"

"Who's that?" I ask as a girl skates up to Austin. She taps his shoulder, and when he looks down, he smiles and pulls her in for a hug.

Shy follows my eyeline. "That's Rose, Austin's ex-girlfriend. No idea who invited her."

"Oh." Heat blooms across my skin. "How long . . . When'd they break up?"

"July or August? Something like that. But they're like *that couple* who's always on-off."

Rose is shorter than me—the definition of petite—with curly blond hair and a loud laugh that I can hear from our table, even over "(I Just) Died in Your Arms." Something tightens in my stomach, and I dig my hand into my pocket for a ginger chew. There are way too many people here. It's sensory overload.

Austin says something to Rose, and she laughs again, her curls bouncing as she nods. When he gets our order of fries, she plucks one off the top and pops it into her mouth. He smiles and nudges his arm against hers; then they skate over to the table.

Sure, Rose is eating my french fries, but why do I feel like I'm having a low-key anxiety attack? Like, *obviously*, Austin has friends outside of just me, and he's had girlfriends. But it never, ever occurred to me until this moment that Austin has a whole other side of his life that I'm not a part of. That I'll never be a part of. Austin dating shouldn't be that surprising. But this piece of Austin Information feels like a sledgehammer hitting me in the ribs.

I chew on the ginger, and it helps calm my stomach. Maybe I'm doing too much, too fast. Like, I went from spending every night alone in the basement playing *RotR* to *this*.

"Hey, birthday girl," Austin says to Shy, and sits across from us.

Rose sits beside him and waves at me. She's even prettier up close. An upturned nose, scattered with freckles, with a single silver hoop through one nostril. Big green eyes. An even bigger smile. "Hey! You must be Eloise. I'm Rose."

"Hi." I busy myself with pulling my phone out of these stupid shorts' ridiculously tight pockets, then open my messages. Because where I want to be right now is home. In my gaming chair, logged into my rogue, in another world.

Austin nudges my foot beneath the table, and I look up. "What?" The word comes out as a snap.

His brow creases with concern, and he pushes the boat of fries closer to my side of the table. "Fry, Lou?"

I shake my head. "I'm actually not feeling well. My stomach . . ."

"Oh no!" Rose's eyes widen in concern. "Do you need some Pepto? I have some of those chew tabs in my purse. They'll turn your tongue black but totally do the job."

"That's okay." I force myself to smile at Rose and slide the boat of fries back toward Austin. She's nice—even though chewable Pepto is the actual worst—and I don't know why I expected her to be an asshole. "They're all yours."

Austin frowns at the fries as if they've personally wronged him. He lifts his gaze to meet mine. "Want me to get you something else?"

"Nah." I'm still holding my phone, my escape just one text away, and my palms are sweaty against its case. My stomach is still topsy-turvy, and sitting here with all Austin's friends makes me feel like I'm at school. An outsider. Under normal circumstances, I'd have already texted my mom. Hell, I'd be on the curb outside waiting for her to pick me up or anxiety puking in the bathroom.

Austin notices my phone, and the space between his brows furrows even deeper. He knows me. Like it or not, he knows *exactly* why I have my phone in my hand. That I'm one text away from noping out of here, hard.

Popping a fry into his mouth, he pulls out his phone.

AUSTIN:
Lou, don't you dare bail on me

I lift my gaze from the screen and look across the table; he's giving me puppy-dog eyes. Pulling out all the golden retriever stops. Austin didn't say I'd be bailing on the party or even Shy, the birthday girl. He said I'd be bailing on *him*. That's what gets me. That I'd be letting Austin down. The person who has never, ever let me down since the day I met him, not even once. He's there for me. For some reason, he's always there for me.

I lock my phone and wiggle it back into my shorts pocket.

Then I grab a french fry and lean my elbows onto the table, listening as Mac and Winston tell a story about that one time they tried to sneak into the aquarium downtown over the summer.

"Thanks for coming." Shy hugs me, the skates in her hand banging against the side of my leg.

"Yeah! Thanks for the invite." I hug her back, then step aside so she can say goodbye to Austin. It's been four hours of snacks, birthday cake, and skating. I have a blister the shape of Florida oozing on my heel, a bruise on my butt from when I fell, and a scraped elbow from when I ran into the wall on my way to the bathroom.

News alert: I'm not coordinated and shouldn't be allowed to operate small machinery like roller skates.

"Sure you don't need a ride?" Austin shoves the Ray-Bans into his messenger bag, then loops the strap over his shoulder.

Shy shakes her head. "Nah. I'm gonna hang out with Xavier for a bit," she says, and waggles her brows, nodding to one of her friends who showed up when we were singing "Happy Birthday." He's tall and handsome and looks at Shy like she's the sole reason the earth turns. "See you at practice!"

Xavier waves before walking out with Shy, the bright laser lights flashing across their backs.

"Shall we?" Austin holds up his skates in one hand.

"We shall." In truth, I'm exhausted. But I'm also really, really glad I didn't go home earlier. Because this exhaustion feels different from when I'm curling up at night after raiding with my guild until I can barely hold my eyes open anymore. This exhaustion almost feels . . . good.

Austin and I walk over to the front counter to turn in our skates. Rose and the two friends she brought with her—I can't remember their names—are already there. One girl is flirting with the guy behind the counter. A baller move, considering they're exchanging innuendos over stinky used roller skates and a bottle of disinfectant, but who am I to judge? I have zero game.

"Hey!" Rose brightens, turning to us. "I was hoping I hadn't missed you."

I slide my skates across the counter, heat pricking at my collarbones. Obviously, she's talking to Austin, and that uneasy, panicky feeling is back, weighing me down. Like, I don't understand anxiety. Sometimes I'm fine—good, even—and then my anxiety flares up and it's asshole hour!

Austin hands his skates to the other guy behind the counter, who looks pissed that his coworker is flirting on the job. Then Austin turns to Rose and smiles. "Yeah, it was awesome you came out. We haven't seen each other in a while, huh?"

Rose's cheeks redden. "Seriously. It was a lot of fun," she says, her eyes practically glued to Austin's.

Cool. This isn't awkward at all.

I dig my hand into my pocket for another ginger chew and shove it into my mouth.

"Um." Rose blushes deeper and turns to me. Like an afterthought. "It was so nice meeting you!"

I smile because Rose has been nothing but nice to me. Maybe even too nice. No wonder she and Austin dated. "Likewise."

Rose gives me a quick hug before turning to Austin. Since she's short, she pushes to her tiptoes to hug him. He wraps one arm around her waist and squeezes her against his chest. Then he clears his throat and steps out of the hug.

"Bye, Rose," he says with another smile, and waves to the other girls. "Lou? Ready to go?"

I nod, and wave at Rose and her friends. Eager to escape this weird alternate reality where Austin isn't the Austin that I know. He's an Austin with a past and an ex-girlfriend, and I don't know why it freaks me out so much. But it does.

Outside Retro Rink, it's cold and dark. The breeze pushes the loose strands of hair from my braid against my face, chilling the sweat from roller-skating for several hours in a warm, poorly ventilated room. Austin and I walk side by side, our arms crossed to try to retain body heat.

He unlocks the murder van; lights flash up the street.

"I'm not sure what surprises me more," he says, slowing down once we reach the van. "The fact that you showed up or the fact that you stayed."

I yank open the passenger door and climb inside, my teeth chattering. "Why're you s-s-so surprised?"

Austin starts the van and turns the heat on full blast, and we wait while it warms up. "Because tonight was the definition of Outside Lou's Comfort Zone."

I tuck my hands into the sleeves of my starry leather jacket, scooting closer to the nearest vent. "Yeah, well . . ." My words trail off and I shrug. I'm not going to argue that it wasn't outside my comfort zone. It totally was. But I did it. And miraculously, I'm still alive, if slightly banged up.

Austin shifts the van into gear, and we head in the direction of home. "You're really uncoordinated."

I laugh and lean back in my seat now that I'm warmed up. "Dude, you shouldn't be talking. You fell just as often as I did."

"Yeah, trying to *help* you."

"And they say chivalry is dead."

He chuckles, then turns on some music, and we drive home, making comments here and there about the night or people we see on the street. The high, frenetic energy in the roller rink has nothing on these quiet, easy moments that are becoming effortless. I don't know when, exactly, the shift happened. When I started feeling *this* comfortable around Austin. But maybe there wasn't one moment. Maybe every moment built off the one before it.

Austin slows alongside the curb in front of my house. The lights are all winked out except the porch light Mom must've left on. I gather my belongings off the floor as he shifts the van into park. The dome light clicks on when I open the door. "Thanks again."

Austin hops out of the van, following me. "Hold up."

I resist the urge to shiver. Even though we're two weeks into the season, it really hasn't felt like fall until this very moment. There are Halloween decorations on my neighbor's lawn. The maple tree above has rusty-orange leaves. The air is bitter and cold but refreshing all at once.

"Tonight was great." Austin says this effusively, as if he's trying to hammer this fact into my pessimistic skull.

"Worth the battle wounds." I smile—a genuine smile. "I'll see you tomorrow?"

"For sure." Austin takes a step forward, then wraps his arms around me.

For a half second, I'm too surprised to respond. But Shy hugged me. Even Rose hugged me. This shouldn't be different. But . . . it's different. His hands slide beneath the leather jacket, his palms hot against my bare waist, my bare lower back, exposed from my knotted-up shirt.

I shut my eyes, press my face against his shoulder, and hold on to him. Austin rests his head against mine, and he smells like boy: sweat from the roller rink and deodorant but also something else, something woozy and warm. And the hug is . . . *nice.* Comforting and completely exhilarating at the same time. Since Austin's only an inch—if that—taller than me, we sort of just . . . fit. We're closer than ever before.

And I don't hate it.

But I say, "I should get inside. Curfew." My voice doesn't sound like mine; it's quiet and thick. Also, I'm lying. Mom won't care if I'm out late, not if I'm off being a normal teenager with friends so she stops fretting over my "social development." But I'm afraid that if I don't say something, I'll just stay like this.

In this moment.

In this hug.

In this *feeling.*

"Right. Yeah." Austin moves first, his hands falling from my waist as he steps back. He palms the back of his neck with one hand, the other hanging limp at his side. "Thanks again. For not bailing."

I burrow my hands into the pockets of my jacket, my stomach flip-flopping. "Bailing on you is like leaving a puppy at the pound. I just couldn't do it."

The nearest streetlamp flickers, and it's dark out on the sidewalk. But Austin's close enough that it doesn't matter. The corner of his mouth twitches and his gaze holds mine. "Joke all you want, but I'm serious."

My knee-jerk reaction is to make yet *another* joke, but he sounds so freaking sincere, I can't do it. "Yeah, yeah. Don't mention it."

Austin steps back toward the van. "Good night, Lou. See you tomorrow."

"Night." I wave, and then I turn toward my sleeping house, my heart a shade less black and a degree warmer inside my chest.

FIFTEEN

The space between the notes is where you'll find me
And I'll dance around these feelings nightly

—The Laundromats, "Lost in Translation" (1981)

I wake up Saturday morning before sunrise. My phone's on silent, no alarm set since it's the weekend, but at seven, I'm tossing and turning and I can't fall back asleep. After I came home last night, I pretty much passed out the second I curled up under my comforter, disjointed clips of Shy's party flickering through my brain.

Even though Austin was teasing me, I'm proud that I stayed. Eloise from a month ago—or even a few weeks ago—would've bailed. Bailed so fast that I would've left a skid mark on the roller-rink floor, a trail of dust *poof*-ing after me.

Groggy, I sit up and take in the darkness. The basement is often dank, but it's even more so now since the sun hasn't yet risen behind the rain-heavy clouds.

I pop out my night guard and set it on my bedside table, flick on my lamp, and then lean against my headboard with my phone. Austin is, undoubtedly, asleep. But lately, texting Austin is one of the first things I do in the morning. Usually for updates on our Marianne schedule, since I rely on him for rides.

But we confirmed our LifeCare plans on our drive home from Retro Rink last night.

There's no reason for me to text Austin.

But do I need a reason anymore, other than wanting to?

ME:
My elbow wound has tripled in size overnight. How're your roller rink battle wounds?

I'm about to toss my phone onto my comforter when it buzzes.

AUSTIN:
are you voluntarily awake before eight?

ME:
I couldn't sleep. Why're *you* awake?

AUSTIN:
is insomnia contagious? I couldn't sleep either 😴

I chew on my cracked bottom lip, thinking back to Rose. I guess if I were Austin, I'd have a lot on my mind. Shy didn't say it outright, but anyone could put the pieces together: Rose showed up because of Austin. Maybe Austin invited her, maybe not; I didn't ask. But she was there for *him*. I don't know anything about them or their relationship, but even I could figure that one out.

ME:
Welcome to my hellish, sleepless world

AUSTIN:
hey at least we have each other

ME:
They do say misery loves company

Austin doesn't reply right away, so I roll out of bed and pull on sweatpants and a baggy UW hoodie of my dad's. Then I stuff my feet into my slippers and walk upstairs. Unsurprisingly, no one is awake, and I get the coffee going.

As it brews, my phone buzzes in my hoodie pocket.

AUSTIN:
what're your plans before Marianne's?

I sit in the window seat by our dining room table, pulling my knees up to my chest as rain smacks against the pane. Most Saturdays, I try to knock out some homework before Marianne's so I can play *RotR* with Austin in the evening, but my college apps have been haunting me lately.

Long story short: the USC essay is not going well.

ME:
Breakfast then setting my essay prompt on fire

AUSTIN:
oh so the usual

ME:
Yup. Who invented college essays?
WHO HURT THEM

AUSTIN:
you're grumpy in the morning

ME:
I'm grumpy all the time

AUSTIN:
true. but it's part of your charm. I wouldn't have you any other way

The coffee maker beeps, and I set my phone on the window cushion to pour a cup. Not like I need it, because I'm suddenly awake. Very awake. When Austin says—or texts—stuff like that . . . I *like* it. The words, the intent, I don't know, it feels good.

Curling back up on the cushion, I reply.

ME:
Why thank you. Not like you have a choice. I'm too stubborn to change

AUSTIN:
any chance you wanna postpone setting shit on fire until after Marianne's? we could leave early and get waffles

ME:
. . . waffles you say?

AUSTIN:
I'll buy 🧇

ME:
Okay I'm gonna ignore the emojis because free waffles sound delicious

AUSTIN:
I'll pick you up in thirty min

I down my coffee and retreat into the basement. By the time I'm out of the shower, the floorboards are creaking above my head as my parents wake up. Even Ana's out of bed before eight on weekends, further proving that we're not related and that my parents probably found her abandoned on the side of the road—or maybe I was the one found abandoned on the side of the road. I don't have enough time to properly style my hair, and I brush out my long waves, frowning at my split ends. My only clean button-down is an off-white one with a Peter Pan collar. I pull a knit sweater on top, then tug on my jeans.

"Hey." I bound up the stairs and walk into the kitchen.

Both of my parents look deeply confused to see me, fully dressed, before ten in the morning on a Saturday.

"Hi, El," Dad says cautiously, with a hint of a smile.

Mom sips her coffee, hair wild with bedhead. "You're up and about early."

I grab my Doc Martens from the rack and pull them on, hobbling on one foot, then the other. "Austin and I are grabbing breakfast before Marianne's. Is that okay?"

Mom and Dad exchange a look.

"Sure," Mom says, and doesn't bother hiding her glee. "But you know, we'd love to meet Austin."

I wrinkle my nose as I finish tying my shoes. "I don't think that's necessary."

Dad chuckles while Mom elbows him gently in the ribs.

"We'll have him over for dinner sometime." She smiles over the rim of her mug. "Have fun, baby."

I put on my rain shell and wait for Austin outside. But I've barely locked up behind me when the murder van rolls to a stop.

I climb into the passenger seat and slam the door shut. "Hi, Orlando."

Austin's hair is damp—from a shower or the rain, I'm not sure—and he's in his usual old-man uniform: the oversized cardigan with a cowl collar, a graphic tee beneath.

"Hey," he says, and smiles. A full-blown, ray-of-sunshine smile. The type of smile that feels deeply unnatural at eight in the morning. But then again, everything about Austin's state of mind is unnatural.

Screw toothpaste ads. He should be used for antidepressant commercials.

"You're awfully awake," I say, barely stifling a yawn. "Emphasis on awful."

Austin huffs an exasperated sigh, which makes me smile. "Good morning to you too."

Not even twelve hours have passed since I said goodbye to Austin last night, but as I settle into my seat and click my seat belt, I realize that . . . I missed him. Maybe I hit my head last night on the rink. Because I shouldn't miss the dork beside me after a measly—I look at the dashboard clock—nine hours.

I feel the back of my head for a lump as Austin pulls away from the front curb. "Where are we getting breakfast?" I ask.

"I was thinking Waft Cove?" He adjusts the speed of the windshield wipers; they scrape against the glass. Then he turns toward me, his brow scrunching in the middle. "You look different."

"No braid." I touch my waves, oddly self-conscious. "I ran out of time. Someone told me I had to be ready in thirty minutes, and I'm not fully functioning before ten on the weekends."

"Wow. This someone—who's not only driving you to breakfast but buying you waffles—sounds like an asshole."

"Oh yeah, he's the worst." My insides are humming. After a pause, I add, "But for real, thanks for the invite. I'm pretty sure my mom was heating up Jimmy Dean breakfast sandwiches in the microwave when I left."

"The ones with the rubbery cheese?"

"Yep." I pretend to gag. "And for the record, you're not the worst. You're—on rare occasions—the best. Before you ask, no, I won't repeat myself, and don't let it go to your head."

Austin readjusts his hands on the steering wheel, steals a glance over at me. "Thanks, Lou," he says, cheeks flushed.

We park a few blocks from the restaurant, and my stomach is rumbling as we walk into Waft Cove, a café on the water. The ceilings are two stories high, and everything is beige, modern. A large breakfast buffet dominates the center of the café, and it's packed. But as I've learned from previous visits, they also have the best breakfast food in a five-mile radius.

Despite the busyness, Austin and I snag a two-person booth in the back without much of a wait. I slide into my seat and grab a menu, even though I'll most likely order the waffles. "So," I say, studying him over the edge of my menu, "what's on the agenda today?"

"Marianne finally called a waterproofer to fix the basement leak. I told her we'd clear the spare room out before Wednesday. Figure we could knock out a chunk today. Wrap up whatever we don't finish on Tuesday?"

I groan, slumping onto our beige-tiled table. "Has it crossed your mind that Marianne is using LifeCare as a front for free manual labor?"

"Project Nostalgia was my idea, Lou, not Marianne's."

"Maybe that's what she wanted you to think. Reverse psychology, dude. You said she keeps firing her house cleaners. Maybe this is why. You and me, free labor."

"Marianne's a millionaire. She's not slacking on house maintenance because of the cost; she just hates strangers going through her shit."

"Lucky us."

"I know you're being sarcastic," he says, and slides me the mug of coffee the waiter just dropped off, "but I consider myself pretty lucky."

I greedily take the coffee mug, which is also beige. "Yeah, well, you're sappy like that."

Austin tosses one of the single-use jam containers between his hands. "Not all of us can be—"

"Don't you dare call me a robot again," I interrupt, and reach out to smack the jam container from the air; it skids across our table.

"I wasn't going to say robot."

I set my menu aside. Who am I kidding? I'm getting waffles. "Yeah, you were."

He just cracks a guilty grin. "Anyways. Should be a low-key day."

"As long as you do the heavy lifting, fine by me."

Austin leans his elbows on the tabletop, the sleeves of his cardigan sliding down his narrow wrists, and rests his chin in his hands. "How goes the digitizing?"

"Pretty good, actually." Over the month, I've digitized hundreds of Marianne's photos. Photos of Marianne onstage, backstage, on tour, in restaurants and hotel rooms, and in front of famous landmarks around the world. Photos of Marianne with Georgie, or Marianne with the band; I recognize each band member by face now. Marianne documented through the ages: young and drunk and sober and aging, and everything in between. "If you ever need help organizing those letters . . ."

"Lou, we both know you only want to organize them so you can read them."

I roll my eyes dramatically. "Come on! Aren't you curious? About Georgie? And touring? And behind-the-scenes band drama?"

"You could try asking Marianne sometime instead of snooping through her stuff. Also, if you're *that* curious about Georgie, Marianne wrote all the lyrics for the Laundromats. A lot of them were about their relationship."

Not like I'd tell Austin—or Marianne, for that matter, since her ego is big enough already—but I listened to all my mom's Laundromats records after I began volunteering. I never knew Marianne wrote all their lyrics, though. "Love the band trivia, Orlando, but if you have a lapse in moral judgment and change your mind about those letters, you know where to find me."

Austin just smiles, and his leg bumps against mine beneath the table.

I wait for him to move his leg, but he doesn't.

What does it mean that I don't move either? Like with the hug from last night and the texts that make me smile and the jokes in the passenger seat of the murder van, I want to gather up these moments. As many as I can have. Because I'm so used to being uncomfortable, and these moments are the few in which I can breathe. They're everything, and I'm afraid I'm taking them for granted. Like Austin might suddenly snap out of it and realize I'm not worth it.

And I'll be alone. *Again*.

I'm surprised how much I don't want that.

Austin's phone, resting faceup on the table, chimes. The screen illuminates, and even though I'm not trying to look, I can see that it's a text. From Rose.

The panicky weirdness I felt at Retro Rink is back. But this time, it doesn't make sense. I'm not at some loud party, floundering in a social situation far above my skill grade. I'm with Austin. My surprising go-to comfort human these days. I *shouldn't* be panicking right now. But I am, and my stomach is twisting itself into a tight, Boy Scout–approved knot.

Austin glances at the screen, his brows drawing together. Then he swipes his thumb across the screen and clears the notification. "Sorry."

"Um. You're fine." The back of my neck is hot. My stomach is acidic. *Rose*. Because what happens if they get back together? Will Austin spend as much time with Marianne? And, by extension, me? "Don't let me stop you from replying. I'm not a five-year-old. I can entertain myself for a few minutes."

Austin spins his phone around on the table. Then he sighs and says, "Rose has barely spoken to me in, like, four months. Between last night and this"—he motions to the phone—"it's a lot."

And for the life of me, I can't tell from his expression if "a lot" is a good or bad thing. Good, probably.

"Shy told me she's your ex." The sentence pops out of my mouth before I can stop myself.

"Right. Of course she did." Austin gives his phone another spin, then asks, "Uh. What else did Shy say?"

"Just . . ." I shrug a little. "I don't know, that Rose was your ex-girlfriend? And you'd broken up in August or something, but you were always getting back together. Or something."

"June, not August. But yeah, we've broken up and gotten back together a few times. . . ." He scrubs a hand over his cheek. "Rose is great, but she broke up with me. And I'm not sure if we really make sense anymore, you know?"

I stare at his phone. Another text illuminates the screen, but I can't read it upside down. Not like I want to read it. "Um. Not really. I've never had a boyfriend."

"Come on." Austin pokes my forearm until I look up—and into his wide brown eyes. "Really?"

"You flatter me," I deadpan, wishing I could take the confession back. My lack of a romantic history is just another way I don't fit in. Apparently, I'm a glutton for punishment, because I add, "I'm not completely pathetic, okay? I've been kissed before."

Two and a half times—don't ask—and yeah, they were both terrible. But I've never had a boy take me on a date or want me or tell me he loves me, disasters and all.

"Oh." Austin's leg jitters beneath the table, almost like this conversation is making him just as uncomfortable as it's making me.

"Yeah. Lydie and Jordan used to drag me to all these parties and stuff with their boyfriends." Why am I still talking? I should stop talking. "Mostly in sophomore year. Homecoming. Even a few pep rallies."

"I can't imagine you at a party. Or a pep rally."

"It wasn't a pretty sight. Trust me."

Austin rakes his fingers through his hair, then drops his hand back onto the table. "Sorry. It's just—sometimes I feel like I've known you forever?" he says with a soft laugh. "But stuff like this reminds me that . . . that I don't know everything."

I think back to last night, my panic over realizing Austin had this whole other life that I wasn't a part of. How shitty that felt. So I say, "You know everything that matters."

I hate how true this is. I hate that I've begun wondering if *anything* before I met Austin and Marianne really mattered. Because lately it hasn't felt like it.

Austin's face softens into a smile. "Yeah?"

"Don't look so smug. I'm not very interesting." Then I gesture to his phone. "And now that we've established I'm not the person to come to for romantic advice, you can text Rose back if you want."

Only when I hear my own words out loud do I realize that if Austin picks his phone back up, something inside me might crack wide open. Because the twisty, knotted feeling in my stomach isn't regular free-floating anxiety. And it's not run-of-the-shitty-mill social anxiety. No. This is fear. Fear that whatever I have with Austin will disappear. Fear that he'll get back together with Rose. Fear that someone else will get to have Austin when I want him all to myself.

"That's okay," Austin says, and puts his phone away. "I'll text her later."

Luckily, our waffles arrive at that very moment, and the conversation shifts from ex-girlfriends and my lack of a love life to a friendly debate on waffle toppings. Waffle toppings I can talk about. Feelings? Not so much.

I'm not a jealous person. Except I'm panicky and anxious and *jealous* right now, shoveling waffles into my mouth like they'll somehow stopper the tidal wave of negative emotion. I'm jealous of Rose. Not just because she might steal away time that I spend with my best friend—because, yeah, I admit it, Austin's the best friend that I've ever had. But because Rose and Austin have a history and more inside jokes than we do and most *definitely* have done more together than kiss two and a half times.

None of this makes sense.

Not like anything about my friendship with Austin has made sense. But seeing him with Rose last night and hearing him talk about her this morning is the emotional equivalent of that one time I got pegged in the stomach by a dodgeball in PE: it leaves me breathless and it fucking hurts like hell.

Last night, I lied about my curfew and ended that hug because I liked it. A *lot*. And it's freaking me out. All this Austin and Rose talk . . . I feel like I'm losing something I didn't even know I wanted. Because if—in some upside-down, backward, alternate universe—Austin had tried to kiss me last night?

I would've kissed him back.

SIXTEEN

What do they say? About the girls
Who lead you astray?

—The Laundromats, "Before You Go" (1973)

You know those nightmares when you wake up and the sweet relief hits as you realize that it was all a dream? Yeah, that's not what happens Sunday morning. I pop out my night guard and sit up, yesterday's realization rushing to the forefront of my consciousness. My realization that maybe, just maybe, I have some not-so-platonic feelings for my best friend.

I'm turning into the worst cliché.

Falling for my best friend, who's in a band *and* in love with another girl?

Even I'm embarrassed for myself.

After Austin dropped me off yesterday, I tried to lose myself in *RotR*. But it didn't work—and it always works. No matter the issue, everything fades away when I'm logged in to my character. I just couldn't stop thinking about Austin.

From those early-morning texts to how Austin bought my breakfast and said *Rose is great*. Annoying, sunshiny Austin, all layered up like an onion so the more I peel back, the more I like. Then Austin logged in to *RotR*, and before I knew what I was doing, I noped out of there, fast. Closed out Discord. Went upstairs and watched a cartoon with *Ana*.

If my mental state could be tracked, voluntarily hanging out with Ana is one step above crying in the library bathroom before my SATs last March. So yeah, not exactly the three-day weekend I was hoping for. Tomorrow is Indigenous Peoples' Day, which means I have a buffer between now and when I have to see Austin next.

Because I *want* to see Austin.

Which is the problem.

I'm so miserable that I didn't even fight my mom yesterday when she asked me to babysit Ana tonight. Apparently, Eloise with Feelings is a pathetic doormat of a human.

I shove my feet into my slippers and shuffle upstairs. I slept like a log last night. Probably because I was *that* eager to escape conscious thought.

Mom's working. Dad's biking. Ana's at a friend's.

Perfect studying conditions.

Once I'm loaded with enough caffeine and carbs to fuel my study session, I retreat into the basement and boot up my computer. After sinking into my desk chair, I click through some Discord and Monsoon notifications, then open my essay prompt.

The blinking cursor mocks me.

I crack my neck and get to work. Because writing about my community or whatever is better than thinking about my feelings for Austin. And I manage to get a few hundred words drafted. No idea if they'll stick, but you can't revise a blank page or whatever.

My phone buzzes with a text after I eat lunch and finally shower.

I sit cross-legged on my bed and stare at the notification, chewing my bottom lip in thought. Then I open it.

AUSTIN:
how's the essay going? 🔥

ME:
Surprisingly okay? I mean, not good but also not terrible

AUSTIN:
whoa that was almost a positive statement

ME:
Nothing is on fire but that's a low bar

AUSTIN:
any chance you're free tonight?

I shift on my bed and lean my back to the wall. Nothing has to change between me and Austin. Just because I've developed some seriously ill-advised feelings for the dude doesn't mean anything will be different. It'll suck once he gets back together with Rose. I'm nothing if not excellent at compartmentalizing. See: the last eleven months. But I need to act normal. Austin is a human empathy meter and he'll notice if I'm acting differently around him.

ME:
I'm babysitting the demon

AUSTIN:
that'd be an excellent band name but what?

ME:
My little sister = the demon

AUSTIN:
of course. no idea how I didn't guess that one

how late? I have something for you

ME:
On a scale of 1–10 how nervous should I be

AUSTIN:
???

ME:
Last time you brought me something it was that ugly ass shirt

AUSTIN:
you love that shirt

ME:
I really don't

AUSTIN:
don't be nervous

it's not a shirt, okay?

ME:
Fine I'll keep you posted. No idea how late my parents will be

AUSTIN:
that's all I ask

ME:
You can also just give me this mystery item on Tues at lunch

AUSTIN:
nah I need to get my daily dose of Lou

ME:
I'm a multivitamin now?

AUSTIN:
you're essential to my daily function

ME:
🖕

AUSTIN:
HOLY SHIT YOU USED AN EMOJI

ME:
To flip you off!

AUSTIN:
you think I care?

look at you. emoting 🥹

ME:
I hate you

AUSTIN:
no

ME:
Yes

AUSTIN:
nope sorry not buying it

don't forget to text me later. I have some grand plans

ME:
That's not ominous at all

AUSTIN:
😇

I toss my phone onto my comforter and rest my chin on my knees.

Trying—and failing—not to smile.

Babysitting Ana has only gotten worse as we've aged. When I first was bequeathed babysitting duty, I was fourteen and Ana was eight. I could stick her in front of the TV for five hours and forget about her existence. At eleven, Ana is not as easily entertained. Because she decided, about a year ago, that *I'm* her entertainment.

"Who're you texting?" Ana leans over my lap on the couch, reaching for my phone.

I shove her shoulder. "Get off me, you rodent."

"Ow!" Ana flails back dramatically and almost kicks me in the chin.

I considered locking myself in the basement, but I don't trust Ana up here alone. Not after the candle fire incident. Also, my mom wants me actually *watching* her, and Ana's a Grade A snitch. I really don't want to deal with a lecture from my mom on being a good sister and how I'm a role model to Ana. Blah blah blah.

With a petulant sigh, she crawls over to the other side of the couch and picks up the remote, clicking through her child-locked Netflix account. And I return to my Austin chat. My parents went to dinner and a movie. They said they'd be back around nine thirty, but considering the fact that nine is Ana's bedtime, I'm hopeful to be rid of her sooner.

ME:
I should be free by 9 or 9:30

The message whooshes off and I set my phone aside. We already ordered dinner—pizza, one of the few meals we can agree on—and I'm hopeful my little sister will fall asleep in a carb coma not long after.

"Sooooo. Who's Austin?" Ana's not even looking at me, just scrolling through shows. But I can see her demonic little smirk.

"Don't. Read. My. Texts."

"Is he your boyfriend?" Ana asks this in a singsong voice.

Don't hit your sister. Don't hit your sister. Don't hit your sister.

I squeeze my eyes shut. Take a deep breath. "No. Austin is definitely not my boyfriend."

"You've never had a boyfriend." She pauses her scrolling to give me a knowing look. "Even my best friend, Macy, has a boyfriend."

"Oh my god." Now my romantic life is more pathetic than an eleven-year-old's? Cool. Awesome.

I slide off the couch and march down into the basement to grab a hoodie. Not because I'm cold, but because if I'm forced to spend another consecutive moment with my sister, I refuse to be held responsible for my actions.

I take my sweet time putting on my hoodie, checking my Discord notifications, and using the bathroom before reluctantly returning aboveground. Forcing one sibling to babysit the other should constitute a violation of child labor laws. Just another reason why I can't wait to get out of here next fall.

Someone knocks as I reach the landing.

"Pizza's here," I yell at Ana, and open the door.

But Austin's standing on my porch.

Not the pizza delivery person.

"Um. What're you doing here?" I don't fully open the door, leaning against the frame and blocking any view Ana might get from the hallway with my body.

Austin's perma-smile droops. "You told me to come over early?"

"Ana!" I swivel around and find the little jerk peeking at us from around the corner. "Did you fucking use my phone?"

"JAR!"

"No one is here to hear me swear—or hear you scream. Don't touch my shit, Ana. I mean it!" I march into the living room and grab my phone from the couch. "How'd you even know my password?"

Ana giggles and dives behind Dad's armchair as I hold a throw pillow threateningly over my head. "It's your birthday," she says. "Aren't you, like, supposed to be smart?"

"Should I go?" Austin hovers in the doorway with a slightly amused—yet concerned—expression.

"Oh, hi, Eloise's-definitely-not-boyfriend." Ana pops over the back of the chair, waving with both hands.

Austin lifts his brows at me, but I turn toward my sister and throw the pillow, fueled purely by vengeance. Ana ducks out of the way and it bounces off the wall behind the armchair. Then she crawls out from behind the chair and plops on the couch, resuming her Netflix scroll. Like she isn't a complete shit-stirrer.

I exhale shakily, then say, "I'll be right back. Don't move, you trashball. I know where you sleep," and walk back to the doorway. I shoo Austin onto the front porch and step outside, shutting the door behind me. "Sorry. If you couldn't tell, Ana used my phone to text you. Why? I think she just loves chaos."

Austin digs his hands into the pockets of his jeans. He's wearing a baggy striped sweater, his too-long hair curling behind his ears and his messenger bag hanging from one shoulder. "Yeah, I figured that out between all the screaming." He pauses, then says, "Eloise's-definitely-not-boyfriend, huh?"

My cheeks redden, and I wait to see if the porch opens up and swallows me whole. Imagine my disappointment when that never happens. "Ana . . . She was peeking at my phone and asking questions—you know what? It really doesn't matter. Hi. Want to wait outside for the pizza delivery person with me?"

The corner of his mouth twitches. "Sure."

I sit on the porch swing, my heart rabid inside my chest. Austin sits sideways, facing me, with one leg bent beneath him. Between Ana's chaos and Austin just showing up, I've felt, like, twenty different emotions in the last sixty seconds.

"So. What'd you want to give me? And I'm serious, if it's

another personalized shirt, you're on an *RotR* ban for three months." I flip up my hood and pull the sleeves down around my hands as a breeze kicks up. The air is slightly damp with a fine, misty rain.

"Wow. You have some seriously strong feelings about personalized T-shirts," Austin says with a laugh. Then he unlatches his messenger bag and pulls out two pieces of paper. "For you."

I take the papers. One is a flyer for A Scare Is Born at the end of the month, with a ton of custom spooky artwork and a list of all the bands participating. The Coinstar Rejects are near the top. The second, smaller piece of paper is an admit-one ticket for the show, the details printed along the bottom: SATURDAY, OCTOBER 28, 7:00 P.M.

"I know you didn't agree to go yet," Austin rushes to say as I study them, "but tickets were selling out—"

I glance up. "Wait. People actually buy tickets to a battle of the bands?"

"Yes, Lou. People buy tickets to battles of the bands. That's why they sell them." Austin tugs on my hoodie strings and it cinches around my face; I scowl. "And now you have a ticket. In case you decide to come."

A battle of the bands—especially a themed one like A Scare Is Born—is a special type of hell, in my opinion. I should tell Austin no. But those hopeful puppy-dog eyes are seriously manipulative. "Thanks. I'll . . . think about it, okay? But you didn't need to bring these by tonight. I would've been equally reticent on Tuesday."

Austin pushes his foot off the porch and the swing sways, us swaying with it. "Sure. But I picked them up after I left band practice, and I wasn't kidding about wanting to see you." He plays with the string on my hoodie. "Anyways, the flyers are sick, right? The guy who did the art is a friend of Shy's. That guy, Xavier, from her birthday party?"

I glance back at the flyer, smiling. "Very cool, and very spooky. Tell Xavier I like how anatomically correct the skeletons are."

"Or you could tell him at A Scare Is Born. I have three weeks to convince you, Lou. And I think my odds are pretty good."

"You'd make a great cult leader, you know that, right?" My cheeks are flushed despite the cold.

"What's up with you and cults?"

I pause, thrown that he remembers our first awkward and hostile conversation. "Nothing? I just find them fascinating."

"They're morbid."

"Um, *yeah*. Morbidly fascinating."

Austin laughs, twirling my hoodie strings around his fingers. The swing chains squeak, and I bite the inside of my cheek. I've never wanted someone to kiss me so badly in my entire life. The kind of want that's a little terrifying—especially after you've spent nearly a year not wanting anything, from anyone, ever.

A car door slams, and I jump, looking over my shoulder. A car's parked on the curb; I didn't even hear it pull up. But I smell pizza before the driver unloads his goods from the backseat.

"I'd offer you some pizza"—I stand abruptly and nearly trip over my own feet, shoving the flyer and ticket into my hoodie pocket—"but then you'd have to eat with Ana. I'm pretty sure you've had enough of my little sister for one evening."

The delivery guy hands over the pizza, and I thank him.

Once we're alone again, Austin unfolds himself and stands,

digging his hands back into his pockets. He shrugs both shoulders up to his ears. "Ana can't scare me away, but my mom's waiting for me to eat. I should head back."

I hug the pizza to my chest. "I'll probably be on later. If you want to play."

"Sounds good." Austin hops down my porch steps and walks backward. "Just text me if I'm not online. And I'll be there."

I wave. Then force myself to turn around and bring some pizza to the world's most undeserving little sister.

SEVENTEEN

Georgia is a state of mind
I wouldn't mind staying awhile longer

—The Laundromats, "The Motor Inn" (1981)

Most teenagers go to their best friends or Google for relationship advice.

I go to a seventy-three-year-old woman whose heart broke forty years ago and never healed.

On Monday, I smash the intercom button on the gate's keypad, cursing myself for never getting the code from Marianne or Austin. The speaker crackles to life, but before Marianne can try to scare me off like some misguided Girl Scout, I say, "Marianne, it's Eloise."

The gate unlocks with a comforting click and I duck inside.

By the time I reach the front door, Marianne has opened it and peers out, one hand clutching the doorframe as she blocks Nox's wily attempts to make a run for it. Her hair is messy, looped in a bun, and she's in loose slacks and a sweater. "I would've sworn today was Monday," she says, widening the door for me, "but come on in."

A laugh catches in my throat and I step inside. "No, it's

Monday. I'm . . . I need to talk?" My voice rises at the end like I'm asking a question.

Marianne's gaze sweeps over me as I shuck off my Doc Martens. "Hurry up," she says, and turns down the hallway. "I'm boiling water for tea."

As she turns, I catch the unmistakable and antiseptic scent of vodka oozing from her pores, strong enough to dampen the scent of vetiver and tobacco. On LifeCare days, Marianne is put together—mostly. But this is Marianne in her natural habitat, not expecting company. And it's so jarring and messy and undone that I almost forget why I'm here.

I follow Marianne into the kitchen, staring at my socks. I didn't put on a matching pair this morning. One sock has a cartoon mouth where my toes are, each toe a tooth. The other sock, which Ana gave me for Christmas, has different emojis printed on it. They remind me of Austin.

The demon commonly known as Ana and I agreed to mutual assured destruction over steaming slices of pizza last night. I won't tell our parents that she broke into my phone and texted one of my friends, and Ana won't tell our parents about our fight or Austin showing up while they were gone. Ana had access to my phone for, like, ten minutes, and I consider myself relatively unscathed. Her text to Austin just said "**nvm come over now ☺**." It could've been a lot worse. Austin should've known it wasn't me from the abbreviation and emoji, but I digress.

Seeing him last night just reminded me how *not* okay I am right now. I have absolutely zero skills to deal with this situation or experience to guide me anywhere but total emotional devastation. Which brings me to this pathetic development. Asking an old lady for help with my lack of a love life.

Marianne coughs, a thick and wet noise, and motions a hand toward the kitchen table. I slide into one of the seats, tucking my hands beneath my thighs so I stop fidgeting. She grabs my mug—because I have a designated mug now—and fills it up, plopping a chamomile tea bag into the hot water. Wise move, that chamomile, since I'm so anxious I'm practically vibrating.

After doing the same for herself, she sits in the seat across from me.

I dunk my tea bag, trying to think of what to say. How to say it.

After a whole minute and a half of awkward silence, Marianne says, "Spit it out, Eloise. I don't have all afternoon."

"Right." Flustered, I sip my tea and burn myself. Then the words blather out of me at an impressive speed. "Austin and I have known each other for a while now. At first, obviously, I thought he was the worst, right? Couldn't stand him. But I followed your advice and didn't write him off. Then, over the last few weeks, we've spent so much time together. And it's just . . . it's gotten really confusing."

Marianne leans back in her chair, holding the mug close to her chest. She raises one thin brow. "If you want my help, you're going to need to give me more to work with than that."

Heat splotches my cheeks. "Um. I went to Austin's friend's birthday party on Friday and . . . I felt like throwing up when I saw Austin hanging out with his ex-girlfriend. Or punching someone. Or both. Yeah, both." Oh my god, what am I doing? This was such a mistake, because now Marianne's looking at me like my head has popped off and rolled across her kitchen floor. "I . . . I'm pretty sure I have feelings for Austin. Nonplatonic feelings. And I'm freaking out."

Marianne snorts, and I widen my eyes. Is she seriously laughing at me right now? In my time of need? Holding a hand over her mouth, she says, "Sorry, sorry. That was rude. I guess I'm just surprised. I thought you knew how you felt." Lowering her voice to a demure purr, she adds, "It's kind of obvious, doll."

"Obvious to *who*?" I'm moments away from spontaneous combustion. "I didn't even know until forty-eight hours ago!"

"Obvious to anyone who's ever been in love before."

"Are you senile? Who said *love*? I have a crush! A teeny-tiny crush." Marianne laughs again, and this is my nightmare. My stomach practically turns itself inside out at the word. Love. I am not—and never have been—in love. No one's ever been in love with me. And I don't see any of that changing anytime soon. Groaning, I lower my forehead to the kitchen table and thunk my head. "This can't be happening. I can't have feelings for Austin. Nope. Not doing it."

"Unfortunately," she says, "that's not how emotions work. Trust me, I've tried. You can't will or ignore them away, Eloise."

I lift my miserable head and glare. "Humor me?"

Marianne just gives me a look, then sips her tea.

I bury my face in my hands, the steam from my mug curling against my cheeks.

"Tell me," Marianne says a few minutes into my silent existential crisis, "what's so awful about having feelings for Austin? You could do worse, you know. He's something special."

I laugh, an unhinged, broken noise, and lift my gaze to Marianne's. "Everything. Austin is the only friend I have. The only friend I've made in a year. There's not a chance in hell I'm risking that. I can't. I'd—" The thought of my life rewinding, to before Austin or Marianne, makes me want to hyperventilate. Austin's woven into the fabric of my life now, and I might unravel without him.

Okay, you win, Ms. Holiday! I need people!

Marianne tilts her head. "Sure. But what if he feels the same?"

I think of Austin and Rose, him nudging her and making her laugh while she stole his—*my*—french fries. How diametrically different Rose and I are, in almost every single way. Rose is petite and blond. I'm almost too tall and my hair is the darkest shade of brown. She's bubbly and nice. I'm an asshole who never smiles. I'm sure I'm someone's type—someone, somewhere out there, who enjoys misery—but there's no way I'm Austin Yang's type.

"He doesn't feel the same way." I drop my gaze and tear at the label on my tea bag. "If I had to bet, he'll be back together with Rose before Halloween. Thanksgiving at the latest. Because that's apparently what they do, him and Rose. Um. I'm not . . . I'm not jeopardizing our friendship over this. I can't."

Marianne sets her mug down with a sigh. "Eloise, you're being ridiculous."

"Okay, that's rude—"

"I wasn't done talking." She kicks my shin beneath the table, and I yelp. Not like she kicked me hard, but she surprised me. "You're being ridiculous. If you feel strongly about Austin, you should do something about it! Don't just assume the worst-case scenario about him and what's-her-face. You have no idea where his head is at. Or his heart."

"Actually, I have a pretty solid idea of where Austin's head *and* heart are at. He and Rose are texting again. I couldn't compete with Rose even *if* he had feelings for me. Which he doesn't." I roll the tea-bag label between my thumb and forefinger. "You don't get it, Marianne. You're . . . beautiful and enigmatic and effervescent. You don't know what it's like to have people not choose you, okay?"

"Are you kidding me? Eloise, I know rejection. I've been rejected by audiences, record producers, the media, partners. My entire career was built around rejection and heartbreak."

"Okay, sure. But what about Georgie? She chose you."

Marianne releases a heavy sigh. "I'm way too sober for this," she mutters, and pinches the bridge of her nose for a moment before continuing. "Georgie and I chose *each other*, Eloise. We weren't a guarantee—we took that leap together."

Shame pricks at me for reopening old wounds. But I'm too selfish, too desperate, not to ask, "Would you do it all over again? Even if you knew how it ended?"

"I've made too many mistakes to count," Marianne says, "but telling that woman how I felt was *never* one of them. Georgie didn't leave me by choice—and my heart broke the moment hers stopped beating—but I wouldn't trade our ten years for anything. . . ." She trails off and runs her forefinger along the lip of her mug. Then she continues. "Even if it was hard in the end, I'm lucky that I got to wake up beside Georgie that final morning, and had the chance to kiss her goodbye, to tell her I loved her. . . . Trust me when I say that holding back because you're afraid of rejection or heartbreak or how it might all fall apart will make for one very lonely life, Eloise."

I don't know what's wrong with me. Because I don't believe it when Marianne says the pain was worth it. I've spent *years* trying to outrun pain. Depression and anxiety and failure and loneliness and shitty friends. Losing my friendship with Austin—all because of some stupid, momentary crush—can't be worth it.

I wrap my hands around my mug and drop my gaze to the steaming, swirling surface. "I'm not . . . *afraid*," I finally say. "But if I don't say anything, we can keep on being just friends and everything will stay the same. I'll get over him. Eventually. Problem solved."

Marianne casts a disappointed look across the table, and my insides squirm. Marianne being disappointed in me is, like, worse than my parents being disappointed in me. "Ignoring your feelings is unfair to yourself and possibly to Austin. If you two just talked—"

"I swear to god, Marianne," I interrupt, and lean across the table, "if you tell Austin about this, I *will* deactivate your Life Alert."

Marianne barks a laugh. "I never set up that Life Alert." Then her face grows serious once again. "I won't say anything to Austin. But you should." She slides a pack of cigarettes closer, playing with the slim box. "I don't know why you came all the way over here to ignore my advice."

"Because"—I slump back in my chair, sinking down a few inches due to the weight of my shame—"I was really hoping your advice would include a five-step guide to ignoring my feelings? And maybe a pep talk about there being plenty of fish in the sea or something?"

"Then you came to the wrong person for advice," she says with a small smile. "I'm a romantic, Eloise. Most musicians are."

I drag my hands over my face and sigh, then drop them in my lap. "Thanks anyways. I'll . . . figure something out. Something that doesn't include me ruining my friendship with Austin."

"And here I thought I'd never meet someone more stubborn than me." She smacks both hands to the kitchen table before groaning onto her feet. "Thank you for proving an old woman wrong."

"You're welcome. Um, I should probably head home." I stand up, then hesitate, something gnawing at my insides. Old Eloise is trying to shove her way forward, but I can't let that happen. I turn and add, "Thanks. I know I'm being a dick right now, but I appreciate you listening and trying to help. I'm . . . not good with this stuff."

"Oh, trust me, that much is clear." Marianne scoops up our mugs and dumps them into the sink. "I'll see you tomorrow?"

"Tomorrow." I say goodbye, then begin my trek back to the bus stop.

EIGHTEEN

With you, I'm me
But I'm nothing in between

—The Laundromats, "Lovesick" (1979)

Curled up on the raggedy corduroy couch, I work through more of Marianne's photos, setting aside those I've yet to digitize on the coffee table. My portable scanner is set up, and the basement is quiet except for Austin's occasional semi-athletic grunt as he lifts a box from the spare room and stacks it alongside the wall to my left.

Today's our last day to clear out the spare room before the waterproofer fixes the infamous basement window leak. When we arrived, Austin volunteered to do the manual labor, and I happily returned to my digitizing project. All the photos are saved to a private cloud folder I set up for Marianne, as well as backed up on an external hard drive. I have no idea what she plans to do with them, but at least they won't be destroyed by neglect and water damage.

I toss aside an envelope of duplicates, then pick up another. And pause. Because stuffed inside are the letters Austin found. The letters between Marianne and Georgie. Violating people's privacy is, from a moral standpoint, not great. I know that; I have a little sister and was on the receiving end of a privacy violation not even two days ago. I fully acknowledge that I'm a snoop, but I desperately want—nay, *need*—to know more about their relationship.

Austin's focused on the boxes, so I upend the envelope onto my lap. The letters cover a range of dates, from the mid-seventies to the eighties. Ten years of letters, most of them likely written while Marianne was on tour. Before the days of cell phones and emails and texts. Pen to paper. Like Marianne said, she's a romantic.

The letter Austin tore from my grasp last week is on the top of the stack. The one from Claridge's in London. March 19, 1981.

Dear Georgie,

Sorry for the delay! Billy picked up our mail when we were in Germany and left it in his guitar case, like the absolute dumbass he is. Anyways. Enough excuses. To answer your question, Europe is fabulous! The food alone, Georgie! Why can't you be here with me? I'm kidding. Mostly. Every time I see something you'd love, I turn to the person beside me, as if I'm expecting it to be you. Shit, I miss you. It's not the same here without you. And I get it. Your mom isn't getting any better. But . . . please don't make me answer you right now. The band. G, you know how much they mean to me. How much I mean to them, the fans, all of it. I'd love to move back home with you if things were different, but the band needs me right now. I'm the front woman. If Billy quit, we could replace him, no questions asked. But you've said it yourself: the Laundromats are nothing without me! Just . . . hang tight, okay? We won't be touring forever. This isn't forever, and I don't understand why you can't be okay with it going on for a little longer.

I stare at the fancy hotel stationery and rub my thumb along the worn-down edges. Georgie wanted Marianne to move back home. And maybe give up the band? If Austin was right—and Georgie died in 1985—this letter was only four years before her passing. What did Wikipedia say? That the band broke up in 1986? Which means Marianne never gave up her career for Georgie.

I peek over the edge of the couch, and once I confirm that Austin's not paying attention, I slouch out of view and keep snooping. The letters are too disorganized to read chronologically, and I jump around. I find a small bundle from earlier in their relationship. Their friendship. How Georgie wrote about Marianne's hand brushing hers when they walked back to her tour bus. About how they laughed until their stomachs stitched and their eyes filled with tears. How Georgie became Marianne's tether as the Laundromats' fame skyrocketed.

I read a letter from 1977:

> With everyone—even the band or my family—I feel like I constantly need to be someone else, to put on a show, to be on nonstop. But with you, I can let go. With you, I'm me. You see what no one else does and you love me for it. How did I get so lucky to have met you? Who would've thought my smoke break would've led to you? Kismet! That's what you whispered into my ear that summer. Kismet.

I skim the later letters, which are shorter and transactional. Mostly because they turn depressing, fast. Gone is the tender sweetness of their first letters. Instead, Marianne writes frequently to apologize to Georgie. To tell Georgie that she'll be back in the Pacific Northwest soon. Between those empty promises, there are talks about money and medical treatments for Georgie's mother. Mentions of a house on Mercer Island that Marianne never visits. Pleas for Marianne to slow down, to take a break, just one summer off. Promises that, it appears,

Marianne keeps breaking. One after another after another. For a decade.

The last letter in my stack is folded in half, one of the corners ripped. I flatten it against the corduroy couch cushion, then scan the lavender parchment.

Dear Marianne,

For over ten years, I have stood by you. Even if, as the world learned your name, no one knew mine. I never minded my quiet life in the background because I had you. My brilliant, talented, fiery Annie. But I have spent a decade waiting for you to come home. To stay with me longer than a week. We both know that this has been going on too long. When you chose rehearsals over my mother's funeral, it proved a point I haven't wanted to accept for years: the band is your priority. Your only priority. Everything and everyone else is disposable to you.

This letter is not an ultimatum. I learned years ago those do not work for you, and I should've never deluded myself into thinking you might step away from the band if I asked and pleaded. This letter is me saying goodbye. This is me saying I love you. And this is me saying I'm sorry we couldn't have a happier ending. I'll be moving out of the house this weekend please give me that space to do so. I hope, from the bottom of my heart, that you're happy with your choices. I will always love you, but I'm tired of loving someone who chooses not to love me the way I deserve. Best of luck with the band.

Love always,
Georgie

The letter is dated April 28, 1985.

The year Georgie passed away.

"Hey." I pop up over the back of the couch. "You said Georgie passed away in 1985, right? Do you know which month?"

Austin lowers another box onto the stack, wiping his brow with his forearm. "Yeah. I actually found her obituary the other day in one of the boxes. May of '85. Why?"

"Hold on." I drop back onto the cushion and rifle through the stack of letters, taking a closer look at several I skipped since they were stamped RETURN TO SENDER, still sealed in their envelopes. They're all addressed to Georgie, postmarked during May 1985.

Marianne lied to me. I don't know why she lied, but she did. And I really don't know how to process this. Like, at all.

Before I can call his name, Austin walks over to the couch. He glances from me to the letters. Then he groans. "Lou, did you read Marianne's letters?"

"Maybe?"

"You're literally holding a letter right now." He sits down and the soft, old cushions dip us closer. But I'm too distracted to appreciate the way his leg touches mine.

"Okay, yes, I read them," I say, exasperated. "But are you really surprised? We both knew it was only a matter of time until I cracked."

The corner of Austin's mouth tugs in a smile. "You know, I figured after Ana broke into your phone, you'd be a little more respectful."

I give him a blank look. "Not the same situation. And I admit it, okay? I shouldn't have read them. But . . ."

Austin lifts both brows. "But what?" His too-long hair curls behind his earlobes.

"I was curious?" Not a lie, but I can't tell Austin I wanted proof—to read about someone who could love a person as prickly as Marianne Landis. To find out more about Marianne's love life. To find out if Marianne was telling the truth yesterday—that telling Georgie how she felt was worth it, despite how it all ended.

"Just read this." I hold out the letter. "And look at the date."

Austin sighs wearily, like I'm taking years off his life, and plucks the letter from my hand. Once he reaches the last sentence, he sets the letter on the coffee table and collapses back against the cushions. "Wow. That's—"

"A Dear John letter. A fucking tragic Dear John letter. And these"—I hold up the RETURN TO SENDER envelopes—"were sent after that letter, but Georgie never got them. See the stamp? Marianne literally told me *yesterday* that she was with Georgie the day she died. That Georgie didn't leave her by choice."

"You went over yesterday? Without me?" Austin's voice is low, caught somewhere between hurt and confusion.

Shit. Leave it to Austin to pay attention to the least important thing I said. My mouth goes dry. "Yeah. Um. I had a quick question and we ended up talking about Georgie. Anyways. That's not the point, dude." Deflect. I'm deflecting. I toss the RETURN TO SENDER envelopes on the table and turn toward him. "The point is, Marianne lied to me. And to you. Aren't you upset?"

Austin shifts on the couch and our knees press together. He's quiet and contemplative for a moment as he stares over my shoulder. Then he looks me in the eye and says, "Not really. I think . . . I think it's one of those lies you tell so often they become truth, you know?"

The low simmer of anger inside me falters as I think of all the lies I've told myself. That I don't have feelings for Austin. That I'm a Human Disaster, the actual worst. That I was the problem, not Lydie or Jordan. Lies that are way, way more convenient than the truth.

"Maybe." I shift on the couch and away from Austin, Marianne's words from yesterday replaying in a tragic loop inside my head: *Georgie didn't leave me by choice—and my heart broke the moment hers stopped beating—but I wouldn't trade our ten years for anything.*

I don't know if I should feel vindicated or depressed. Because Georgie left Marianne, and Marianne lied about it.

NINETEEN

You're the dream and I'm the dreamer

—The Laundromats, "Bedsheets" (1981)

Shy invited me to go Halloween costume shopping.

I said yes. Something I regretted immediately. Like, the *second* I replied to her text last night, I tried turning on airplane mode so the message wouldn't go through. But I was too late. So, on the Wednesday before Halloween, I take the bus and meet her in the University District.

I spot Shy before she sees me. She's leaning against a bike rack, taking Very Artistic Selfies. We've texted a few times since her birthday party, but that's been it. The line between my friends and Austin's friends has become upsettingly blurry.

I'd be lying if I said I didn't enjoy texting with Shy. Or smile when one of the twins likes my Instagram posts. I've spent so, so long on the outside that I forgot how safe it feels to have people. To have *friends*. But if I lose Austin, I lose everything I've worked for over the last two months.

My discovery about Marianne and Georgie has done nothing except reinforce my stubbornness: I am not telling Austin how I feel and will take this secret to my motherfucking grave.

Marianne's heart is still broken, both from the breakup and Georgie's passing. So broken that she can't even tell the truth about what happened between them.

Excuse me for not buying whatever romantic bullshit she's selling.

If I never tell Austin, then I will never have my heart broken.

Problem solved.

"Hey." I yank off my headphones and tuck them into my backpack.

Shy finishes snapping the photo. "Hey yourself!" She hugs me, then motions up the sidewalk. "There's this supercool vintagey store that has great costumes. Sound good?"

I adjust the collar of my pumpkin-patterned button-down. "Sounds great."

We fall into step, and I squash the little flare of fear inside my chest. *Shy* invited *me.* She wants to be here. This isn't pity. "So, um. What's the costume for? Do you still trick-or-treat?"

Shy sighs wistfully. "I wish. I tried last year, and half the houses refused to give me candy. I was dressed up and everything! Such bullshit."

"Wanna borrow my little sister?" I offer, and she giggles. "Oh, I'm serious. You can have her. Halloween is, like, the only time she's useful. My mom always has me take her around the neighborhood, but people usually give me candy since I'm with her."

Shy taps her chin in thought, and we slow at a crosswalk-free intersection. "I have a cousin I could borrow," she muses, and I laugh because she's actually considering it. "But I'm getting a costume for A Scare Is Born. I convinced the band to dress up. You're coming, right?"

"To the battle of the bands?" I step out into the street during a lull in traffic and when a car doesn't stop for us, Shy yells at their bumper. The flyer and ticket Austin brought over are tucked into the edge of my vanity mirror, among my comic con wristbands. The fact that they're not in the trash means I'm *maybe*, possibly, considering it, but I say, "Probably not."

"No, you have to come!" Shy loops her arm through mine and steers me down another street. Maple trees arch over the sidewalk, dropping umber and pumpkin-orange leaves onto our shoulders. "Austin said he invited you."

"Oh, about a dozen times. He even bought me a ticket, but . . ."

The roller rink was one thing. A concert is another giant, anxiety-inducing concept my brain has yet to wrap itself around. I doubt Austin will be disappointed if I don't show up. He'll be busy all night, and I'll just end up standing in the back of the crowd for a few hours. But every single time I try to bail, I stop myself. I feel too bad. Which is very unlike me.

We reach the storefront—a light-up sign advertises one-of-a-kind costumes, rentals, and vintage dresses—and duck inside. It's warm compared to the October-chilled air, and it's so stuffed to the brim that it's like being at Marianne's house. But I'd bet there aren't any snuffboxes with vintage cocaine in them here.

"What's the issue?" Shy asks, and I follow her to the costume section in the back corner of the long, narrow store. "Is it Rose? Because I doubt she'll be there. She usually avoids Coinstar Rejects shows. Not her scene."

I focus on a rack of scale-patterned leggings. "Why would Rose be an issue?"

Beside me, Shy pauses and tilts her head in confusion. "Because you and Austin . . ."

"Are just friends." The words come out more forcefully than I intended, and I pull out leggings with a fish-scale pattern. I pretend to be interested in them when all I can think about is how fish don't have legs and how I definitely have feelings for Austin.

But Shy's still staring at me. "Are you serious?"

I return the fish leggings to the rack and pause my riffling. "Yeah. Why is this so surprising?"

"I mean . . . shit, *really*? You're seriously telling me all that chemistry has led nowhere?"

Heat rushes up my chest and neck to my face. The old beveled mirror on the wall behind the fish leggings reflects my tomato-red cheeks. *"What?"*

Shy tosses her hands in the air. "Don't get mad at me. You two act like a couple!"

My mouth opens and closes in horror as I scrape around my brain for a proper response. "Yeah. A couple of friends! Austin and I are just friends. He's not . . . He doesn't look at me that way, okay? So drop it."

Something shifts in her expression, and I realize my mistake. "Oh," Shy says softly. "You like him."

I turn back to the array of weird leggings. "Austin's my friend. Obviously, I like him."

"Please don't make me ask if you like-like him, Eloise. We're not twelve."

I wither up and die inside. But I can't be too combative, or it'll look like I'm hiding something. Taking a deep breath, I try to calm down. Shy doesn't know what she's talking about. Shy isn't in

Austin's and my relationship. Not like we have a *relationship*. Fuck.

"You totally misread the situation," I say as calmly as possible. "We're friends—which is a miracle in itself, since I can't stand him half the time. I'd probably need a full-on lobotomy to date him."

Shy watches me as I flick through the leggings. "Okay," she says simply. "I'm sorry. But that's all the more reason to come to A Scare Is Born! He's really nervous, and as his *friend*, I know he'd like you to be there."

I ignore the extra inflection she puts on "friend" and force a smile. "Yeah, maybe. I'll need to ask my mom."

Either my straight-up denial broke Shy or she actually believes me, because that's the end of our Austin chat. She just motions me over to another section of costumes in the back corner. Shy unearths a zombie bride costume—a tattered white gown splattered with fake brain matter—but I end up buying a simple pair of devil's horns for five dollars. The headband they're attached to is thin, and I think I can braid my hair around the band so it looks like horns are sprouting out of my head.

Seems appropriate.

Shy walks me to my bus stop, and we talk about how she's going to do her makeup for the big night and how she's super excited-slash-nervous that Xavier's coming and how the other bands who'll be performing measure up. But honestly, it's all in one ear and out the other.

Do Austin and I act like a couple? Other than some . . . accidental moments, we rarely touch. We've certainly never kissed. The question chews at me. Until I realize it doesn't matter. Who cares if some people think we're together? We're not. We never will be. End of story.

I hug Shy goodbye and take my bus home.

Luckily, I have my house key, because no one's home when I arrive. Mom's working. Ana has art camp on Wednesdays. Dad's on a biking trip in Canada with his friends. The front door clicks shut behind me and I grab a semi-stale muffin from the kitchen before retreating to the basement. I turn on the space heater, dump my backpack in the center of my room, and boot up my computer.

I'm raiding with Unarmed Rage in thirty minutes, and I quickly review my planner and calendar. Midterms are right before Thanksgiving break. I have a Computer Science Club meeting at the end of November. My application essay still isn't done, but I have roughly five weeks to finish it—and I've actually made some progress over the last two weeks. I have around fifty hours done for LifeCare. All in all, I'm on top of things.

Monsoon dings with an alert, and I switch from my school email to the gaming client.

baselessinseattle 5:29 p.m.
Looooouuu

esioledoesntcare 5:30 p.m.
Whaaaaaat

baselessinseattle 5:30 p.m.
wanna play?

I toggle over to my guild server, where everyone's getting ready for the raid—talking about repairing items in the main city, asking if anyone has any extra starflower so they can craft a stamina potion—and I type that I'll have to miss out on tonight's festivities. They'll be fine without me.

esioledoesntcare 5:31 p.m.
Sure. Discord?

baselessinseattle 5:31 p.m.
one sec

My Discord app pings as Austin logs on, and I readjust my headphones.

"Long time, no chat," Austin jokes.

"Oh yeah. What? Six hours since lunch?"

"I missed you making fun of me," he says, in a faux-serious voice. "It was five hours too long."

I roll my eyes, even though he can't see me, and log in to my alternate character, Fasia. "What? Want me to text you insults every hour?"

Austin laughs, and he pauses to drink something. "You offering?"

"Go log in to your character," I say, because I'm alone in the tiny village where we last logged out. And because he's not serious. Or if he is, maybe Austin's developed slow-progression Stockholm syndrome with me.

A moment later, Austin's Moon Elf rogue appears before me. He jumps up and down a few times, then uses the wave command.

I type */insult* into our chat.

In the chat, it says, *Fasia thinks you're the son of a motherless satyr.*

Through my headphones, Austin starts cracking up.

Grinning, I open my quest log and check my map, directing us where to go next.

"How was costume shopping with Shy?" Austin asks. While I read, his character roams around town, accidentally stepping into the bonfire outside the blacksmith. I snort as his character sizzles and his health bar drops a few points.

"Fine." I track the quest marker and stock up on poisons for my blades. "She found an awesome costume for your battle of the bands." I refuse to utter the phrase "A Scare Is Born."

"You ever gonna answer me about whether or not you're coming?" Austin's character, Zadreal, summons his mount—this weird antelope-cat hybrid that's an abomination of nature—and I summon mine. We take off toward the quest marker. "The show's in three days, Lou."

I loll my head back, then put my character on backslash-run and stretch my arms overhead. From my desk, I stare over at my mirror. The flyer and ticket. "You really want me there? What if I'm bad luck?"

Austin snorts. "You're not bad luck. And yeah, I want you there. Remember what I said about live shows? They're stressful as fuck."

"And me being there would somehow make it less stressful?" I ask dubiously.

"I can't believe I'm saying this, but yeah, it would. C'mon. Please."

I sigh heavily, the feedback from my mic booming. "If it means that much to you . . . *fine.*"

"Fine? I'll take it." Zadreal dismounts and uses one of the toys we picked up in a dungeon loot drop last week. It's a kazoo. Then his character starts dancing. "Next step is convincing Marianne."

"Mm-kay, I'm logging off now."

Austin mounts the antelope-cat and takes off toward the marker. "Like you'd miss out on watching me try to defeat the Dreadscion."

"I do love watching you get frozen to death."

We reach the quest marker and I stuff all my worries about Austin and the battle of the bands and school into the back of my brain and get lost in my virtual world.

I can't sleep.

I count sheep. Listen to my meditation app. Down a melatonin tablet.

But nothing works.

I slide on my slippers and pad upstairs to the kitchen, where I microwave a mug of water and drown a Sleepytime tea bag in it. Then I quietly creak my way down the wooden staircase, sit cross-legged on my bed, and unlock my phone. I must really hate myself, because I open Instagram and search for Rose under Austin's friends. There aren't any photos of her on his account—almost all of it is band promo. And one really horrific photo of me eating a croissant with the caption "Lou-ser" that he refuses to delete.

But I find her almost immediately.

Rose Gembalski. Her profile is public, and I scan through the photos, very careful not to accidentally like any of them. Unlike Austin's account, hers features several photos of her and Austin over the last three years. Austin and Rose on paddleboats in Lake Washington. Austin smiling into a cup of coffee, his head ducked away from the camera. Austin, Rose, and Shy outside Brickline for a high school production of *A Midsummer Night's Dream*. Rose is dressed as Tatiana, with a flower crown in her hair and glitter on her cheeks.

I low-key hate Rose. I shouldn't. But it's not in a girl-hate-y, competitive way. Trust me, I'm well aware that we're in vastly different leagues. Playing different sports. Or whatever. I just hate that she broke up with Austin. Not like I know the whole breakup story or anything, but I know Austin. According to my LifeCare app, I've spent nearly fifty hours with him over the last two months—and that's not even counting school, *RotR*, or Shy's birthday. He's . . . *good.* The best. And I can't understand how you'd voluntarily let someone like him go.

After another self-loathing scroll through Rose's account, I switch over to Discord and open my Unarmed Rage chat. We have players from all around, and there's a good chance that someone's online at any given moment.

If I can't sleep, might as well rage-kill some fire griffins and level up one of my other alt characters.

But not a single member of Unarmed Rage is online right now; a few are set to "Away," but no one is actively around at two in the morning on a Wednesday. Or is it Thursday? I send a few DMs, then raspberry my lips, drop my phone onto my comforter, and drink my lukewarm tea. I could play alone. But playing *RotR* by myself at two in the morning is a level of gaming addiction sadness even I don't want to wrestle with.

The middle of the night is when I'm at my loneliest. Like I'm the only person alive, especially in a house of well-functioning sleepers. As I sip my tea, I try to unwind my brain. Forget about Shy's comment at the costume store. Or Austin saying he missed me making fun of him. When I reach the bottom of my mug—just the lone, soggy tea bag remains—my phone screen lights up. I slide the mug onto my bedside table and scoop up my phone. But it's not a Discord notification.

AUSTIN:
go to sleep, Lou

That depressing, only-person-alive feeling fades as I read his text message. Because I'm not alone, not really. Not when I have Austin.

ME:
What do you think I've been doing for the last three hours? Also how'd you know I was awake? Should I be creeped out right now? Because I kind of am

AUSTIN:
you logged on to discord, dummy. I was talking to my brother and saw you come online. logic told me you were awake or finally figured out how to play video games in your sleep

ME:
If only. But nope, insomnia strikes again

AUSTIN:
anything I can do to help?

ME:
Nah. Unless you want to play rotr?

AUSTIN:
I'm not enabling you

go to sleep

ME:
I've taken 5mg of melatonin, counted a hundred sheep, listened to my meditation app for 30min, and just downed a mug of sleepytime tea. I'm trying

AUSTIN:
what goes on in that brain of yours?

ME:
Wouldn't you like to know

AUSTIN:
actually yeah

keeps me up at night

I'm too tired to fight back my smile. I really doubt I keep Austin up at night the way he keeps me up at night. Instead of counting sheep, he probably counts all the ways he can embarrass me or turn me into a walking, talking ray of sunshine.

I stretch out on my bed.

ME:
You're not missing out on much. Mostly my brain feels like that "Don't Open: Dead Inside" door from The Walking Dead

AUSTIN:
your brain is full of zombies? 

ME:
More like thoughts that won't die and a warning I never ever listen to

I always open the door

Austin doesn't reply right away, and my phone screen dims, then turns off.

I shut my eyes for a moment, but I don't feel any different.

Fucking Sleepytime tea. That bear in pajamas is a marketing gimmick.

My phone buzzes, but when I open my eyes, no new text alert brightens the screen. An incoming call does. An incoming *video* call. I almost panic reject the call but end up staring at the screen as it rings twice, three times . . . By the sixth ring, I hit accept.

"You almost didn't pick up, huh?" Austin's voice is nighttime soft. He's also in his bedroom, all the lights off, and his face is shadowy, grainy.

Grateful I removed my night guard—it gives me a major lisp—before drinking my tea, I say, "Can you blame me? I hate video chats. No one needs to see my face while talking to me."

And in the tiny square in the corner of the screen, I can see myself. My screen is also grainy and dark, my hair swooped back into a bun on the top of my head. A blob of toothpaste is on my chin, and I quickly wipe it off. Luckily, I'm not dressed in the unicorn pajamas Ana picked out for me for my birthday, which I usually wear when it's cold at night. I'd never live that down.

"But you picked up."

"I was worried you were in duress and needed help. But now

that I see you're fine . . ." I pretend to reach forward to end the call.

Austin laughs, shifting his pillow around and tucking his arm beneath it; the pillowcase creases against the side of his cheek. I soak the image in, almost guiltily, as he says, "Just so you know, I like seeing your face when I talk to you."

Oh boy.

We're not flirting. Mostly because I don't know how to flirt. Ipso facto: not flirting. My brain is probably addled from too many natural over-the-counter sleep aids and the fact that I feel the tiniest bit less alone with him.

"Um." I swallow hard. "I might give this sleep thing another try—"

"Shit. Was that weird?" Austin pushes his hair back from his eyes. "You just . . . you make all these really funny facial expressions. And wrinkle your nose when I annoy you. It's entertaining."

Yeah, definitely not flirting. Okay. Chill out. I wrinkle my nose and say, "Whatever." Then I grab my weighted blanket, tug it over my legs, and change the topic of conversation. "Why were you talking to Ethan so late?"

"We're always missing each other, with our school schedules and stuff, but he had time tonight. Felt like forever since I'd talked to him."

"Trying to lure him over to the dark side to play *RotR* again? We could use a third for arenas."

Austin cracks a sleepy smile. "Maybe." Then he yawns, so I yawn too. "We just talked about school, the band . . . brother stuff."

"Ah, yes. Brother stuff." I yawn again, which just makes

Austin yawn, which makes *me* yawn again, and we both dissolve into muffled laughter. "You're like a human sedative tonight, dude."

"Thank you?"

"You're just"—I flutter my hand around at the camera, gesturing to him—"very calming when you're not annoying me to death. You contain multitudes, Austin Yang."

"Happy to be of service." He pushes his hair back again, fluffs his pillow. "Also, I wanted to let you know that I'm an excellent zombie killer. You know, for your undead thoughts. If you ever need any help."

I'd laugh if it weren't so stupidly sweet. "Thanks."

Austin smiles. "Anytime, Lou."

I fall asleep like that, curled on my side with my phone propped up against an extra pillow, listening to Austin's breath evening out into sleep on the other end.

TWENTY

This isn't the love story
Our hearts set out to tell

—The Laundromats, "What's Left" (1984)

I'm not sure what's more impressive: that Austin convinced me to attend A Scare Is Born, or that he talked Marianne into coming. Honestly, at this point, I wouldn't be surprised if he were shoving flyers into the faces of every single person he passes on the sidewalk. I found over twenty randomly hung up at Evanston High, some even in the women's bathroom, which was questionable. The dude is *hyped*. And I get it. The winning band gets a recording session at a studio and a sit-down with a local music manager for industry advice and tips.

Since the band needed the van to transport their entire set of equipment, I volunteered to drive Marianne to the venue, an all-ages bar in Wallingford, where we'll meet up with everyone else.

I finish braiding my hair around the devil horn headband, making microadjustments until it looks perfect, and forgo my usual button-down for a black T-shirt with red piping. My go-to pair of high-waisted jeans and Doc Martens stay the same and match my half-assed costume. When I can't stall any longer, I head upstairs.

"Wow!" Mom looks up from the kitchen table, where she's working on the accounting side of the dog- and cat-grooming business. "You look great, baby."

I grimace, pointing to the horns. "I feel ridiculous."

"You look ridiculous," Ana says from the couch, and inside my head, I flip her off.

"Oh shush," Mom says to Ana, chuckling. Because, apparently, when *she's* a jerk, it's cute. "Eloise is gorgeous."

I grab my rain shell from the hook by the door, lingering. "You sure I can take the minivan?"

Mom shoos me with her hand. "Go, go. We're ordering in for dinner. You go have fun, okay? And tell Austin I said to break a leg."

"Will do." I grab the keys off the side table. "I'll be back before curfew, okay?"

"Call or text if you need me." Mom pats her cell phone, which is on the table beside a notebook. "Be safe."

I wave and head out to the driveway. I clean Mom's car trash and make sure the passenger seat is tidy enough for Marianne, then make my quick jaunt over to Green Lake. The entire drive, my heartbeat is pounding faster and faster, the silent alarm bell of anxiety clattering around between my ribs.

As much as my nervous system wants me to bail, I can't. I'm responsible for Marianne, for one. And for another, Austin wants me there. And I want to be there *for* Austin.

Marianne's waiting on the sidewalk for me when I pull up, and I unlock the doors for her.

I roll down the passenger window. "Want some help?"

"I'm perfectly capable of getting into a car by myself, thank you very much." She opens the door and lifts herself into the seat with a grunt. The entire interior of Mom's minivan immediately smells of tobacco and vetiver.

Mom's never going to clean that seat ever again.

"You ready?" I ask, my insides itchy and jumpy.

Marianne nods, clicks her seat belt, and gazes around the inside of the car. "Thank you for picking me up. The Man revoked my license *years* ago."

Probably a good call, considering she has cataracts. I enter the Starbird Lounge into Google Maps and wait as it routes us. The inside of Mom's minivan is quiet, and all I can think about is how today's the first time I've been alone with Marianne since I barfed my unrequited crush feelings all over her kitchen table.

"The thing I talked about," I begin uneasily, "you know, a few weeks ago?"

"About you being in love with Austin?"

"Oh my god, that's *not* what I said. Is your memory finally crapping out? I never said love! You did—I only said it was a crush. Because it's just a crush. That's it." My voice is high-pitched with frustration. Or embarrassment. Both, probably. "And I'm over it—over *him*. So can we just forget that the conversation ever happened?"

Yes, I'm lying. But if Marianne thinks I'm no longer into Austin, maybe she won't harass me about him.

"What conversation? I'm just so old. . . . I can't remember anything these days." Marianne gives me a curious look across the car, widening her blue eyes. "Who are you?"

I shake my head. "Not funny."

"My memory is excellent. But sure, we can pretend you don't have feelings for Austin if you'd like."

"Thanks. You're very kind," I say with as much sarcasm

as I can muster. Then I just shift the car into drive, following Google Maps, intent on my semidelusional denial. My feelings for Austin will fade. They're like a fire—if I pay attention to them, feed them oxygen, they'll burn out of control. But if I smother them? They'll die out. Like that one time I accidentally started a fire in our microwave—I left the door closed, and the flames snuffed out. Problem solved.

Marianne humors me, though, and for the entire drive to the Starbird Lounge, she makes small talk. Asks me about my college applications. About the trip I'm planning down to USC over winter break. Tells me about how Nox needs to have a dental and get her nasty kitty teeth cleaned; I recommend a vet Mom sometimes works with. Safe, emotionless topics.

A few times, during the conversational lulls, I almost ask about Georgie. About the letters. Ever since I read them, I've waffled between pity and confusion. I feel *bad* for Marianne. But I also don't know why she lied to us. As much as I want to pry, I keep my mouth shut. On our drive home that night, Austin and I agreed we wouldn't tell Marianne that we know the truth about what happened. Doesn't mean I'm not tempted, though.

The all-ages bar is a beacon on the corner, with a bright neon marquee, the colors flashing orange and black. The light box is also lit, advertising tonight's event:

A SCARE IS BORN: Seattle's Annual Battle of the Bands!

After circling the three-block radius around the Starbird Lounge, luck strikes and I snag street parking near the entrance. I take a whopping five minutes to parallel park alongside the curb and break out into a nervous sweat. Thankful for my prescription-strength deodorant, I hop out of the van, circle to the other side, and open the door for Marianne. I help her down onto the sidewalk and she pauses, adjusting her outfit.

Leave it to Marianne to dress to the nines for a local battle of the bands. She's in a long, black, gauzy skirt, pointed-toe boots, a cream-colored camisole, and three separate shawls, draped over her shoulders. Necklaces layer her neck and collarbones, and her lips are painted a dark, dark red. Some might mistake it for a costume, but this is classic Marianne.

"Let's go find Austin." Marianne tilts her head back as she takes in the chaos. The people on the sidewalk, smoking and laughing. The bump of music from inside the Starbird. The air, slightly damp on our skin thanks to the recent rain. Even I can admit it's a little magical.

I offer my arm to Marianne, and she loops hers through mine. We walk to the entrance, where we hand over our tickets, and a bouncer stamps our hands with glow-in-the-dark pumpkins.

Immediately, I'm overwhelmed. It's dark and warm and loud in here. Like Retro Rink but on steroids. *Austin,* I remind myself. *I'm here for Austin. I'm here because—for once in my life—I'm going to be a good friend.*

"Eloise." Marianne pulls on my arm. "Over here."

I stumble beside Marianne as we weave our way through the crowd. The inside of the Starbird isn't large. There's a stage on the opposite end of the wide room, where someone in a Starbird Lounge T-shirt is setting up equipment. A dance floor is directly in front of it.

Marianne leads us into a back corner, where there's a bar and a half-dozen tables set up with candles.

"Isn't this a fire hazard?" I ask, not sure if I mean the candles or the sheer number of humans.

Marianne laughs. "Oh, you sweet, anxious child." I scowl, and she just smiles. Then she bops one of my horns. "You know what, Eloise? You're adorable, and it's a shame you won't talk to Aus—"

"Oh my god, Marianne! Seriously?" I bug my eyes out at her, and she just laughs and laughs. Too old for this, my ass. Marianne's having the time of her life. Probably because she gets to torture me all evening.

I unloop our arms and cross mine over my chest. We're standing off to the side, beside a door marked PRIVATE. "Did Austin tell you where to meet him?"

Marianne pushes onto her tiptoes, not like she needs the extra height. "No, but they're probably backstage." She gestures to the door. "I think he said they're on third. Why don't you text him?"

I shift on my feet, then pull my phone from my back pocket. But before I can unlock it, someone says, "Lou, we said you had to wear a *costume*," and Austin bear-hugs me from behind.

"Oh!" My voice comes out as a pathetic squeak because my back is pressed against Austin's chest and his hands are on my hips. "Um. Hey."

Austin lets me go and I turn around, prepared to argue against him calling me the devil. But my mouth drops open. "What the fuck are you wearing?"

Austin runs a shaky hand through his hair, and then he shrugs. "What does it look like?"

He's wearing a blue shirt. But not any ordinary blue shirt. Oh no, it's a blue, screen-printed shirt that says MISERABLE LUMP OF A HUMAN BEING with a bunch of skull emojis patterned around the lettering. Unlike my ugly yellow shirt, his fits snug, clinging to his body.

I clasp my hand over my mouth, not like it's doing a good job of muffling my laughter. "Please don't tell me you had that *made*."

"I'm all about supporting small local businesses." He grins—practically ear to ear. "I tried to braid my hair but it's too short. What do you think? I haven't quite mastered your scowl, though."

I shove his shoulder, laughing. And when I'm laughing, all those little anxieties float and fade away. "This is *so* weird. I hate you."

That grin, somehow, gets even wider as he smooths his palms down the world's second-ugliest shirt. "You wish you hated me."

If only he knew the half of it.

"ELOISE!" Shy slams into me and we topple into a nearby speaker, her arms wrapping around my waist. "You came!"

I hug her, then untangle myself. "Someone had to drive Marianne."

Shy's dark eyes widen, and she looks at the woman standing beside me. "Holy shit. Austin, you didn't tell us"—she lowers her voice—"Marianne fucking Landis was coming tonight!"

Marianne's smile is bemused. "Let me guess. Shy?"

Shy's cheeks darken and she nods. "Hi. Yes. Hello." Her fingers fret nervously with her bangs. "I'm a big fan. Huge."

"Thank you." Marianne's blue eyes twinkle in the dim light, and Shy is so blatantly starstruck it's hilarious.

The twins are the last out of the private door, and we do the whole "Holy shit, it's Marianne Landis" rodeo for a second time. As Winston and Mac fangirl and Shy shows Marianne her tattoo—a few lines from the Laundromats' hit

"Midnight"—Austin grabs my wrist and pulls me deeper into the room, back near the bar.

"Not gonna lie," he says, stopping when we're far enough away from our group that I can hear my own thoughts again, "I didn't think you'd show up."

I lean my hip against the wall and cross my arms, my nerves thrumming. "Well. Marianne has cataracts and can't drive."

He tucks his hands into the front pockets of his jeans. "Rideshares exist. I'm just really, really, really glad you're here."

"Wow. Three reallys."

"Three reallys." Austin hesitates, then steps closer until the toes of his Converse are touching the toes of my Doc Martens. He reaches out and adjusts my horns, brushing back the hairs that have already escaped my braided headband, his fingers trailing my temple and then my jaw. "Your horns were crooked."

I gulp, then stare down at our feet. "Thanks."

The Converse don't step back. They stay there, right against my combat boots, as Austin mirrors my position and leans against the wall, our bodies facing each other and inches apart. The heat and anxiety and nerves of it all are making me dizzy. I squeeze my eyes shut for a moment, try to ground myself. Shy's words—*You two act like a couple*—buzz around in my head. I should step back and create some much-needed distance. But I don't.

I like this way too much to be the first one who pulls away.

Austin clears his throat. "Hey, uh, after this—"

Microphone feedback crackles and cuts him off. I look over my shoulder at the stage, which is barely in view from back here. A Starbird employee is leaning into the microphone. "Witches and ghouls, it's time to get spooky! Will bands one through three return to the graveyard—I mean, the *greenroom*. We're on in ten minutes!"

"That's you, right?" I stand up straight and cross my arms even tighter. Like my anxiety is making me collapse in on myself like a dying star. "Marianne said you're on third?"

"Yeah." Austin looks past me at the rest of the band. Then he turns to me. "You're not going to run off halfway through the show, are you?"

I bat my eyelashes in innocence. "That doesn't sound like something I'd do."

"Yes, it does."

Shy yells at him to hurry up, and he holds up one finger.

I take small steps backward. "I'm here for the long haul. If you don't believe me, I'll give you my car keys."

This makes Austin smile, and he pushes back from the wall. "Nah, I trust you."

"Don't be nervous," I tell him, and we walk back to the group together. "You're going to be great."

Austin studies me for a second, then must decide that I'm being serious. "Thanks, Lou. Seriously," he says, those kind eyes searching mine. His hair's a mess and he's so nervous that he's practically vibrating with energy and that stupid shirt is tight around his biceps and *shit*, I like him way too much.

"Come on," Shy says, and grabs Austin's forearm, dragging him toward the private door. "Wish us luck!"

Marianne and I both tell them to break some arms and legs. Then Shy, Austin, and the twins disappear through the door.

Tilting her head at me, Marianne says, "You two looked awfully cozy."

"Fuck off."

Marianne laughs, then points toward the bar. "Let's get something to drink. It's hot as balls in here."

I don't know who's babysitting who, but I go with Marianne to the bar. She orders a vodka tonic with cranberry, and I get a ginger ale since my stomach's currently inverting itself. We stay in the back as the first band takes the stage and A Scare Is Born begins.

For the first two bands, Marianne and I stick to the back of the Starbird. Marianne gives dry commentary, criticizing the bands, from their singers to the types of guitars to the lyrics. I have a feeling she's being a dick for my amusement and my amusement alone, since it's clear I'm one accidental Austin touch away from a full-on emotional breakdown. And it's also clear Marianne knows I'm full of shit.

I'm not over Austin. No matter how hard I wish I were.

As much as I crave those close moments, I can't keep doing this. I can't keep finding myself in these weird, confusing situations with Austin. He's my friend. Because the way he looks at me? Platonic as hell. The way he looked at Rose at Retro Rink? Romantic as fuck. Our banter is just that—banter. Unlike most people, Austin can stand me for more than five minutes at a time. It doesn't mean anything more than that.

The second band—Eventual Ghosts, how on brand—leaves the stage, and we wait for the Coinstar Rejects to begin their set; there are five minutes between each performance. The people in the crowd are restless as they wait, funneling toward us for the bar or ducking into the bathrooms down the hall to our left.

Marianne sips her vodka tonic with one hand and uses the other to poke me in the small of my back with her pointy fingernail. "Go on," she says. "You don't have to hang out here with me during their set, you know. Go! Have fun!"

"I am having fun," I say, way too defensively.

Marianne raises one brow. "Eloise. Get out of here. I'm tired of looking at you."

"You sure you'll be okay back here?"

"Oh, yes. I'll be fine." She pats the fanny pack, which is somehow fashionable, around her waist. "I have my phone if you can't find me. But seriously, go be a teenager. You don't have to babysit me all night."

"Fine, fine." I finish my ginger ale and set it on an empty table, wipe the sweat off my palms, and then push through the crowd. The lights dim as I make my way forward and Austin, Shy, and the twins take the stage.

As glad as I am to be here for Austin and the band, I kind of want this night to be over. The sensory overload. Marianne's knowing looks. Austin's confusing . . . well, *everything*. Tonight has been a lot. And it's only just beginning.

"Hello, Seattle!" Shy leans into the microphone, wrapping her orange-and-black-painted fingernails around the stand. She texted me pictures earlier—each one has little webs painted onto the nail. Her zombie bride costume is amazingly spooky beneath the lights, the effect even more badass due to the fog machines spouting eerie mist across the stage. "We're the Coinstar Rejects and we're here to play a few songs for all you lovely people!"

Someone in the crowd whoops and a few people laugh, conversation rippling as everyone waits for the music to begin. Several people repeat the band name with confusion; maybe Austin's right and the worst thing a band name can be is forgettable.

Shy beams and turns to Austin, her tattered skirt twirling around her legs. He loops the strap of his bass guitar over his shoulder and says something in her ear. Shy nods, then turns to the twins. For an awkward, quiet minute they tune their instruments, trade a few more whispers. And then they begin.

Watching the band onstage is way different from watching them practice in Austin's garage. Shy dances like she's lighter than air, and the veins in Mac's biceps bulge as they frantically slam their sticks onto their drum set, and Winston bobs his head so much that I'm afraid he might pass out, but Austin is calm. His hands move slowly, purposefully, along the neck of his bass guitar.

I always thought Austin was at ease and comfortable wherever he was—forever in his element. But it's clear that *this* is Austin's element.

I force my attention away from Austin and to the crowd. People are smiling and dancing and a few are taking videos. As I watch strangers watch my friends, all that panic in my chest softens. Ugh. What is this feeling? Pride?

I slide my phone from my back pocket and film a quick video of the crowd to show the band later. When the song ends, I clap, cheering—even though there are actual judges, and the winners aren't decided by one of those giant clap-o-meters. But my whoops are drowned out by the people in the audience, who're *loving* this. Watching your friends succeed . . . feels pretty good.

They transition into their second song, which is slightly less dancing material, but the crowd rolls with it, and I snap photos, of both Austin and the band. I swipe through them. Maybe I can become the Coinstar Rejects' social media manager or something, because these aren't half bad.

After the second song ends and the crowd claps and cheers, Austin rests his bass guitar against the wall and grabs a swig of water. He scans the crowd and I clock the moment he sees me: his face stretches into that goofy grin. I lift my hand in a small wave—proof of life, that I didn't run—and his smile stretches even wider. Even if a huge part of me wanted to bail earlier, I'm glad I didn't. Austin's expression alone is worth it.

I can be his friendly face in the crowd.

The third and final song has Austin on the keyboard, singing a duet with Shy. It's the same song they practiced in Austin's garage. And as I listen, I realize it's a love song. That fucking four-letter word has been inescapable, thanks to Marianne being a complete asshole. When I first heard the song, I was too distracted that Austin could sing to pay attention to the details.

Now the details are all I can pay attention to.

Austin doesn't write their songs, I know that. Shy and Mac do. But when Austin's gaze locks onto mine halfway through the song, it's difficult to remind my brain of the facts. That Austin's not singing *to* me, that he didn't write the lyrics, that it's just a love song Shy and Mac probably wrote on the back of a Taco Bell receipt while high off edibles.

I know all this. But like the pathetic sap I've become lately, I can't help but fall for Austin a little more during his solo. What can I say? There's something undeniably attractive about a boy on a stage, singing a love song, wearing a really weird shirt that's an inside joke only you would understand.

Then Austin shuts his eyes, his voice syncing back up with Shy's as they bring the song to an end. A final crash of Mac's cymbals and it's over. Shy thanks everyone and grabs Austin's hand, who grabs Mac's hand, who holds on to Winston's hand,

and they all bow theatrically before walking off the stage and out of view.

The lights brighten during the five-minute intermission.

And two rows in front of me is a familiar head of blond curls. *Directly* in front of me. So directly that it's entirely possible Austin wasn't looking at me at all. He was looking at Rose, the ex-girlfriend who showed up for him even though it's not her scene. Rose, the girl he can't stay away from for more than a few months.

And I have a sick, nauseating feeling that they're already on again, or, by the end of A Scare Is Born, they will be.

TWENTY-ONE

This is how we end
We were never more than friends

—The Laundromats, "Fools" (1981)

Austin wasn't looking into my eyes while he sang his heart out—even if, for a hot minute, I convinced myself that he *might* be. I'm not the girl you croon love songs to. I inspire hatred and derision, not love. The disappointment swoops low in my stomach, but it's not exactly surprising. I don't get love songs or romance or the guy. *Especially* if the guy is, well, the best and kindest person I've ever met. If I continue on my miserable path, I'll probably end up with a bounty hunter or a lawyer or someone equally terrible.

I'm jostled and bumped into as people wander for the bathroom or the bar. The movement snaps me out of my depressing spiral, and I turn, eager to make my escape, when a hand closes around my wrist.

"Eloise, hey!" Rose halts me in place, and when I turn, she's all smiles. Her pretty blond hair is loose around her shoulders and she's wearing an angel costume, complete with tiny wings and a halo. Subtle, universe. *Subtle.* "It's so awesome to see you."

I pull my arm back. People continue to bump into us, and my anxiety rises. "Um. Yeah. Same." Lies. I'm lying.

Rose's smile wobbles; guess I'm not selling the lie, but I'm barely trying. She recovers quickly. "C'mon! Let's get out of the crowd. I think they'll be coming out over there. . . ."

Maybe there's not enough oxygen in the Starbird, but I follow Rose toward the backstage entrance and the bar, and I see that Marianne is no longer where I left her. I scan the tables and bar for any sight of her, but she's nowhere to be found. Between her height and her bone-white hair, she's hard to miss.

Shit. I can't exactly bail without Marianne. I might be the worst, but I'm not going to strand a seventy-three-year-old woman at a bar without a ride. Even if bailing is all I want to do right now.

I scrounge through my pockets for a ginger chew and shove one into my mouth, then cross my arms. Rose and her two friends—the same girls from Retro Rink—are chattering on about the show and the first few bands. Despite the ginger chew, I feel like puking when Rose comments on how good Austin looked tonight but *what the hell was up with his shirt?*

Anxiety is short-circuiting my brain. Like, why the hell am I standing here, listening to this conversation? Do I hate myself that much? But I'm too overwhelmed to move, to do anything else. Sensory overload and panic and teeny-tiny cracks in my heart—they all immobilize me.

My eyes dart around the Starbird, but Marianne's vanished.

Eventually I pull my phone out, and as I unlock it, my last application opens. The photos and videos of Austin. My cheeks warm, and before I can second-guess myself, I delete them all. I have a feeling—a really good feeling—that I won't want to remember tonight. Because even if no one can see it, I'm dissolving on the inside. For a few hopeless minutes, I had hope.

And now the hope is gone, and I'm emptier than I ever was before.

ME:
Where are you? Set's over. We should go

The message to Marianne whooshes off and I tuck my phone back into my pocket.

The door we're loitering beside opens and Shy practically flies out of it. She jumps up and down excitedly, her tattered zombie-bride skirt swirling. "Holy shit! That was amazing!" She pauses her jumping when she notices Rose and her friends beside me. "Oh. Hey, Rose."

Rose hugs Shy, and the rest of the band exits, the door slamming shut behind them. Austin's last to appear, and he pushes back his flop of messy, sweaty hair as he scans our group. When he notices Rose, his eyes widen. Before he can say her name, she pushes past Winston and Mac and tosses her arms around his neck.

"Whoa—hey!" Austin hugs Rose, and his hand settles in the small of her back, his chin resting on her head. The gesture is so intimate, so familiar, that I almost want to cry. Stepping out of the hug, he smiles. "Thanks for coming."

Rose flicks back her curls, then readjusts her halo. "Like I'd miss this."

Shy rolls her eyes and walks over to me, hovering alone by a trash can. She drops her voice and asks, "You okay?"

I meet her gaze. "Why wouldn't I be?"

"Denial isn't a good look on you," she mutters, but bumps her hip into mine. "Let's grab some waters."

Marianne still hasn't texted me back, so I follow Shy to the bar to grab waters for the band. Once we're alone—well, away from the band—she tries to talk, but I cut her off.

"Don't, okay? I'm fine." I motion to the bartender and Shy orders six waters. Grabbing a napkin on the bar, I begin twisting and shredding it as a distraction. "You guys were great," I say, and try to infuse some enthusiasm into the sentence. Because last song aside, I enjoyed myself. They're talented, and even if I feel stuck between crying and anxiety puking, I hope they win. They deserve it.

Shy and I gather the water bottles. "Yeah? There are still three more bands, but . . . I feel good? Did we look good?"

I force a smile, because this isn't Shy's fault. "Amazing. Iconic. All of you. That costume was a great idea."

We rejoin the group and I hand Austin a water, avoiding his gaze as he thanks me. The group moves to a free table on the opposite side of the lounge, and I consider my options since Marianne is MIA. At what point do I become concerned about her absence?

There aren't enough chairs but I'm too antsy to sit anyways, flipping my phone around in my hands. The second round of bands begins, and Winston and Mac leave the table to get a closer eye on the competition.

"Eloise." Rose pats the now-empty seat beside her. Austin is on the other side of her, and he flashes me an oblivious smile, his eyes shining from the high of performing. And, if I had to guess, the girl beside him.

I sink into the seat like an obedient dog. Spin my phone around on the table.

When it lights up, I lunge for it.

AUSTIN:
what's wrong?

I glance to my right and Austin meets my gaze, that smile dimmed.

ME:
Can't find Marianne

There. A good excuse for my shit mood, and it's not a lie. Because if I could find Marianne, I could leave. I exit Austin's message and open my conversation with Marianne, sending her yet another message.

ME:
WHERE DID YOU GO OLD WOMAN

Then I lock my phone and ignore Austin staring at the side of my face. Rose quickly distracts him, pulling him close—her hand curling around his bare forearm—as she shows him some photos and videos she took during their set. Because that's her role, not mine. I sip my water and scan the crowd, keeping my eyes open for Marianne. Shy shoots me worried looks before Xavier shows up and pulls her onto the dance floor.

After a few minutes of absolute torture while Austin and Rose flirt, I say, "Hey, I'm going to look for Marianne. I have no idea where she went, and she's not replying to my texts."

"I can help," Austin offers, half getting out of his seat.

"Nah, I've got it," I tell him, and force a smile. Try my hardest to keep up the illusion that the only thing wrong is the missing former front woman who's under my care tonight. I wave and take off toward the other side of the lounge. As I walk, my eyes burn, my brain branded with the image of Austin's chin on top of Rose's head as they hugged. Rose pulling Austin closer, laughing as she flicks through photos, his head so, so close to hers. That stupid song and the eye contact and all these useless feelings that are ruining everything.

Oh! And I've apparently lost Marianne.

Fuck tonight.

I do a useless lap around the lounge and check the bathrooms before finding an exit. Because I need fresh air. I need some distance. And if the exit automatically locks behind me and I can't get back inside, that's just an added bonus.

The exit leads to an alleyway beside the Starbird Lounge. It's quiet out here. And cold. Today's rain faded into a foggy mist, and it feels nice against my overheated skin. I lean my back against the side of the building and tilt my head up, staring at the cloudy, starless night sky. I take slow, deep breaths like my old therapist taught me and try to calm down. Enjoy the goose bumps that aren't emotionally charged like the ones I had inside.

After a moment, I let my eyes fall shut, and I breathe until the urge to cry passes. Blinking my eyes open, I reach for my phone, but still no word from Marianne.

The door a few feet away from me creaks open.

"Hey, there you are." Austin steps into the alleyway.

"Just, um, taking a breather." I force my voice to be calm, then motion toward the lounge. "I couldn't find Marianne inside."

Austin tucks his hands into his front pockets and walks over to me. "She'll turn up. Probably signing autographs for some adoring fans who recognized her."

I force myself to laugh. "Probably."

He slows to a stop, eyes narrowing as he studies me. "Tell me what's going on, Lou. Because something's wrong."

"Nothing's wrong." I hold his gaze and do what I do best: compartmentalize. After all, I've done this every single day at school, whenever I see Lydie and Jordan. Whenever Mom or Dad asks if I'm okay. Show the world that it can't hurt me, even if I'm breaking on the inside.

Austin takes a step closer. "Nope. Something's wrong."

"I'm fine, okay? Why won't you believe me?"

"Because you're a shitty actor." The corner of his mouth tugs upward, but his eyes are still darkened with concern. "Were we *that* bad?" he jokes.

A surprised laugh catches in my throat. "No, you were actually decent."

Austin moves even closer, and once again, our shoes are toe to toe. He rakes his fingers through his hair, studying me. "Hey, you know that you can tell me anything, right?"

But I can't. Not when the one thing I want to say will ruin our friendship. "Yeah, I know. It's just, um—" My brain goes painfully empty as I search for an excuse. Something emotionless and believable.

"Is it me? Did I do something?" Austin's voice is soft, cracks a little.

The earnestness of this boy almost does me in. "You didn't do anything," I say quietly, and I shiver as a breeze funnels down the alleyway. "This is about me, not you, okay?"

"Are you giving me the 'it's not you, it's me' speech right now?" Austin laughs like it's a joke, but he sounds way, way too exasperated for it to land.

"No, because we're not dating." I shrug casually, but the tone of this conversation is morphing. "Obviously."

"Obviously?" He blinks. "What does *that* mean?"

I groan and press the back of my head against the brick exterior of the Starbird. "There's no hidden meaning. We're not a thing, Austin. Because if we were, you wouldn't have spent the night hanging out with your ex-girlfriend."

Heat floods my face, and instead of the flow of traffic on the other side of the alley and the distant thump of music from inside, I only hear the rush of my blood and my heartbeat. I didn't mean to say that last part. It kind of slipped out with the rest of my word vomit.

Austin drags his hand along his jaw, then braces himself against the wall behind me. Leans the tiniest bit closer. Close enough for the heat of his body to warm the coldness of mine. He drops his voice low. "That's what this is about? Rose? I didn't invite her."

"I don't care if you invited her or not," I say, and the odds I anxiety puke right now are upsettingly high. My heart is racing, and my stomach is turning, and I hate the way he's looking at me. Like he's searching and puzzling and reading between the lines. "This isn't about Rose or you or us—"

"Can we not talk about Rose right now?" Austin interrupts, his cheeks flushed red. This is my first glimpse into Upset Austin. No smiles or sunshine, a version of Austin I had no idea existed. "What's so wrong with me? Because you seem pretty disgusted by the idea of us being together."

Did I offend his fragile male ego or something? "Dude, are you kidding me right now?" I cross my arms over my chest. "Nothing's *wrong* with you. Also, if anyone should be disgusted, it's you, not me. Because I'm so far from your type, it's almost funny. Now, can you fucking move? I need to find Marianne."

Austin doesn't move. If anything, he's frozen in place, his gaze locked onto mine. "What're you talking about?" he asks, voice rough with confusion. "Lou—"

The door to the Starbird Lounge bursts open and Shy steps into the alleyway. Her phone's in her hand and her mouth drops open into a surprised O as she stares at us. I know how this looks—my back to the wall, Austin leaning over me. A conversation crashing to an end before it even started.

"Shit, um, didn't mean to *interrupt*." Shy laughs nervously, taps her phone to her palm. "But Austin? I texted you. The judges are about to go over their scores."

I push past Austin and he stumbles, tripping on his Converse. "You're not interrupting anything," I say, and practically run back into the Starbird Lounge.

Before Austin and Shy can follow me inside, I pivot toward the bathrooms and shamelessly cut in line, a chorus of people complaining as I lock myself inside. Inside, I perch on the counter and hang my head over my knees. I'm out of breath, my wheezing loud and labored in the claustrophobic bathroom with holographic bird wallpaper twinkling in the dim overhead lighting.

I have feelings for Austin. Giant, confusing, and complicated feelings.

I don't want them.

And I definitely don't want *him* if he doesn't want *me*.

When I squeeze my eyes shut, all I see is Austin leaning over me, his face saying something that doesn't match up with his words. But he's also flirting with his ex-girlfriend and has never, ever looked at me the way he looks at Rose.

They're perfect for each other, and Austin and I couldn't be more different.

I slide off the counter and splash some water on my face. No idea why people always do that in movies, because it doesn't do a thing to help calm me down and now my shirt is wet. Painted cursive loops across the mirror—*Take a Selfie & Tag @ starbirdloungewa!*—frame my bloodshot and wild eyes, the hair escaping my braided crown and the devil horns.

What the fuck am I even doing here?

I unlock the bathroom and ignore the complaining from the people I cut in front of, turning left toward the front entrance. Maybe the universe doesn't totally hate me, because, miracle of all miracles, I spot Marianne by the coat check.

"Marianne!" I yell over the music, and wave my arms overhead. "Let's go!"

"But they're about to announce the winners," Marianne says once I reach her, her dark lips curling downward. "Won't Austin—"

"It's, um, an emergency. My mom needs her car back," I interrupt, and hold up my phone, like she just texted me. "I'm sure Austin will fill us in later."

Before Marianne can call out my lie or protest, I loop my arm through hers and drag her out of the lounge. I keep my head down as we walk along the sidewalk toward the minivan, its lights flashing as I hit the key fob. Silent, I climb into the car and turn on the engine, letting the heat blast until I'm no longer frigid.

Marianne's equally silent beside me as I turn on Google Maps and begin driving.

The whole mess in the alleyway, unshakable and upsetting, repeats in my head as I cross Seattle's darkened streets. I feel like I'm splitting in half, fracturing. There's the part of me that wants more, the part of me that wants to cross the blurry line of friendship and romance with Austin, just to see what happens. And there's the part of me that wants to shove it all deep down and be grateful for what I have: a best friend.

Tears blur my vision as I slow to a stop in front of Marianne's, but I blink them away.

"Eloise," Marianne says, unclipping her seat belt.

I turn toward her, drumming my hands on the steering wheel. Sniffling, I force a smile. "Yeah?"

"I overheard you and Austin." At my horrified expression, she rushes to add, "Not intentionally. God no, I hate teen angst. I was having a smoke out front. . . . Anyways. Let me give you some advice: Be brave for those you care about, Eloise. Brave and vulnerable. Otherwise, you might miss your chance and regret it for the rest of your life. If you really care about Austin, tell him."

"I'm *not* telling Austin. Especially not after tonight."

"Because that little ex of his showed up?" Marianne shifts in the passenger seat to face me. "Austin didn't invite Rose, did he?"

"Who cares if he invited her or not? Austin's face lit up like a Christmas tree when he saw her, Marianne. He wanted her there."

Marianne lifts one thin, pale brow. "You don't know that. But what you do know is that he wanted *you* there."

My throat tightens. "As his friend. Please. Please stop trying to convince me that I have a chance. I don't, okay? Because no one would choose me when Rose Gembalski is standing right there!"

"Gembalski? Now that's a terrible last name." When I don't even crack a smile, Marianne groans. "Talking to you is like talking to a brick wall sometimes."

"Gee, thanks."

"Take it from an old woman who has made a lot of mistakes," Marianne says in that deep, husky voice, like velvet on leather. "When it comes to love, you don't want to always wonder *what if.* It'll eat you up, and you'll hate what's left behind. Stop being a coward, Eloise, and tell him how you feel."

I stare at the woman across the car, heat flooding my body. Shame and anger and embarrassment—all blending together until I can't tell where one emotion ends and the other begins. "I'm not a coward for trying to protect my friendship. Even if Austin feels the same, we're not going to have some happy ending. Not when I'm . . . *me.* You should understand that better than anyone. I read your letters, Marianne. I know that Georgie left you before she died."

Marianne's shadowed expression shifts from earnest to shocked and . . . something else. Something far too similar to what I'm feeling right now. But the words continue to pour out of me.

"You made it seem like you and Georgie had this . . . perfect love story. Like you were soul mates. You told me you kissed her goodbye the morning she *died.* Who lies about something like that? What the fuck is wrong with you?" My body strains against my seat belt as I twist to face her, all this anger filling the gaping wounds my hurt left behind. "Georgie rejected you in the end, and after reading all your letters, I can't say I blame her. You're selfish and a drunk and a liar, Marianne, and I don't want any more of your shitty advice!"

For one impossibly long moment, Marianne doesn't move. Then she opens the car door, gathers her skirts, and steps onto the sidewalk. But she turns to face me, and the minivan's overhead dome lights up the scene. Marianne's eyes, red and wet, and her mouth, all twisted and tight. "We're more alike than I thought, Eloise." She looks away, toward the glassy lake, before returning her gaze to me. "But I understand. I understand more than most. You have no right—*none*—to speak to me like you know my story. My life is none of your fucking business."

Then Marianne slams the car door shut.

The dome light clicks off, bathing me in darkness.

I drop my forehead to the steering wheel.

And I cry.

SHY:
HEYO WHAT DID I JUST WALK IN ON?! 👀

AUSTIN:
where did you go? they're about to announce the winners

AUSTIN:
Loouuuuu

AUSTIN:
did you leave?

SHY:
Austin thinks you left. Did you bail? Where are you?!?!

AUSTIN:
are you kidding me? I texted Marianne. she said you both left?

AUSTIN:
what the fuck

I read the text notifications first thing the next morning and roll onto my back, my sheets tangling around my legs. Muted sunlight filters in through the egress window, slanting across my body, and I wipe at my eyes. Last night feels like a fever dream. Or like I was drunk—not like I've ever been drunk before, but I have a great imagination—the memories coming back in disjointed, confusing segments.

But I was sober and all that happened and *fuck me*.

I didn't spend long outside Marianne's. I cried with my forehead pressed against the steering wheel for five, ten, maybe fifteen minutes; I'm not sure. When I finally made it home, everyone was asleep. I tiptoed down to the basement, and the emptiness of my bedroom, the loneliness, unhinged something inside me once again, and I cried myself into a fitful sleep.

Nothing is clearer in the light of day. If anything, I feel worse. It's an emotional hangover.

I made a mess and I have no idea how to pick up the pieces.

I sit upright and lean against the wall, unlocking my phone again. Stare at the messages both Austin and Shy sent last night. What do I even *say*? Austin and I . . . fought, or whatever you want to call it. I bailed on him and Shy. I yelled at Marianne. Yeah, I'm the worst.

After a few false starts, I reply to Austin.

ME:
Sorry, didn't mean to bail. I felt sick. How was the rest of the show?

Not exactly a lie.

Then I open Shy's messages.

ME:
You didn't walk in on anything, nothing happened. And yeah, I bailed. I'm really sorry and I hope the rest of the night went well

Shy's reply comes in before I finish putting on my slippers.

SHY:
Not buying it but thanks! Did Austin text you?

ME:
Not since last night

SHY:
We won 🎉 but someone was super emo after you left

I'm not trying to be mean but like . . . did you even think of Austin when you bailed? He was really upset

ME:
He was mad?

SHY:
Nope. Hurt

I stare at the messages, pain aching across my chest. No, I didn't think of how Austin might feel. I don't reply to Shy, and she takes the hint, so I finish putting on my slippers and grab a sweater, then trudge upstairs. The kitchen is empty and quiet, a note on the counter. Apparently, everyone went to brunch for fried chicken and waffles and decided to let me sleep in. For once, I wish they would've woken me.

I pour myself coffee and grab a stale bagel, then sit down at the kitchen table.

Shy's words batter me, and I'm already bruised. I get it. Bailing was a bad call. But how could I stay?

My phone buzzes.

AUSTIN:
oh you're alive

ME:
Was that ever a question?

AUSTIN:
I dunno, you disappeared and didn't reply to any of my messages last night

ME:
I went to bed

AUSTIN:
we won. sucks that you decided not to be there

ME:
I told you, I felt sick

AUSTIN:
right

I frown at my phone. This isn't how it's supposed to be. This isn't how Austin and I talk.

ME:
I'm sorry

Congrats on winning

Austin never replies.

TWENTY-TWO

I loved you more, but
You loved walking out that door

—The Laundromats, "Outside of Me" (1984)

Rock bottom.

I'm not an addict—well, unless I'm addicted to hating myself—but I don't think I've ever felt so low. Not even in the darkest depths of a depressive episode. When I'm depressed, I feel almost nothing at all. In the days since A Scare Is Born? Yeah, I've felt every single miserable second. And I miss Austin like hell.

Austin's avoiding me. When I signed into *RotR* yesterday, he wasn't online. And he never texted me about lunch today; I had to eat in the computer lab. Ms. Deaver is hitting up the dating apps now that her divorce is final, which meant she was in a mildly better mood; that made one of us.

I fucked up. The kind of fuckup that'll be ten times worse when we go to Marianne's tomorrow. Because, as far as I know, Austin has no idea what happened between me and Marianne Saturday night. I regret all of it, but yelling at Marianne wasn't my finest moment, not even close.

Tomorrow will be torture if both Marianne *and* Austin are pissed at me.

Sure, Marianne's a liar. But she's not an asshole like me.

After class on Monday, I walk to the upperclassmen's lot where Austin always parks, and I actually *feel* the tightness in my chest lighten when I spot that creepy van in the last row on the left. Austin's loading his school stuff into the back.

"Hey," I call out when I'm closer, and he looks over his shoulder.

"Hey." Austin's face is guarded as he slams the door shut, turning to me. The response is so shocking, so unlike Austin, I almost can't breathe. He doesn't have a jacket. Rain dampens his hair and patters on his shoulders, drops rolling down his cheeks and nose.

I smile. *C'mon, Austin.* But nothing. "I'm glad I caught you."

Austin opens the driver's-side door, but he doesn't get in. "What do you want?" His words are clipped and exhausted, like he'd rather be anywhere than here talking with me.

My mouth goes dry, and that *I can't breathe* feeling intensifies. "Um. I've barely talked to you since Saturday. I kind of feel like you're ignoring me or something."

"I had a busy weekend." The words are flat, and somehow, I know that Austin is lying.

I readjust my grip on my backpack strap and bob my head. "Okay. Are we still on for tomorrow, after Marianne's?"

Tomorrow is Halloween, but my favorite holiday of all time has been overshadowed by the absolute clusterfuck that was my weekend. Last week, Austin and I made plans to have a horror movie marathon at my house. He's never seen a single title from my horror movie spreadsheet, which is unacceptable.

Austin rakes his fingers through his damp hair. "I don't

know. . . . There's no Marianne this week. Didn't Donna email you?"

"No, Donna didn't email me. Marianne canceled? Marianne never cancels." Wow. Is literally *everyone* avoiding me now? Maybe I deserve it, but ouch. And Austin didn't even really answer my question.

"Yeah, well. Guess she doesn't want company." He won't even look in my general direction. Shy's text races through my mind—about how I *hurt* him. But seeing the hurt is way worse than just hearing about it. Austin without the sunshine is a deeply upsetting sight. "Look, I need to go. I have to run errands for my mom. But I can . . . I'll give you a ride home. If you want." He ducks into the van without waiting for my answer.

I bite the inside of my cheek, shame turning my stomach inside out, and walk around the van, then climb inside.

"Hey, um, congrats again on winning," I say as he pulls away from the curb, as if forcing the conversation along will somehow make things normal. Like we'll regain our rhythm if I pretend hard enough.

"Thank you." Austin turns on the radio, signaling the end of the conversation.

The ride from the school lot to our neighborhood is short, and I'm actually relieved when we hit the elementary school traffic. While we stare at the sea of bumpers, I turn off the radio and say, "Hey, I'm really sorry about Saturday. Seriously."

Austin glances at me from the corner of his eye. "What exactly are you sorry for?"

I pick at my nail polish, tiny red flakes landing on my jeans. "Everything? Bailing on you before the announcements? That stupid fight in the alley? Take your pick. I'm sorry for all of it.

I was . . . having a shitty night. I shouldn't have taken it out on you, okay?" I try to smile, but he's turned away from me. "I'm sorry," I say again, more forcefully, earnestly, this time.

Austin lifts one hand from the wheel and drags his fingers through his hair. "I heard you."

I brush the nail polish off my jeans, anxiety hot inside my chest as I flounder for something else to say. But my brain comes up empty, and I'm panicking.

The light turns and we roll forward. He doesn't say anything for a minute. Then: "Rose came to the show because she wants to get back together."

The words are a knife between my ribs, searing and aching. I mean. That's more or less what I thought. But hearing it out loud hurts like a motherfucker. "Oh."

"What do you think I should do? Should I get back together with her?" Austin asks, and the knife twists. His tone is calm, rational. As if we're talking about homework or what we want to pick up for dinner after volunteering. Like a friend talking to a friend. Except one friend has some seriously non-platonic feelings for the other friend, and that friend is getting back together with his gorgeous, nice, well-adjusted ex-girlfriend.

"I don't care." I try to keep the hurt out of my voice, but I'm sure it bleeds through. "Do whatever you want."

Austin doesn't respond, and I can't even look at him as he parks on the curb outside my house. I'm oddly on the verge of tears as I fumble with my seat belt.

Austin and Rose fit together. They're the same, perfect for each other. I'm Austin's friend. Or I used to be. Maybe I managed to fuck that up too. Because things were good between us until Saturday night.

We had a rhythm.

I pushed, he pulled.

I was grumpy and he was sunshine.

Now it's all messed up.

"I said I was sorry." I finally unlatch my seat belt and grab my bag from the floor. "I'm not sure what else I can do except say I'm sorry."

Austin flexes his hands on the steering wheel and still doesn't look at me. "You bailed. We weren't even done talking and you fucking *ran away* from me. Then left." He finally turns toward me. "What're you doing, Lou? What're *we* doing?"

I blink at him in confusion. "I'm not—I don't know. And last I checked, you were dropping me off."

"Forget it." Austin sighs and shifts the car into park. Then he says, "Do you know how hard it is to be your friend?"

"Wow," I say, and my throat is tightening and my eyes are burning because Austin's always had a knack for pushing my buttons—but I never thought he'd push *these* buttons. "No one's *making* you be my friend, you know that, right?"

A car alarm blares down the street, and my vision goes blurry, and Austin's face falls as he reaches for me. "Shit. Lou, that's not—"

I shove open the door and stumble out. Swinging my backpack over my shoulder, I walk-run up the sidewalk toward my house. But I've barely made it to our mailbox before Austin catches up with me.

"Lou, hold on." He grabs my sleeve, and I turn around.

Yanking my arm back, the fabric of my hoodie slipping from his grip, I say, "You know what, Austin? Fuck you. If it's so terrible being my friend, consider our friendship over. Look at you, off the hook! You're welcome."

Austin holds my gaze, and there's so much hurt there. The level of hurt I didn't think someone as kind and happy as Austin had a capacity for. Hurt I caused. I always knew Austin would realize that I was a bad friend, and it plays out on his face live as he stares at me. "You don't mean that."

I cross my arms tight over my chest. "Like you'd be that upset. You wouldn't even look at me ten minutes ago. You haven't been online. You didn't text me about lunch."

"Yeah, because you hurt my fucking feelings, and I needed some space, okay?" He plays with the little flag on our mailbox, jiggling the metal. "That doesn't mean—you're my best friend, Lou."

"Which is it, Austin?" I can actively feel myself falling apart, my mind spiraling away from me, the heaviness setting in. "Is it too hard to be my friend or am I your best friend? Because it can't be both."

Austin squeezes his eyes shut and drops his arms to his sides. "That's not what I meant. Being your friend isn't hard, okay?" He opens his eyes, and they're glassy. "You're difficult and confusing and infuriating. Usually, it's worth it. But sometimes, yeah, being your friend is shitty because . . ."

"Because *what*?" I dig my fingernails into my arms, trying not to cry. Not here, not in front of him. And when Austin doesn't reply, I take a step backward, toward my house. "You know what? It doesn't matter. The fact that you can't answer me tells me all I need to know. Thanks for the ride."

Then I turn and hurry up the pathway to my house, almost

drop my keys as I unlock the front door with shaking hands, and slam it shut behind me. A sob catches in my throat and I squeeze my eyes shut, taking a shuddering breath.

What the fuck did I just do?

TWENTY-THREE

Tell me, honey, was it worth it?
This chance you took on me?

—The Laundromats, "Last Chance" (1981)

The upside of having a basement bedroom is it's almost too easy to wallow in the darkness. With the blinds snapped shut and all my lights off except for my laptop, I curl up in my bed with a hoodie pulled over my head, a handful of stolen candy from the bowl upstairs on my pillow, and more self-loathing than I know what to do with. You'd think I'd be a pro at this by now, but apparently not.

I shove an entire fun-size Snickers into my mouth and start *Halloween*. Last week, I spent an hour picking the perfect movies to show Austin my favorite genre of film, and it feels appropriately self-loathing to watch them by myself.

Over the last twenty-four hours, I've only felt worse about my fight with Austin. Normally, I'd feel self-righteous. I'd be telling myself I made the right decision. Except the look on Austin's face was way more haunting than Michael Myers's creepy skin mask. And what he said? About how being my friend is hard? *That's* what I can't shake. Austin's not a mean person—clearly, I filled that role in our friendship—but that was the most hurtful thing anyone has ever said to me.

I'd rather read a hundred cruel texts between Lydie and Jordan than hear Austin talk about how hard it is to be my friend. Austin was supposed to be the one person who understood me. Who *got* me. And I have no idea what happened. None of it makes sense, and not in the normal our-friendship-doesn't-make-sense way.

The tiger finally ate the mouse. Sorry, viral video fans.

"Eloise?" Mom knocks on my door. "Can I come in, baby?"

With a groan, I pause my movie. "Yeah?"

Mom pokes her head inside. She's dressed up as Bad Sandy from *Grease*, skintight pants and all. She takes a look around my depression cave and sighs. "I take it Austin isn't coming over?"

"Nope." I begin unwrapping a Reese's.

"Do you want to talk about it?" She leans one hip against my doorframe, illuminated by the hallway light. As cringey as her outfit is, she looks way too good for forty-five. I shove the peanut butter cup into my mouth in response. "Well. Since your plans fell through, then you're free to take your little sister trick-or-treating."

I choke on the candy. After I manage to swallow, I say, "Mom, no. I'm having a terrible Halloween, okay? Don't make me leave my den of wallowing."

"You know, maybe it'll be good for you to get out of the basement." Mom turns on her red heels and walks back upstairs before I can fight or make a counteroffer.

I shut my laptop and slide off my bed, scurrying after her. "Can't you take Ana?"

Mom reaches the landing and grabs the bowl of candy, balancing it on her hip. "Ana asked for you to take her."

I roll my eyes so hard, I almost fall over. "Nice try. You just don't want to go."

"Believe it or not, Eloise," Mom says, turning as our doorbell rings, "Ana likes spending time with you."

"No, she doesn't." I snort and cross my arms. "I'll answer the door all night if you take Ana. Please, Mom. Don't make me do this."

"Trick or treat!" The chorus fills our entry hall and Mom oohs and aahs over all the costumes while I sneak a mini bag of M&M's from her backup supply on the floor. Yes, I'm stress eating. But that's what Halloween is for when you're depressed, friendless, and full of regret.

Mom shuts the door and sets her bowl of candy onto the hallway table beside the Swear Jar. "Eloise, Ana would really like you to take her. It'll be an hour, max. Then you can hide in the basement for the rest of the night instead of telling your mom what's wrong."

"Nothing's wrong." I pop an M&M into my mouth, and Mom holds her hand out; I pour a few into her palm. "Fine. Austin and I got into a fight yesterday after school."

Mom munches on the candy. "I figured it was something like that. What happened?"

"I don't really want to talk about it. At least not right now."

"Oh, Eloise." Mom pulls me closer and gives me a hug. "While I empathize," she whispers into my ear, "you still need to take your sister trick-or-treating."

I groan and untangle myself from her. "Fine. Where is the little brat?"

Mom shoots me an admonishing look. "Ana's finishing getting into her costume. I need to help her with her hair, if you don't mind watching the door."

With that, Mom shoves the candy bowl into my arms and disappears upstairs. The doorbell rings before she's made it to the second-floor landing, and I sigh, put on an incredibly fake smile, and open the door.

Ana's dressed up like a mermaid. Her skirt is this shiny, sequined monstrosity that tufts out with tulle around her ankles and is a major tripping hazard, and she has on a matching sequined top. Mom pinned back her long blond locks with seashell clips, and her candy bag is a crab-shaped bucket. Where did our mom even find a crab-shaped candy bucket?

Children, parents, and kids my age swarm the lamplit streets, rain shells unzipped and flapping since it's supposed to drizzle later, but so far, the rain hasn't made an appearance. I'm carrying Ana's rain jacket draped over my arm, my hoodie still pulled up over my head.

I trail behind but keep an eye on Ana, feeling dead inside. Getting out of the house has done exactly nothing for my mood and overall mental state. Without a movie to distract me, I replay that stupid fight over and over again inside my head. The entire exchange has haunted me since yesterday.

Do you know how hard it is to be your friend?

The only conclusion I can come to is that I broke Austin. After over two months, I finally broke him. Whatever energy he had to deal with me tapped out, and he was done. But that doesn't explain why he looked so fucking sad. This is when I could use another friend to talk to. Even Marianne is off the table after our showdown in my mom's minivan. Shy is Austin's friend first—her loyalty lies with him, not me.

I have no one. Again.

And it's all my fucking fault.

"Where to next?" I ask listlessly as Ana skips down the cobblestoned steps of our neighbor's house, crab bucket swinging. We've hit the last house on our street, but it's only eight, and there's plenty of room in that bucket. Maybe I can take some of Ana's candy as compensation for my time.

"Um." Ana unwraps a Dum-Dum from her bucket and pops it into her mouth. "Can we go to Macy's neighborhood?"

I lift a brow. "Macy with the boyfriend?"

Ana giggles. "Yep! She lives over there. It's really close." Then she jabs her pointer finger over our heads.

"Sure." I pull my sleeves down over my hands and motion for Ana to lead the way. But she stays in step with me.

"What's wrong?" The candy bucket bangs into my legs. "You seem sad."

I glance down at my little sister. The perfect daughter. A mini-me of our mom. Popular, with more friends than she knows what to do with and—for now at least—balanced brain chemicals. Ana's always been a walking, talking example of everything I'm not, which is super fucking depressing since she's eleven years old. And more perceptive than I give her credit for.

A few raindrops plink down onto us, and I hand Ana her rain jacket, which she tugs on with a petulant little sigh. "Not having the best Halloween," I tell her, and nearly get bodychecked by a kid in a Frankenstein costume.

"Oookay." She tilts her head to look at me. "Why not? Aren't you having fun?"

I force a tortured smile. "So much fun."

Ana's blue eyes narrow, as if she's trying to figure out if I'm being sincere. At this point in our lives, she should know that I am very rarely sincere. "Are you sad 'cause you're not hanging out with Austin?"

Oh, for fuck's sake. I can't catch a break. "What? No."

"Uh-huh."

"Shut up, Ana."

Ana tugs my sleeve to guide me down our cross street, and I follow. Shrieks and laughter fill the air, and I'm too damn depressed to enjoy the spooky atmosphere, exorbitant lawn decorations, or costumes that pass us on the sidewalk. "Mom said you had to be nice to me."

"When has that ever stopped me before?" My hoodie isn't waterproof, and rain dampens the fabric. If this continues, I'll be a wet rat by the end of the night. Awesome. Maybe I'll catch a cold and avoid school tomorrow. I really can't stomach another lunch with Ms. Deaver.

When we turn onto Fletcher Drive, my stomach does a little flip-flop. "This is where Macy lives?"

"Yeah, the big gray house." Ana points with her free hand; it's maybe five houses past Austin's. Like our street, Fletcher is swarming with kids. Due to our neighborhood's central location and relatively flat streets among a city of hills, we're in prime candy country.

"Why aren't you trick-or-treating with Macy?" I ask Ana after she hits up the first house.

Ana spins, her sparkly skirt swooshing around her legs. "Because she's at her dad's this week and he lives in West Seattle." She sighs, as if it's possible for her eleven-year-old brain to understand the complexities of Seattle traffic. "But she's the best and told me her mom would give me extra candy if I went to her house."

I grunt in response. How nice for Ana, to have such a good friend. Not jealous at all. I hang back on the sidewalk as Ana methodically makes her way up Austin's side of Fletcher, hitting each and every house. If I were in a better mood, I'd go to the door with her and try to scam my own candy out of our neighbors. It usually works because Ana's so—*ugh*—adorable.

Ana chatters on about her after-school art camp as we approach Austin's house, and I loiter near his driveway as she walks up to the porch with a gaggle of other kids and preteens.

From the sidewalk, I hear the chorus of "Trick or treat!" as the door opens.

Austin stands illuminated in the doorway, and my muscles tighten. I figured he'd be off with the band or—if I want to get real dark—Rose, once our movie marathon plans fell through. But there he is, wearing a witch's hat that most definitely belongs to his mom, holding out a giant basket of candy. He kneels down when he sees Ana, smiling at my demonic little sister.

Before I can dive behind the half-dead shrub bordering his driveway, Austin looks over Ana's shoulder and spots me. He doesn't wave or really acknowledge me. But he saw me. My stomach hurts. All the candy was probably a really bad idea.

Austin stands back up and the door snaps shut, and I'm still standing in the rain, feeling like my stomach is being pulled inside out through my belly button.

I'm mad at Austin for what he said.

But I also really, really want to cry right now.

Ana skips toward me, swinging her crab bucket with reckless abandon. "Austin lives here! Wanna say hi?"

"Nope." I force my gaze from the shut front door and give my little sister a blank look.

Ana's tiny pink mouth pinches together. "Are you not friends anymore or something?"

I shrug my rolled-forward shoulders, curling more into myself. "Honestly, Ana, I have no idea. And I don't want to talk about it."

The sigh that escapes Ana's lips is so eerily similar to my own that I almost laugh. "O-kay, *whatever.* But Austin told me to tell you that he didn't mean it. Whatever that means."

I glance over at the red house, the big windows with the curtains drawn, my throat tightening up. That eager softness I've felt lately, the part that longs to connect, wants to forgive him. But I keep hearing it—*Do you know how hard it is to be your friend?*—echoing loud against my eardrums, and I can't do it. There's only one way to interpret that, and even if Austin regrets what he said, he still said it. He feels that way, on some level. I always knew he would. It was just a matter of time.

When I don't reply, Ana continues along the sidewalk and I follow, all but dragging my feet. "You've been a lot nicer since he became your friend, Ellie."

You know what's worse than talking to your mom about boy problems? Talking to your little sister about boy problems. "I said I don't want to talk about it."

"You haven't been as grumpy."

A kid in a gigantic blow-up T. rex costume almost knocks me over, and I trip on the curb. Too bad he didn't knock me into the road and unconscious. "Ana. What did I just say?"

We stop in front of the big gray house, and Ana turns to me. Rain slicks her sequin scales, and the bright yellow rain jacket clashes with her mermaid costume. "You're just sad all the time. Don't you wanna be happy? I saw how happy you were when Austin came over when you babysat me."

I narrow my eyes. "Were you spying on us?"

Ana grins, bats her eyelashes. She swings around the crab and knocks me in the knees with it by accident. "Maaaaybe. That's why I texted him. You actually smile when he's around."

"Oh my god." I pinch my brow and squeeze my eyes shut. I am never, ever having kids. How does anyone deal with this, willingly, on a day-to-day basis? "Do you ever mind your own business?"

When I open my eyes, Ana's already halfway up the cement steps to the gray house's front door, and I sigh. I always knew Ana was paying more attention than I gave her credit for, but hearing her say I'm sad all the time is a blow. And it hurts, hearing that other people—like my little sister—notice a difference in me when Austin's around. Because Austin isn't going to be around anymore, and I really, really don't know how to handle all this.

My eyes burn, and I sniff, blinking rapidly. But it's too late, and fat tears blur my vision, hanging from my eyelashes. Maybe I messed up yesterday. I shouldn't have told Austin to fuck off or declared that our friendship was over. But I also don't know how to protect myself any other way.

Not many people in this world have the power to hurt me—I've been very intentional about that—but Austin is one of the rare few who can. Maybe that's why it hurts like hell. I *trusted* him. So I responded the only way I know how: I pushed Austin away before he could hurt me again. I pushed him as far away as possible.

Metaphorically speaking, that is. Austin does live only two blocks from me.

My miserable little brain wanders back to Jordan's comment in AP Bio. After our awkward Fast Plants lab, I switched partners and found myself paired with a jock on the football team; it was a lateral move. But I haven't been able to forget Jordan's comment.

Jordan said I acted like she didn't exist after the whole ghosting drama, and that it was messed up. Did I really do that? Jordan didn't defend me to Lydie—but she also didn't send those messages. And yet, at the first sign of hurt, I pushed Jordan away and closed the book on our friendship.

Maybe Jordan and I could've repaired things if I let her. But I never gave her the chance.

I push people away. I don't listen to apologies. And I don't give second chances.

Yeah. I'm the fucking worst.

I swipe back my tears before my little sister can see—skipping down the moss-covered staircase—and decide something. I'm done being the worst. As mad as I am at Marianne, she was right that day in her kitchen. Pushing people away before they can push me away only guarantees my loneliness. I can't expect anyone to give me their all when I always, always have one foot out the door of our friendship.

For someone so outwardly focused on success, I'm a pro at setting myself up for failure.

"You have to go to the bathroom," I tell Ana when she stops in front of me, already biting into a full-size Kit Kat bar.

"Huh?" Chocolate crumbles out of her mouth and smears on her chin. "No, I don't."

"Do you want me to talk to Austin or not?" I lean down and wipe her chin off with my thumb. "I need an excuse, okay? And your tiny bladder is going to be my excuse."

Ana blinks a few times in confusion. Then she grins and shows me her chocolate-stained teeth. "Okay! Let's go!" She grabs my hand and drags me back the way we came. Involving Ana is probably a terrible idea, but it's too late to back out now.

As we backtrack down Fletcher, I also make a deal with myself: I'd rather have Austin as my best friend than not have him at all. My life has been better with him in it, and I'm not ready to let him go. Even if it'll hurt my heart sometimes, I will be a good and supportive friend. Even if watching him get back together with Rose will be more painful than a stake through the heart. I won't hold a grudge over that comment, even if it sliced me up. I said some mean shit too. But that doesn't mean it has to be the end of our friendship.

Austin's front door has a giant Halloween-themed wreath hanging from the knocker, and an assortment of carved jack-o'-lanterns crowd the front step. We missed a huge wave of kids, and there's no one waiting for their candy fix. I hesitate on the BADDEST WITCH ON THE BLOCK doormat—because I don't know how to apologize, not really—until Ana sighs loudly and leans forward, pressing her tiny finger to the doorbell.

Footsteps echo on the other side of the door, and then it swings open.

Austin glances from me to Ana, who is doing an impressive potty dance. "Um, it's one candy per trick-or-treater—"

"Can Ana use your bathroom?" I blurt out, and peel back my soggy hood.

"I guess." He looks confused but flashes my little sister a smile. "Down that hall, okay? Door on the left."

"Thank you!" Ana skitters past him and disappears into the hallway.

Austin adjusts his weight from one foot to the other. "You can come in and wait. If you want."

"Thanks." I step into the Yangs' house, and I'm immediately surrounded by the sweet smells of pumpkin and apple cider. "Monster Mash" plays faintly in the other room, interrupted by bursts of laughter.

"My mom's having a party." Austin scrubs a hand through his hair, not looking at me. The witch's hat he was wearing earlier is on the floor by some extra bags of candy, and he's wearing what I can only describe as the spooky version of an ugly Christmas sweater.

"I'm sorry, okay?" The words come out clipped and not genuine. At all. Sighing, I try again. "I shouldn't have, um, told you to fuck off and said that our friendship was over. And I really shouldn't have bailed at A Scare Is Born."

Austin glances up from the floor. "Are you trying to apologize right now?"

"'Trying' is the operative word, but yeah, I am." I cross my arms and commit to the apology. Go big or go home. "You were right—I was upset at the show. You were the reason I was there and I felt like you were spending more time with Rose than me. Which is, like, *fine*. I totally get it. You two are getting back together, which is . . . awesome."

"It is?" Austin tilts his head, and the soundtrack in the other room shifts to "I Put a Spell on You."

"Yeah," I say, way too effusively, "but I'm an insecure

asshole, so. I just—I sometimes do this thing where I push people away. I'm really sorry for pushing *you* away. Like, I'm still not sure what to think about what you said yesterday. But either way, you didn't deserve that."

Austin swallows; his Adam's apple bobs in his throat, and he leans back to glance down the hallway. The bathroom door is still closed. Stepping toward me, he lowers his voice and says, "Being your friend isn't hard, Lou. At least, not in the way you might think. But I'm really sorry."

I hug my arms tighter around myself. "Well. I don't make it easy."

"Maybe not," he says. "But you're worth it. I should've never made you feel otherwise."

Heat flushes my cheeks. "Sorry for being a complete asshole."

Austin palms the back of his neck and gives me a shy smile. "Thanks. But this time, I think I deserved it."

The bathroom door creaks open, and Ana skips out into the hallway, a blur of pastel sequins and yellow. She glances between me and Austin. "Did you guys make up or do I need to go to the bathroom again?"

"Really?" Austin laughs. "You used your little sister as a ruse to get into my house?"

"What? She's useful every once in a while."

"Hey!" Ana pops both hands on her hips. "You're welcome," she adds with more sass than I've ever felt in my entire seventeen years.

"I think we should go now." I unwind my arms from myself and grasp Ana by the shoulders, steering her toward the door, which Austin opens for us.

"Bye, Eloise's-definitely-not-boyfriend," Ana calls over her shoulder, and I shove her onto the front porch. Even if Ana's insistence led to me making up with Austin, comments like those are going to get all her Halloween candy stolen.

"Sorry." I turn toward Austin and linger in the doorway. A clump of kids begin to make their way up the pathway. "She's demonic. Anyways. We're . . . good?"

Austin grabs the candy basket from the floor. "Yeah, we're good. I'll see you tomorrow, okay?"

The trick-or-treaters take over the front porch, so I wave goodbye and follow Ana back to the sidewalk. A tiny part of me aches during our walk home. But the thing is, Austin will never be more than just a friend. And that's okay.

The rain picks up and Ana shrieks, running ahead of me once we're in sight of our house.

Austin and I made up, which is great.

But I still need to find a way to make things right with Marianne.

TWENTY-FOUR

I'm the lightning in your sunshine

—The Laundromats, "The Storm" (1973)

November is quick to remind me why it's one of my least favorite months. Don't get me wrong, I love fall; it's the superior season. But I love October and its pumpkins and maple lattes and tangible daylight. The start of November is wet and cold, and the sun rarely makes an appearance.

November: welcome to misery.

And miserable, I am. Because I didn't listen to Ms. Holiday at the end of junior year and signed up for an *absurd* number of AP classes. Midterms are in two weeks, and my first day back at LifeCare is tomorrow. I'm swamped, stressed, and pounding ginger chews. I used my unexpected free time last week to study rather than volunteer on the phones. If I log my six hours a week between now and application time, I'll have my seventy-five hours completed. But I can't wait until tomorrow to apologize to Marianne.

Well. I *shouldn't* wait. I've already put it off long enough, and I can't exactly apologize with Austin hovering around. Even if he forgave me for what I did to him at A Scare Is Born, I'm less sure that he'd be as forgiving about me blowing up at Marianne, one of his favorite people, all because I'm too emotionally immature to deal with my feelings for him.

I should spend the hours before dinner studying, but on Monday, I take the bus after school and head to Marianne's.

Even with a weeklong break in our LifeCare duties, Austin and I have hung out. Both at school during lunch and online. We've moved past the A Scare Is Born and Halloween Eve drama, but I can't shake the feeling that we're not where we used to be. I'm worried that the effortless ease of our friendship before A Scare Is Born is gone.

Maybe it's just me. Heart-bruised and hawk-eyed, searching for any sign of Austin and Rose's reignited relationship. Not like I've been stalking their social media accounts or anything. Because that'd be weird. Okay, I totally am. But I've sworn to myself not to interfere. I'm not going to stand in the way of Austin's happiness. Even if his happiness lies with Rose Gembalski. They're like a fucking Disney cartoon couple; they belong together.

The bus drops me off at the stop two blocks from Marianne's, and I dash through the rain with my backpack thumping against my spine. I stop at the garden gate and—once again—curse myself for not knowing the code. Hopefully, Marianne isn't so upset that she won't let me inside.

I flip open the plastic case and press my finger to the call button on the keypad.

"Can't you read? No solicitors!" Marianne's grizzled growl is staticky through the tiny speaker.

"Hi, Marianne. It's, um, Eloise." I shiver, rain slicking off my coat and dampening my jeans, and stare at the brand-new NO SOLICITORS sign affixed to the gate. "Can I come in?"

The intercom's buzzing quiets and there's no reply. I always knew the odds of Marianne not letting me inside—or giving me a chance to apologize—were pretty high. But I still had hope. Hope that's rapidly dwindling. Then the gate unlocks with a faint click, and I scramble to push it open before the gusty wind blows it shut and locks it again.

The teal-blue house and its yellow door are both welcoming and intimidating. The overgrown lawn is even more wild and unkempt, plants sprouting to life with all the extra rainfall over the last week. The front door opens as I step onto the porch, with its cluttered frog statues and cracked Buddha, and Marianne peers out at me. I barely get a glimpse of her; the entry hall light is turned off.

"Eloise." That's it. That's all the greeting I get. But Marianne opens the door and rolls her wrist, motioning me inside the creaky, cold house.

I step inside and untie my boots. As I straighten, I study Marianne as she studies me. A lit cigarette burns between her fingers, and she's wearing a glamorous housecoat that looks as if it belongs on the pages of a 1970s spread of *Vogue Italia*. Unbrushed bone-white hair hangs loose around her shoulders, and she's barefoot.

Rarely does Marianne look her age. But today, all I can see is the seventy-three-year-old woman with the stiff hip and sporadic cough that I made *cry*. Yeah, I really hate myself sometimes.

"Can I make you some tea?" I say after I realize Marianne's just going to stare at me like a ghost in her own house and not initiate conversation.

Marianne nods, then turns and pads to the kitchen, her cigarette trailing ash along the hardwood floor. She flicks on the overhead light once we reach the kitchen and tosses her cigarette into the sink, then collects a few unwashed old cans of cat food and dumps them into the recycling.

Awkwardly, I set my backpack on the table and step to the stove, filling her mint-green kettle with water. Once the stove flame licks around the bottom of the kettle, I return to the table, where Marianne has taken a seat. She's crossed her legs, exposing the leathery, pale skin of her thighs.

"How can I help you, Eloise?" Marianne asks.

"I came to apologize. What happened after A Scare Is Born . . . I should've never, ever spoken to you that way. Or read your personal letters." I press my palms beneath my legs, trying not to fidget. "You trusted me with your belongings—your *story*—and I turned around and used that against you. You were just trying to help me, and I hurt you. And I'm really, really sorry."

Marianne pulls out a pack of cigarettes from her housecoat pocket and removes one. Her eyes are trained on mine, and I want to look away. On a good day, eye contact can worsen my anxiety in social situations. And today is far from my best day.

"Thank you," she says after a moment, then uses her lighter to spark the cigarette.

"I don't . . . I don't expect you to forgive me or trust me again. But I wanted you to know how sorry I am." Unwanted emotion thickens my voice, and I look away, studying the glass tabletop. "Whatever happened between you and Georgie is your own business. And as much as I read into things, it has nothing to do with my own . . . situation."

"Still haven't told Austin how you feel, I take it?" Marianne taps ash into her huge crystal ashtray.

I glance up from the table. "Nope. We fought after A Scare Is Born. . . . Things are okay now, but I'm not here to talk about Austin." Hesitantly, I unzip my backpack and remove the wrapped gift, sliding it over toward Marianne.

The old woman studies the box, the crisp corners of the swirly blue gift wrap. "You got me a gift?"

"An apology gift. Actually, I was going to buy you this anyways, but I wasn't sure when. Given how huge of an asshole I was last week, I figured now was as good a time as any."

The corner of Marianne's mouth curls with a demure smile. She sets the cigarette into the ashtray and rests her hands on the gift. "I shouldn't have been as insistent about you and Austin. Especially when I saw how upset you were during the drive home. You're just so . . . *stubborn*."

"I'm very set in my ways, yes," I say with a nod. "I'm going to make an excellent curmudgeonly old woman."

Marianne chuckles. "Yes, you will. You'll give me a run for my money." She drums her fingers on the gift, then says, "You're a bright girl, Eloise. Smart. Ambitious. And very stubborn. You remind me of myself when I was young. You fight like hell for what you *think* you want, but you don't fight for what you already have. You value accomplishments over connections."

I open my mouth to defend myself, but . . . shit, Marianne might be right? I mean, I only volunteered because it was crucial for my escape plan to Los Angeles. When I started at LifeCare, I told myself I just needed my hours, and then I'd get out. When Lydie and Jordan ditched me, I didn't bother trying to repair my relationship with Jordan, who'd been my best friend since middle school. I was always obsessed with college, but the second my friends dropped me, it became my only focus.

Until two months ago, that is, when I stepped foot in this house.

The teakettle whistles, and I stand up, pour us each a cup of tea, and then return to my seat. "I think I push people away because I don't want to find out if I'm worth fighting for. I don't want to . . . embarrass myself by assuming people care when they don't. So I make sure it's not an option."

"And how different is that from assuming people don't care and losing them?"

"Pretty much the same thing. Trust me, I'm well aware that I'm responsible for most of my misery after everything that happened," I say with a sigh, and blow on my steaming tea. "But I'm trying to do better. I'm here, aren't I? And I apologized to Austin. I'm . . . trying. Trying to do better."

"That's all we can really do." Marianne lifts her mug and clinks it against mine, then takes a sip.

I cup my mug between my palms and roll Marianne's words around in my head. Maybe I have been too focused on school. Too focused on an out. But apologizing to Austin and Marianne is a step in the right direction. Hopefully.

"I also want to apologize for calling you, um, a drunk and a liar." Internally, I cringe at my own words. Seriously. I'm the worst.

Marianne sighs and sets down the mug. "Eloise, I've struggled with both drugs and alcohol for almost my entire life. I was in rehab after I lost Georgie. Then again, several times, between then and the nineties. None of it . . . stuck. I don't think I wanted sobriety hard enough. I was a little too comfortable self-destructing. And I am a liar, doll. I lied to you and Austin. But I lie to myself more than anyone else."

"You could, you know, still get sober." I tear at the tea bag label.

Marianne drops her gaze to her hands. "Oh, I'm sure I could. . . . But what I'm trying to say is, it's okay to be mad at me, Eloise. I did use my history with Georgie to try to sway you to open up to Austin. In hindsight, that was very manipulative.

"But I meant what I said, when you came to me for advice. I don't regret telling Georgie how I felt about her. I just regret everything that came after. Georgie was the love of my life, and she deserved so much better than what I gave her. I took advantage of her. I lied to her. I chose the adoration of strangers over her." Marianne pauses for a long sip of tea, then adds, "After Georgie ended things, my manager checked me into rehab, so I wrote her letters. They were all returned to sender, but I wasn't deterred. When I was discharged, I had this romantic grand plan where I was going to apologize to Georgie and win her back. Treat her right."

I tamp down the urge to interrupt, to ask all the questions I'm dying to ask, and just listen. Because I have a feeling Marianne has never told this story before, and she deserves an audience.

"But I never had the chance. Four days into my treatment, Georgie went on a run and was hit by a drunk driver." Those bright eyes stare beyond me, beyond this room, beyond this decade. "I found out when I arrived at her sister's apartment downtown, where Georgie had been staying. We had a house together, on Mercer Island, until she left. . . ."

Even if I'd been able to piece together some of their story, it's a thousand times sadder hearing Marianne tell it. All those letters, returned to sender. I can feel the hurt and pain laced between each syllable. The regret, still weighing on her over forty years later. "I'm so sorry."

Marianne's mouth twists, like she's trying to hold back tears. "Thank you. I'm sorry too. I never meant to lie to you or Austin about Georgie. The lie sounded so much, I don't know, nicer than the truth. And I wish I'd been with Georgie until the very end.

"I always wonder *what if.* What if I'd left the band in '81? Maybe Georgie would still be alive. What if I'd been a better person, kinder? What if I'd realized what a loving partner I had before she was gone? I made so many mistakes, and I wasn't a very good person, Eloise. I shouldn't have lied, but . . . it was nice to pretend." She wipes at her eyes, then smiles across the table at me. "Apologies. I doubt you came over here to listen to my tragic life story."

"I don't blame you for trying to rewrite the past," I say gently. "If you ever want to talk about Georgie, you can. To me or to Austin."

"Good to know. Thank you, doll." She plucks the now-dead cigarette from the ashtray and lights it again. For a moment, I just sit with Marianne as she smokes, tendrils curling up to the dusty ceiling fan, the echoing tick of the starburst wall clock filling my ears. Once the cigarette's burned to the filter, she clears her throat and says, "That's enough about me. Why don't you tell me what you and Austin fought about?"

I chew on the inside of my cheek. Then shrug. "I don't know. Austin was upset about me bailing, which is more than fair. But then he told me that being my friend was hard. Which . . . is honestly the worst thing he could say to me."

Marianne lights another cigarette, nodding to herself. "Did he explain why being your friend was hard?"

"Not really. I mean, I get it. I don't make being my friend easy." I empty my mug but continue playing with the tea bag label. "Austin apologized and said that wasn't what he meant. But it still fucking hurt."

After a long drag, Marianne leans forward. "Have you ever wondered if Austin has a hard time being your friend because he wants to be more than your friend?"

I blink across the kitchen table at her. "Um. No? Why would I wonder that?"

"Maybe I was wrong about you being smart," she says with a sigh. "That boy is so hung up on you it's embarrassing to watch."

My heart pounds like I've just half-assed my way through running the mile in PE. "Did Austin tell you that? Because at this point you're legally obligated to tell me if Austin has feelings for me."

Marianne leans back in her chair, readjusting the housecoat around her legs. "Austin and I haven't ever spoken about his feelings for you or anyone, for that matter. I might have cataracts, but even I can see how he looks at you. You're just too insecure and afraid to see it."

"But . . . Austin asked me a week ago if he should get back together with Rose. He wanted my *advice*." I've fully shredded the tea bag label now, little bits of damp paper littering the glass tabletop. Ninety percent of me is positive Marianne is full of shit right now. But that ten percent . . .

"Maybe he wanted you to react? Or tell him no? I don't know, Eloise." Marianne tips back the rest of her tea and sets the mug aside. "You're a hard read. But Austin isn't. If there's even the *smallest* part of you that thinks he might feel similarly, you should go for it."

"And if he rejects me?"

"If your friendship is as strong as you think it is, then you'll move past it." She says this with so much certainty, I almost believe her. I'm pretty sure I'll die of embarrassment, and maintaining a friendship will be a moot point since I'll be a ghost. But still. "If your feelings are genuine, you'll never regret sharing them. Okay?"

I manage to nod. And my feelings are genuine. Annoyingly genuine. That's why it's fucking scary. I've never done this before. "Just so we're clear, if Austin rejects me, and I die of embarrassment, I'm haunting your ass."

Marianne chuckles, and the corners of her eyes crinkle. Inside my head, I hear her calling my humor a defense mechanism. She's not wrong. After another drag, she asks, "Does that mean you're telling him?"

"Maybe? I don't know. I need to think about . . . all this." I scrub both palms over my cheeks. "I really wasn't expecting an emotional deep dive when I came over here."

"Speaking of . . ." Marianne snuffs out the cigarette and then picks up the forgotten gift. "May I unwrap this now?"

"Shit, yes. Sorry." I offer up a small smile. "I wanted to apologize to you and we ended up talking about me. I'm a selfish asshole."

"No, you're not. I brought up Austin, not you." Marianne carefully peels back the tape. "You're not selfish for talking about yourself or your problems. And I'm glad I got to talk to you about Georgie . . . the *truth* about Georgie and me. I love your company, Eloise. No more apologies, okay?"

I manage to nod, my throat tight with a weird, surprise emotion. "Okay."

Marianne unwraps the gift. I bought her the nicest digital frame my babysitting allowance could afford, and already linked it to the online account I set up with all her digitized photos. While I'm not fully done with my contribution to Project Nostalgia, there are hundreds already uploaded and ready for viewing.

As I explain this, Marianne's eyes well up and she sniffs back some tears. "This is very thoughtful."

"I can set it up for you. Where do you want it?" I get up and collect our mugs first, setting them in the sink. Then I follow Marianne's instructions and set up the picture frame by her toaster, in view of the kitchen table. It only takes me five minutes to get everything hooked up to her wireless and logged in to the account I already made. I write down the login info, just in case, on a note and stick it to the back of the frame.

Marianne groans to her feet and stands beside me, smiling at the frame. The slideshow begins, showing a photo from her childhood. A tiny, pre-fame Marianne standing on a tire swing, golden-brown hair fanned out around her like flower petals. Marianne wraps an arm around my waist and hugs me to her side. As I hug her back, I realize this is the first time we've hugged. She's thin and bony beneath my touch; I hug her even tighter.

Marianne plants a kiss on the side of my head and lets me go. "You're a caring person, Eloise, even if you pretend not to be. Thank you."

I roll my eyes, sniff a little. "Yeah, yeah. You're welcome."

Marianne walks me down the hall and to the front door. My mom needs her minivan back before dinnertime, and I have a lot of thinking I need to do. Ideally with leftover Halloween candy.

"Good luck with Austin," Marianne says as I tug on my shoes, slide on my rain jacket.

"I might not say anything. Ever. And die alone." I zip my jacket and hoist my backpack onto my left shoulder. "Maybe I'll get a few cats."

Marianne winks, then opens the front door for me. "Whatever you say, Eloise."

Laughing, I step outside. "I'll keep you posted." Then I wave and step out into the downpour of rain.

Dad knocks on my bedroom door a few hours after I return from Marianne's. "Hey, El. The Chinese food is here," he says. "I thought we could have a family dinner. What d'you think?"

"Family dinner?" I repeat dubiously, and glance up from my textbook. Mom took Ana and Macy to the ballet downtown tonight. "With just the two of us?"

"Yeah, why not?" Dad's overgrown eyebrows bump over the ridge of his glasses as he smiles hopefully. He's in an old UW T-shirt and sweats, the brace he never, ever washes strapped to his lower back, which he threw out yesterday.

I tap the butt of my chunky highlighter to the spread-open page of my textbook. "Um, sure. Just give me a minute."

Dad shoots me a thumbs-up, then disappears upstairs.

I reach a stopping point in my chapter, cap my highlighter, and set it in my pencil holder. Rubbing the heels of my hands on my eyes, I groan. When was the last time Dad and I even ate dinner together? Or spent more than five minutes alone together? I'm not exaggerating when I say I can't remember. Mom's usually always there, or Ana. I love my dad, but he couldn't have picked worse timing for some daddy-daughter bonding. There's way too much on my mind to participate in awkward small talk.

In the hours since I returned from Marianne's, I've oscillated between stress eating mini bags of Skittles while thinking about Austin, and halfheartedly studying for midterms while thinking about Austin. Rather than doing one thing successfully, I'm half-assing both. None of the study material is sinking into my brain, and I'm no closer to figuring out what to do about Austin.

Is Marianne right? Am I too afraid and insecure to see what's right in front of me? Like, I'll be the first to admit that I have the self-esteem of a soft-shelled turtle. But I'd know if Austin had feelings for me. I *want* Austin to have feelings for me.

My stomach grumbles, and I trudge upstairs.

No way I'm figuring this out on an empty stomach.

Dad's at the kitchen table with an array of different Chinese food take-out containers spread before him, the tops popped open. Steam curls out of the containers, and my stomach grumbles even louder in response to the sweet and savory smells. The fire in the adjacent living room is roaring, and since the house is sans Ana and her chaotic demon energy, it's quiet.

I kneel on the bench and inspect my options. "Jeez. Did you order their entire menu?"

"What? The best part of Chinese is the leftovers." Dad tilts a white container to the side, piling sweet-and-sour chicken onto a paper plate.

No argument there. I serve myself Szechwan garlic chicken and a few plump pot stickers, piling a small mountain of fried rice on the edge of my overflowing plate.

"I can't remember the last time it was just the two of us," Dad says through a mouthful of egg roll.

I'm oddly comforted by my dad acknowledging how not normal this is. "Me either."

For a few minutes, we just eat, and the silence isn't too uncomfortable.

But then Dad asks, "So, how's everything going in the life of Eloise?"

I squish rice between the prongs of my fork. "Busy. Senior year is . . . busy."

"School's good, though?" Dad sips his beer, studying me over the smorgasbord of takeout. "Austin's good?"

"Yeah." I bob my head, focused on my rice. I'd rather die, be resurrected, and die again than talk to my dad about boys, and I pivot to a safer topic of conversation. "School's intense—I signed up for way too many APs—but I have around fifty hours done with LifeCare. Marianne took a week off, but I should still have enough by the end of the month."

"I'm really proud of you." Dad offers me the last dumpling, and I pop it into my mouth. "You've really taken initiative the past few months with your college applications. I wish we were in a better situation where you didn't have to worry about scholarships, but you're killing it, kid."

If Dad and I were having this conversation two months ago, I would've lapped up the compliment like the attention-starved eldest child that I am. But the praise feels empty after my conversation with Marianne. "Thanks, but . . . I don't know, sometimes I wonder if I've only focused on school as a way to avoid all the hard stuff. Like how Lydie and Jordan ditched me, and until two months ago, I had zero friends. If I was so focused on school, I didn't have to focus on how lonely I was."

Dad pauses mid-sip of his beer. "I had no idea you felt that way, El."

"Marianne said something today that got in my head." I play with my dad's chopstick wrapper, twisting it between my fingers. "All things considered, I could have some worse coping mechanisms, right?"

Dad chuckles, then adds, "Sometimes it's a helluva lot easier to throw your focus on something else—where you *excel*—rather than deal with your problems. Why do you think I'm constantly on my bike these days?"

"I always figured you were a fan of the spandex shorts," I deadpan, and my dad smiles.

"I love biking. It's a community, where I have friends. I have apps where I can set up goals and targets to hit every day." He taps the side of his head with a chopstick. "Mentally, it feels great to achieve, to do well. But at the end of the day, I'm still unemployed and nowhere close to finding a new job."

Huh. Mom always joked that biking was Dad's midlife crisis, but it sounds like it's been his own obsessive coping mechanism. Finding one small area to succeed—like me with school and, at times, with *RotR*—to mask the pain of the areas where we've failed. Or, more appropriately, where we *feel* like we've failed.

"And here I thought we had nothing in common," I say. Okay, humor is definitely one of my coping mechanisms. But one thing at a time. "Thanks, Dad. I hope you know that I'm not mad or anything about you losing your job. I'll be fine. Scholarship or no scholarship, I'll figure it out."

Dad's eyes soften behind the smudged lenses of his glasses. "That means more than you know, Eloise. Thank you. But did you really think we had nothing in common?" He points to our dark hair. "You take after me, kid."

"Physically, sure." I ball up the wrapper and flick it across the table. "But I guess I've never felt really close to you or Mom. She has Ana, who's—"

"Her mini-me," he interrupts with a nod, and when I meet his gaze, he smiles. "I never can decide if it's creepy or cute."

"Right? And I'm . . . I don't know, not *anything* like Mom? Or Ana, for that matter." I shrug, my hands now fidgety with nothing to pick at. "And I never thought we were alike. You weren't home a lot. And when you were, you mostly watched sports. I hate sports."

Dad laughs, a deep belly laugh. He sips his beer, then munches on the last soggy egg roll. "I know you hate sports, kiddo. Remember when I tried to convince you to join the soccer team?"

I wrinkle my nose at the memory. This was back in middle school, when my parents were cycling through after-school activities to help my "social development," which is both ironic and comical in hindsight. "Don't remind me. I hate playing sports more than I hate watching them."

"We don't have similar interests, but that doesn't mean we don't have other things in common. You're driven. Focused. As much as I love your mom, she has the attention span of a goldfish." I snort, and my dad laughs. Because it's true. "Your mom is creative—big-picture stuff, you know? You're like me. A numbers person."

I hadn't thought of it that way. Dad's worked in tech for so long that it kind of just blended into the background of my mind. I never took a step back and realized that, yeah, he's kind of a nerd too. Even if he's a nerd about finance and data, not video games and computers. "Okay, okay," I say with a fake groan and a real smile, "I get your point."

"I never want you feeling alone, El. Not at school, but especially not at home." Dad pushes his glasses up his nose and then begins to condense our leftovers, tidying the empty containers into stacks. "There's nothing wrong with independence. Just know that we're here for you. Even if you end up moving over a thousand miles away next year."

"Thanks, Dad." I slide off the bench and hug him, wondering why the thought of a thousand miles no longer sounds as appealing as it did two months ago.

TWENTY-FIVE

You should've never let me closer
You should've never let me love you

—The Laundromats, "Unaccountable" (1984)

AUSTIN:
you. me. cafeteria. BREAKFAST FOR LUNCH!

Once a year, Evanston High has Breakfast for Lunch day. The cafeteria serves up halfway decent pancakes, rubbery scrambled eggs, and too-crispy hash browns. I don't know when the tradition began, but it predates my freshman year. Even if the food isn't that good, the novelty has a certain appeal.

I hide my phone beneath my desk during AP English and reply.

ME:
I'm not a breakfast for any meal other than breakfast person

AUSTIN:
yeah I'm gonna pretend I didn't just read that

meet me outside the caf

I lock my phone and tuck it into my hoodie pocket, smiling.

I'm no closer to figuring out what to do about Austin than I was last night. But rather than dwell in my emotional soup of despair, I refocus on my class and finish taking notes on what the midterm might cover. Maybe I'll have a grand epiphany about what to do with my feelings. Maybe Austin will tell me how he feels or break my heart by getting back together with Rose, and the universe can take care of this for me.

I'm definitely not procrastinating.

Ten minutes later, the bell clangs over the PA system and I dump my books, notebooks, and four-color note-taking pen into my backpack. Then I hoist the ridiculously heavy bag onto my shoulders and enter the stream of students filtering into the hallway. Since Austin doesn't drive me to or from school, I haven't seen him since lunch yesterday. And I'm weirdly nervous as I walk toward the cafeteria. Nothing has changed, not really, since yesterday.

Well. I guess things are a little different, since I'm seriously considering Marianne's advice.

As the mass of hungry students bottleneck at the wide staircase leading to the ground floor, I catch sight of Jordan ahead of me. She's alone, typing away on her phone as she walks, somehow managing not to trip or slam into anything. Like she can sense me, she glances up from her phone and over her shoulder. And very, very awkwardly, I raise my hand in a wave. Jordan's thick brows arch in surprise. Then she returns my wave, gives me another odd look, and continues down the stairs.

My palms are sweating, but that wasn't too bad. I'm not entirely sure if I can repair my friendship with Jordan—or if I even want to, at this point—but she was right. I shouldn't have pretended like she didn't exist. Maybe I wasn't to blame for them ditching me, but I definitely have some culpability for making sure it stayed that way.

I reach the bottom of the stairwell and turn left toward the cafeteria. Austin's leaning against the wall with his ankles crossed, flipping his phone around between his hands. The oversized maroon sweater he's wearing is rolled up his arms, and his jeans have about two holes too many to be intentional. An ugly and lumpy scarf, knitted for him by Shy, is looped around his neck.

Austin catches my eye and waves. Then he mimes rubbing his stomach as if he's starving and I've taken too long, when the bell rang literally three minutes ago. As I reach him, my phone buzzes—and so does Austin's.

I unlock my phone and read.

DONNA!:
Hi kiddos, please don't worry too much, but Ms. Landis is in the hospital. You won't be needed at her house today as planned. Doctors aren't sure, but they think it's a stroke. She's at UW Medical Center on NE Pacific if you'd like to visit

I lift my gaze from my phone to Austin, whose facial expression mirrors mine.

"A stroke?" I manage to say, and it's like I missed a step going down the stairs, my stomach whooshing.

"Fuck Breakfast for Lunch day," Austin says, and grabs my wrist. "We're going to the hospital."

I almost trip over my boots as he tugs me back the way I came. But I dig my heels into the tile. "Um. I can't ditch class."

I feel like I'm on the verge of puking, and every time I blink, the word "stroke" flashes before my eyes.

Austin rakes his fingers through his absolute mess of hair. "Seriously, Lou? Marianne is in the hospital. Even if Donna checked in on her, she'll have to go back to the center. Marianne's alone." Those big, doleful brown eyes widen, as if trying to unlock some sympathy door inside my brain.

I've never skipped class. Called out sick? Yes. Had a few mental health days? More than I'd like to count. But I've never ditched.

Austin's grip slides from my wrist to my hand, his fingers weaving with mine. "Maybe it's not convenient, but we need to be there for Marianne. No one else will be. We're all she has."

I stare at our hands. The last time we held hands was at Retro Rink, and that was for balance. This . . . this is for comfort. Comfort I didn't know I needed right now. Because fear over tarnishing my spotless attendance record is way easier to confront than the other reason why I'm panic spiraling: I don't know how to lose people.

Marianne's so vibrant, so *alive*, that it's been easy to ignore the coughing and pill bottles and doctor appointments marked on the wall calendar in her kitchen. I've never lost someone—not entirely, not forever. But avoiding the hospital and walking into the cafeteria for Breakfast for Lunch day won't save me from losing Marianne.

If I stay, Austin might forgive me.

But I'd never forgive myself.

"Okay. Okay, yeah, let's go before I change my mind."

Austin doesn't hide his surprise. But he squeezes my hand. "Good. Also, I hate hospitals, and I don't want to go by myself. C'mon."

I grip my backpack strap with my free hand and let Austin lead me down the halls, out into the upperclassmen's lot, and we climb into the van. While Austin pulls up directions to the hospital on his phone, I text my mom. Not like she can cover for me with the school; excused absences require a student signing out of the front office with a guardian. I fill Mom in because when the school calls, she'll probably assume the worst—and more likely—scenario and worry that I'm dead. Not ditching.

Austin zips out of the student lot, and we head toward the hospital, which is an excruciating fifteen-minute drive.

"Do you think this is why she canceled last week?" Austin stares straight ahead, hunched forward with both hands grasping the wheel. The tension radiating off his body is so unusual, so not like Austin, it's disarming. I'm the anxious one, not him. "Maybe she wasn't feeling well?"

I shake my head. "I mean, I don't know. But I'm pretty sure she canceled because of me."

"What?" He still doesn't look away, hyperfocused on the rainy roads and direction prompts from his phone. "Why?"

"You weren't the only person I pissed off at A Scare Is Born." I squeeze my eyes shut, mentally picking through my entire conversation with her yesterday. Looking for a sign—any sign—that something was wrong. A sign or symptom I would've missed. "When I saw her yesterday, she was fine. I mean, I think she was fine."

"You saw Marianne yesterday? When?"

"After school. You also weren't the only stop on the Eloise Deane Apology Tour." I slump against the door and rest my temple on the cool glass. My eyes well up, and I don't fight the tears. Marianne is in the hospital. Maybe if I'd stayed longer yesterday or paid closer attention . . . *Fuck*. I should've made her set up that stupid Life Alert weeks ago.

Austin is quiet beside me. When we slow to a stop at a light, he releases his death grip on the wheel and flexes his fingers. "Why didn't you tell me you two fought?"

"Because I figured you were mad enough at me for bailing." I swipe at my eyes with the sleeve of my hoodie. "Marianne's, like, your favorite person, and I didn't want you to hate me."

"You know I was never *mad* at you, right?" From the corner of my teary eyes, I watch his expression shift. "And, as much as I care about Marianne, you're my favorite person, Lou." The light turns and someone behind us honks. He sighs, then rolls through the light.

I don't know if I've ever been someone's favorite before. Ana is clearly the more beloved daughter. Jordan preferred Lydie over me, and vice versa. Sure, I'm a teacher's pet, and a handful of my teachers probably view me as their favorite student. But I'm Austin's favorite *person*.

"Oh." I grab a hopefully clean napkin from the cup holder and blow my nose. Emotion still thickens my throat, and my eyes are glassy, but I take a tight, achy breath. "You're my favorite person too."

Austin doesn't look away from the road, but he smiles.

Austin parks in the visitor lot outside the emergency room, and we tumble out of the van into the rain. The entire sky is gray and November levels of miserable, as if it understands that today is a shitty day. Austin told me I'm his favorite person, but Marianne's still in the hospital, and my emotions are still a chaotic mess. But as we approach the hulking tan-brick building,

I grab Austin's hand. His fingers tangle with mine and I'm the tiniest bit calmer at his touch.

The ER is busy. And as Austin leads me to the check-in, I realize that I've never been in an emergency room. Ever. Once, we went to urgent care when Ana fell off her bike when she was four, but that's it. The Deanes are surprisingly healthy stock. But I have no idea where to go or what to do.

I don't know if I should be sad or grateful that Austin knows everything I don't.

"We're here to visit Marianne Landis," Austin tells a nurse in pink rubber-duck scrubs seated behind a large circular desk beyond the entrance. "She was taken in earlier today. Possibly for a stroke?"

The tired-looking nurse clacks on her keyboard. "Okay, one minute . . . Landis, you said? She was just moved out of the ER and into a private room. See that blue line there? Follow it to the elevators, then go to the second floor and take a left. Room 207. Here, take these visitor passes."

Austin and I thank the nurse, slap the VISITOR stickers onto our chests, and follow her directions to the second floor. We enter the elevator and the silence is oddly comforting. I don't even care if my definitely sweaty hand is wrapped in his. He's gripping my fingers tight, and I can't help but wonder if his hatred of hospitals is because of his dad.

Rather than lie and promise that Marianne will be okay, or say something empty and useless, I squeeze his fingers as tightly as possible, and Austin shoots me a grateful smile.

Marianne's room is beside the nurses' station. It's large with big windows, two couches, and bright, colorful paintings. But all the niceties can't hide the fact that it's still a hospital room, and Marianne's on the bed in the center. The hospital bed has her elevated, a few pillows behind her back. Her pale arms rest on either side of her body, the blue veins bright under the fluorescent lighting, and wires snake out from beneath the blankets, electrodes on her chest, an oximeter on her finger. A wheeled monitor beeps rhythmically with her vitals.

And Marianne looks . . . Marianne doesn't look like Marianne at all. That bone-white hair is matted, braided back from her face. Her skin sags and is naked of makeup. No rich burgundy lipstick. No shawls or cashmere sweaters. Just a flimsy hospital gown that's two sizes too big. Or maybe she's just that thin.

"Marianne?" Austin tugs on my hand for me to follow, and we approach the hospital bed together. He said her name quietly, and she doesn't stir. Just slowly breathes in, then out.

"Knock knock." A Black nurse in pineapple-printed scrubs steps inside. "I'm Arisa, Marianne's nurse. Donna mentioned you two might come by. Eloise and Austin, right?"

We both nod, and Arisa smiles. She has a warm, crinkly-eyed smile. "Marianne's sleeping right now, but I'm sure she'll wake soon. We gave her a light sedative before her CT and MRI scans, but it's wearing off."

"What happened?" I ask Arisa. "Donna said you thought it was a stroke?"

Arisa circles Marianne, checking a few wires and adjusting an IV bag. "We'll know more when the scan results come back and the doctor has a chance to review them. But Marianne presented with common signs of a stroke. She's a smart cookie, though, and called 911 when she began to feel dizzy this morning."

I pull my hand from Austin's and lower myself onto the nearest couch. "So she didn't have the stroke yesterday?"

"Whatever symptoms or event Marianne had began early this morning." Arisa tucks the blanket tighter around Marianne's hips, then smooths back her hair. "While it's possible she felt unwell last night, nothing occurred until earlier today."

A tiny bit of guilt fades from my chest and I press my palms between my knees, hunching forward. Okay. Well. I couldn't have stopped it. Or stayed long enough to have been there when it happened. But I'm still incredibly sad. I can't imagine how scared Marianne must've been this morning to pick up the phone and call an ambulance.

Austin sinks into the cushion beside me. "Is it okay if we wait? Until she wakes up?"

"Of course." Arisa beams at us. "It's so nice that you two are here. I'm sure she really appreciates it." Then she excuses herself and steps out into the hallway.

Once we're alone with Marianne, my eyes well with more tears. Even if I couldn't have been there for Marianne in the moment, I'm panic worrying. Like, what if our fight stressed her out so much that she got sick? Or what if that night out was too much for her, like she warned us? What if, these past two months, I wasn't helping Marianne thrive, but putting her in a worse situation than before?

"If I were a meaner person"—Austin scoots closer on the stiff hospital couch and wraps his arm around my shoulders, tucking me against his side—"I'd make a joke about finally having proof that you're not a robot."

I hiccup-laugh and grab a tissue from the box on the closest end table to wipe at my eyes. "Fuck you."

But I lean into Austin. Maybe this is just comfort—two people waiting bedside at a hospital together—or maybe . . . I don't know, maybe it's something more. Even if I don't know the difference right now, I don't care. I need him in this moment more than I've ever needed him before. So I rest my temple against Austin's, and he holds me even closer.

And together, we wait for Marianne to wake up.

TWENTY-SIX

This love is a wildfire
And I'm ready to burn

—The Laundromats, "Fireline" (1981)

Four hours, five cups of coffee, eight vending-machine candy bars, and three bathroom breaks later, Marianne wakes up. The doctor visited while she was still asleep and confirmed that she had a stroke. A small stroke, but a stroke all the same. But she assured us that Marianne was out of the proverbial woods.

Marianne flutters her eyelids and turns her head toward the small plasticky couch where Austin and I are seated, a mess of wrappers and empty paper cups on the small end tables flanking us.

"Hey, Marianne," Austin says softly, and stands up. He approaches the bed and wraps his hand around hers. "How're you feeling?"

Marianne mumbles something, and suddenly too nervous to sit still, I hop to my feet and step into the hallway. I spot Arisa at the nurses' station and wave to catch her attention. "Marianne's awake."

"Excellent! I'll be right in," Arisa says, and points at some paperwork she's in the middle of filling out.

I return to Marianne's room and walk over to the bed. Every nerve and muscle and emotion inside is telling me to run in the opposite direction. Every tiny fear and worry transforms my feet into lead. But I don't stop, don't run. Maybe I don't know how to do this, but I'm trying.

"Hi." I lay my hand over Marianne's. "I'm here too."

Marianne turns her head on her pillow, those spotlight blue eyes hazy. "Eloise." She smacks her lips a little, like she's thirsty. "Hi, doll."

My sinuses burn as more tears well up, but I smile. "The nurse will be here in a second. Are you doing okay? Can I get you anything?"

"No. I . . . I'm just tired." She twitches her fingers against mine, and I study her face. The left side sags, as if someone pressed their thumb into clay and swept downward, while the right is untouched. As the drugs wear off, the brightness returns to her blue eyes.

Arisa bustles into the room, and Austin and I step back as she performs some routine tests and checks Marianne's vitals again. I slump down onto the couch and wipe my eyes. I feel like I've been in the hospital for twenty-four hours, not four.

I grab my phone and reply to my mom's texts. She's concerned but surprisingly understanding. The school did call. I missed three classes. Goodbye, valedictorian. Evanston High uses attendance and difficulty of classes to determine who is valedictorian in a tie or close call. Mindy Channing probably just edged me out of the race completely.

I'm weirdly okay with this. Maybe it's the emotional exhaustion talking. We'll see how I feel tomorrow.

Austin plops down beside me and drags both hands through

his hair. Dropping his arms on his lap, he says, "Well. She's awake. That's good."

"You were right, coming to visit her. I'm glad she didn't wake up alone."

A slow, soft smile crosses his exhausted face. "I love it when you say I'm right."

I roll my eyes. "I was trying to be sincere."

"Yeah, I know." He bops his shoulder with mine. "How long do you want to stay?"

I check the time. It's only 4:37 p.m. If it were any other Tuesday, we'd be in the middle of our visit at Marianne's. "Not sure. We'll need to eat real food eventually."

Arisa glances over her shoulder and says, "Our visiting hours are all day, but Marianne needs her rest. I'm sure she'd love it if you came back tomorrow. What do you think, Marianne?"

"Hmm?" She turns her head toward us, and even through the medical haze, she's calculating the distance between Austin and me. The closeness. I swear, if Marianne accidentally says something because she's all drugged up, I'll expire on the spot. "You can go, don't worry about me." The tone and essence of Marianne is still there, but she speaks slower, more haltingly.

"Are you sure?" Austin shoots her a worried smile, despite her insistence not to worry. Pretty sure apathy goes against his nature. "We're in no rush."

"Can you—can you feed Nox?" Marianne asks. "You know how to get inside."

"Of course," Austin says, and it's obvious how relieved he is to do something useful, to help Marianne in some way. "Are the instructions the same as last time I fed her?"

Marianne nods jerkily, then flicks her hand—which still rests on the bed—at us. "Go on. I'll be fine. Come visit tomorrow."

Austin and I stand. As he hugs her goodbye, I clean up our trash and tidy the matching plasticky pillows. Then it's my turn. I hover beside Marianne's bed and take her right hand in both of mine.

"I'll be back tomorrow, after school." I squeeze her hand gently, so gently, because she feels breakable. "Anything I can bring you from home?"

"My cigarettes?" Marianne wheezes at her joke, and I scowl.

"Nice try. I'll bring you some books or magazines." Then I lean down and gently hug her. Instead of tobacco and vetiver, Marianne smells like isopropyl alcohol and the starchy detergent on her pillowcases. "Before you ask, I haven't yet, but I will. Soon," I whisper into her ear.

"Good." She smiles, her lips uneven, as I pull away. "If you don't, I will."

"Way to ultimatum me into a major life decision, Marianne," I mutter, and she wheezes another laugh.

"Okay, okay." Arisa shoos us away after I step back from the hospital bed. "Let's give Marianne some time to rest."

Austin grabs his messenger bag and we thank Arisa, wave goodbye to Marianne, and return to the bank of elevators. I yawn, pushing back all the loose hairs that have fallen against my cheeks from my braided crown. Emotions are exhausting.

Austin catches my yawn, and we exchange a smile. "She's okay," he says with a relieved nod.

I'm relieved too. Marianne is seventy-three. She's a smoker and a drinker, a lonely overindulger. What did Donna's pamphlet say? That loneliness increases your risk of stroke by something like 30 percent? Maybe this will finally convince

Marianne to stop chain-smoking and drinking vodka like it's crucial to her everyday survival; loneliness definitely wasn't her only risk factor.

Marianne's lucky.

I sneak a look beside me at Austin. And yeah, I'm pretty lucky too.

I lean my temple against the window as Austin drives us home from Marianne's house, where we fed Nox an extremely stinky can of cat food, and I watch the rain-smeared traffic lights flash by. Unlike earlier in the van, I'm not on the verge of tears. I'm exhausted from the crying and the worry and the unavoidable sugar crash from all those vending-machine candy bars. But in a weird way, I'm really, really okay. Because I didn't run away. And because Marianne's okay. Our fight didn't factor into her stroke. Five decades of drinking, smoking, drugs, and lonely self-loathing did. Probably her genetics too, but hey, I'm not a doctor.

Austin and I don't talk much during the drive home. The silence isn't bad. If anything, it's comforting to find a person who can enjoy the quiet with you. And I don't mind not talking. I have too many thoughts jumbled inside my head, competing for attention. I meant what I said to Marianne. I'm telling Austin. If anything—in *such* a clichéd way that it's embarrassing—today was a reminder that life's short and time isn't a guarantee.

I don't know if I'm doing a selfless or selfish thing. Telling him how I feel is selfish if it ruins our friendship or causes a shift we can't recover from. But *if* Austin feels the same, then I'm putting it all out there, for him. Making myself uncomfortable as hell, for him. Opening myself up, for him. I just have no idea which way this will go. Unlike Marianne, I'm not confident. Not in any facet of my life, and especially not with Austin—or romance in general.

Austin slows and hits the blinker, turning off Fifteenth Avenue and navigating into our neighborhood. A moment later, we're on my street. The porch light is on, no doubt left for me by my mom. Her texts were surprisingly understanding, but I'm not sure if it's because I was doing the right thing, or because she cares more about Marianne Landis's health than my attendance record.

"Hey." Austin stops alongside my curb, shifts the car into park, and looks across the van. "Thanks again, for coming with me. You made a pretty shitty day tolerable."

"Yeah, of course." I play with the straps of my backpack, which is resting between my feet on the floor. "I don't know if I've ever thanked you for letting me volunteer with you and Marianne. I wasn't very nice to you; you didn't have to do that."

Surprise awakens Austin's sleepy face. "No thanks necessary, Lou. I couldn't have you terrorizing seniors on the phone." He lifts one shoulder in a lazy shrug. "But you're welcome."

I brush back my hair—my braid is more undone than done at this point—exhale away my anxieties, and say, "Can I talk to you about something?"

"Sure, yeah." The befuddled expression on his face is earnest and sweet. "You can talk to me about anything."

"Right." I force myself to stop fussing with my backpack and look at Austin. "You really are my favorite person. Pretty much in every sense of the word. I was actually jealous of you when we first met. You're just so likable and comfortable being yourself . . . and you're happy. I've never been happy, not really, until I met you." My vision blurs as a few unexpected tears break free.

Austin turns toward me. Even in the dim light, I clock his concern. "Lou—"

"I'm not done. Just . . . hold on." I swipe at my eyes, take another breath, and continue. "Marianne and I fought after A Scare Is Born because I haven't been honest with you. Not as honest as I should've been, anyways. . . . I don't want you getting back together with Rose. Because I love you—and not as a friend. I'm *in* love with you. It's okay if you don't feel the same way, or if I'm too late. I just needed to tell you the truth."

A moment passes. Then another. A car drives by and the interior of the van floods with light, illuminating his widened eyes. "You're in love with me?"

"Trust me, I was surprised too," I say with a watery smile. "I'm sorry if I've ruined everything—ruined *us*—but I don't regret telling you. I don't regret how I feel about you."

"Lou, you didn't ruin anything," Austin says, then he bridges the remaining distance between us and kisses me.

I've spent many sleepless nights wondering what it'd be like to kiss Austin, but my imagination could never do this moment justice. The heat of it. The tenderness. The way he smiles against my lips.

Austin rests his forehead against mine and says, "I love you, Eloise. I just . . . never thought you'd love me the way I love you."

I tangle my fingers in his too-long hair and, this time, I kiss him. Because this is real and happening and *Austin loves me*. I didn't see this one coming, but maybe I should have.

The car rides and coffees and late nights playing *RotR* and The Shirt and hugging in my driveway and early-morning texts and three reallys, and *what's so wrong with me*, and Marianne was right. I'm a dumbass. I'm the girl who thinks she's smart because she has a 4.1 GPA but in reality is as emotionally intelligent as a hamster.

Austin loves me, though. Disasters and all. He *gets* me. And when our lips finally part and his tongue caresses mine, I think I finally understand what Shy meant about *chemistry*.

TWENTY-SEVEN

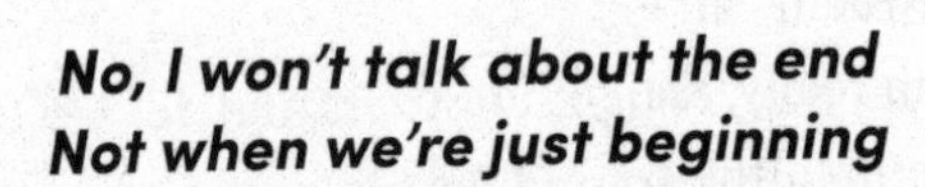

No, I won't talk about the end
Not when we're just beginning

—The Laundromats, "Sausalito" (1979)

"Put the shirt on, Lou." Austin shoves the green T-shirt at my chest.

I bat the wad of fabric away from me like it's on fire, then dart to the other side of Marianne's kitchen for safety. "No. Stop it. This is weird."

Austin had custom WELCOME HOME, MARIANNE shirts made. She was discharged from the hospital this afternoon—she was only admitted for five days—and the nurse she hired is driving her home. For the occasion, I suggested a banner. Or a tastier option, like cupcakes. Austin went with shirts.

"You'll only have to wear it for thirty minutes, tops." Austin chases after me, and his arms catch around my waist and pull me closer. I laugh, scrambling and shoving at his chest. But then he twists me around until my back presses against the counter, and he kisses me. The kiss is so good I almost forget what we're arguing about.

In the four days since Marianne was admitted to the hospital,

Austin and I made the easy transition from best friends to boyfriend and girlfriend. There wasn't really a conversation about it. After we kissed on Tuesday, I invited him inside for dinner and introduced him as my boyfriend. As loath as I was to admit it, it was time he met my parents. I spent two months hiding Austin from them, afraid of what might happen if it all fell apart. But I'm really, really tired of being afraid.

Down the hall, the front door opens, and I reluctantly end the kiss. "Fine. Give me the shirt," I tell him, "but know that you manipulated me. You're a very good kisser."

Austin presses the shirt into my hands and grins. "Thanks—you're not half bad yourself. But I just wanted to kiss you. No ulterior motives."

"Yeah, I don't believe that for a second." I quickly unbutton my shirt and tug the ugly green one over my tank top. Then I hold out my arms. "Happy, you freak?"

"Extremely. Green's really your color, Lou." He kisses my cheek. "C'mon, let's say hi to Marianne."

We poke our heads into the hallway just in time to see Marianne and her nurse, Jia, head our way. We met Jia briefly at the hospital yesterday; she's a young Chinese American woman with a perky bob and an even perkier personality. I hope Marianne doesn't break her spirit.

Marianne has a walker now, but she's dressed in her own clothes, which makes her appearance less shocking. Even though we've visited her at the hospital, it's jarring to see this new version of Marianne in these familiar halls.

"Welcome home, Marianne!" Austin's practically bouncing on his toes. We already told Marianne we'd be here—it felt like a bad idea to try to surprise a seventy-three-year-old woman recovering from a stroke—but he still declares the sentence like we're at a surprise birthday party.

Marianne pauses her walker-shuffle and looks us up and down. "What the fuck are you wearing?"

Austin isn't deterred. "Your welcome-home shirts. Don't worry, I got you one."

"Phew," she mutters sarcastically, but a small smile plays on her lips.

While she looks stronger and healthier than she did that first day in the hospital, the damage of the stroke is apparent. The stroke affected the right hemisphere of the cerebrum. She has weakness as well as facial paralysis on her left side now. It also worsened her vision, causing partial blindness in her left eye. Her speech was affected, but luckily, it's nothing major. She speaks slower now, but everything that makes Marianne *Marianne* is still there.

"Welcome home," I tell Marianne, and give her a hug as she reaches us. "Fridge is stocked. The great room is set up with the hospital bed. Nox is probably hiding in a closet somewhere, but she's going to be happy to see you. I think she's sick of me and Austin."

Marianne chuckles, but it's a slow wheeze. "I thought I said no to the hospital bed," she says, and I step aside so Austin can hug her. I grab the kettle to make us tea as he helps her to the kitchen table.

Jia leans her hip against the doorframe and smiles. "Even if you said no, Marianne, the doctor said yes. Just until you're recovered, okay? Those three to four months will be over before you know it!"

"Sure, sure." Marianne shoots me an annoyed look from her seat, and I smile in commiseration.

The great room was outfitted to be Marianne's temporary bedroom during recovery, hospital bed and all. We helped put the room together over the last few days. Needless to say, Marianne isn't pleased to be treated like, you know, a stroke patient. Poor Jia. She's going to have her work cut out for her. The doctors also strongly suggested Marianne stop smoking and drinking. To my utter amazement, she agreed. We dumped all the booze in the house, and she has enough nicotine patches to kill a rhinoceros.

Jia excuses herself and steps into the great room, leaving the three of us alone.

Once the water's ready, I set Marianne's mug on the kitchen table, then bring two over for me and Austin. I sit beside him, across from Marianne, and he wraps his arm around the back of my chair. Marianne smiles. She knows, of course. Somehow, she knew we were together when we visited her in the hospital on Wednesday, before either of us said anything. We weren't holding hands or even touching. Somehow, she just knew.

Marianne looked between us and said, "I told you so, Eloise."

Seventy-three and still petty. I respect it.

Now Marianne uses her right hand to lift the mug of tea. "Thank you both for helping out around the house while I was gone."

"Not a problem. We moved all the organized boxes back into the basement room too. With the window fixed, you could actually use the space, if you want?" Austin pumps his brows. "I'm envisioning a tribute to the Laundromats and your overall amazingness as a musician. I could hang up some photos, display your old guitar—"

"I don't need a museum in my house," Marianne says with a wheezy laugh. "Not even I'm that self-absorbed. Just having a safe place to store all those memories is good enough. Thank you for organizing everything and making that possible."

"Anytime." I nod to the digital frame, angled toward the table. "It was really fun, looking through all those photos. I can only aspire to live half the life you have, Marianne."

"I've made many mistakes, but I can't lie: it's been a wild ride."

"Still is," I say, because even if she's recovering and older, Marianne still has plenty of life to live. And—for the first time in decades—maybe she'll be sober enough to enjoy the time she has left. "Ride's not over yet."

Marianne lifts her mug in cheers. "Look at you, Eloise, being positive for once in your life."

Austin laughs and we all clink our mugs together. "Yeah, she's even happy sometimes? It's really taken some getting used to."

"Fuck you both," I say, and sip my tea. But I'm smiling. Of course I'm smiling.

EPILOGUE

FIVE MONTHS LATER

Where did we go, how can I find you
When the pieces of me shattered and scattered
Ashes in the wind, trying to find their way
Home, but I'm alone without you

—The Laundromats, Unreleased Lyrics

Simon & Garfunkel's "The Sound of Silence" plays on a mental loop inside my head.

The curtains over my egress windows are snapped shut since Seattle decided, for once, to participate in a season called spring; the sun is out and everything. I'm completely prone on my bed—face buried in the mattress—but I don't feel like crying. Actually, I haven't cried at all. Which is weird because I should be devastated right now.

I heard back from the University of Southern California this morning. Not only did my months of community service not impress the scholarship application committee, but they didn't impress the admissions board either. I was so focused on the scholarship and affording college that I didn't even consider that the school wouldn't want me.

For someone with pathetically low self-esteem, I should've seen this coming.

My phone chirps and I reach out for it on my bedside table. Smushing my cheek to the mattress, I read the messages.

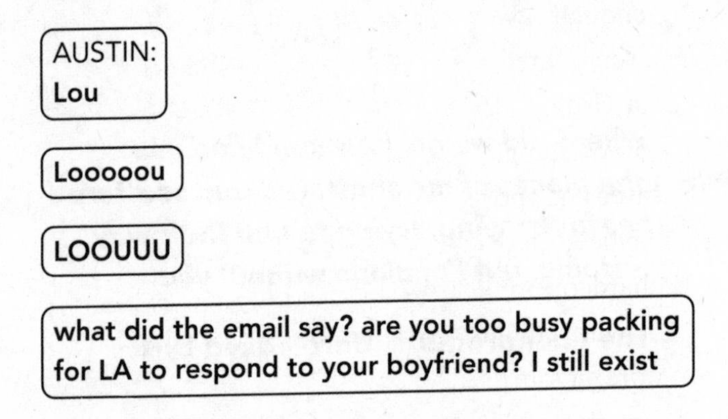

A strangled laugh catches in my throat and I sit upright. Then I pull open my email, screenshot the message from USC, and send it to Austin.

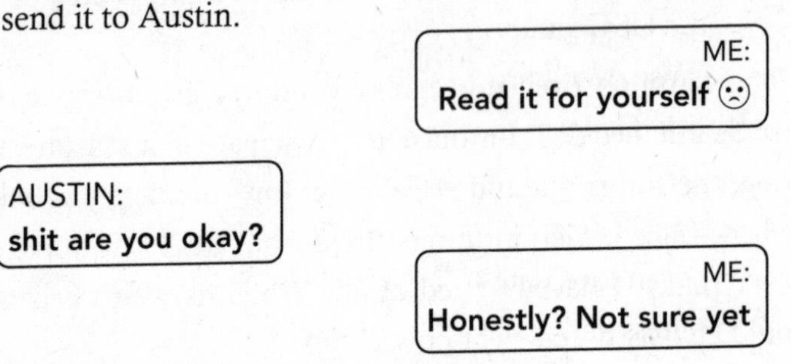

Austin doesn't reply, which is ominous.

For a moment, I sit there and reread the email. A form rejection. They didn't even use my name. Since freshman year, I envisioned myself in Los Angeles, 1,137 miles away. And, as of junior year, I craved the distance with an obsessive hunger. The chance to start over. I was so absurdly confident I'd be accepted, but I'm holding the reality of my situation in my hands.

Ms. Holiday insisted I apply to a few backup schools, and I did. At the time, it was just to humor her. Because I wouldn't need a backup college. Backup colleges were for slackers. Comically enough, every single school except USC accepted me. A few even offered me scholarships.

UC Santa Cruz. Georgia Institute of Technology. Parsons. University of Washington.

Yeah. I caved and applied to UW. And it's *not* because of Austin.

Okay, maybe it's a tiny bit because of Austin. But Mom and Dad were hardcore pulling for UW. It was never an option, though, not with USC on the table. Except USC isn't on the table anymore; it's in the fucking trash. Literally. I move the email into my trash folder and lock my phone.

I should be melting down right now, right?

With a pathetic groan, I stand up and walk over to my desk. The various USC paraphernalia stare back at me. As I take them down, I pause over a brochure I got during my campus visit over winter break. Dad was the one who went with me to Los Angeles. I remember LAX and all the traffic. The unrelenting heat, even in December. The campus, right in the heart of the city. And I was . . . not in love with it. I thought I'd take one look and sigh with happiness and contentment, finally in my element. But all I can remember is being uncomfortable and sweating a lot.

I never told anyone this. Not Dad, who seemed to pick up on some of my lackluster vibes during the trip, but he never pushed me about it. Not even Austin, who was enthusiastically rooting for USC because that was my dream.

I collect the rest of my paraphernalia and tuck them into one of my desk drawers.

Relief. I'm almost *relieved*.

My phone chirps again and I scoop it off the comforter.

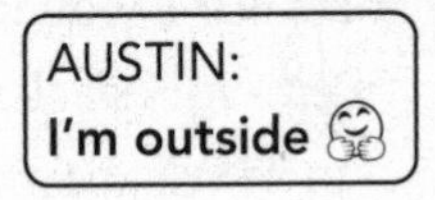

ME:
Of course you are. Hold on ♥ gotta get dressed

I swap my pajamas for a button-down and jeans, slather my face in sunscreen because my skin hasn't seen the sun since last September, and climb upstairs. We're three days into spring break. Ana's at Macy's house, Mom's in the laundry room with a cat named Izzie, and Dad's at work. Three months ago, he got a job as an accounting manager for a local bicycle shop chain. And he loves it. Mom loves it too, since he's home by dinner every single night. She's even started cooking, which is the only downside.

After lacing up my Doc Martens, I step onto the front porch and shut the door behind me.

"Hey," I call out, hopping down the steps.

Austin's leaning against the side of the van with a to-go coffee, his legs crossed at the ankles. His hair is shorter now, swooped up in the front, and everything about him right now—the oversized sweater and skinny jeans and a smile that warms me from the inside out—is so quintessentially *Austin* that I almost forget why he's here.

Oh, right. USC.

"Hey yourself." Austin lifts both brows, as if amazed I'm fully dressed and *not* sobbing. When I reach him, I wrap my arms around his neck and hug him. He puts the coffee on the hood of the van, then hugs me back. "Hanging in there?"

"Yeah. Been a weird morning." I shift in his arms until I can grab the coffee off the hood. "Thanks for the coffee."

"Croissant's in the van." Austin kisses my temple before letting me go. "Can I steal you for a bit?"

I narrow my eyes. "Why?"

"Humor me."

"That's all I do in this relationship."

"Ha ha." Austin nods toward the van. "I'm serious. You free?"

"One sec." I text my mom and ask if I can hang out with Austin, and she quickly replies with a bunch of thumbs-up emojis. Both my parents *love* Austin—quite possibly more than I love him—and the "effect" he's had on me. I also consider five months of therapy, which I returned to after Marianne's stroke, to be a factor in my improved moods and decreased anxiety, but whatever floats their boat. "Yup. Let's go."

I slide into the passenger seat and grab the waxy white pastry bag off the center console, then tear into the buttery chocolate croissant. Austin steers out of our neighborhood and heads east.

"So, where are we going? Marianne's?" I ask once I've demolished my croissant, brushing the crumbs off my jeans. I ball up the empty bag and shove it into one of the cup holders.

"Nope. She has that tai chi class with her recovery group today." Austin unrolls the window a few inches, and cool, pollen-laden air whips inside the van. I sneeze. Ugh. Spring is the fucking worst.

Once Marianne finished physical therapy, her doctors

suggested a support group. Austin and I goaded her into attending at least a few sessions, and to our mutual surprise, Marianne loves it. She's made *friends*. They do tai chi and yoga on Green Lake, unironically. They paint pottery together; Austin and I each have several very ugly mugs she's painted at Color Me Mine. Despite the stroke, this is the happiest and healthiest I've seen Marianne since meeting her last September. Austin even says it's the best she's been since he met her. She's also five months sober.

"Then where are we going?" I shift in my seat to face him and sip my coffee. "You have to tell me, otherwise this is kidnapping."

Austin just laughs, the light breeze ruffling his hair. "Oh please, you got into this van willingly."

I lean the side of my head against the headrest. "I thought I'd be devastated," I say after a moment. "Maybe it hasn't sunk in yet."

"Or maybe you're not the same person who set their mind on USC in freshman year?"

I grunt, unwilling to admit that he might have a point. But Austin changes the conversation, catching me up on the newest gig the Coinstar Rejects booked—another high school's prom, which sounds absolutely terrible, but they're excited—and I don't even realize we're driving onto the University of Washington's campus until Austin's parking in a visitor lot.

"You brought me to a school during spring break? Even I don't love learning that much." I'm joking—and deflecting—because I can only think of one reason why Austin brought me here. In the last five months, Austin has never *once* asked me to go to UW with him or acted like I'd consider any other school except USC. In a weird way, it almost bummed me out, like maybe he was perfectly fine with me leaving. But Austin was just being Austin—unfailingly supportive.

"Look. You can go wherever you want for college, but you said you'd humor me, remember?" Austin turns off the van, leans into the backseat, and passes me a bag.

I peer inside. And no, it's not an ugly personalized shirt, but a UW hoodie. The exact same style that Austin's mom bought a few weeks ago when he got his acceptance. Mine dinged my inbox not long after, but we never really talked about it. "When'd you get this?" I ask, because there's no way he had time to run to the campus bookstore and back this morning.

Austin's cheeks darken. "My mom bought it. I accidentally let it slip that you also got into UW, and she was excited." Austin's mom and dad met at UW because, apparently, everyone in this freaking city went to that school. Binna really likes me, and yes, it weirds me out. "I was planning on returning it. I still can—"

I unzip the soft purple sweatshirt, pull it on over my button-down, and then rip off the tags.

Austin grins, then leans into the back for his matching sweatshirt, because—oh god—we're that couple now, and swaps his cardigan for the hoodie.

We climb out of the van, and when I reach Austin, he grabs my hand and leads me toward the quad. The cherry blossoms are in full bloom this time of year, soft pink-white petals swirling through the air. Since it's spring break, the quad is quiet. Just a few other onlookers admiring the cherry blossoms like us.

Austin plunks down on a bench beneath one of the trees and squeezes my fingers. Even I have to admit it's beautiful. Not just the trees, but the campus. I take a deep breath and the air is sweet.

"While my motivations are seventy-five percent selfish," Austin says, nudging my knee to get my attention, "the other twenty-five percent aren't. UW is a great school, Lou. There are tons of gaming companies that offer internships and even college credit—yeah, I looked some up. Also, you love the weather, you depressed freak. And there's good coffee and food and—"

"Slow down," I say with a laugh, then bite my lip. "I've thought about it, okay?"

Austin stops his sales pitch and almost looks stunned. "Really?"

"Yes, really." I pull his hand into my lap, running my thumb along his knuckles. Honestly, I've thought about it way more than Austin knows. The thought of leaving him in five months—not only as my boyfriend, but as my *best* friend—makes me want to throw up and cry. "USC was my dream for so long, though."

"Doesn't mean you can't have new dreams," Austin points out, and plucks a cherry blossom petal from my hair. "I know USC isn't an option anymore, but that doesn't mean you have to choose UW or anything. I'll support you no matter what, okay?"

I look up from his hand and smile. "You're the best, you know that, right?"

"Nah, you're the best." He kisses me then, sweetly and briefly.

And I let myself envision it. Staying in Seattle this fall. Watching the leaves turn from my classroom windows and visiting my parents on weekends and sneaking Austin into my dorm, falling asleep all intertwined beneath my comforter. Staying in touch with Marianne and having tea at her kitchen table, Nox wending between our legs. Standing in the crowd at Coinstar Rejects shows because, yeah, the entire band is going to UW like the bunch of codependent musicians they are. Continuing to grow with Austin, the boy I've managed to fall more in love with every single day.

I pull back and say, "Okay."

Austin blinks away the hazy expression he still wears, all these months later, when we kiss, like he's not entirely sure how he ended up with his mouth on mine. It's objectively adorable. "Okay, what?"

"UW. Let's do it."

The hazy cuteness gives way to shock. "Wait. Are you serious, Lou?"

"Yeah," I say, nodding, because the more I think about this, the more *right* it feels. Maybe this is why I'm not currently balled up in the fetal position in my bed. "I didn't . . . Okay, I never told you this, but I didn't really like USC when I visited with my dad. LA is kind of gross? But if they'd accepted me, I don't know, I think I would've maybe made myself go?"

"Well, you're incredibly stubborn," Austin says.

I ignore him and continue. "I love this city, and sure, the idea of USC was cool. A fresh start and finding my people in college, being on my own. But maybe I don't need to leave to do that. UW is a great school, and I am *not* saying that I'm staying for you, but you'll be there, and I'm kind of wildly in love with you, so. Yeah. Let's do it."

"You really sure about this?" he asks, more serious.

I look past Austin toward the rest of the campus, then to the familiar skyline I've known and loved all my life. And back to *him*. "Yeah, I really am."

Something about my expression must convince Austin, because he stops asking questions and kisses me. Then he slings an arm around my shoulder and holds his phone out in front of us. "Smile for the camera, Lou."

I make a face, scrunching up my nose. "Ew. No. Why?"

"I promised Marianne that I'd update her on your college plans! She knew you were hearing back this week." Austin turns the phone into selfie mode and knocks his head against mine. "Hey, zip up your sweatshirt so she can see the logo."

Laughing, I readjust my hoodie until the UW logo is dead center, curl closer to Austin, and cheese for the camera. "Happy?"

Austin takes the photo. "The happiest." He kisses my cheek before texting Marianne.

Her reply arrives a minute later, both a text and a photo.

MARIANNE:
Told you she'd choose UW

The photo's a selfie; Marianne's much more tech savvy these days. Green Lake's in the background, as are some of her tai chi stroke buddies. But Marianne's smiling, joyful and vibrant. Healthy and, for the first time in a long time, not alone.

I tug the phone from Austin and send myself a copy of the photo. "You ever think a seventy-three-year-old woman is *too* invested in our relationship?"

"Oh yeah, all the time. But it's only fair. Marianne is kind of why we're together." Austin locks his phone when I'm done and sets it aside. After a moment, he says, "I'm really glad USC rejected you."

I shake my head, laughing. "You know what? Me too."

ELOISE DEANE'S "SENIOR YEAR IS A DUMPSTER FIRE" PLAYLIST

1. “Reinvent”—Phoebe Green
2. “Running Up That Hill”—Kate Bush
3. “Lonely Girls”—TV Girl
4. “More Than This”—Roxy Music
5. “Witchcraft”—Graveyard Club
6. “Love Will Tear Us Apart”—Joy Division
7. “Another Play”—Bark Bark Disco, Joon
8. “And She Was”—Talking Heads
9. “Standing in the Back at Your Show”—Wild Ones
10. “Mad World”—Tears for Fears
11. “Empty Streets”—Diamond Thug
12. “Happy Loner”—MARINA
13. “Dreams”—Fleetwood Mac

Acknowledgments

Every author has a pandemic book, and fittingly, *All Alone with You* is mine. As a self-proclaimed loner, I learned the hard way that there's a difference between *choosing* to be alone and being lonely. While I wrote (and rewrote, then rewrote again) Eloise and Austin's story, I finally accepted that People Need People. Who knew? So. If you've found your people, hold on to them tight. And if you've yet to find your people, know that they're out there and will accept you exactly as you are.

All the thank-yous and boxes of chocolates to my agent, Melanie Figueroa, for taking a chance on me and the messy sample chapters that would eventually become *All Alone with You*. Thank you for being my proverbial seat belt on the roller coaster that is publishing! Without you, I would've been flung off this ride months ago and would still be crying over cotton candy in the parking lot. To Root Literary and its inimitable roster of agents and assistants—you are all magical, talented human beings. And thank you to Heather Baror-Shapiro at Baror International and Mary Pender at UTA, for your advocacy on the foreign and film rights side of publishing.

Many thanks to my team at Simon & Schuster Books for Young Readers, specifically my editor, Jessi Smith, publicist Alex Kelleher-Nagorski, and cover designer Krista Vossen. Thank you to Sarah Long for the beautiful Easter egg–filled cover that continues to delight and warm my heart.

Thank you to Britney Brouwer, Erin Cotter, Elora Ditton, Sabrina Lotfi, Emily Martin, Emily Miner, Page Powars, and Rachel Simon for being friends, cheerleaders, and readers. All the love to my real-life not-publishing friends, Becca, Cooper, and Phil. Thank you for Monday nights, also known as my favorite day of the week. Here's to more adventures, dice rolls, taco feasts, and wizard-themed restaurant outings. I am incredibly lucky to call you three my friends.

As always, a big thank-you to my family—Mom and Dad, you're still the most supportive and wonderful advocates of these books, and I can't thank you enough. A special thank-you to my cat, Sofiya, for easing many a lonely night over the past (almost) fourteen years. And the biggest, cheesiest, and most effusive thank-you to Steve. I might be the worst sometimes, but you're definitely the best. Thank you for being the sunshine to my grumpy day.

About the Author

Amelia Diane Coombs is the author of *Keep My Heart in San Francisco*; *Between You, Me, and the Honeybees*; *Exactly Where You Need to Be*; and *All Alone with You*. She's a Northern California transplant living in Seattle, Washington, with her spouse and their Siberian cat. When she isn't writing or reading, Amelia spends her time playing video and tabletop games, road-tripping, and hiking the Pacific Northwest.